Acclaim for Chris Bohjalian's

trans-sister radio

"[A] sexy, exquisitely sympathetic novel . . . a fascinating read about trans-sexuals and small-town life." —*Mademoiselle*

"Bohjalian doesn't write novels so much as he weaves them, one thread into the next. The result is a fine tapestry, delicately and perfectly constructed. . . . There's nothing tawdry or sensational here, unless you believe . . . that an enjoyable literary work in an age of Harry Potters dominating the best-seller list is a sensation."
—*The Milwaukee Journal-Sentinel*

"A thought-provoking story, on all kinds of levels. . . . [A] fun read, and it raises some very good questions." —*The Oregonian*

"Relentlessly pull[s] the reader into the story. . . . [An] addictive read."
—*The Denver Post*

"Transsexuality goes mainstream in this *Scarlet Letter* for a softer, gentler but more complicated age. . . . Bohjalian humanizes the transsexual community and explains the complexities of sex and gender in an accessible, evenhanded fashion, making a valuable contribution to a dialogue of social and political import." —*Publishers Weekly* (starred review)

"Bohjalian's stock in trade is tapping into the ethical dilemmas of modern day life in a way that shows their human dimensions, the price we pay for being who we are. . . . [*Trans-Sister Radio*] challenges easy assumptions about love and gender in a way that will keep people talking."
—*The Times-Picayune*

"[Bohjalian] writes well, and constructs his story seamlessly."
—*The Washington Post*

"Eminently readable. . . . [If] you love a speedy read, a look at how the other half lives and lots of provocative questions and moral mind-benders, then *Trans-Sister Radio* will come in loud and clear."

—*The Miami Herald*

"Bohjalian is a social scientist accustomed to exposing the stories of people caught in marginal situations they can't ignore and against which they will be forever measured. In *Trans-Sister Radio*, he has taken an Erlenmeyer flask, filled it with The People Next Door, added a dash of Trans-sexual, and stirred. . . . [A] page-turner that sheds a mainstream light on a well-hidden part of America." —*Lambda Book Report*

"Love stories are common. Original love stories are rare. Creative and well-told love stories are a treasure. Chris Bohjalian's new book . . . fits the latter description. . . . [A] beautifully told story."

—*Fort Worth Morning Star-Telegram*

"[Bohjalian] uses his extraordinary gifts for storytelling and character development to delve into further controversial areas—the acceptance (or not) of transsexuals in today's society and the endless complexities that gender adds to our lives. . . . Bohjalian is a master at exposing the emotions of a highly charged situation and carefully dissecting controversy." —*Library Journal*

"In *Trans-Sister Radio* Bohjalian makes us confront significant matters and consider how they shape our lives." —*The Burlington Free Press*

"Plausible and entertaining . . . sincere." —*People*

"Bohjalian is especially good at domestic scenes and dialogues. As in his earlier stories, he has each major character give expression to his/her individual version of and reaction to what is happening, drawing the reader into their lives and emotional states. It is something like a well-composed opera: First one character sings what is going on, then another has a solo, while a third does a reprise of the plot in a different key."

—*Vermont Sunday Magazine*

Chris Bohjalian

trans-sister radio

Chris Bohjalian is the author of seven novels, including *Midwives* (a *Publishers Weekly* Best Book and a New England Booksellers Association Discovery title), *The Law of Similars*, and *Water Witches*. He lives in Vermont with his wife and daughter.

trans-sister
radio

trans-sister radio

a novel by

Chris Bohjalian

Vintage Contemporaries
Vintage Books
A Division of Random House, Inc.
New York

FIRST VINTAGE CONTEMPORARIES EDITION, AUGUST 2001

Copyright © 2000 by Chris Bohjalian

All rights reserved under International and Pan-American Copyright Conventions. Published in the United States by Vintage Books, a division of Random House, Inc., New York, and simultaneously in Canada by Random House of Canada Limited, Toronto. Originally published in hardcover in the United States by Crown Publishers, a division of Random House, Inc., New York, in 2000.

Vintage is a registered trademark and Vintage Contemporaries and colophon are trademarks of Random House, Inc.

The Library of Congress has cataloged the Crown edition as follows:
Bohjalian, Christopher A.
Trans-sister radio / Chris Bohjalian.
I. Title.
PS3552.O495 T72 2000
813'.54—dc21
99-049250

Vintage ISBN: 0-375-70517-1

Author photograph © Victoria Blewer
Book design by Lynne Amft

www.vintagebooks.com

Printed in the United States of America
10 9 8 7 6 5 4 3 2 1

⇒ *for Victoria* ⇐

"If the body and soul are comely, who am I to quarrel about the color of wings or the speed of flight?"

THOMAS BURNETT SWANN

"Should one deal with our sister as with a harlot?"

GENESIS 34:31

trans-sister
radio

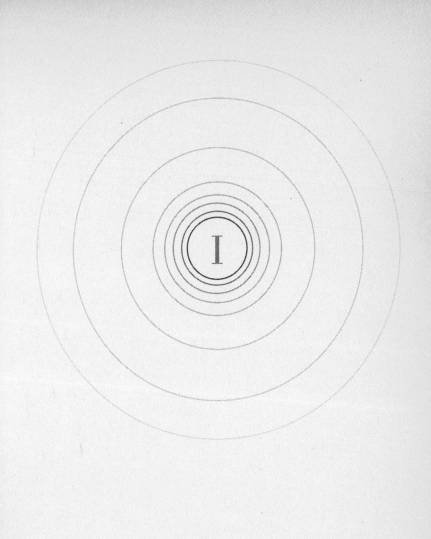

I

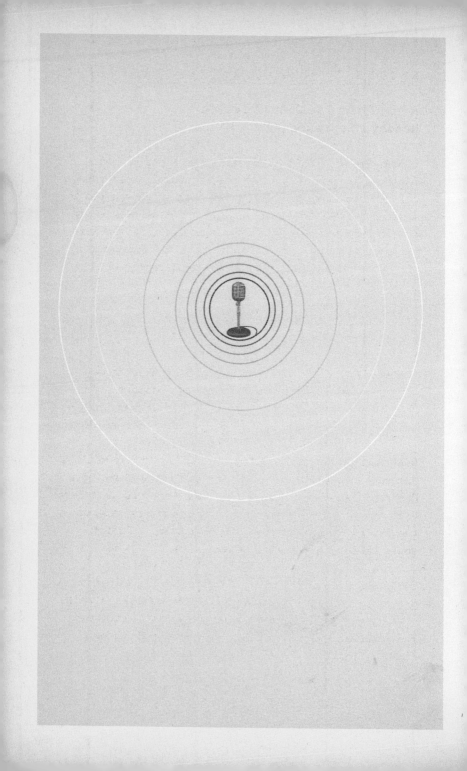

NATIONAL PUBLIC RADIO TRANSCRIPT:

All Things Considered
Monday, September 24

LINDA WERTHEIMER: Periodically this year we have
explored what we've called the Nature of Love: those
strange and wondrous ways we find our soul sparked by
somebody else. This afternoon we continue that series
with the first in a five-part story that begins with
gender dysphoria——the clinical term for individuals
who believe their sex at birth is in error——and ends
with——

NOAH ADAMS: Well, we won't tell you that, at least not
today. You'll have to wait until Friday.

LINDA WERTHEIMER: Carly Banks is nineteen, three
weeks now into her sophomore year at Bennington College in Vermont. Her father, we will tell you, is the
manager of one of our affiliate public radio stations.

NOAH ADAMS: But this is her mother's story as well as
her father's——though her mother and father have been
divorced for eleven years now. This week you will meet
Will and Allison Banks, Carly's parents, as well as
the fellow Allison met who she was sure, at first,
would be the man of her dreams.

LINDA WERTHEIMER: This part of the series was written
by Carly——with the guidance of NPR's own Nicole Wells
——while Carly was with us this summer in Washington.
The engineer was Sam Coleman, and the producer was
Kirsten Seidler.

carly

I WAS EIGHT WHEN MY PARENTS SEPARATED, AND
nine when they actually divorced. That means that for a little more
than a decade, I've watched my mom get ready for dates. Sometimes,
until I started ninth grade, I'd even keep her company on Saturday
afternoons, while she'd take these long, luxurious bubble baths. I'd put
the lid down on the toilet and sit there, and we'd talk about school or
boys or the guy she was dating.

I stopped joining her in the bathroom in ninth grade for a lot of
reasons, but mostly because it had started to seem a little weird to me
to be hanging out with her when I was fourteen and she was naked.

But she has always been pretty cool about bodies and sex, and for all
I know, she wouldn't mind my joining her in the bathroom even now
when I'm home from college. For better or worse—and usually for
better—my mom has always been very comfortable with subjects that
give most parents the shivers. A couple of days before my fifteenth

birthday, she took me to the gynecologist to get me fitted for a diaphragm, and told me where in her bedroom she kept the spermicidally lubricated condoms. (Of course, I already knew: God, by then I even knew where she'd hidden a vibrator.)

I hadn't had sex yet, and my mom made it clear that she didn't want me to in the foreseeable future. But she had a pretty good memory of the hormonal chaos that hits a person in high school, and she wanted to do all that she could for my sake to ensure that she wouldn't become a grandmother any sooner than necessary.

When I think back on it, my parents' divorce was very civilized. At least it has always seemed that way to me, though it's clear there are things I don't know.

The way my mom tells it, I was in second or third grade when they realized they just didn't love each other anymore the way they had when they were first married. They'd worked together at the radio station then, and they'd shared everything. My mom insists they both came to the realization at about the same time that they should separate: My mom was thirty-two and my dad was thirty-three, and they figured they were still young enough to hook up with someone who, in the long years ahead, could keep their motors humming the way they were meant to.

Sometimes my dad hints that it wasn't quite so mutual. Most of the time he toes their party line, but every so often I'll get the impression that when he moved out, he was figuring they'd both change their minds and reconcile in a couple of weeks. I think he might have thought he was just being cool.

Once when he was visiting my mom, I overheard him telling her that he knew her heart had never been into the counseling they went through when I was eight.

Still, he was the one who got remarried.

Sometimes, when I was little, I'd help my mom pick out her jewelry or clothing for a date.

"Wear the pearls," I might suggest.

"It's a clambake," she'd remind me.

"Too formal?"

"And they might scare the oysters."

One time she especially indulged me. I was eleven years old and convinced there was no fashion statement more powerful than a kilt. And so she wore a red-and-green Christmas kilt to a backyard cook-out, even though it was the middle of August and the air was just plain sticky. That night my baby-sitter spent most of the time standing in front of a fan, with her T-shirt rolled up like a halter.

If I were to count, I'd guess my mom probably had five serious boyfriends in the decade between my parents' divorce and the day she met Dana. Dana had been in pre-surgical therapy for two years by then and had probably endured close to fifty hours of electrolysis. He'd been on hormone therapy for a good four or five months.

Unlike a lot of pre-op M2Fs, he wasn't trying to pass as a woman yet, he hadn't begun his transition.

Of course, he didn't tell my mom any of this—not that he should have. When they met, he was simply the professor for a film course at the university that she was taking that summer as a lark, and she was one of his students.

What was he supposed to do, say to the class, "Hi, I'm Dana, and I've spent a good part of the last year with my upper lip deadened by Novacaine"?

Or, "Good evening, I'm your professor. I'm about to start developing breasts!"

Or, if he wanted, for some reason, to be completely candid, "You folks ever met a lesbian with a penis? Have now!"

He had no idea he was going to fall in love with my mom, even when they started to date, and she had no idea she was going to fall in love with him. It just happened.

My mom's a sixth-grade teacher at the elementary school two and a half blocks from our home. When she went back to work after I was born, she decided she didn't want to be in broadcast anymore, and she sure as heck didn't want to be commuting thirty miles—one way—to Colchester or Burlington every day. And so she decided to see if she was meant to teach, and clearly she was.

She's excellent, truly gifted in front of a blackboard, and her kids always adore her. There are some parents who think she's too lenient, and every year there will be one or two who will complain about something in the class play she organizes each spring: The girls' costumes are too revealing. The boys' dancing is too provocative. The subject matter in one of the skits is inappropriate.

Ironically, the one show that really sent the school board over the edge didn't bother the more conservative parents in town. It was actually a group of very liberal parents—the sort who usually stood by her—who complained. My mom had been taking African dancing one night a week in Middlebury for a couple of months and decided to incorporate some of what she had learned into her end-of-the-year show. The kids loved the dancing as much as she did and really got into it. And so in the finale she had all the boys drumming and all the girls dancing, and some of the more progressive parents in town thought she was encouraging some kind of reactionary and unfashionable sex-role stereotyping. Although the boys had no shirts on and the girls were wearing two-piece bathing suits and grass skirts they'd made from the tall reeds that grow out by the watershed, all anyone was concerned about that year was the notion that the girls weren't drumming and the boys weren't dancing.

Nevertheless, despite my mom's popularity with her students and her reputation as a teacher, before I turned eleven I was still scared to death that I'd wind up in her class. Bartlett's a pretty small town, and each grade in the elementary school has only two classes, so I figured there was a one-in-two chance that I would have my mom as my teacher.

I didn't understand then that there was no way the school would allow that to happen. I didn't realize they even thought about such things.

Sometimes I considered telling my mom that I didn't want to be in her class, and trying to explain to her why. But at nine and ten I didn't fully understand words like *favoritism* or *preferential treatment,* and I'd probably never even heard the term *paranoia.* Moreover, my mom and dad hadn't been divorced all that long, and I was afraid that voicing my desire to be in Mrs. Chapel's class instead of hers would feel to my mom like rejection. Desertion. Even though my parents still seemed to be friends, I didn't want her to get the idea that her daughter was taking sides, since that wasn't the case at all.

Not long after the divorce was final, when it was clear they weren't going to get back together and he was never going to move back in, my dad bought a house on the other side of the village. Why not? His friends still lived in the town, and so did I. His place was about a ten-minute walk from Mom's.

The custody arrangement was pretty loose. I was supposed to spend weeknights with Mom and weekends with Dad, but it never really worked out that way. I was as likely to be with Mom on a weekend as I was with Dad on a Tuesday or Wednesday night. On some level, I think, I was trying to rebel against the unnatural formalism that marks any custody agreement, and pretend, in some way, that we were still one happy family. But on another level, my reason for being one place or the other was mere pragmatism. My mom's house wasn't buffered by the cliffs to the north, and so she had much better TV reception: That meant I really wanted to be there on Saturday and Sunday nights, when I could pretty much watch all the TV I wanted.

Occasionally, I'd spend a night at Dad's simply because I could tell that Mom wanted to bring her current squeeze home for the night. No one ever moved in with us until Dana, but she certainly got serious often enough that some men would sleep over.

Likewise, until Dad married Patricia, there were those Saturdays when I figured he needed a quiet evening with a prospective girlfriend more than he did one with his daughter, and so I'd hang with Mom.

But the fact is, my main home base has always been my mom's house.

For virtually my entire life, my dad worked for Vermont Public Radio. Most of the time he was the president and general manager, which must be among the most thankless jobs in the world: It seems like you spend your life raising money, and trying to explain to a lot of elderly blue-hairs why VPR has so much news and commentary, and then to a lot of political junkies why the station has so much classical music.

And then there are the fund-drives three times a year. Those weeks, you just don't sleep.

Sometimes, if the light is right, my dad looks a little bit like Dana did two years ago. Same straw-colored hair. Same grayish-blue eyes. Same build.

Of course, they look nothing alike now. After all, you can still see my dad's Adam's apple.

I probably know as well as anyone what it's like to have a crush on a professor.

Unlike my mom, of course, I've never acted on one, I've never actually slept with a teacher. But I know what it's like to sit in a classroom and forget about the material or the text, and just sort of gaze at the guy at the front of the room.

And Dana was a very handsome man. I wouldn't be surprised if my mom saw in him some of the same things that first attracted her to my dad. But Dana was more delicate looking, and smaller boned. The first time I met him, when he came to a party my mom gave at our house, I wouldn't have described him as effeminate, but I might have said he had fine—perhaps even beautiful—features. And when a guy has no hair or stubble on his face, you're bound to notice a pair of really nice cheekbones, or a chin that's shaped a bit like the smaller half of a pear—and just as smooth.

I'm sure some people picked up on the fact that he had begun judiciously plucking his eyebrows, but I didn't. I just thought they were shaped like the most remarkable sickle moons.

He wore his hair back in a ponytail then, held together with the sort of thin rubber band a supermarket is likely to wrap around scallions. And he was dressed pretty much like generic professor: jeans, a summer-weight navy blazer, and a work shirt made of softened blue denim. Loafers.

He was tall and thin like my dad, and still drinking his beer from a bottle—again, just like Dad.

The party was the third week in July, and my mom had been in his class for three or four weeks. I was working at the garden nursery that summer, hoisting juniper trees in buckets, and helping people choose between Saint Cloud and Jersey blueberry bushes. It was a great summer job for a kid, especially for a kid who has finished high school and is about to start college, because it meant I had my evenings completely free.

There were probably a dozen of my mom's friends at the house that Friday night. It wasn't exactly a sit-down dinner party, but there were massive amounts of food—salads and cheeses and bread—and plenty of beer and wine. There were a few folks hovering behind the screen door in the kitchen, pouring themselves glasses of wine or bringing out food from the refrigerator, but the majority were on the stone terrace in the backyard.

Most of the people there had known my mom for years, and a few had been her friends back in college. My mom was part of a whole crowd of people who went to Middlebury College together in the 1970s and ended up staying in the area.

Dana was, essentially, the odd man out at the party—which, in all fairness, was probably a role he was used to. I thought I'd scoop up a plate of the strawberry pasta before heading out for the evening, and he was beside the two long picnic tables with the food. He was sipping a beer, and near enough to Jody and Graham that from a distance it might have looked like he was part of their conversation, but when you got close, it was pretty clear that he wasn't.

I wasn't sure then where he fit into my mom's life, and I thought it was possible he was merely a friend of a friend, perhaps a person who had been dragged to the party because he was a houseguest of someone who had been invited. My mother often had strays like that at her parties. And so I said hello.

"I'm Carly," I said. "Allison's daughter."

"I'm Dana," he said. "Your mother's teacher."

"Film?"

He nodded and smiled. "I guess she fears I don't get out enough. So she invited me here tonight."

I knew my mom got a charge out of the course, but I'd had no idea she liked the teacher enough to invite him to our home. When I'd asked her Wednesday night who was coming, she hadn't mentioned her professor.

"She enjoys your course," I said, unsure what else I should say. Here I'd been viewing Dana as merely some stranger in our house in need of company, when actually he was my mom's latest candidate for a new boyfriend.

"Oh, she is just a delight. But I'm sure you know that."

The class was exactly the sort of interdisciplinary shambles I've come to love now that I'm in college. Basically, my mom was reading a couple of nineteenth-century New England novels and then watching the twentieth-century movies that were based upon them. It was supposed to offer a really cagey window onto how Puritan New England affects our culture, but it was clear the class spent most of the time dissecting the fact that Louisa May Alcott had written a novel about a boy named Laurie and a girl named Jo, or making fun of Demi Moore's Hester Prynne.

"Well, I know she's really good about her homework," I said. "She likes the reading."

He ran two fingers abstractedly along the rim at the top of the bottle. I'd never noticed an adult man's fingers before, unless he was a logger and was missing a few, but I certainly noticed Dana's. They were long and slender, and the short, square nails seemed to gleam.

The fact that his fingers were largely without hair didn't register with me then.

"She tells me you start college in five or six weeks. Congratulations."

"Thanks."

"Scared?"

I paused. Most of the time that summer, adults merely babbled to me about how much fun I would have, or how smart I must be. No one had ever touched on the fact that I might be scared to death— which, of course, I was.

"A little."

"I was, too. I was a basket case just about this time, oh, seventeen years ago now."

I did the math instantly in my head, but figured I'd confirm his age just in case. Maybe, I hoped, he'd bummed around Europe for a couple of years before starting college.

"How old are you?"

"Thirty-five."

As far as I knew, Mom had never been involved with a younger man. Once, she'd been pretty serious about an older man. When I was in eighth grade, she saw a guy named Foster, who was in his mid-fifties, which at the time had made him seem downright primeval.

"I'm not *that* much younger than your mom," he said, grinning, as if he'd sensed what I was thinking.

"No, not at all," I said. Mom had just turned forty-two.

He reached for a cocktail napkin from the table beside him and surprised me by dabbing it against the edge of my lips. "You had a little drop of strawberry there," he murmured. "Can't have that, now. Do you have a date tonight?"

"Nope. I mean, I am going out. But it's just with a group of friends I hang out with."

"Boyfriend?"

"Not since May."

He took a sip from the bottle in his hand, and for a moment I thought I'd seen him extend his pinkie as if he were holding a cup of tea.

"You know," he said, "most kids your age who are about to start college are scared right now, too."

"I guess."

"Except for the drama jocks. Nothing scares a drama jock."

"I don't act."

"And there will be a lot of drama jocks at Bennington, won't there?"

"Mom told you where I'm going?"

"It did come up. What are you scared of, may I ask? Is it making friends or doing the work? Or is it, I don't know, just being away from home?"

I thought for a moment. "I'm not sure."

"I can tell by the way you just introduced yourself to me that you're a real shrinking violet," he said, rolling his eyes. "Clearly you'll *never* meet anybody."

"Kids are different."

"Yeah, they're younger. And here's the big secret about colleges: They only try and accept people who can do the work—especially a place like Bennington. Those incredible dullards in admissions? Well, one of the few things they're actually very good at is figuring out who's going to make it and who isn't. The last thing they want is for someone to fail. Besides," he went on, "I can't imagine you have any problems in the classroom."

"My mom's biased."

"Your mom and I have never talked about your academic strengths or weaknesses. I just have a good feeling about you," he said, and then he did something that in hindsight seems pretty minor, but at the time was one of the more astonishing things an adult male had ever done to me. He touched my hair.

"You wear your hair a bit like your mother, don't you?" he murmured, and with the fingers of only one hand he fixed the barrette, which had fallen askew. "So many young girls insist on a Barbie do. But short hair becomes you. You have such a lovely face—just like your mother."

Had any man in the world other than Dana touched me that way, I would have felt it was a come-on. I would have felt threatened. And given the fact that this man was my mom's friend—perhaps even a man she was interested in—it's likely I would have been pissed.

But none of those thoughts passed through my mind at that moment. I was simply flattered that this attractive older man thought my face was lovely. And I was glad that a person who apparently thought about hair felt I'd made a good decision with mine.

It was, in some way, as if one of my mother's close female friends— one of the women she'd known since Middlebury, and whom I'd known my whole life—had complimented me. The small remark was meaningful. Powerful. Reassuring.

"Thank you," I said.

He shrugged. "No problem. Girl can't have a barrette with a mind of its own."

I was home that night in time to help my mom load the dishwasher.

"You didn't mention you were inviting your teacher," I said as I emptied wineglasses into the sink. I tried to sound casual.

"I didn't know I was until yesterday. It was very spontaneous."

"Did you invite anyone else from the class?"

"Most of the other students are nineteen and twenty. They're closer to your age than mine."

"Not that doctor you told me about. Not the woman who works for the phone company."

She placed a sheet of Saran Wrap over a glass bowl filled with couscous. "I guess I could have invited them. But I didn't."

"You like him?"

"Who?"

"Dana!"

"Sure, I like him just fine. That's probably why I invited him."

"Do you like him as a friend? Or as something more?"

She placed the couscous in the refrigerator and closed the door with her hip. "Too early to tell."

"I like him."

"I'll sleep easier."

"He likes you."

If I'd said something like that to a girl my age, she would have been unable to resist asking me how I knew such a thing. But my mom had a generation on me, and merely nodded unconcernedly as she reached over my shoulders for the sponge at the edge of the sink.

"He grew up in Miami. Did you know that?" I asked.

"I think I did."

"He went to school in Massachusetts—Hampshire College, he said—because he wanted to be as far away from home as possible."

She wiped the crumbs off the counter she'd cleared, and turned to me. I was pleased that I'd finally said something that had gotten her attention. "How in the world did that come up? How long were you two chatting?"

"Not too long. But we talked about college."

"Personally, I've never been wild about Florida. I can't blame him for going to school in New England."

"I think it was more about his parents. He didn't say anything about Miami one way or the other."

"Your father once had a job offer from a station in Gainesville. I guess you were five or six," my mom said, clearly hoping to steer the conversation away from Dana. She never liked talking about the men in her life until she'd made a decision about them one way or the other.

I considered letting her off the hook, but it was a Friday night—almost Saturday morning—and I was having fun watching her sweat. And so I plowed ahead.

"Want to know why he picked a place in the Berkshires?"

She rinsed the sponge. "Sure. Tell me."

"Because his nearest relatives would be a thousand miles away in Atlanta, and his mom and dad would have to change planes at least once if they ever wanted to visit. Getting there would be a major ordeal."

"Well, then," she said, "I guess I should be flattered that you're only going to be two or three hours away."

"Want to know something else about him?"

"You're dying to tell me, aren't you?"

"He thinks you're pretty. And he likes your hair."

She smiled and gave me a small hug. "I'm happy you like him," she said, her voice serenely maternal. "Really, I am. But right now we're just friends. That's all. If it ever becomes anything more, you'll be the first to know. Okay?"

Her hands were wet from the sponge, and the back of my shirt grew damp.

"Okay," I said.

As we pulled apart, I found myself looking carefully at her mouth, and I wondered if I'd ever be brazen enough to dab someone else's lips with a napkin.

All Things Considered
Monday, September 24

BACKGROUND AUDIO: The sound of teacups on china saucers, the clinking of spoons. Small murmurs of conversation.

CARLY BANKS: Montreal's majestic Hotel Pierre sits across from an entrance to Mount Royal, the elegant park designed by Frederick Law Olmstead in the midst of Quebec's largest city. Here the International Association for Gender Diversity is holding its annual conference, this year themed "Trans-Am: In Praise of Gender Expression Across the Americas."

Raymond and Vanessa Packard are two of the nearly eleven hundred conference attendees who have arrived in Montreal. They've been married for five years—a demographic detail of little distinctiveness.

What makes their marriage unusual, however, and what has drawn them to Montreal is the fact that until six years ago, Vanessa was a man.

RAYMOND: Oh, I knew she wasn't a "genetic" female the night we met. But she'd been on hormones awhile, and it was about as close to love at first sight as I believe you really get in this world.

BANKS: Raymond, forty-one, owns an automobile dealership in Oak Brook, Illinois. Vanessa, thirty, is an accountant just outside of Chicago. You would never guess today that this slim young woman in a blue blazer and a beige business skirt was genetically male at birth, and had lived the first two decades of her life as a boy and a young man.

VANESSA: We met at a bar, just about seven years ago now. Ray was taking two salespeople out for a drink after work, and I was there with a friend. You know, unwinding.

BANKS: Raymond says that despite his immediate attraction to Vanessa, the notion never crossed his mind that he might be gay.

RAYMOND: I never, ever viewed Vanessa as male. Not for a second. Don't get the wrong idea, I'm not an idiot: I understood the plumbing, I realized she had a penis. But I could also see there was a beautiful woman inside there, and she was working her way to the surface.

VANESSA: The night we met, I was wearing a black stretch velvet dress that fell to my ankles. It had long sleeves and a princess seam—a little formal for that particular bar, as I recall, but when you're trying to pass, you don't want to cut any corners.

RAYMOND (laughing): See what I mean? Even then, she was ALL woman!

dana

HOW DO YOU SPEAK LIKE A WOMAN?

I've read all the books and I don't know how many articles. A lot. I've read all about adverbs and qualifiers (women, supposedly, use lots more of both than men) and how females are more likely than males to phrase a statement in the form of a question:

"Shall we go to dinner?"

"Aren't those shoes lovely?"

"Have you ever seen such a gorgeous day?"

And while I've made small changes here and there, I don't believe I've really done anything especially significant. I speak the way I always have.

And I don't believe I speak like a transvestite or a transsexual struggling to pass. I don't think anyone ever left one of my lectures on Flaubert or George Sand and murmured, "That professor sure talks like a fruit."

Or, these days, "That professor is *so* butch."

The fact is, I've always been female and so I've always had a natural inclination to speak a bit like a woman—but not, I believe, like a caricature of a woman.

It's just that simple.

I've never liked caricatures of women. I've never, to be honest, liked the way a transvestite looks—which is probably among the main reasons why I chose to go through such a precariously short period of pre-operative transition. The medical standards of care for transsexuals suggest that a patient spend a year living as the opposite gender before undergoing the final surgery, but I limited myself to barely three months.

That was it: twelve weeks. The last thing I wanted was to be perceived as a guy in a dress. And while my therapist wasn't pleased with the length of my transition, not for one single moment did she doubt either of our diagnoses, and she wrote all of the necessary referrals and recommendations. She'd known me for years, and there wasn't a question in her mind that I was indeed (and I've always loved the phonetics of this expression) gender dysphoric. Same with my surgeon. He knew what I was the moment we met, and I am quite sure he assumed I had spent more than a season—though a season is still, of course, sufficient time for whole ecosystems to transform themselves completely—in transition.

I think the fact that I was never a public cross-dresser was a big reason why my family was always able to convince themselves that my gender dysphoria was some kind of phase. Maybe a brain fog that would eventually lift. Go away. Disappear.

After all, as a teenager I was never caught in one of my sister's miniskirts or a blouse, and I wasn't hiding waist slimmers or lace brassieres in my closet. It's not as if I was concealing breast forms in my bureau. The five or six times I tried dressing up, I was so incredibly disappointed by the results that I'd wound up even more depressed than I'd been before I had crawled inside a pair of panty hose and a dress.

And I wasn't brazen enough to try shaving my legs until college.

Moreover, I always had girlfriends. In Florida. In Massachusetts. In Vermont.

Before I went through with the surgery, a gay friend of mine in the Sociology Department who knew my sexual history would shake her head and sigh. "Oh, good, Dana," she'd say. "Just what the world needs: another lesbian in a man's body."

In my late twenties, I had a therapist who was always trying to convince me that my interest in women was a sign that I shouldn't be considering surgery. But whenever I fell in love, it just reinforced in my mind how much I was missing, and I would fall into a funk as deep as the moat that had surrounded my adolescence.

Ah, but then I started on hormones, and it was amazing. The glimmer of heaven, the Northern Lights. Three months on estrogen and progesterone and a testosterone blocker, and I had flushed my antidepressants down the toilet. I was happier than I'd ever been in my life.

And it seemed as if my body hair was just melting away. Even though I was on a pretty low dosage of everything, I spent less and less time plucking, and the electrolysis grew considerably less painful. I took this as further proof that I was making the right decision: My body knew well what it wanted.

Still, sometimes Allison would ask me if I hated my body—meaning, specifically, my genitals. We talked about that often in the months before we flew to Colorado for the operation. One autumn night when we were at her house in Bartlett, maybe a month and a half after Carly had left for college, we were lying in bed after making love, and she wrapped her fingers around my limp penis. "Do you really hate it that much?" she asked.

We had had an exquisite Indian summer that year: Even though it was October, it was so warm at night that we were actually sleeping with the windows open a crack, and I could feel the moist, evening air on the small, wondrous hillocks that were just starting to rise from my chest.

"I don't think hate is the right word," I said.

"Because I have to tell you, it works really well," she said, a tiny quiver in her voice. Allison had only known my plans for a couple of weeks then, and she was still a little wobbly.

"Thank you."

"I mean, I've been with a lot of men. Maybe not a lot. But easily seven or eight. And trust me: You use yours very well."

"You can't count the college boys."

"Have you ever . . ."

"Yes?"

"Have you ever had trouble getting an erection?"

"Around women? God, no."

"Never?"

I squeezed her. "Well, the female hormones have begun to make them a little less common. We've both noticed. But before I began hormone therapy? No, never. I've always been a bit of a rarity in that regard: a relentlessly horny trannie."

She cupped my bottom with her free hand and pressed her long fingers between my cheeks. "You're getting hard now," she said.

"Tell me about it."

"If you don't hate it . . . then why do this?"

Why? It has been the question of my adult life, hasn't it? I've answered it for my parents and my sister, I've answered it for doctors and counselors and friends. I've explained it to therapists. To cousins. To acquaintances who are particularly bold.

Interestingly, I was never asked why by a college administrator. Perhaps they feared their questions might trigger the sort of grotesquely unpleasant sexual harassment suit that generates all manner of bad press. Or maybe they simply thought they were supposed to be open-minded.

Personally, I think I just gave them the creeps: Dana Stevens, the tenured transsexual.

"Why?" Allison asked me again.

"Because," I told her, "I'm a woman. And a woman isn't supposed to have a penis. I'll be much happier when it's gone."

She stopped fondling me and kicked off the lone sheet that was resting upon us. For a moment I feared we were going to have a fight, or a scene like the one we'd had when I first broke the news to her. But then I understood she was simply going to show me, once more, that she loved my penis enough for the both of us, and was about to give me the blow job of the millennium.

3

carly

My mom's film course met on Tuesdays and Thursdays. Dana asked her out for the first time right after the class that followed my mother's party.

"Are you the matchmaker who encouraged him?" my mom asked me at breakfast the next day, a Wednesday, as she painted her toenails red.

"Nope."

"Well, I hope you're pleased. We're going out to dinner Friday night."

Breakfasts were strange that summer, because I had a job to get to and my mom didn't. As a schoolteacher she had the summers off, and so we had grown accustomed to strolling through our summer mornings together in slow motion.

But that summer my mom was always up and dressed with me, as if she felt a motherly responsibility to see me off to my high-powered job watering baby lilac trees. Of course, *dressed* for her at six forty-five in the morning usually meant shorts and a bulky T-shirt: Although I had to be at the nursery by seven-thirty, Mom didn't have to be anywhere ever seven days a week.

Still, my mom can make ugly shorts look good. She has long slender legs that a lot of girls my age would kill for. I have them, too, but between field hockey and lacrosse, throughout high school they were usually swollen somewhere or bruised.

And while my mom seemed to begin the day that summer in shorts, at some point she would slip into a sundress, because she had invariably changed her clothes by the time I would come home from work.

"In Burlington?" I asked.

"Yup."

"Can I have some friends over, then?"

"Sure. Just the usual rules."

The usual rules meant no drinking, no drugs, and no identifiable proof that anyone had had anything that even resembled sex. And no more than a half dozen kids.

"What time do you think you'll be back?"

"It won't be late. We're meeting at seven o'clock. So I'm sure I'll be home by ten-thirty or eleven."

"There might still be a few kids here then."

"That's okay." She dipped the brush back into the bottle for the last time and screwed on the top. "Are you coming home tonight after dinner with Dad and Patricia?" she asked.

"I doubt it. But I'll call if I change my mind."

She nodded. "Will Michael be here Friday?" She tried to sound casual, but Michael had become a pretty loaded word in our house. My mom thought I'd made a tremendous mistake when I broke up with him back in May. She certainly agreed we should separate before college, or at least come to what she called an accommodation, but she also feared I had dumped him for no other reason than a desire to get the inevitable over with early on.

Not true. I had broken up with Michael because I didn't want to spend my last summer before college like I was married. I didn't want to feel a moral obligation to spend every minute with the boy when I wasn't wheeling shrubs in and out of the sun.

Besides, it's not as if there was this incredible spark. Michael was just a nice guy who was always willing to use a condom. Sometimes, I think, my mom liked him more than I did.

"Probably not."

"Miss him?"

"Nope."

"Well. Good for you."

I swallowed the last of my juice and gave my mother a quick kiss on her forehead. And then I left for the fast-track world of philodendron.

My mom lives in a tri-gable ell that was built in 1885. It has three stories, a Queen Anne porch with fish-scale trim on the clapboards, and a set of bay windows on both the first and second floors. It's been white for at least as long as I've been alive, and the shutters on the windows are green.

My dad's house is a two-story Greek Revival cottage that dates all the way back to 1851. It has its original slate roof, gingerbread trim, and stained-glass windows around the front door. These were added toward the end of the nineteenth century. The house is a very light yellow.

I know these details about my parents' houses because my eighth-grade class did a booklet together on "Historic Bartlett," and I wrote the chapter on architecture.

It seemed like the radio was always on in my dad's house when he was home, and it seemed like it was always tuned to Vermont Public Radio. Sometimes it was on just loud enough for a person to tell whether the station was broadcasting music or talk, and sometimes it was like there was this other person in the room with you who was constantly trying to interrupt—and constantly being ignored.

Occasionally, my dad would raise his hand and signal time-out, and Patricia and I would make faces at him while he listened intently for a brief moment.

By the time I got to his house that day, *All Things Considered* was long over, and even *Marketplace* was winding down. In my dad's house, we often told time by the shows on the radio:

"What time is it?"

"Let's see, *Fresh Air* is ending. It must be a few minutes before five."

In reality, my dad isn't all that psycho about work. He just thinks he should know what's on the air at any given moment.

He was outside barbecuing when I got there, and so the kitchen window was open with the radio aimed toward him. Patricia was standing up by the dishwasher, thumbing through the mail, and I figured she must have just arrived home herself because she still had on the skirt and blouse she'd worn that day to work. She was a lawyer in Middlebury.

Though Patricia had been married to my dad for five years, we still hadn't figured out how physical our relationship was supposed to be: I had no idea when I was supposed to hug her or kiss her, and it was so clear that she hadn't a clue either. We liked each other just fine, but we both understood on some level that my loyalty was always going to be with my mom, and we would never be very close—sort of like college roommates freshman year who understand from day one that they're never going to be great pals. They might know all sorts of personal details about each other—what that other person sleeps in at night, and the kinds of shampoo she will use in the shower—but they don't really talk about those things that matter.

"Hi, Patricia," I said when I walked into the kitchen, beelining straight for the refrigerator so I'd have something to do with my hands and my mouth.

"Evening, Carly."

"Dad outside?"

"Mr. Barbecue."

"Dead things?"

"And plenty of vegetables for you," she said. My dad and Patricia viewed my decision to become a vegetarian largely in terms of the way it seemed to complicate their dinner menus. For the first few months after I gave up meat, they tried to convince themselves that birds weren't animals and I'd eat chicken if they served it. And when that didn't work, they tried to persuade me to eat fish. It had only been since Easter—when I'd refused to eat the lamb my dad had spent all of Good Friday trying to butterfly—that they finally realized my resolve was unwavering.

She put down the last of the mail and looked up at me. "You haven't been wearing sunscreen, have you?" she said, and she compressed her lips together the way she did whenever she was worried about something.

"I did the other day," I told her, but I knew my answer sounded pretty lame.

"You should wear it every day," she said. "You don't know the damage you're doing."

I did, of course, and in all honesty it wasn't vanity that kept me from wearing sunscreen. I really didn't care that much about having a tan. But my hands were always covered with peat moss or dirt, or I was wearing these big heavy gardening gloves, and I just never seemed to remember sunscreen when it was convenient.

"I'll try tomorrow," I told her, and I took my can of diet soda and joined my dad on the patio. His house sat at the very base of North Mountain, which meant that the woods began at the edge of the backyard and then climbed straight up a solid fifteen hundred feet. Even though the front yard got a reasonable amount of sunlight, the backyard was always dark and depressing, in my opinion.

Mom's house was smack in the middle of the village—only a block from the commons and the gazebo, and right across the street from the library—which meant that while there was considerably less privacy, it was also a lot less gloomy.

"How's Mom?" he asked after he'd hugged me. He rarely asked about Mom in front of Patricia. Sometimes Patricia would bring her up, but it was always in very general terms. School budgets. Class trips. Single women.

"Fine. She's thinking about going bicycling for a couple of days in Maine next month."

He nodded. "With whom?"

"A couple of girlfriends. Maybe Nancy Keenan. Molly Cochran."

"She like her film course?"

"She does." I watched him use his index fingers to flip a skewer with red and green peppers. The skewer was hot, and so he touched the metal for just the tiniest second: A quick flick with two fingers, and the peppers were turned.

"She always liked movies," he said.

"This one's filled with dogs. But I think that's the point."

"A whole course devoted to bad movies?"

"Well, it's books and movies. The guy who teaches it put it this way: 'It's not whether the books or the movies are any good that matters. It's how the movies were changed from the books.'"

"You've met him?"

Instantly I realized my mistake. The only thing I hated more than talking about Patricia with Mom was talking about Mom's latest boyfriend with Dad. For a person who hadn't lived with his ex-spouse for over a decade, he still seemed to have an awfully strong interest in her new squeeze.

"Once. It was real informal."

"Where? Did you join your mom for a class?"

"Not exactly."

"Not exactly?" I'm sure he thought he sounded unconcerned, but his interest clearly was piqued and his voice had an edge.

"Mom invited him to her party last Friday night."

"Really?"

"Yup. But I think it was just because she thinks he's sort of pathetic."

"Old guy?"

"Oh, you know. Middle-aged. Like you and Mom."

"In his forties?"

"Sort of," I lied.

"What's his name?"

"Dana. I don't know his last name."

He flipped the swordfish with a spatula. "Nice guy?"

I wondered if Dana ever barbecued, and decided that he didn't. It wasn't that barbecuing was so clearly man's work in my mind and Dana wasn't manly. But barbecuing is communal cooking: People who live alone aren't likely to fire up the hibachi.

"I guess."

"Well, I hope he is. I only want your mom to be around nice men."

The coals were spitting from the moisture that was dripping onto them from the fish, and the smoke was starting to make my eyes water. I backed away from the grill, hoping Dad could sense my discomfort with the subject of Mom's professor. I certainly didn't plan on mentioning the fact that the pair were going out to dinner in a couple of nights, or that Dana resembled my dad.

"Dinner looks just about done," I babbled, deciding that their fish and my vegetables were close enough to cooked that I had an excuse to cut short our conversation. "I better go inside and wash up."

Patricia usually went up to bed before Dad—at least when I was there—and so my dad and I watched one of those police dramas on TV. Unlike the rest of Vermont, Dad and Patricia hadn't broken down yet and bought a satellite dish, which meant they only got two stations and there wasn't a whole lot of programming choice.

But it really didn't matter, because the TV show was just an excuse for us to be together and chat. I always felt a certain duty to stay up with Dad when I was at his house, because by my last years in high school I was spending so much less time with him than with Mom.

Most of the evening we talked about my departure for Bennington at the end of the summer, and what sorts of things I planned to bring with me. But we also discussed a public radio conference he'd attended over the weekend, and then—as the program on TV was winding down—we talked some more about Mom. I knew it was coming the moment he took off his eyeglasses and rubbed the bridge of his nose.

"You know I'd never, ever tell your mother how to live her life. But do you think it's safe for her to go bicycling in Maine?"

I shrugged. "Sure. She'll have one or two other women with her."

"Will it be part of a bicycle tour? Will there be guides?"

"No, I think it's just her and her spandex."

"How long will she be gone?"

"I don't even know if she's decided to go for sure. She may not bother. It's just an idea she had with Nancy Keenan the other day, because her film course ends next week, and she was trying to figure out what to do with the rest of her summer."

He shook his head. "You know something? Your mom and I just don't talk enough anymore."

"Divorce will do that."

"We're still friends, Carly, even if we don't live together. I mean, I didn't even know she was interested in this professor character—that fellow she had to her party."

I almost told him that I wasn't sure she was interested in Dana, but then I remembered the two of them were going out on an honest-to-God dinner date in a couple of nights. And so I stared at the TV and tried to nod ambiguously.

"Dana, right?" my dad asked.

"Uh-huh."

He didn't ask me any more questions; once again he knew exactly how far the interrogation could go. But I didn't miss the fact that he had brought up my mother a second time that evening, and that he had remembered Dana's name. I hadn't sensed any tension between Patricia and him at dinner, but they had both been unusually quiet and the idea crossed my mind that—as the radio shrinks like to put it—the two of them were having some problems and their relationship needed some work.

All Things Considered
Monday, September 24

CARLY BANKS: . . . and so Dr. Meehan has been per-
forming what is now called sexual reassignment surgery
since 1981. Last year, his Waterman Gender Clinic in
Trinidad, Colorado, helped eighteen women become men,
and a hundred and fifty-nine men become women—including Dana Stevens. Meehan estimates that over the last
two decades he has performed sexual reassignment
surgery close to four thousand times.

DR. THOMAS MEEHAN: Gender dysphoria is as old as
time. Let's face it, Eve was made from Adam. Herodotus
was chronicling what he called the Scythian illness—
the decision by Venus to change the Scythian men into
women—some twenty-five hundred years ago. It may only
be the surgery that's new. And, in some ways, the concept of surgery isn't even all that modern. It's only
the techniques that are new. But the Greeks, the
Romans, and the Phrygians all did their fair share of
castration. Philo of Alexandria describes it. Cedrenus
cites it. Priests were regularly castrated in worship
services for Cybele.

BANKS: The Waterman Gender Clinic is one of a half
dozen sites in the United States where the vast majority of sexual reassignment surgery is accomplished,
but it is among the oldest, having been founded by
Meehan's predecessor in 1971. And though the number of
patients Meehan sees every year has fallen as a result
of newer competition in Pennsylvania, California,

Oregon, and Wisconsin, he still does about a third of the procedures.

MEEHAN: We all know the "big" names. Tennis pro Renee Richards. Writer Jan Morris. The real pioneer, Christine Jorgensen. But most transgendered people are simply anonymous members of their communities. They're lawyers and firefighters and bureaucrats. Ever heard the name Leslie Nelson? Lady on death row in New Jersey. She had her sex change in 1992.

BANKS: Dr. Meehan says that perhaps half the transsexuals who come to the Waterman Gender Clinic are involved in a relationship, but adds that a relationship should never be the reason for a reassignment.

MEEHAN: I can only think of one case in which a person underwent the procedure for that reason, and I can assure you he wasn't a patient of mine. I'd never have done it. He didn't fit the guidelines for surgery, it was that simple.

BANKS: But Dr. Meehan did meet the candidate when he flew to Colorado for a consultation.

MEEHAN: Male stockbroker, lived somewhere in Boston. Married for three years, when his wife decided she was gay. Well, he loved her very much, and he finally found a surgeon who would do the procedure—which was just ridiculous. Insane, completely insane—on both their parts.

About six months after the surgery, the wife decided she was wrong, she wasn't a lesbian. And so she walked out. And now there's this poor guy in Massachusetts who's trapped for the rest of his life in a woman's body. Oh, we could re-create for him a limp penis, and we could take him off hormones. Remove the implants in his chest. But he'll never have working testicles again, he'll only be at his best a cosmetic man.

My point? Gender dysphoria and romance don't have a damn thing to do with each other. Transgendered people fall in love exactly the way you and I do, but it should never be the reason for surgery.

4

allison

I REMEMBER LYING CURLED UP IN A BALL IN MY bed that fall after I heard Dana's plans, and trying my best to be reasonable. But reason doesn't come easy, especially when you're awake in the middle of the night.

Maybe, I would think, I *could* be a lesbian. Wasn't it conceivable that I might still love Dana after the surgery? Perhaps love had absolutely nothing to do with sexual preference. Perhaps you just fell in love with a person—gender be damned—and it just so happened that I had always fallen in love with men.

Or, perhaps, it was all nurture: I'd been conditioned from an early age to be heterosexual. Once I renewed my relationship with a post-op Dana Stevens, I'd see how possible it was for me to fall in love with a woman.

But then I would back off. I was forty-two: Did I really want to travel down that path at midlife? Not likely.

After all, I'd certainly never had those sorts of desires.

But alone in one's bed, the mind wanders into some very strange corners. Once, I climbed out from under the sheets and turned on the light, and took an antique silver hand mirror from the top of my dresser. I then sat on the edge of the bed and spread my legs, and used the mirror to study my vagina. How in the world could a doctor build such a thing? It wasn't like breasts; it wasn't the sort of item you could fake with a pair of silicone implants.

Maybe a surgeon could shape skin into labia, but how do you begin to construct a clitoris? How do you fabricate a G spot, a cavity, inner walls that grow moist?

It was beyond me, completely unfathomable.

And while I thought I loved Dana, would I really want to make love to a doctor-built vulva? I wasn't even sure I wanted to make love to one made by God.

None of this would have been an issue, of course, if I'd known Dana's plans when I met him that summer. I know I would not have grown interested in him if I had realized he was on female hormones and planned to have a sex change soon after Christmas.

And the fact is, at first I wasn't romantically interested in him anyway. I merely saw him as a professor who was smart and funny and just a little bit catty. I thought he was cute, but I also thought he was gay.

I should be precise: I thought he was a gay male.

The signals? No wedding band. No references to a partner or spouse. Eyebrows that clearly were plucked.

When I invited him to my house for a party, it never crossed my mind we might wind up as lovers. Inviting him was a spontaneous gesture, because I thought there might be a friendship in the offing. He made me laugh in class all the time, and I was certainly learning a good deal more from his course than I'd ever expected.

At some point at the party, however, it crossed my mind that he might be straight after all. Clearly my daughter thought so. I'm not exactly sure what he said or did that changed my mind, but it may have been as simple as the way he touched my side at one point when we were chatting. We were outside on the terrace, and he was holding his plate and telling me how wonderful he thought the pasta was, and with his free hand he touched the small of my waist—just above my hip, his pinkie within a millimeter of the elastic at the top of my panties. And then he held his hand there for a long moment, and I felt a slight rush. I was wearing a thin cotton dress, and I could almost feel how warm his fingers were through the fabric.

And when he asked me out after class on the following Tuesday, it felt nothing at all like a platonic overture. I remembered well the feel of his touch from my house Friday night, and I was open to whatever possibilities he had in mind.

Looking back, if anything at all surprises me about our first date, it's the idea that somehow we managed not to make love. I've always been a sucker for smart men, and the first thing he did at dinner was seduce my mind. We had dinner on the deck of a restaurant in Burlington that looked out upon Lake Champlain, and we had a glorious view of the sunset over the Adirondacks. We talked about teaching children and teaching adults, and how one taught that murky group in between: college students of traditional age. We talked about Carly and college and my fears of wandering alone for months at a time through my musty old house in the village.

He told me little bits about his adolescence in Florida, and the relief he felt when he arrived in New England. He didn't tell me why his teenage years had been difficult—why, I know now, they had been a horror—but I understood that his adolescence had not been pleasant.

It would be some months later before I would learn about the drinking and the drugs and the powerful self-loathing. Toying with the notion of suicide after he saw a photograph of a transsexual in a magazine when he was seventeen, and realized that was what he was—minus the requisite surgery.

He took me back to his apartment for coffee and dessert after dinner, and we had the very last fresh strawberries of the season. He made whipped cream for them, and he put out a small plate with melted chocolate. And then, as if we were teenagers, we actually necked on the couch. He lived on the top floor of the closest thing Burlington has to a luxury high-rise, a seven-story co-op smack in the center of the city. His living room faced the hill section of town, and when I would open my eyes, I could see the lights on in the windows of the one- and two-century-old houses to the east.

We never left the couch for the bedroom, but I would have followed him if he'd made the slightest gesture in that direction. I had never in my life been with a man whose hands were that gentle or whose mouth was that soft. He would spend long minutes tracing my lips with his tongue, before probing just the tiniest bit inside me. Men sometimes have a tendency to offer substantially more of their tongue than is really necessary, but not Dana. Not at all. And he would massage my body with his fingers as we kissed, at one point actually pulling me off the couch and onto his lap so I was straddling him, and he rubbed my back that way until I was—for the first time in my life—aroused and satiated at once.

I'm not sure how or why we stopped. I have a feeling I said something about having to get home. I believe I said such a thing because that part of me that was the mother of a teenage girl thought it would be an inadvisable moral precedent to sleep with a man on a first date.

There was an E-mail from Dana waiting for me the next morning when I logged on to my computer at home. We'd talked a good deal about movies the night before, and in his E-mail he'd listed exactly when the films I wanted to see were showing at different cinemas. He suggested we go out Sunday evening, but he said he was open to any nights at all when he wasn't teaching.

Initially, I considered writing back that while Sunday night would be fine, why wait another whole day? Why not go out again that very night? But I concluded that that draft was too forward, and never sent it. Instead I simply agreed that Sunday night would be lovely.

We chose a movie that was showing in Middlebury, so he could pick me up on the way. And then I decided to invite him to dinner at my house first, at least in part so I wouldn't have to miss my daughter two out of three nights in a weekend. Though I would be going out on a date, at least Carly and I would have dinner together Sunday night.

Dana and I made all the arrangements without speaking a single word to each other. We did it all by computer.

Sunday afternoon Carly surprised me by knocking on the bathroom door while I was taking a bath. She hadn't joined me while I'd bathed in a very long time, and though I immediately told her to come in, I found myself slipping under the bubbles that remained on the surface of the water. Had I really aged so much in four years that I'd grown uncomfortable with my body? Had I really grown shy?

Carly, too, was uneasy, I could tell. She sat on the john the way she had when she was younger, but she stared out the window at the afternoon sky as we talked, instead of looking at me.

"A second date with the prof," she began, and I understood instantly why she had felt compelled to venture once more into the bathroom while I was taking a bath. "I know if I were one of the other kids in the class, I'd expect a really good grade just to keep my mouth shut."

"Trust me: It's okay if Dana fails me."

"You like him now, don't you?"

"I do."

"Is he the first man you've ever dated with a ponytail?"

I thought for a moment, and reached for one of the brass handles at the edge of the tub with my foot. I let the hot water run for a couple of seconds and warm the tub. "As a matter of fact, he is," I said finally.

"Do you think it's sexy?"

"No, not necessarily. But I like his hair."

"Either his shampoo or his conditioner has a ton of fragrance in it."

She was right, and I nodded. I tried to recall the aroma from Friday night. It was definitely from an expensive brand: Dana certainly wasn't using some lonely guy's price club shampoo.

"And his hair's longer than yours," she continued. "A lot longer. Is that a first, too?"

"I think so. Your father had pretty long hair in college. But back then so did I. And your father would never have put his back in a ponytail."

She curled one of her legs up on the seat and toyed with the leather straps of her sandal. "Dad doesn't think you should go biking in Maine," she said.

"I don't know if I will. The fact is, I probably won't. It was just an idea Nancy and I were tossing around. But whether your father thinks I should go really doesn't matter."

"Guess not. How come you changed your mind? Dana?"

Carly has always had astonishing instincts, and I was impressed that she had, yet again, understood something about me before I had. Until that moment, I hadn't realized that I had changed my mind. But I had. Clearly. It wasn't that the idea of biking along the Maine coast no longer interested me: It was that I now had a more interesting play-mate than Nancy Keenan.

"Maybe. Maybe I'll just go for a day or two in the Adirondacks in the fall—over Columbus Day weekend."

"Maybe you'll go with Dana."

"Maybe. He's about to begin his very first sabbatical. When he fin-ishes teaching this summer, he won't be in the classroom again until next September. Thirteen months. So he'll certainly have the time."

"Is a sabbatical paid?"

"You bet."

"What a racket. Remind me to become a college professor."

"I'm sure he'll be working. He's already published two books, you know. I'm sure he'll be researching. Writing—"

"Biking with you."

"I'll have a lot of time on my hands, sweetheart. You know how much I'm going to miss you."

For the first time since venturing into the bathroom, she looked at me, and she gave me the smile of hers that I've loved her whole life—a grin that is impish and mischievous and knowing at once.

"Yeah," she said, "so I guess you'll just have to replace your daugh-ter with some hunk who wears a ponytail."

will

THE YEAR ALLIE AND I SEPARATED WAS A NIGHT-mare. On the surface it was all very congenial, and I put on a good face. And while, looking back, it's pretty clear that Allie wasn't happy, I'm not sure I knew at the time that I was leaving for good. It was one of those decisions we made after a counseling session had gone particularly badly, and we were livid with each other.

Before I found an apartment—and then the home in which I live now—I moved back in with my father in Montpelier. I was there about a week and a half, and I stayed in the room I'd lived in as a boy. Thirty-three years old, I thought, and I'm living in a room that still has thumbtacks in the wall from Grand Funk Railroad and Moody Blues concert posters. Worse, the dog my parents had gotten when I'd left for college had grown used to sleeping on what had been my bed, and the animal—geriatric by then—was flatulent. The mutt was a biohazard, but it would have been inhumanly cruel to kick him out. The result? One night I went to bed wearing swimmers' nose plugs, and while I eventually nodded off, I woke up a moment later gasping for breath as if I had sleep apnea.

The next day, Allie and I met for coffee after school, and when she broke down sobbing in the little bakery café on Main Street, I realized we really were finished. She insisted I hadn't done anything wrong, which was a sure sign. She said she just didn't love me the way she had when we'd met, and we'd probably gotten married too soon. We'd been, pure and simple, too young.

It was most likely a defense mechanism of sorts, but I decided she was probably right. I said so to myself, and then I reached across the little glass table and took her hands and agreed with her. I stared for a long time at her wedding ring, and then at mine.

The fact was, I'd spent the last year or year and a half unreasonably angry at something I never could quite identify: My mother's losing battle with Lou Gehrig's disease. The construction firm that was behind the radio station's new home and was constantly finding reasons to go over budget. The station's board of directors, who seemed to want me—a very young and green station president—to listen to every whiner who sent in his twenty-five-dollar annual membership check.

I was even squabbling with my older brother that year, snapping at him without reason whenever we'd speak on the phone. I was giving him parenting advice that he certainly didn't need, and telling him how I thought he should deal with the building contractor who was adding a couple of dormers to the west wall of his house—and, because he was only working on the project every third or fourth day, had been at work on it all summer long. The scaffolding had been there since Memorial Day, making whole rooms shady even at noon.

Given my attitude, I decided right there in the bakery that perhaps it was time to try something new. Maybe, like Allie, a part of me longed for something more.

Or, perhaps, somebody else.

Maybe that would even be best for Carly. It can't be healthy to watch your parents snap at each other like angry turtles in a terrarium, or to see your mom sad.

This is, of course, what every parent in the midst of a divorce says to himself. At least every decent one: I'm actually doing my kid a favor by leaving. In the long run, she'll be happier, right? Right?

A little more than a decade later, long after my ex-wife and I had settled into a pretty terrific friendship, I think I began to understand what Allie had been feeling back then. And while I didn't believe I was especially morose the summer that Allie started to see Dana, I probably wasn't a great blessing to be around. I was growing so desirous of being alone that instead of going straight home after work, some evenings I'd stop and park at a patch of dirt just beyond the high wire fence that marked the edge of a runway at Burlington Airport, and I'd watch the planes swoop down just above me. I'd tell myself I'd only stay for one more Saab 340, one more Dash 8, one more Boeing 737—a jet that seemed absolutely massive, compared to the commuter planes, with their primitive propellers, that linked Burlington with Boston. But I never kept my word to myself, and some nights I would get home half an hour or forty-five minutes late.

One evening when Patricia asked me how work was, and I mumbled—as I did always that summer—that it was fine, she accused me of being incommunicative.

"Why do you say that?" I asked.

"Because your own radio station reported the battle you had with protesters today over your tower on Mount Chittenden!" she answered, referring to the hikers who were complaining, yet again, about the radiation from our broadcast tower on a mountain that was a part of the state's Long Trail.

"Oh."

"Well?"

"Well, what?"

"How was work?"

I shrugged. "It was fine," I repeated, and on one level I was telling the absolute truth. I'd been president of the station since I was thirty-one. It would have taken an earthquake that brought down the building for work to be anything but fine.

Looking back, it's easy to see that I, too, was ready for a change—at work, maybe, or perhaps at home. Maybe simply in bed.

Of course, I didn't see it that way at the time. I merely assumed I was going through a phase.

dana

THERE ARE TWO WORLDS OF PEOPLE AROUND ME. There is a world in which everyone knows I was born a man, and there is a world in which no one has any clue whatsoever.

Sometimes the two orbits will overlap, and a person will discover rather suddenly my history with gender. If that person is particularly brazen—or, it seems, a reporter—he (and yes, in my experience, more times than not it has indeed been a *he*) will ask one or both of two questions:

Does it work? (Translation: Do you have orgasms?)

Did I ever assume I was merely a homosexual? (Translation: Isn't this just about penetration? About wanting *to be* penetrated?)

The first question is actually much easier to answer than I imagine it is to ask. Yes, I can answer honestly, it works just fine. (Translation: Touch me right and you'll have to peel me off the ceiling.)

The second question is more complicated, and it seemed to me that some of the folks from NPR—one engineer in particular—were always coming back to it. It was clear they were trying to be tolerant and open-minded, but their inquiries implied they suspected that I'd been driven to my decision by an army of unbearable homophobes.

Always, of course, they were forgetting completely one teeny-tiny detail: I *was* gay! I just happened to be a gay woman.

Now, in all fairness, I had indeed toyed with the notion that I might be a gay male at different times in my life, but it was always a desperate, and increasingly pathetic, fantasy. After all, even in *this* world it's a hell of a lot easier to be a gay male than a transsexual.

But three times I had sex with men, and each event was an almost unimaginable disaster. The fact is, I simply wasn't attracted to men or interested in gay male sex. To be perfectly honest, I had always been the sort of man who would absolutely dread his prostate exam for days in advance, so the whole idea of anal penetration was going to be problematic for me at best. It was only after a trio of homosexual liaisons failed to elicit a single ejaculation—regardless of who did what to whom—that I figured I'd had my three strikes and was out.

More important, that second question assumes that gender is all about sex, or that sexual preference is at the core of our gender. I can't speak for other transsexuals, but there is no way on God's green earth I would have become a born-again woman just so the sex would be hot. No orgasm in the world is worth all that electrolysis.

Truthfully, I became an external woman because I have always been an internal woman. That's all there is to it. And I've known this most of my life. I think I had the first solid clue when my sister was born. I was five, and my parents put her in my arms on the couch in our living room, and I was absolutely enchanted. I told them I couldn't wait to have a baby emerge from my tummy, too.

Quickly—almost curtly—my father reminded me of the few, rudimentary biological imperatives I had been taught during the preceding nine months. My mother rubbed my back.

Outside our living room was a screened-in porch with a small pool, and outside the porch was a wall of lush tropical foliage that separated us from our neighbors. I handed my sister to my mother, stood up, and went stamping my feet outside into our backyard. I clawed my way into the brush, found a spot in the dirt to curl up in, and then I started to cry. Soon I was howling like a toddler.

"It's not fair!" I screamed over and over. "It's not fair!"

And while my parents took comfort in the notion that my tantrum was simple panic because I had lost a monopoly on their attention, I knew the awful truth. The things I wanted most in the world were going to be forever denied me.

Worse, when I started elementary school, I learned that even small manifestations of femininity would be out of the question, too, and that my desires were, apparently, perverse. Yes, I wanted someday to have a real baby and real breasts, but at six, I would have been pacified with a plastic doll that looked like a newborn, and a couple of pretend diapers.

I knew, however, not to speak up.

I knew not to ask for dolls that were babies, and I knew not to ask for dolls that looked like Amazon models with eating disorders. I knew not to ask for dress-up clothes and little-girl makeup, I knew not to pretend I was a princess or a mermaid or a bride. I knew not to be a girl.

At least I knew not to in front of my family or friends.

Sometimes in my room, however, when I had shut my door for the night, I would go to the store. I placed my desk chair behind my toy chest and put my plastic cash register upon it. And then I would be the sales assistant one moment and Dana the customer the next, and I would pretend to buy a frilly dress with pink floral edging along the collar and sleeves. I would purchase a handbag, long shiny hair like my mother's—a chestnut-colored apron my parents never used would suffice—and I would leave the emporium shaped like an hourglass Barbie. Then I would crawl back into bed and press my little penis and my little balls deep behind the fat on my six- and seven-year-old thighs, and finally I would fall asleep.

Some nights I'd be crying. Some nights, not.

Sometimes I would take off my pajama bottoms and sleep in only my pajama top, pretending the loose shirt was actually a little girl's nightgown.

Invariably, my last thought would be the hope or the prayer that when I awoke in the morning, I would discover it had all been a dream. I would wake up clothed in a cotton nightdress covered with flowers, and my room would be draped in all manner of pink and lavender and rose. My closet would be rich with dresses and skirts, and my mother would help me get ready for school by brushing the tangles from my hair, and slipping a colorful barrette in place. Maybe that afternoon I'd have ballet class.

I stopped hoping and praying when I turned nine. I didn't know the word *deviant*. But I knew the word *bad*.

Jordan was on hormones, and so were Pinto and Marisa. Pinto and Marisa were lovers. Pinto was the only one in the group on male hormones, and the only person who planned, someday, to have the artists in Trinidad or Palo Alto sculpt a penis from forearm and calf muscle.

The first time I went to a meeting, I offered Pinto my penis and suggested we simply swap genitalia, but of course they aren't doing transplants yet.

The rest of the group were cross-dressers, drag queens, and a few conflicted souls who talked a lot about hormones and surgery, but admitted they weren't sure what they should do. I recognized two young folks from the university, and they recognized me. We promised not to tell anyone our little secret until we wanted it out in the open.

Altogether, there were about thirty-five of us in the Green Mountain Gender Benders, but there were usually no more than fifteen or twenty in attendance any given week. I'm a case in point. The whole time I was a member, I don't think I went to more than a dozen meetings: I went five or six times before I started on hormones, and five or six times after. I only went once after I met Allison.

We gathered in a party room at the back of a very tolerant bar on Colchester Avenue, but there were no windows and the place always smelled like keg beer gone bad. On the bright side, the room was dark—it actually had wallpaper that was supposed to look like wood paneling—which meant that most of us looked better than we had any right to.

I'm not sure why the group wasn't as helpful as Dr. Fuller thought it would be. Part of the problem may have been configuration. I don't have the same problems as a heterosexual man who likes to pass in women's clothing in public, or a gay man who likes to parade for the world in drag.

Okay, I had some of the same problems: Finding a pair of dress sling-backs that fit a man's size-nine flippers. Discovering a chenille sweater broad enough for my shoulders.

By and large, however, we probably would have been better off with three separate support groups. But in a city as small as Burling-ton, Vermont, that just wasn't going to happen. There weren't enough of us for three different groups.

At least there weren't enough transsexuals.

Still, I did get something out of the meetings. It was through the Benders that I found my electrologist, a woman who wasn't flustered by the challenges posed by a man in her chair. That was nice. And I'm sure it was healthy to be reminded that I wasn't the only human being on the planet who'd had a miserable adolescence, or who'd been born the victim of a howling chromosomal error. And it was probably very helpful to see how much the basics in life were huge to people like us: Pinto's desire to pee standing up; Marisa's yearning to wear a B-cup without padding; Jordan's hunger to fall in love with a man, and for that man to fall in love with her as a woman.

But I've never been much of a joiner. And once Allison had said she would stick by me, at least until I came back from Trinidad, I lost interest in the group. I still had drinks now and then with Jordan, and once Allison and I went out to dinner with Pinto and Marisa. But I no longer needed their shoulders to lean upon, and I no longer needed their advice. Suddenly, I had an honest-to-God genetic woman by my side to make sure I didn't inadvertently choose clothing that made me look like a harlot.

When do you know you're falling in love?

I think you know pretty fast.

I knew I was falling in love with Allison Banks by the time she left my apartment after our very first date. And so I almost didn't ask her out a second time, because I didn't want to pull her into the unpredictable gravity of the world on which I was planning to land and rebuild my life. I had everything in place for the final step in my sexual reassignment—sabbatical, surgeon, a date with the knife just after the first of the year—and I didn't want to risk the possibility that she might fall in love with me, too. That wouldn't be fair.

But I did ask her out again, didn't I? I simply couldn't stop myself, and Saturday morning I sent her an E-mail.

Was that selfish? Of course it was. Indefensible.

But the heart does many things well, and rationalization is right up there with powering the circulatory system. If you don't connect with her, I told myself, she'll think it's her fault. She'll think she did something wrong, she'll think there's something about her that you found unappealing.

Which simply wasn't the case. There was nothing about Allison that I found unappealing.

By early August I was completely smitten, and by the middle of the month, when the leaves were starting to turn in the hills surrounding Bartlett, I'd reached that wondrous point of no return where I would think of her constantly when I was awake, and then dream of her incessantly when I slept. I imagined us transcending—or, perhaps, simply ignoring—those little details that I, too, would soon be a woman, and Allison wasn't gay. I hid from her exactly who I was, as I hid it from almost every person I knew.

Why? Was it simply the realization that I would lose her once she knew? Surely that was a part of it. But that was only one of my reasons for remaining underground.

First of all, it would suggest a massive ego to presume that she was thinking of me in the same way, and was beginning to fantasize that we were destined to be together forever. And while people who've conditioned themselves to hide who they are can be many things, ego-monster isn't high on the list.

I also kept my arrangements to myself because I didn't want to make the month of August any more difficult for Allison than it already was, on the off chance that I really was more to her than a mere summer fling.

Let's face it, we met when Carly was about to leave for college, and she was more than a little shaky. This was, after all, her only child who was about to depart. And while Allison was used to being alone in her house a couple of nights every week, she wasn't prepared to be on her own for weeks and weeks at a time. She wasn't sure she was ready to go months without seeing her daughter.

I could also see there was all that baggage that must come with looking at your daughter one morning and discovering she's an adult. Suddenly, Allison realized, she was Mom to a grown-up. Here was a woman who still liked painting her toenails a fireball shade of red, and abruptly she had to cope with the notion that her little girl was her height and allowed to vote.

And so I didn't want to make August any more difficult for her—or for Carly—than it already was. She was planning to take Carly to college on the thirtieth, the Friday that began the Labor Day weekend. And so I vowed I would tell her no later than the end of the second week in September. By then, I figured, we couldn't possibly be so profoundly entwined that she couldn't unfasten the knots and get on with her life. Me too.

Clearly I figured wrong.

A woman takes her index finger and presses the nail or the fleshy print at the tip against her cheek, and she raises her eyebrows and smiles. She dips her chin just the tiniest bit. Without opening her mouth, she has just said, "Moi? Little ol' me? You can't be serious!"

A man—at least one who wants to be taken for a heterosexual—needs words to convey the same idea:

"Give me a break. You're out of your mind!"

I was in a phase where I was toying with mannerisms and gestures when I met Allison's ex-husband, and so I probably made a bad situation worse. We didn't get off to a very promising start.

It was the second week in August, a Sunday afternoon, and Allison and I were outside on her terrace. Earlier that day we'd had brunch with a group of her friends, and we really hadn't been back at her house for very long.

About four o'clock, Will arrived. He'd taken Carly to Burlington, where the two of them had been shopping for the higher-tech toys she wanted to bring with her to college. A new CD player was the big item, but they were also getting a floor lamp and a new printer for her computer. Will, it seemed, helped Carly hunt for those consumables that were rich with wiring and plastic and silicon chips, while Allison escorted her on the pricier clothing excursions.

I imagine there was a chance that Will would have come in and said hello to Allison regardless of whether there was a car he didn't know parked in the driveway. But the fact that an unfamiliar Honda was sitting smack in front of the little horse barn that Allison used as her garage guaranteed it.

We didn't hear them pull into the driveway, but we did hear them in the kitchen. Allison raced inside to greet them, and I watched from the terrace as she took from Carly what looked through the screen door like a tiki torch, and then gave her daughter a hug. Will put a pair of pretty good-sized cardboard boxes down on the floor. I considered venturing inside to say hello to Carly and meet her father, but at that moment they looked like such a cozy and intimate family unit that I decided to wait outside.

Probably, I should have stood. I should have paced around the wrought-iron table, or hovered with my hands along the back of the wrought-iron chair. I should have sent a body message into the kitchen that said in a polite but manly sort of way, "Don't forget to say hello to the guy outside on the porch."

But I didn't. I sat in my chair and crossed my legs and sipped my cranberry juice.

Then, when Carly and Allison finally brought Will out to meet me, I considered for just the briefest moment responding to the introduction the way I would in a few months, once the surgery was behind me. I considered remaining in my seat. Perhaps extending my hand to Will. Perhaps not.

It was a stupid idea. Inane. Selfish.

And so quickly I stood, but already it was too late. It wasn't that I had seemed feminine to Will by refusing, at first, to stand and greet him: On the contrary, I must have seemed almost threatening. Confrontational. Downright combative. I must have seemed like the new male in the pride, the young lion who can't wait to show off his fangs and his claws and his newly found power.

"Will, this is Dana," Allison said. "We met at the university."

"It's a pleasure," he said, taking my hand in his and attempting to make flour from my four metacarpals.

"My dad just bought me the coolest CD player," Carly told me, shaking her head and rolling her eyes toward heaven.

"Oh, good. You'll need that at college," I said, surprised that my voice sounded normal with my hand in a vise.

"I know she's only going to listen to classical music on it," her father said lightly, finally releasing my fingers.

"Can you stay for a drink?" Allison asked him.

"Yeah, I have time. Sure."

"Want a beer? Juice?"

"A beer would be great."

"Hungry?"

"I can always eat."

"I'll see what we have."

Carly and I sat down when Allison returned to the kitchen, and I know I expected Will to sit down, too. Nope. Oh, he went to a chair, but only to pull it out for his daughter. Instead, he remained on his feet right beside me, so I got to look up at him as if I were a recalcitrant elementary-school student, or perhaps a suspect being questioned about a string of serial killings.

And then the interrogation began. He wasted barely a breath on the weather—we agreed we could both feel the fall coming at night, but that was the extent of our meteorological commonality—before getting to the agenda that really mattered to him. Was I in the English or the English and Communications Departments? Where did I go to school, did I have my doctorate? Where did I live? Was I as friendly with all my students as, apparently, I was with Allison?

Now, it would be very unfair of me to imply that Will Banks was some sort of bully that day. He wasn't, at least not consciously. But he was on the terrace behind the house he'd once owned, and he was a mere fifteen or twenty yards away from the woman with whom he'd once lived. He was sufficiently belligerent that Carly said her mom would probably need some help carrying the food and the drinks, and chose to leave us for the kitchen.

In all honesty, I wasn't much better. I was angry about his juvenile power games, even if, inadvertently, I had triggered them by failing to stand. In any case, I decided I could be testy, too.

Just before Allison and Carly returned with a plate of cheese and crackers and a tray of drinks, Will began circling around the foremost issue on his mind. Did I have any children? An ex-wife? And then, boom, ground zero:

"So," he said, "I gather you're dating Allison."

I wondered if he had ever before used the tone that he put into that little observation: dubious and condescending and protective at once. Certainly he would use it again someday, when Carly brought home the man who had asked her to marry him:

So, I gather you want to marry my Carly.

Clearly I'd been thinking about affectation and gender more than was healthy or normal or wise. It seemed to me that if Will could be threatened by the notion that his ex-wife was dating another heterosexual, he would be devastated by the idea that she was dating a fruit.

And so instead of answering his question with words, I recrossed my legs, swinging my left over my right with great histrionics, and planted the tip of my finger deep in my cheek. Then I raised my eyebrows like the two sides of a drawbridge, dipped my chin, and—for good measure—batted my lashes like butterfly wings.

Moi? Little ol' me? You can't be serious!

It wasn't a kind thing to do and it wasn't a smart thing to do. But Carly had spent Saturday night at her father's home, and Allison and I had spent our very first night together. In her home. In her bed.

For better or worse, the Sunday afternoon I met Will, I was feeling pretty damn ballsy.

All Things Considered
Monday, September 24

CARLY BANKS: How do you tell a lover you're not the person she thinks you are? It's a question that can haunt a pre-operative transsexual. How, for example, would Dana Stevens tell a woman before reassignment that he was sure in mind and in spirit . . . he was a woman?

DANA STEVENS: It was never easy—at least for me. But I always wanted to be honest. I always wanted to tell the woman I was seeing that I was, in reality, a part of the tribe. It seemed only fair. But how? How do you begin?

Well, the fact is, usually you beat around the bush. At least I would. You know, you drop hints. You want to gauge your partner's tolerance for this sort of thing. How does she feel about homosexuality? Bisexuality? Cross-dressing? What kind of transgender urges has she experienced?

With one partner, I remember, I shared my dreams. And when my actual dreams weren't clear enough, I made up some new ones:

"Wow! You can't believe the dream I had last night. I was in the most hideous automobile accident—just awful! The only good news? I suffered only minor injuries. Scrapes. Bruises. Castration."

The thing is, sometimes I really would have dreams like that, and they weren't nightmarish at all. I'd wake up, and in that never-never land between sleeping and waking, I'd believe for just the briefest moment that it hadn't been a dream at all, and I would be so happy!

BANKS: Dana recalls once leaving a newspaper story out for her partner.

STEVENS: It was one of those alternative newsweeklies, and it had an article in it about a male-to-female transsexual and her female lover. I left it out on the kitchen table, and I circled all the parts about the transsexual's unusual brand of teenage trauma and angst.
    Of course, I circled all the deliciously filthy parts, too.

BANKS: That particular strategy worked well: Dana's girlfriend understood what the pre-operative transsexual was trying to tell her . . . and that the lifestyle in the offing wasn't for her.

STEVENS: Fortunately, she knew herself well enough to know that what I was driving at wasn't going to be her cup of tea. And so we broke up. But we're still friends.

BANKS: And my mother? How did you tell my mother?

STEVENS (sighs audibly): Badly. Oh, Lord, Carly: really and truly badly.

allison

At first I thought he was joking.

Then I thought it was a fabrication to let me down easy: We were about to break up.

And then I began to fear I was insane, because I was in love with a lunatic.

The mind, I can tell you, reels. It reels, then recoils. It begins a retreat into a series of images and ideas that are clearly related to the news you've been given, but not exactly relevant. He is sick, he is ill, he is deranged. He needs help.

No, he is beyond help, he is way too far gone. He is a deviant beyond therapeutic salvation. He is delusional.

Then: He can't possibly be serious. He is, outwardly, much too normal for that sort of surgical mutilation.

But because you don't instantly stop loving a person—our history, albeit a short one, didn't simply evaporate on that ledge at the edge of the woods—you begin to wonder about yourself. You wonder first how you missed all the signals, because certainly the signals were there. They had to be.

Hadn't your ex-husband warned you?

And then you begin to consider the possibility that, on some level, you didn't miss a thing. You heard the hints, and you understood them. But you didn't care, because, deep down, you are *that way,* too.

Whatever *that way* is.

Finally you just get sick. At least I did.

I didn't vomit, but I did put my head between my knees and stared down at the white and silver and gray of the rock, and allowed the waves of nausea to roll over me. And when he tried to touch me, when he tried to rub the back of my neck, I believe I told him to get his hand off me.

His *disgusting* hand off me.

I was angry, and I wanted to hurt him.

Before Dana told me his plans, we had a glorious late summer together. His course ended on the first day of August, and he wouldn't be in a classroom again for over a year.

And so we were like two teenagers for the entire month: four-plus weeks with no jobs to attend to, and really very little responsibility. Oh, I was going by my own classroom for an hour or two every day— getting the room the way I wanted it, revising my lesson plans, weaving what I had learned the past year into my curriculum—but I've never viewed my August responsibilities as work. I'm too excited about the imminence of a new semester, and the arrival of my new students.

And so Dana and I went to movies and dinner two and three nights a week, we read on my terrace in the afternoons, we went for hikes all over the state.

My best friends—women, all—told me they no longer saw me, and the single ones confessed they were jealous.

Dana and I were making love, it seemed, all the time. I'd never had a lover as attentive as he was, I'd never been with a man who was so relentlessly focused on me. My pleasure. What I wanted. We didn't spend a whole night together until the second Saturday in August, but as I recall, we saw each other every single day up until then that month, and almost every time we were together, we would find a moment alone to seduce each other. Once, in a largely empty movie theater in Middlebury, of all places, when our interest in the film was starting to flag, he crouched between my legs on the floor of the cinema and pushed up my dress, and I shocked myself by coming in public.

I would never have allowed a man before Dana to do such a thing. I would certainly have been incapable of an orgasm.

But—and this matters in ways that say much more about me than about Dana—he was the first man I'd ever been with who had absolutely no hair on his chest. (At the time, of course, I assumed it was simply genetic. I hadn't a clue it was hormones and electrolysis.) There was something about Dana that was at once exotic and safe and— almost like an aura—tender. He was, without question, the most unthreatening man I'd ever been with.

We spent lots of time with Carly, too. I knew I was going to miss her madly when she went away to college, and I was prepared to spend considerably less time with Dana in those weeks if the two of them hadn't gotten along. But they had. Dana, obviously, spent a large part of his professional life around teenage girls, and he was at once completely at ease with my daughter and capable of making her comfortable with him. The three of us went biking on her days off, we went to band concerts at the gazebo on the green. Dana had a friend with a sailboat, and he still remembered enough about sailing from his childhood in Miami that he took us across Lake Champlain one day, and bought us lunch at a marine restaurant on the New York side of the water.

And though he never actually went shopping for clothes with us, he did accompany us twice to the mall, when we embarked upon shopping expeditions in the weeks before Carly was due at school.

I know now he was indulging one of his favorite whims. While

Carly and I were picking out sweaters and shirts and jeans, he was at a lingerie store. Ostensibly he was there to buy something slinky for me—and on both occasions he did—but he spent most of his time just rubbing silk and nylon and spandex against the sensitive skin on the palms of his hands.

Will and I drove Carly to college. I thought it was inappropriate for Dana to join us, and he agreed. Though there was no question in my mind by those last days of August that I had fallen in love with Dana, he had still been a part of my daughter's life for barely a month.

I had assumed there was a pretty good chance that Patricia would take the day off and join us, too. I hadn't relished the prospect, though that certainly wasn't because I disliked Patricia: I simply took pleasure in the notion that the family unit that would send Carly off into the world on her own would be the very same one that had conceived her in the first place, and nurtured the newborn that was now almost five and a half feet tall.

A week before we were to leave, I asked Will if Patricia was going to come along, and the idea that she might seemed to surprise him.

"No, I think she thought it would just be us," he'd said. "Besides, I'm pretty sure she has depositions that morning."

And so the last Friday in August, the three of us piled into Will and Patricia's massive Explorer. It was the first time we had been alone together in an automobile in almost a decade. Once, two years earlier, the three of us had been in a car with Patricia, when we were driving to and from Will's father's funeral. But Carly hadn't even been old enough to be one of my students the last time the Banks family had soloed inside an automobile. Almost reflexively, therefore, I hopped into the backseat before Carly: I didn't want my daughter to feel like the little kid in the back on her first day of college.

Since much of the freshman class had considerably longer drives before them than we did, we didn't leave until late morning. Carly didn't want to be the first kid on campus.

For most of the two-hour trip she was quiet, and Will and I babbled about our memories of our freshman year—though we did not, I noticed, discuss the fact that we had met soon after we'd arrived at Middlebury, and were seriously involved by the spring. Since our stories were meant to offer Carly one final booster shot of confidence, we both focused instead on how we had met the different adults around her who had been our friends for over two decades, and the strategies we'd employed to manage a workload that seemed, at first, overwhelming.

Occasionally, I studied the boxes and suitcases that were piled beside and behind me and inventoried their contents in my mind. I think I was trying to reassure myself that Carly had everything she could possibly need.

By the time we arrived, the unloading was well under way. It was early afternoon, the sun was warm, and I felt impossibly old. The Volvos and minivans stretched like wagon trains along the thin roads that surrounded the lower campus, and snaked between the renovated barns and white clapboard dormitories. We parked on a patch of grass perhaps thirty yards from the entrance to Carly's new home, and I focused on the parade of consumption and privilege of which we were a small part so I wouldn't wind up weeping because my child was leaving home and I was irrevocably middle-aged.

Instead I joked about the skis and snowboards that sparkled in the summer sun, and the Frisbees and tennis balls that coursed through the air all around us. I noted the different makes of computers that were carried in by fathers and sons, and the easels and butterfly chairs that were carted inside by mothers and daughters. There were endless boxes of CDs and CD players, televisions and VCRs and—protruding from the pockets of sundresses and shorts—their black plastic remotes.

And, of course, there were armloads and hangers of clothes. Like those remotes, frequently they were black, too, because this was, after all, Bennington. Carly's new friends would have hair that was purple and orange and green, some would have literally dozens of studs in their ears. But their clothes would largely be black. Some would, in fact, dress like a close branch of the Addams Family.

"There's Morticia," Will observed at one point, when Carly was not within earshot. Sure enough, wandering toward the front door of the dorm with a silver mountain bike in her arms, was a young girl with waist-length black hair wearing an ankle-length sheath the color of soot.

Will and I were younger than many of the parents, but that helped little as I stood in the frame of the door to Carly's room and watched her decide where on the bureau to put her coffeemaker, or in which drawer she should place her bras and panties and socks. And though I managed to say good-bye to her without crying, Will and I were barely beyond the stone pillars at the edge of the campus when I could feel my eyes starting to tear.

Sometimes we joked about age on the way back to Bartlett, and sometimes we reminisced about how little the ritual of the first day of college had changed in a generation. Sometimes I just sat back in the seat and closed my eyes behind my sunglasses and tried not to think about how awful it would be when I got home and saw so much of Carly's life gone from her room.

We'd been in the car a little over an hour when Will surprised me by bringing up what he described as my new beau. Both times he'd dropped by my house in August, Dana had been there.

"I wouldn't have guessed he was your type," he said, shrugging.

"The ponytail?"

"That's part of it."

"Sometimes you need a change."

"And he's so theatrical."

"Theatrical?"

"He's always using his hands when he talks."

Certainly I knew what Will was driving at, but Dana's sexual orientation wasn't a question in my mind. I hoped if I ignored the insinuation, he would understand that I didn't want to discuss my new boyfriend with him. And so I simply stared at the hills that rolled up toward the mountains to the east.

"Look, I know it's none of my business," he went on when I was silent. "But you know how much I care for you."

"You're right. It is none of your business."

"But I can't help myself. I want you to be happy."

"Then you'll change the subject. Or you'll let me change it."

"Can I say one more thing?"

"Not if it's about Dana."

"Well, I'm going to, I have to. And it's the last thing I'll say, I promise. But some people I know at the university think he's a tad odd. They say he's changed over the last year or two."

"I really don't care to discuss this."

"They say he's started to look different. They say—"

"*They?* Who are *they*? Is *they* your idiot friend in the Poli-Sci Department? The one who does your Wednesday-morning radio commentaries? Well, of course she's not going to like Dana. She's a baby step away from bombing Planned Parenthood!"

"Oh, she is not."

"She is! And if she's your *they,* I just don't care."

"And if she's not alone?"

"I still don't care."

"Look, I just think you should know there are people at the school who believe he shouldn't be teaching. There are people there—"

"Will!"

"There are people there who say he's a transvestite!"

"Dana? Oh, please."

"Have you noticed his eyebrows?"

"Clearly you have."

"Look, I'm sorry I had to tell you."

I shook my head and sunk as low in my seat as I could. "You're not one bit sorry," I said.

"I am."

"Well, in that case, let me reassure you: Dana has never worn a dress in his life. And he is an absolutely fabulous lay."

I know now I was wrong about the first part. But the second part remains undeniable. Indisputable.

I am cocksure.

Certainly I thought about Will's allegations off and on in the first two weeks of September, but I never gave them much credence. I was busy with the start of the new school year: nineteen new students, the committee meetings that appear out of nowhere, the first field trips of the fall—including an excursion to a maritime museum on Lake Champlain, which was in reality an absolutely terrific day, but seemed to strike everyone who hadn't been there as a disaster.

We were in the midst of a glorious September heat wave—one of those last, wondrous tastes of high summer—and the temperature must have hit ninety degrees. The kids always love the replica of the Revolutionary War gunboat and the actual artifacts that have been pulled from the deep water, and that class was no exception. Unfortunately, when it was time to return to school, the bus driver couldn't get the vehicle to start, and it was clear it was going to be an hour before another bus would arrive. Since there wasn't a whole lot else to do at that point, I let the kids go swimming in the lake in their school clothes. I was present, and so were four adult chaperones, and only nine or ten kids chose to dive in. No one was going to drown. But two of the girls decided to take off their shirts so they were swimming in what amounted to sports bras—the sort of opaque halter tops in which grown women exercise all the time. And though I insisted that both girls put their shirts back on immediately, the rumors that spread throughout town were astonishing. Two parents called the school, and I ended up spending more time dealing with the aftermath of the field trip than I'd spent planning it.

Meanwhile, when I wasn't at school, I was getting used to living in my house without Carly. I was not, however, getting used to living alone. Dana spent three nights with me the first week Carly was gone, and four nights with me the second. He would be there when I returned home from school, and he would insist on cooking me the most astonishing meals. This wasn't dinner, this was dining: Smoky pumpkin soup and sweet potato vichyssoise, a loaf of walnut beer bread he baked himself. A wild mushroom tart, with hen-of-the-woods sickle puffs he found growing on one of our hikes. Pastas with salmon and pine nuts and fennel.

Once, when I'd had a few glasses of wine, I found myself examining his face in the candlelight—first with my eyes, and then with the tips of my fingers—and I believe I almost asked him something. *Why are you so beautiful?* perhaps. *Why are you so smooth? What is it about your face that I love?*

But I didn't. A big part of the allure was the mystery: A magic trick loses its luster once you know the secret.

In the middle of the month we went for a picnic up in Lincoln. High in the mountains, yet no more than a half-hour hike from the road that coils through a gap near the summit of the four-thousand-foot Mount Abraham, is a ledge that faces west. Its views of sunsets and smaller hills are certainly not a secret, and yet only once in the dozen times I've been there have other people stopped to picnic, too. It may be too close to the road for the hikers who want to take on the Long Trail or venture to the top of the nearby mountain.

But it is indeed a wonderful spot. We went there on a Saturday, and Dana insisted upon preparing everything. The only contributions I was allowed were the plastic wineglasses he'd found in a kitchen cabinet, and the ratty cloth napkins I saved for exactly this sort of occasion.

"So, you plan on bringing along a little wine?" I asked, half kidding, when I was turning the plastic goblets over to him that Saturday morning. I actually assumed we'd be drinking bottled water from them, and he simply wanted to add a little elegance to the event.

"Nothing like getting a really good buzz at the edge of a cliff," he said, and he surprised me by pulling from the refrigerator a bottle of wine he'd hidden there the night before.

We set off from my house in his car just after noon, and we were settled in at the ledge before one. Midway through lunch a young couple with a golden retriever wandered near our perch, but they hadn't brought a lunch and it was clear that they didn't plan on staying. And so we were, most of the time, completely alone.

We had probably been at the cliff for close to an hour when he told me. I had never completely emptied my glass in the time we had been there, but I'd still consumed a good third of the bottle of wine: Dana had topped off the goblet almost every time I'd taken a sip.

When he leaned over once more with the bottle in his hand, I blanketed the rim of my glass with my fingers and shook my head no.

"You either think you're going to get lucky up here, or you have something on your mind," I said. I hadn't planned on adding the second part, it just came out. But he had been unusually quiet that morning, and I had the distinct sense that it was because there was something troubling him that he wanted to share.

"Get lucky? No, I'd be afraid we'd roll off the cliff," he said.

"And I don't think it would do my career any good if somebody saw us."

"Probably not."

"So you do have something to tell me, don't you?"

"I do."

"And it's the sort of bombshell that demands a little wine."

"Oh, I wouldn't say that. Actually, I think it might be the sort that demands a lot of wine."

I nodded, and a litany of possibilities crossed my mind. He was married. He had a child—no, he had children. He had teenage children, fathered when he himself was in high school or college.

He'd been involved with a student, and there was going to be some legal problem.

He had a criminal record.

Perhaps—and Will's allegation in the car came back to me—he really was a transvestite, and he'd been caught in some public and embarrassing way.

If that was the case, I wondered how much I would care. If I would care. No, I knew it would disturb me; I knew, on some level, it would frighten me.

But would it lead me to push him away? I doubted it. I doubted it seriously. At that moment on that ledge, I doubted seriously that there was anything he could tell me that would lead me to break off our affair.

And so I told him that. I realized how desperately I loved him, and I told him. I said that short of informing me that he wanted us to be merely friends—short of putting an end to our two-month romance— there was nothing he could possibly say that could upset me.

"Maybe now is exactly the wrong time to tell you this," I heard myself murmuring, a quiver of need I wasn't sure I'd ever noticed before in my voice, "but I love you. I love you more than I've ever loved anyone except Carly."

I had surprised myself with my frankness, and I found myself looking into the sun so I wouldn't have to look at him.

And, ironically, it's clear now that I had surprised him, too. My sense is he would have led me to his confession with greater care if I hadn't told him how I was feeling. He would have told me a story about his childhood or his adolescence, he would have tried to describe for me the horrific longing for something he had thought for most of his life he couldn't have—but something he needed almost like air.

Perhaps he would have gingerly worked his way through the drinking and the drugs, and how, somehow, he had finally come out on the other side, unscathed. Miraculously.

Maybe he would have recalled how much he had hated his erections when he was a teenager, how much they had reminded him that his body was wrong. All wrong. An error that howled every time he felt himself growing hard.

Maybe he would have told me the fantasies he had now when we made love, he would have confessed to me where his mind roamed when he was inside me.

But he didn't. He didn't say any of that. He reassured me that he loved me, too, and then he plunged ahead, assuming—in the euphoria that enveloped us both like a fog after my candor—that our particular love could shoulder anything.

"Okay, then," he said.

"Okay," I said.

"Well," he began, and he blinked. "You're in love with a woman. In a little less than four months—just after the first of the year—I'm going to Trinidad, Colorado, to have a sex change."

"You're kidding," I said, though I had a sense that I didn't get the joke. Clearly what he had said was meant to be funny, and I was missing the point.

"No. I'm not. I've been on female hormones since Valentine's Day."

I turned to face him. "If this is some bizarre story because you want to break up with me ... I'd rather you just told me the truth."

"No, that's not it at all! I love you, too, Allison! My God, you can't begin to imagine how much! That's why I'm telling you this. I'm telling you because I want you to know everything about me. I'm telling you—"

"Telling me—"

"Look, I'm a woman: a woman who's been saddled since birth with the body of a man. But in my mind, it's a fact: I'm female. Just like you. Well, not exactly like you, because you're straight and I'm gay. At least you've been straight up until now. But my hope and my prayer is that none of that matters anymore, because in a couple of months, I'm finally going to take care of it. The penis. I'm finally going to have the surgery that will make me as much of a woman on the outside as I am on the inside. And I know this is a huge stretch for you, but I'm hoping with all my heart you'll still love me. After all, I'll still be me. Dana. I'll be the exact same person I've always been, except I'll be dressing the way I'm supposed to, and I won't have to endure public bathrooms with urinals."

He'd tried a joke because he must have seen he was losing me. He must have seen I was slipping away. I heard what he was saying, but I was no longer listening. I was listening instead to my ex-husband's accusations in the car, I was listening instead to my instincts from July. I was listening instead to the sighs he would make when we would make love, and wondering at the way his body, abruptly, had begun to repulse me. What sorts of people had he been with, what kinds of hands had stroked him? Whose mouths had been there before mine?

What, exactly, had Dana done?

It suddenly seemed that I'd been sleeping with a person who was either deeply perverse or profoundly insane.

A person who, either way, was capable of harboring inside himself all manner of errata. Insanity. Secret.

I think that's when I started to feel ill, and I think that's when he tried to touch me.

And I think that's when I grew angry and told him to get his hand off me.

But I wasn't nearly that polite.

All Things Considered
Monday, September 24

DANA STEVENS: I told her when I told her for a lot of
reasons. Honesty. Decency. The fact that in a couple
of weeks I was going to start wearing a dress.

CARLY BANKS: Transition?

STEVENS: Girl's gotta start sometime.

8

will

ALL IN ALL, I THINK I TOOK THE NEWS RATHER well. Rebecca Barnard told me toward the end of October.

"I assume this has something to do with Halloween," I said.

"Nope. Mental illness," she said.

Rebecca knew Dana Stevens from the university. She didn't know him well because they were in different departments, and they were constitutionally likely to have very different friends. Rebecca teaches political science, and she's built a career rehabilitating the reputations of Coolidge and Harding and Hoover. But certainly their paths crossed periodically.

"You saw him?" I asked.

"Everyone saw him; there must be fifteen of us on the committee. He arrived a few minutes late, and the only seat left was across the room from the door. And so he had to sashay past us all."

"And he was wearing a dress?"

"No, he was wearing a skirt."

"Oh."

"And a blouse."

Rebecca was at the studio taping her Wednesday-morning commentary. Twice a day the station broadcasts essays and opinions by a fairly diverse group of people from Vermont and New Hampshire, and at the time Rebecca was the resident right-wing conservative. I rarely agreed with her, but she was always good theater.

"Any idea why?" I asked.

Though there wasn't a need—the engineer hadn't arrived yet in the booth—she pushed the microphone away from her face. "He's going to have a sex change. He's going to become a faux female."

Rebecca was aware that Allie was dating Dana, because back in August I'd asked her if she knew him. Something about him had struck me as odd. And while I knew that what Allie did wasn't supposed to be any of my business, I couldn't imagine why she was romantically involved with a man who was so outwardly—obviously—gay. And so I'd thought I would see what Rebecca could tell me about him. At the time, she had suspected he was merely a transvestite: disgusting, in her opinion, but not particularly dangerous, since he only taught literature and film.

"A faux female," I repeated.

"A transsexual," she said.

"I thought he was on sabbatical."

"He is. But he's still a member of the library building committee. He can still come to meetings if he wants to."

"Is he supposed to?"

"Not necessarily. I think he was showboating."

"Advertising?"

"Informing us of his intentions."

"I see."

"I mean, he didn't tell me. He told his friends. But he's out, it's official. From now on, he's über-trans."

"Does that mean he's going to . . ."

"Chop it off? You bet. He says he's going all the way. Surgery's sometime in the next couple of months." She shook her head and added, "I will be absolutely furious if the university health plan is funding this sort of mutilation."

Ironically, while Rebecca thought even less of Dana now that she knew the truth, I was actually relieved. Now, I assumed, there was absolutely no chance that Allie would mistake her summer infatuation with the fellow for an affair with a future. How could she? She liked men.

Likewise, I presumed, so did Dana. And if I had been wrong and he hadn't liked them before, well, clearly he did now.

Why else would he be planning to spend all that money to build a vagina?

That night when I came home from work, Patricia was in the garage. The lights were on and the door was up, and I saw she was by the wall where we stored our skis. She was still in the dress she had worn to the office that day, but over it she was wearing a bulky cardigan that I knew came from the drawer in which she kept her more casual sweatshirts and sweaters. She had a bottle of mineral water in one hand and a ski pole in the other.

I parked in the driveway.

"I think I'm going to break down and buy a new pair of skis this year," she said when I joined her. She hung the pole on the wall, tossing the loop around the nail with the same athletic ease with which she did practically everything. "Downhill, that is."

"No reason not to," I said.

I noticed that she had rearranged our skis and boots when she was examining them. We preferred downhill to cross-country skiing, but we had the necessary skis and the gear for both sports. That meant that we both owned two sets of skis. Usually, we lined up our alpine skis in one spot and then our Nordic skis in another. That evening, however, I saw that she had put her two sets of skis together, and then my two sets beside them. There were Will's skis, and there were Patricia's skis.

It looked oddly foreboding to me, but I told myself that I was reading more into it than was there. It was, I concluded, inadvertent.

"How was work?" she asked.

"Fine."

She looked at me for a long moment, and I knew she wanted more. I knew she deserved more. I wished I had kissed her when I had walked into the garage.

"Well," she said finally, "you can tell me all about it at dinner."

I smiled and said sure. Then, because she was entitled to more than a series of monosyllabic responses, I told her that I'd heard a very funny story that day about the professor Allie had been dating.

Dana Stevens came out to Rebecca Barnard and her peers in October. It would be eleven more months before the professor would come out before the whole country on National Public Radio's *All Things Considered*.

There would be a middle step, however, between one university's faculty and a sizable part of the United States: my radio station.

There were actually two versions of what I would come to call the transgender tapes in the memos I would write as a station president. There was the story that ran over five days one September on National Public Radio. But six months before that, in the middle of March, there was a considerably less ambitious version that ran for two nights on my affiliate station in Vermont.

I tend to doubt the NPR feature would ever have occurred without the Green Mountain trial run. It was sort of like previewing a Broadway show out of town—though of course that wasn't the original plan. No one anywhere in the NPR universe was hoping to try out "transgendered" material in the hinterlands before taking it national. The fact is, no one in the NPR studios in Washington was even aware of the two-day story we did in Vermont until after it aired.

I should also note that only the initial programming idea was mine. That's it. And clearly that changed before NPR went into production.

My original idea was pretty basic: a story on gender dysphoria. Nothing more. That's pretty much what we did on Vermont Public Radio the March after Dana came out. We produced it ourselves, twenty-two minutes altogether. Dana and Allie were the focus then, just as they would be later in the year when NPR jumped in. But so was the school board. Our version turned out to be as much about the fracas in Bartlett as it was about transsexuality.

Moreover, Carly didn't have anything to do with the VPR production. She was away at Bennington at the time, and working a few hours a week for a little radio station in the southwestern corner of the state.

After our version was broadcast, I would have been completely content to wash my hands of the whole topic. I certainly wasn't lobbying to see the story go national, or to have *All Things Considered* start shoveling money into it later that year—especially after some of the more bizarre encounters I had in the days immediately after the Vermont account aired.

One crisp March morning I was stopped on Main Street in Bartlett. I was emerging from the gas station with a cup of coffee on my way to work, and I must have been focused on the way the lid for the Styrofoam cup didn't quite fit because I didn't see the fellow until he was in my face.

"Your ex-wife's a terrific teacher," he said to me, wagging a finger, before he had even introduced himself.

"I think so, too," I said. He was a little younger than me, and he was wearing a tan trench coat over a bulky ski sweater. His loafers were stained with white road salt, and the frames of his eyeglasses were a metallic yellowish green. He had a lamb's-wool and leather aviator cap on his head—the kind with the flaps that flip down over the ears—as if he thought he was Charles Lindbergh.

He seemed harmless enough, but it was clear he was slightly eccentric. "I gather you have a child in her class?" I said.

"Sure do," he said, and he volunteered the information that he was a graphic designer. "But I have to tell you," he added, "my wife and I both think your plan is a little kooky."

I tried to smile. "What plan is that?"

And so he told me, and for the first time I realized that there were actually people in town who knew bits and pieces about my life and Allie's, and who therefore presumed that I was using the radio station that March to try and mastermind a reconciliation with my ex-wife. This particular fellow had heard through the grapevine that Patricia had moved out on me, and so he reasoned that I was now trying to move in on Dana.

In his opinion, the sole purpose of the transgender feature on VPR was to show Allie the error of her ways.

That was never the case, and I suppose that's become pretty obvious now. If I'd known then how our story would end, I imagine I would have done all that I could to prevent any radio programming at all about transsexuality and gender.

The truth is, I have never seriously believed there was anything I could do that would bring Allie back into my life as anything more than a friend. If as a result of some unaccountable twist of fate we actually wound up together, well, fine. But I would never—at least not consciously—have tried to sabotage her relationship with another person.

Nevertheless, I was concerned about her: I have never, ever stopped caring about Allie. We were a couple for almost fifteen years, including college, and most of my memories of that decade and a half are pretty darn good.

Obviously I never made any secret of the fact that I disapproved of Dana's lifestyle before the operation, and I wasn't happy with the idea that he had moved in with my ex-wife. That's clear to everybody who knows me. But the reason I didn't support Allie's choices is pretty basic: Say what you will about Dana and transsexuality, it's not normal. And she's a teacher. That's not a promising combination.

Here's an indisputable fact: Dana Stevens had to be diagnosed with a demonstrable mental disorder before he could have his surgery. And just as I would have been concerned if Allie had gotten involved with a man who—for example—had some form of schizophrenia or depression that couldn't be treated with medication or therapy, at that point in my life it was inevitable that I would worry about her interest in Dana.

I worried about what her friends would think, and what the school board would say. I worried about what the parents of the kids in her classroom would do.

I worried, in essence, about what sort of effect he might have on her life.

Still, my concern was never the catalyst for the programming.

Nor, I should add, were the NPR stories that aired the following autumn a part of some Machiavellian scheme to boost my daughter's profile in Washington (as if I *even had* that kind of clout).

Certainly Carly was growing more and more interested in broadcast, and because I am her father, it was inevitable I would take notice. She followed up her part-time job at the Bennington-area radio station with a summer internship at NPR. (I can take some credit for getting her the interview in April.) Early on, the ATC folks took a liking to her, and some very terrific—and powerful—people took her under their wings.

And why not? She's a wonderful kid.

She spent the Fourth of July that summer with Linda Wertheimer and her husband, Fred. Cokie Roberts introduced her to the Vermont congressional delegation—two Senators and a Congressman. And Elizabeth Arnold and Nicole Wells became like big sisters to her. They still are.

But did I suggest that my nineteen-year-old daughter be the point person for a series on NPR? No way. They asked Carly about how best to approach Dana, and how her mother and I might feel about their doing something more with the story. After all, they knew me. They knew what was going on.

Carly herself took it from there. Carly, I am proud to say, was the one who went to Linda Wertheimer and said, essentially, "Look, Coach, I'm your go-to girl. If you really want to do this story, give me the ball."

And that's exactly what NPR did. They gave her the ball. And she ran.

All Things Considered
Monday, September 24

DANA STEVENS: . . . and I think that's why most people at the university tolerated me in dresses that
fall. They rarely had to see me. And so there weren't
all those uncomfortable issues about which bathroom I
should use, or whether my students would be able to
deal with the fact that Professor Stevens had shown up
for class Monday morning in a burgundy broomstick
skirt.

I mean there were some dirty looks, especially the
first few times I appeared on campus. But I like to
believe by, I guess, a week or two after Thanksgiving, I was passing. Passing completely. You know,
I was invisible. I didn't ever want to be one of
those pre-ops who wears his wanna-be gender on his
sleeve.

CARLY BANKS: For some transsexuals, and for Dana
Stevens, that moment when they first "pass" in public
is almost an epiphany.

STEVENS: It was a Friday afternoon, and I emerged
from a grocery store in Burlington with a big brown
bag in each arm. Out of the blue, this very distin-
guished older man—a retired banker, I imagined—
raced over to me and insisted on carrying both of
my bags to my car. He even opened the front door for
me, once I'd placed my groceries in the back! You
could have knocked me down with a feather. No, I
take that back: You wouldn't have needed a feather.
You could have knocked me down with a puff ball: a

dandelion puff ball. Poof! And I would have been on
my knees.

LINDA WERTHEIMER: When our series continues tomorrow,
Dana Stevens leaves Vermont for Colorado, and prepares
for sexual reassignment surgery.

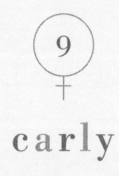

carly

I<small>T WOULD HAVE BEEN SIMPLE TO GET ON A BUS</small> any Friday in autumn and go home for the weekend. It takes a mere two hours and forty-five minutes for even a slow-moving motor coach to slog between Bennington and Middlebury. But I didn't. I didn't want to get into the habit of going back to Bartlett anytime I got home-sick or depressed, or fell into a panic because it just seemed like there was more work than I could handle.

Besides, I would have felt a moral obligation to invite my roommate to join me if I went home, and there was always that off chance she might say yes. Not likely. But it was possible. And the idea alone of having to entertain June Ramsey for a weekend in Bartlett was torture. June and I were simply not meant to live together, even in the context of college. She was very smart and—when she wasn't hopelessly unhappy—she may have been very nice. I'll never know about the second part, because I don't think I ever saw her in the mood to smile.

The problem was that she was all wrong for a place like Bennington. It was obvious she came from gobs of money—which, actually, is pretty normal for the place—but she didn't belong at a school in which a third of the students do really scary things to their hair and most of the faculty don't know the meaning of the word *requirement*. She was from a ritzy suburb of Boston, and she would have been much better off at a college that had lots of mandatory freshman courses, embarrassing hazing rituals, and parties with guys in blazers who served everyone gin and tonics.

The only reason she'd wound up at Bennington was that she fancied herself a poet, and there had been two high-profile poets in the English Department there when she'd been choosing a college in high school. Unfortunately, one of them had left by the time June arrived, and the other was taking the year off.

And so she was miserable. A couple of times I tried taking her with me to the battery factory not far from the college gates. As part of a film course I was taking, I was making a documentary on the closest thing Vermont had to proletarian factory degradation, and I thought June and I might become friends if we left the environment of our dorm room. Nope. She was every bit as angry and irritable off-campus as she was on it, even when I let her do whatever she wanted with the college camcorder I was using.

By Columbus Day, it seemed, the only thing we talked about was whether she should try and endure a second semester at Bennington or transfer to another school.

In any case, I didn't go home until Thanksgiving break. The school shut down the Friday before the holiday and didn't reopen for ten days.

I wasn't sure what to expect from either of my parents that week. I knew that both of their lives were in chaos, but they'd both been so secretive and coy on the phone that I didn't know exactly what was going on.

Certainly I had inklings: I knew, for example, that my dad and Patricia had begun to see a couples counselor, but my dad hadn't said who had initiated the sessions. And while I figured he would have told me if he or Patricia were about to move out, on the bus home I began to fear that they'd begun sleeping in separate bedrooms, and they would both be unbearable to be around.

Likewise, I knew that my mom and Dana had split up at some point in September, but it didn't sound like their breakup had lasted very long. I had the impression that once more they were an item. Yet my mom had also said she had some news to share with me about Dana, but whenever I'd tried to press her for details, she had vehemently refused to tell me a thing on the phone.

My suspicions? At first I'd surmised they were going to get married, but my mom had denied it. Then I'd asked if he was sick— cancer or MS or some weird hair thing that gave him rainbow-shaped eyebrows—and she'd said that wasn't it either. But she had paused, and so I'd wondered if I was getting close.

And when I'd finally asked her to tell me simply if it was good or bad news, she'd become downright incoherent, babbling about how it wasn't for her to say whether it was good or bad, it just . . . was.

Still, it was clear to me that it wasn't great news in her opinion, and I was confident that it had something to do with whatever had occurred between them in those first few weeks after I'd left for college.

Sometimes on the bus home I would doze, and sometimes I would just watch the snowflakes floating to the ground outside the bus window. It would be dark by the time we got to Middlebury, and a lot colder than when I'd left Bennington after lunch. I realized at some point north of Rutland that I'd gone from being uneasy to being nervous: The difference, it seemed to me, was one of degree. The closer we got to Middlebury, the more uncomfortable—and awake—I became.

My mom met me at the bus, and all the way home and for much of the night we talked about college. She made me my favorite dinner (French toast that she actually bakes in this honey-pecan sauce), and she asked me all the right questions: My roommate, my classes, my movie. My friends.

But although she was pretty candid about what she knew about Dad and Patricia's problems, she was vague about Dana. Moreover, she never once brought him up. Always it was me who would initiate any conversation about the man who, it was evident by the time we had finished with dinner and wandered into the den, was still a very big part of her life.

Finally, when we were settled on opposite ends of the couch, both of us in our nightgowns, I asked, "Will I get to see Dana this week?"

"Do you want to?" she asked.

"Sure. Why not?"

She was sipping a mug of hot tea, and she placed it on the table beside her. I thought she was about to touch me—she started reaching her hands toward me, as if she was going to pat my curled knees or rub one of my ankles—but then she let her hands fall into her lap.

"Just how much has your father told you?" she asked.

"About Dana? Why would Dad be talking about Dana?"

"He hasn't told you?" She sounded almost incredulous.

"No. I don't think Dad's mentioned him."

She shook her head, surprised. "Well. I guess he really is focused on his own troubles."

"Patricia?"

"Uh-huh."

"So: What's going on? I'm a big girl, Mom, I can deal."

She smiled. "You think so?"

"That awful?" I asked, and for the first time I got a little scared. Her smile was anything but reassuring.

"Oh, I think that depends on your perspective. Dana's actually very happy."

"Good. I like Dana."

"I do, too. Very much."

"Are you in love?"

She hesitated. "With the man we both know? Absolutely. And it's clear he loves me."

"But there's a problem . . ."

"If you're okay with this," she went on, as if I'd never interrupted her, "I'd like him to move in with us."

"Is that what the big deal is?" I asked, almost laughing out loud. "Is that why you've been so freaky about him on the phone? God, Mom, I don't care. It's your house! You can live with anyone you want to. Besides, I'm away at college nine or ten months of the year, I'm—"

"That's not what the big deal is."

"Oh."

"He won't move in until after Thanksgiving—if it's okay with you. He won't move in until after you've gone back to school. And he might only be here for a couple of months. He'll be in Colorado for at least the first part of January, and I don't know quite what will happen when he returns."

"This all sounds fine," I said.

"His living here will be an experiment."

" 'Cause you haven't lived with a man since Dad?"

She sipped her tea, and then did something I'd never before seen her do: She slipped her pinkie into her mouth and gnawed off a piece of her nail. I noticed for the first time since I'd been home that she'd begun biting her nails.

"Because I haven't lived with a woman since college," she said.

I nodded. For a moment, it seemed, that explained everything: The fact that Dana's face was as smooth as mine, the way he'd fixed my barrette the night we had met. The smell of his shampoo. Dana, I concluded, was actually a woman who for some reason was trying to pose as a man. Maybe she had something to hide. Maybe she had someone to hide from. Maybe, pure and simple, she was a lesbian who was still figuring out what it meant to be butch. I had already met a girl like that at Bennington.

But then my mom added the relevant details, and what for a few brief seconds had started to make sense grew confusing.

"Maybe I don't understand," I said. "Dana's a man?"

She puffed out her cheeks and sighed. "Most people would say so."

"But he doesn't think so?"

"No," she said. "That's what I meant when I said he's a transsexual."

"Woman inside. Man outside."

"In this case, yes. But it can work the other way, too."

In my mind I saw a penis—flaccid, a pretty generic unit at first, but then I saw it dangling below Dana's torso. And then I saw it in women's panties underneath a dress. A bright dress with flowers. Maybe the sort of flowers I'd cut at the nursery that summer.

And then I saw it gone.

"He's been living that way for well over a month now," my mom was saying.

"In women's clothes . . ."

"Yes."

"Have you seen him?"

"In women's clothes? Yes, of course. Any number of times. We're still dating."

"So when the two of you go to movies, you're both wearing dresses?"

"No, not necessarily. Wednesday night he was in stirrup pants. And I was wearing a tunic top over a nice pair of jeans."

I wanted to ask what people were saying, but I was disappointed in myself for caring. And so I tried to phrase my question a little differently. "Do people think you're a lesbian?" I asked. I had tried to sound grown-up and progressive and open-minded, but I know the word *lesbian* had caught in my throat.

"I don't think that matters."

"I guess not."

"What matters is whether I think I'm a lesbian."

I expected her to say something more: *Which, of course, I'm not.* Or: *And, obviously, I'm not.* But she didn't. Instead she took a long sip of her tea, her eyes focused on nothing but the tea bag on the surface of the amber-dyed water.

"Do you still want to see Dana?" she asked finally.

I wasn't at all sure that I did, but I also didn't think I had a choice. Although Mom had made it clear that this was my call completely, it seemed to me that I would be letting her down if I passed. Moreover, it would be like I was, somehow, less hip than my middle-aged mother. And so I shrugged nonchalantly. "Sure," I said. "Why not?"

"Brunch on Sunday?"

"If it's real late."

"Absolutely. I know you need your beauty rest."

"Can I ask you another question?"

"You can ask me a thousand questions."

I noticed a small drop of blood near the tip of her pinkie. "Does it hurt?" I asked.

She thought for a moment. Then: "Yes. Less now than when Dana first told me. But I'm still disappointed. And I still feel betrayed."

I nodded as if she had answered my question. I decided not to tell her that I'd only been wondering about the surgery.

No one likes to imagine their mom or dad making love—not with each other, not with other partners. So to keep those images at bay when I went to my room that night, I tried to concentrate upon my mom's remark that she hoped Dana would still change his mind. She doubted he would, but she said that a part of her fantasized he'd be so happy once he'd moved in with her that he'd postpone his surgery indefinitely.

I also tried reassuring myself that my mother couldn't possibly be a lesbian. After all, she was forty-two. One would think she'd have figured out her sexual orientation before midlife.

But then I began to wonder. I began to wonder about her, and I began to wonder about me.

She'd said that she'd fallen in love with a person named Dana. After his surgery, she had observed, he would still have the same brain, the same soul, the same sense of right and wrong. The same sense of humor. The same understanding of exactly how much fresh mint should go into a summer pea salad. Why, she had asked me, would the things that she loved most about him have to change once he'd had his surgery? The fact is, she had said, they wouldn't.

And so it was at least a possibility that the two of them would stay together after his operation. They'd certainly remain friends. As for the rest? She just didn't know.

Which, in the dark of the night, made me begin to doubt myself. I didn't assume lesbianism was genetic, but that evening I did find myself questioning my own sexual orientation. Why had I been so quick to break up with Michael last spring? Why didn't I have a boyfriend at Bennington?

I hadn't really given a whole lot of thought to exactly what lesbians did sexually, but when thoughts of a post-operative Dana and my mother crept into my head against my will, it dawned on me that most of what would go on in their bed wouldn't be dramatically different from what went on between heterosexuals.

There was that penis, of course . . . or lack of one.

But even Michael and I had done more than simply fornicate. And he was an inexperienced high-school boy!

I thought of the half dozen lesbians I knew at Bennington, and I decided they probably weren't lesbians the way I might be a lesbian. For them, it seemed, it was more of a political statement than a sexual orientation. I had a feeling at least two of them were actually closet heterosexuals and would probably come out once they'd outgrown the thrill of being marginalized.

I'm not sure how long I had lain in my bed before finally falling asleep, listening to the rumble the furnace would make when it would kick on, or to the sound of the leafless hydrangea branches as they scratched against the bay window below my bedroom. I was exhausted, but it still took me forever. The last thing I remember before finally nodding off is the feeling I'd had the night Dana and I met, when he gently touched my lips with the edge of a paper cocktail napkin. I had felt, I decided, cared for and happy and warm. If he made my mom feel that way, it probably didn't matter whether or not he had a penis.

10

dana

HOW DO YOU HIDE YOUR PENIS?

It depends upon what you're wearing.

I started cross-dressing that autumn in Vermont, so it's not as if I had to hide it under some risqué tank suit or slinky bikini. (Reason #1,701 why I fled sunny Florida before coming out . . .) And Allison and I did not exactly have a calendar jam-packed with proms and cotillions that fall, so there were no events that would have demanded that I try to pour myself into some champagne flute of a gown.

Most of the time, a quality pair of panty hose or tights would flatten the penis out to my satisfaction.

Of course, it's possible that my standards weren't very high or I wasn't particularly demanding. Jordan and Marisa, for instance—two girls from my support group—insisted that they couldn't possibly wear even stirrup pants without looping a little string around the tip of their penis, and then pulling the string back between their legs. They'd attach the string to a thin band they'd wear about their waist like a belt, tying it to the cord at the very base of their spine. The result? Balls and all would be tucked like a little baby between their thighs.

Was I nervous when I first started wearing women's clothing? Lord, yes. But I also felt movie-star fabulous. I'd been dieting, I'd been on hormones, I'd grown my hair long. And, I discovered, wearing women's clothing in public because I was in transition was a very different sensation from wearing it in private because I was experimenting. You can't imagine what it's like after a lifetime in the wrong attire to finally feel the right clothing energizing your body.

And *energizing,* it seems to me, is exactly the right word. Dressing the way you were meant to is very, very invigorating, the first time you do it.

It is not, I should add, erotic. At least it wasn't for me. I'm sure there are transvestites in this world who get very turned on once they're cinched inside some sleek little ottoman rib dress—and, in all likelihood, some transsexuals as well—but this wasn't a sexual experience in my case. Not at all.

But it was exhilarating. Downright rejuvenating. This, I was practically singing to myself in my head, is what it feels like to dress like a woman! To dress the way I was meant to!

I felt like I was in a movie musical.

And while I had most certainly been frightened the first time I walked into a meeting at the university, or the first time I walked down North Winooski Avenue in Burlington, it always was worth it. Even when, the first few times, I'd hear some teenager on the street calling me names.

The moment that fall that probably gave me the worst case of the shakes was the first time Allison was to see me in a dress. I wanted to look good. I wanted to be attractive. I didn't want to, once more, scare her away. I'd done that back in mid-September, and I didn't want to do it again.

Earlier that fall, she'd taken my confession (what a horribly unfair word!) about as well as could be expected: She'd been furious. We had walked back to my car in absolute silence, and she didn't say a single word to me as I drove her home. I had assumed we were finished, and when I got back to my apartment mid-afternoon, I just collapsed on my bed and sobbed.

I sobbed because I had lost a woman I loved, and I sobbed for the reason I'd lost her. I sobbed because, yet again, a person hated me the moment I stopped living the big lie.

But then she called me two days later. That Monday night I was home alone, missing her so much that I actually wished I had a stack of papers to grade or a class to prepare for. I don't think I had spoken to anyone other than my sister in Florida and a waitress in a downtown diner since we had parted on Saturday. Ah, but then she called, and in an instant I went from gloomy to giddy.

"I want to understand more about your plans," she said. Then: "I want to see you again. If you still want to see me."

"God, yes!"

She told me how angry she was that I hadn't told her sooner, and I admitted it was indefensible. She told me she didn't have any idea what wanting to see me meant.

"Maybe I just want closure," she said.

"I could see that," I said. "But I hope that's not the case."

"I know you do. So be warned: Maybe I'm just calling you to get your hopes up so I can dash them—the way you dashed mine."

"That wasn't my intention. I just wanted—"

"You just wanted a lot of things. You wanted someone to hold your hand through the next four or five months. You wanted someone to be your guide when you started to dress up. You wanted someone to teach you to be a woman. We both know that."

"No, that's not it," I insisted. "I fell in love. That's all. I fell in love."

"I believe you. But let's be honest: You fell in love with me because you *needed* to fall in love. I don't know who your friends are, but I haven't met any. And everything you've told me about your family suggests they're not going to be particularly supportive. So you needed someone. And, if only because I was there, you chose me."

"It didn't work like that."

"Maybe you didn't plan it like that—"

"Trust me, no one ever plans it like that. No one plans to fall in love, period—at least the way I've fallen for you."

"Perhaps not. Still . . ."

"If you really believe that, then what is it you need from me? Tell me. What did you need in July? What do you need right now?"

She was silent for a long moment at the other end of the line. "I don't need anything," she said finally. "I only want to see you."

We saw each other four times in late September and early October. I was dressed as a man on each occasion, though I was spending more and more time dressed as a woman. And when I showed up at a meeting of the Green Mountain Gender Benders for the first time in months, I appeared in a button-front skirt and suede zipper boots. Some members of the group were a little cold to me, since I hadn't shown up in so long, but they were still proud of me for finally coming out.

In hindsight, I wore way too much makeup that night, but most girls go overboard when they first start experimenting with lipstick and mascara. (Of course, most girls get to make their cosmetic explorations when they're teenagers, not when they're flirting with middle age.)

I had a sense that that meeting would be the last one I would ever attend: My surgery was barely a season away, and already I was viewing myself less as a transsexual and more as a woman. My chest was starting to bud, thanks to the hormones, and the hair on my head seemed thicker and more lustrous. I felt the muscles in my arms and my legs starting to melt, I felt my skin beginning to grow young. Truly: young. I could see it in the mirror.

And, best of all, Allison had called. The support group met on Thursday nights, and Allison had phoned me that Monday. We had dinner together on Friday, the night after I'd donned boots and a skirt for the Benders.

For Allison, of course, I wore blue jeans and penny loafers. The evening when I would spend literally hours throwing clothing onto my bed, and then—when I had finally found something that didn't

make me look like a construction worker in drag—applying and reap-
plying makeup, was still a few weeks away.

"As far as I can tell," I told Allison Friday night, "transsexuals either
go into a deep denial and overcompensate like crazy, or they just give
up and start planning for surgery."

"Women transsexuals, too?"

"You mean boys born in a female body? I can't speak for them, but
it's probably true. Still, I can only speak for girls like me."

I'd chosen an Italian restaurant near the office parks that ringed
Burlington's southeastern suburbs—the sort of place that depended
upon a business lunch clientele and was virtually deserted for dinner.
This way we could be assured of some privacy. Moreover, because the
restaurant was far from my downtown apartment, the turf would be
vaguely neutral, which seemed to make sense. I didn't want Allison to
have any fear that I harbored some delusion that we'd go back to my
apartment and make love.

"What do you mean they overcompensate? They try and be super
macho?"

I nodded. "We're talking construction worker macho. I know one
girl who was a Navy SEAL, for God's sake! And the doctor who will
be doing my surgery has done army sergeants, an air force colonel, and
a submarine commander. For a group that wants to make our penises
disappear, we spend a lot of time with phallic symbols, don't we?"

"But not you."

"No, I just gave up early on. As a teenager, I was simply one endless train wreck—oops, there's another one of those symbols. We just
can't help ourselves, can we? Still, I'm quite serious about this: You
cannot imagine how unhappy I was. How miserable. There were
months in my last two years of high school when I spent far too much
time gazing longingly at razor blades, steak knives, and big bottles of
aspirin."

Allison was nursing her wine, sometimes resting the edge of the
goblet abstractedly against her lower lip. It was clear that she wanted a
second glass, but she was too far from home to risk getting potted.

"You didn't ever really try killing yourself, did you?" she asked softly.

"When I was a teenager? No, I never actually tried it. Thank God. It's just that I had a pretty good idea what kind of future loomed before me, and I wasn't happy. I remember one afternoon I came across nude pictures of transsexuals in some adult skin magazine. Eureka! I thought. There you are, Dana: Superfreak."

"I'm sure they weren't transsexuals like you. Not if they were posing for an adult magazine."

"No. Though one was really quite pretty. But they were still presented as disgusting outcasts, and they certainly didn't do a whole lot for my self-image. The pictures weren't exactly designed for men to get off on."

"Probably not."

"And already I was drinking way too much. I'd begun sneaking my parents' scotch in eighth grade when I started getting chest hair, while all the girls around me were getting these perfect little breasts. It was awful. Oh, God, did I hate my body—did I hate myself. It wasn't until I began to realize that surgery was a genuine possibility that things began turning around."

"Did you have friends then?"

"In high school? Certainly not boys. I wasn't into that compensation thing."

"Girls have boys who are friends."

"But those girls are still treated as girls! Or at least viewed as girls! Whenever I hung out with boys, they'd want to do boy-type things that didn't interest me. It had been that way my whole damn life. Let's play combat! Let's play race car! Let's go build a tree house! Oh, please. And it certainly doesn't get any better when you're a teenager. In fact, it gets worse."

"At least they're not playing soldier anymore."

"Hah! The soldier's just on leave now. He's got his four-day pass, or he's gone AWOL. But with all that testosterone coursing through him, he is still every cell the warrior. Of course, by then, even if I'd wanted to play football or drink beer or talk about some poor girl's hooters, the boys wouldn't have wanted me hanging around."

"Too . . . effeminate?"

"I was considered quite the girly boy. Naturally."

"Well, did you have friends who were girls?"

"A few. And I always seemed to have a girlfriend, which at least gave me a little power in the eyes of the boys. But it was all very, very difficult. Especially when I was still trying to figure out what was going on. I'd see a beautiful girl, and I'd want her sexually, but I'd also be desperately envious of her. My sister said it's like this friend of hers, a man who can't walk, and she's absolutely right. That guy is incredibly jealous of people whose legs work, and sometimes he gets seriously pissed off at life. He was in some sort of accident when he was nine or ten, and now he's stuck in a wheelchair. It just doesn't seem fair."

"You'd desire a woman? And be jealous of her?"

"Still do. God, Allison, I look at your body, and I just want every part it, and I want it in every imaginable way. I wish my feet were as petite as yours, and I wish I could dab red polish on my toes while watching TV—just like you do. I wish my waist were your waist, and I wish I had hips—"

"Trust me, you don't want my hips."

"I do! And forgive me for confessing this, Allison, but half the time when I lick you, I'm turned on and resentful at once. After all, even when I have a vagina, it will never be as creamy as yours! I'll never be naturally moist! I'll never—"

"I get it," she said. "Thank you."

"I'm sure you do, but it's only because you're very intuitive and very smart. I haven't begun to tell you how shitty my years in high school really were. I haven't told you a thing about the eating disorders and the dieting and the vomiting—anything to prevent my body from bulking up and becoming a man's. I haven't told you about the times my mom would start crying when I would get drunk and try to tell her what I was feeling. Or the way my dad couldn't stand to be in the same room with me for more than five minutes—and, in fact, still can't. He's not mean to me: He just doesn't know how to deal with his pansy son."

"And your sister?"

"She's terrific. But she's five years younger than I am, so she wasn't much help two decades ago. When I was fifteen and sixteen years old, she was still in elementary school. So I would spend days and days alone in my room with absolutely no one to talk to, because, basically, I had nowhere to turn and no one to confide in."

I watched her drain the last of her wine. "I shouldn't have another glass," she said, "but I think I will."

"I have that effect on people," I said, and I motioned for our waiter to return.

When we were waiting for our check after dinner—long after we'd finally given in and ordered and finished a bottle of wine—Allison reached across the table for my hands and wrapped her fingers around mine.

"What will it look like?" she asked, the worrisome urgency of a mother in her voice. *Honey, do you really think a tattoo's a good idea? Do you really think you should dye your hair purple? Maybe you'd like to talk to someone about this self-mutilation thing?*

Of course I knew exactly what she meant. I'd asked it myself of doctors in three states and in Montreal. And each time I'd used that very same word. *It.*

What will it look like?

Each surgeon had known instantly what I was talking about.

"Will it look like . . . any other woman's?" Allison asked when I didn't answer right away.

I shrugged and then repeated what the surgeon I had chosen in Colorado had told me. "It will look exactly like what it's supposed to look like," I said, and then added what he'd said to reassure me. "Apparently, it will fool anyone but a gynecologist . . . and even gynecologists, at first, will assume it belongs to a g.g."

"G.g.?"

"Genetic girl."

We had both had way too much to drink, but with the little reason that remained we agreed it was inadvisable for her to try to drive back to Bartlett. We decided instead we would leave her car in the parking lot of the restaurant, and she would spend the night in my apartment in Burlington.

There, at her urging, I showed her my special closet with my secret wardrobe, and then we made love on the bed. The next morning, I knew, we'd regret both decisions. But it was late and we were drunk, and we were just two chicks having the best time in fantasy land.

Our next three dates were very different. We went to dinner. We went to the movies. And then we went to our separate homes. We knew I was in my waning days in Jockeys for Him, and neither of us could cope with the notion that our passion might not survive my transition. My castration. My rebirth.

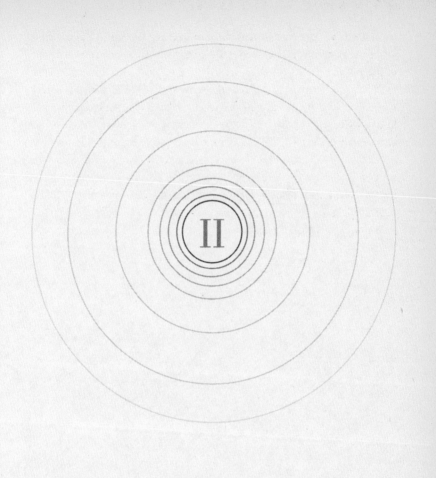

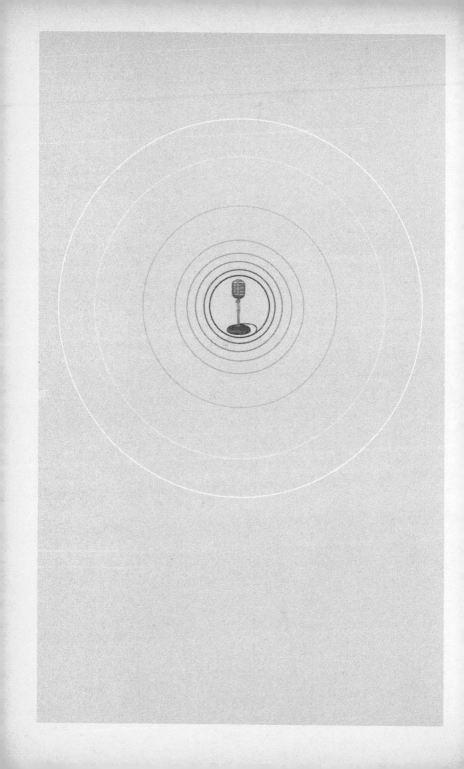

All Things Considered
Tuesday, September 25

CARLY BANKS: Stevens says she honestly didn't know whether Allison Banks would accompany her to Colorado.

DANA STEVENS: Really, I didn't. But I hoped she would. I wasn't afraid of the surgery—I was actually looking forward to it. But I wasn't sure I could bear being alone. I'd spent so much of my life as a male that way that I wasn't sure what I would do if I woke up as a woman and my world was as empty as ever.

carly

"GENDER MATTERS," DANA ONCE TOLD ME. "SEX-ual orientation doesn't."

And while that mantra makes sense to me now, the bombshells my mom dropped on me the night I came home from college had left me shaken. The fact that I thought Dana was a pretty good-looking woman Sunday afternoon didn't help. He'd come over for brunch, and I wasn't honestly sure what to expect, but I certainly hadn't antic-ipated a tall, attractive woman in jeans and boots and a sweater.

Dana was wearing more makeup than my mom wore, perhaps, but this was still no Cockney aunt from a Monty Python sketch.

Apparently, he hadn't always looked so good in women's clothes. The first time my mom had seen Dana in drag, she said there was no way he could have passed for a woman. This was despite their decision to meet in some dive on Colchester Avenue with rotten lighting. By the time I came home from college, however, my mom had had six or seven weeks to whip him into shape. They spent whole afternoons at the big-and-tall-girl shops in the strip malls outside of Burlington when my mom was done teaching for the day, and once they went to some big-and-tall-girl factory outlet near Montreal.

Dana was in heaven: racks and racks of dresses just his size.

I wasn't sure what to say when he arrived early Sunday afternoon, despite having lain in bed most of that morning trying to figure it out. Fortunately, Dana made it easy for me.

"It's my hair," he said, hanging his leather pocketbook along with his jacket on the coatrack just inside the front hall. "That's what's different. I've let it grow out." And then he hugged me, and I smelled his perfume.

It was only the three of us that afternoon, so my mom was probably more comfortable with Dana physically than she would have been had there been other people with us. Nevertheless, I was still struck by the way they touched each other. After he handed her a big wooden salad bowl he'd gotten down from a cabinet high above the oven, Dana swirled his hand on her back, like her back was a window he was washing. I saw my mom squeeze his fingers after she'd given him the corkscrew for a bottle of wine. And they must have kissed each other at least three or four times.

Once, I saw Dana kiss the tips of my mother's fingers where she had bitten the nails down to the cuticles and the skin was ragged and raw.

My mom, I knew from experience, wouldn't have been that physical with a regular boyfriend in front of me. Dana, of course, wasn't a regular boyfriend: He had some of the advantages of one, such as the height to get down the salad bowl without needing a stool, and a lifetime of pulling corks from bottles of wine. But he was softer than a man, and he moved more gracefully through a room. His jeans may have been androgynous, but his blouse and his sweater were very delicate. Once or twice when he moved quickly in the kitchen and his cardigan flared behind him like wings, he reminded me of a dancer.

And when my mom and he touched, it was like they'd been friends since childhood: just a pair of women who'd played tea party together at four and Barbies at five, now putting together a brunch on a lazy Sunday afternoon. Two women who'd been pals forever.

When we sat down to eat, the two of them were so busy asking me about college and the film I was making at the battery factory that for long periods of time I completely forgot the strangeness that loomed before the two of them. I complained about my roommate, my lack of sleep, and about the way so many kids at the college were from cities and suburbs and couldn't cope with rural Vermont.

I could have been talking to my mom and her friend Molly Cochran. In some ways, I could have been talking to Dad and Patricia.

By the time Dana left late that afternoon, I was actually more comfortable with the notion that Dana the Transsexual was going to move in than I'd been a few days earlier with the idea that Dana the Man was going to live with us. It wouldn't, I realized, feel like my mom's male lover was in the house when I'd wake up in the morning—my hair a rat's nest, my breath poison gas. Rather, it would seem like her roommate from college was there. Maybe a friend from childhood had arrived. Perhaps some female cousin she hadn't seen in years, but with whom she had once been very close, was going to stay with us awhile.

I understood something sexual would be going on when they disappeared into my mom's bedroom at night, the door closed when I was home, perhaps open wide when I was at college or at Dad's. But that no longer mattered—or, at least, it mattered less. When my mind neared the notion of my mom and Dana in the same queen-size bed, inevitably it would latch onto the realization as well that Dana was neither a female cousin nor a lesbian lover. At least not yet. And something about the whole equation would then make me shudder.

Mostly, however, I was reassured. I was fine. I'd watched Dana, and a big part of me had concluded that he wasn't completely insane. Maybe, on some level that mattered more than most, he really was a woman.

My father tried to put up a good front, but let's be real: His life was a natural disaster. At least it must have seemed that way to him, whenever he looked at the two adult women in his life. Patricia, it was clear even to me, wasn't wild about the idea of seeing a therapist: She thought it was only postponing the inevitable. And my mom, a woman he'd once been married to, was about to start living with—in his eyes—a man who wore makeup.

I'm not sure what he was fearing more as winter approached: the idea that Patricia would leave him and he'd be seen by the world as a two-time loser, or the fact that his first wife was involved with a transsexual.

The irony, of course, is that a big reason why Patricia was so unhappy was that she believed my dad was still in love with my mom. Despite the fact that they'd been divorced for over a decade, Patricia could see clearly that fall that my dad was still thinking about his "Allie" a good deal more than was wise for him or her or, no doubt, even my mom.

I stayed there Monday and Tuesday when I came home from college, and while the two of them were civil at breakfast and dinner, both nights they fought. Neither one yelled—no one in my family is a real screamer—but I could hear them hissing at each other in their bedroom while I tried to read in my bed.

"I don't know why you'd think that," my father insisted. "Do I talk about her? No. Do we have lunch? No. Do I even see her now that Carly's in college? No."

"And it's killing you."

"Killing me? Hardly."

"You drove past her house last week."

"I just wanted to see if her creepy boyfriend was there. I find it unfathomable that they're back together."

"That's exactly what I'm talking about!"

"We're still friends. It's only natural to care about what she does with her life."

"There are degrees, Will. There are degrees."

"And she's Carly's mom. I have to think about her, too."

"Carly's in college, for God's sake. She's not some impressionable preschooler."

By the time I got up Tuesday morning, Patricia had already left for her office, but my dad was still home. He was finishing the first section of the newspaper while listening to Bob Edwards interview a Peruvian soccer star on *Morning Edition.*

"Did you hear us last night?" he asked.

"Hear what?"

He folded the newspaper into a small rectangle and smiled: "Yeah, right."

I shrugged.

"You know, I didn't tell you about Dana this fall because I figured your mother would have ended the relationship long before you came home from college. I'm sorry. I should have told you."

I poured myself a cup of coffee and sat down with him. "Why?"

"Why what?"

"Why should you have told me?"

"So it wouldn't have been such a shock."

"I can deal."

He stretched his legs under the kitchen table and rested his hands in his lap. "All right, then: What do you think of Dana?"

It was eight in the morning, a pretty early hour in the day for me that semester. I considered taking the easy way out and being completely noncommittal and vague. And my dad seemed so pathetic that fall that I seriously considered the uncommunicative-teenager route out of sympathy. A grunt would probably have sufficed.

But that didn't seem fair to Dana, and so I answered with what I thought was a compromise. "Well, she's a little weird and I have my doubts. But I like her. I like her a lot."

"She? Her?"

I realized instantly that I'd chosen exactly the wrong pronouns for my dad. "I guess I could call Dana a him. But I know that's not what she wants."

My dad nodded. "You're very diplomatic. But I think there's a biological imperative here that transcends preference."

"You don't think Dana could be a woman in a man's body?"

"I think Dana could believe such a thing. I think he could believe it with all his heart. But Dana is no more a woman than I'm an NFL linebacker. I could go around all day long in a New England Patriots jersey, but I still wouldn't be six and a half feet tall, I still wouldn't be two hundred and eighty pounds of rock-hard muscle. I still couldn't tackle an NFL running back if my life depended upon it."

"It's not exactly the same thing."

"Maybe not. But Dana's delusions will still affect your mom's life. That's my concern. I don't care what Dana does. Really, I don't. I only care if his actions take a toll on your mother."

"I wouldn't worry so much about Mom. She'll be okay."

"You sound like your stepmother."

"Well, she's right."

"I don't think either of you realize what people will say. What people already *are* saying."

"About Mom and Dana?"

"She's a schoolteacher, honey. She's a schoolteacher in a little village in rural Vermont. This isn't West Hollywood. It isn't even Bennington College."

"They'd do fine there," I agreed.

"People lose their jobs over this sort of thing. They lose their friends. Their families. They lose everything," he said, shaking his head as he spoke.

That night, my dad and Patricia took up exactly where they had left off on Monday, but they were more conscious of my presence down the hall this time, and so they spoke much more softly. Nevertheless, I still heard select words and phrases, and sometimes I'd overhear a whole sentence.

"You're in love with her, admit it," Patricia said at one point, and it sounded as if she was on the verge of tears. Then, a little while later, she said, "I won't quiet down. It's not fair, and you know it. It's not fair and I shouldn't have to take it."

The next morning, my dad and Patricia had both left for work by the time I awoke, and I wouldn't see them again until Friday night. I knew they were seeing their couples counselor during lunch that day, and my hope was that the therapist would find a way to reestablish peace in our time. I wasn't confident, but even a nineteen-year-old hates to see parents fight.

12

will

PATRICIA AND I WENT SKIING EVERY SATURDAY AT the Snow Bowl that December, and not simply because Patricia had purchased a new pair of skis. We donned our goggles and parkas because our therapist had encouraged us to do more things together.

Ironically, at the Snow Bowl I found myself focused even more on Allie and Dana, despite the fact that Allie had never once slipped either of her little feet into the cavernous plastic shell of a ski boot, or looked down from a chair lift and watched her skis bounce like airplane wings in a bumpy sky.

But, I learned, I was always going to associate the Snow Bowl with Allie. It was simple transitivity: I was on the ski team at Middlebury and we practiced at the Snow Bowl, and so the Snow Bowl would always remind me of college. College, in turn, would connect me with Allie.

There were other reasons, too, of course. We all have moments when we think we're at our best, and when we like ourselves just a little too much. Many of my moments like that occurred those winters when I was a very young man, and I'd squeeze in a dozen runs—a dozen runs minimum—a day, and then I'd return to Allie's dorm room, as attentive as a prodigal lover. I'd feel badly that I'd deserted her, and I'd be unfailingly attentive and present.

At least I think I was present.

Present is one of those words that came up a lot when Patricia and I were in counseling. Apparently, I'm not always as *present* as I think I am. I'm not exactly *absent*—even those months when Dana and Allie were becoming an item, I wasn't *always* alone in my car at the edge of the airport—but it seems I don't always listen.

"What I think Patricia is saying," our therapist constantly said, "is that you hear her. But you're not listening to her. Do you see the difference?"

Certainly I did. Our counselor was a woman about a decade our senior, who was still very attractive. Unfortunately, she took great pride in what she called "active listening," which meant two things. First of all, it meant she was always nodding her head when either Patricia or I spoke, as if she were one of those wooden mascot dolls with a bobbing noggin you buy at the ballpark. You couldn't stare back at her without getting seasick.

Second, it meant that any problems Patricia and I had could be reduced, in her opinion, to my inability to pay attention to what my wife really was saying. Patricia could have had an affair with the seventeen-year-old son of a client—which she most assuredly did not—and in the eyes of our therapist it would have been because I wasn't listening.

Of course, it's easy to be catty about the counselor now. Even then, however, I think I understood she was onto something, if only because of those Saturdays Patricia and I spent together on the ski slopes. I'd recall college and my first years with Allie, and I'd remember how, once, I probably *had* been a better listener.

One Saturday that winter, a couple of weeks before Christmas, I was waiting for Patricia at the bottom of the mountain and watching the other skiers motor downhill. I found myself ogling a slim young woman in navy blue ski pants. I noticed her midway down her final descent toward the base lodge, and I could see that she had terrific form. Then she abruptly cut her skis into the powder and came to a stop about twenty yards distant. She was chatting with another woman, facing away from me as she pulled off her goggles and her headband. Her parka was yellow and only fell to her waist, which meant I stared for a long moment at her rear.

Forgive me: Any man would have.

Then she turned toward me and I realized she wasn't a woman at all. She was a young man. A young racer. Me, perhaps, two decades earlier.

My hair, too, had been long.

Patricia suddenly pulled up beside me, jabbing her poles into the snow and leaning upon them.

"See someone you know?" she asked, catching her breath.

"I thought I did," I said. "But I was wrong."

I have a friend who insists that every man who marries multiple times essentially marries the same woman. This guy went to college with Allie and me, and now he's a professor and psychological researcher in the Northwest. In the study for which he's probably known best, he surveyed literally thousands of men who married two and three times, and then "profiled" their spouses. He determined that these men's wives had much more in common than might have been apparent if you had just glanced at the women as they strolled toward wedlock in churches and synagogues and city halls. Even those men who handled midlife particularly badly and convinced young things half their age to witness their physical declines up close and personal were usually marrying much younger versions of their first wives.

There were exceptions, of course. There always are. But, he insisted, the idiosyncrasies of what we love as we age don't really change.

Either I'm one of those exceptions or my friend's research is hokum. I think I first fell in love with Patricia because she was in so many ways so very different from Allie. We met at a car wash in the waning days of yet another northern New England mud season. I don't think Allie took any of our vehicles to a car wash in all the years we were together or married. It just never crossed her mind that she might want a car that was cleaner than it could get from a night out in the rain, or that a backseat wasn't in reality a massive knapsack in which one tossed all the small necessities a person might need on the road: A box of tissues, an extra lipstick, an aerosol can of an "instant tire repair." The old cassettes you no longer listened to, and that book on tape you haven't quite finished. A pair of winter weather wiper blades, and all those books you've been meaning to donate to the library. Dozens of Magic Markers, small (and large) slabs of oak tag. Maps of Vermont and maps of New England and maps of New York. A map of, of all things, Arkansas that AAA sends you by mistake. ("Where else would you keep a road map?" Allie had asked me when I inquired why in the world she had a map of Arkansas in her automobile.)

The day Patricia and I met, one of the water jets at the car wash needed to be unclogged, and while an attendant took a few minutes to repair it, the two of us climbed from our seats and stared up at the surprisingly warm March sun. And then, still beside our cars, we started to chat. After a moment I wandered over to her—it would have been rude not to, I decided—and I stood beside her.

Resting upon the backseat of her car was a burgundy leather briefcase, clasped shut. Nothing more. Nothing else on the seat, and nothing on the floor. The passenger seat was empty, too.

And in the cup holder just off the dashboard was an official Vermont Public Radio plastic auto-mug with safety lid.

"New car?" I asked, and I motioned through the glass windows.

She knew instantly why I was asking, and she smiled and offered a self-deprecating shrug. "I've had it a little over a year," she said. "Isn't it awful to be so compulsive?"

We had the chance to speak for a good ten minutes before the water jet was fixed, and I learned then that she was a lawyer and that her office and her town house were as tidy as her car. I learned that she swam and she skied, and she wasn't dating anyone seriously.

The following Saturday we went skiing together on the heavy spring slush that exists at the tops of the mountains, and it was so warm that we were able to ski in only windbreakers and turtlenecks. Already the sun felt higher at noon than it had earlier that week over the car wash, and the snow was dazzlingly bright.

That car wash, incidentally, is very near the Burlington airport. It is on the opposite side of the runway edge where some years later I would find myself stopping to watch the planes come and go. But when the wind is right, the planes climb and descend just above that car wash, too, their wheels stiff-legged below their bellies, and the wind was right on the day Patricia and I met. Twice when we were speaking turbo props zoomed over us—one coming to Vermont, and one leaving.

If, somehow, I could watch a film of the two of us standing together at that moment, I wonder if even then my gaze was straying up toward the planes as they passed overhead. I tend to doubt it. But one can never be sure.

Everyone knows someone who knows someone who knows a trans-sexual. Or is related to one. Remember that notion that only six degrees separate any two people on the planet? Well, you can halve the number between any normal person and a transsexual.

That autumn and winter at work, I was asked constantly about Dana Stevens. Vermont is an extremely small state, and the university and public radio communities are particularly close. And so people around me seemed to know quickly that my ex-wife was dating a transsexual, and then living with one.

"What do you think?" they'd ask, and—my voice indifferent—I'd tell them it was her life.

"Look at this," my assistant, Rita, said about three weeks before Christmas, and she showed me a holiday card the station had received the day before from a graphic design firm in Montreal that we used periodically. They'd created their card in the shape of an apple, and included inside a photograph of the staff that had been taken at an orchard. There must have been fifteen employees in the picture, and it was clear that the shot had been posed in the picking season in early autumn: Everyone was wearing a heavy sweater and a comfortable jacket—everyone except the thirty-something redhead in a sleeveless sundress. The redhead who stood a head taller than everyone else in the photo. The redhead with the creamy white skin on shoulders as broad as mine.

No. Broader.

"Transsexual?" I asked Rita.

"Yup."

And Kate Michaels, perhaps our foremost expert on classical music, kept finding me CDs in our collection by transsexual and drag performers. Every other day she must have discovered another one. Rarely—never, actually—did she find an artist we played on the air, but they were still talented musicians on reputable labels. I saw the word *diva* on the CD title a little too often for my taste, and to this day I don't understand why so many of them insisted on wearing feather boas, but there was usually nothing inherently wrong with their music.

Any number of times I almost asked Kate to stop, or told her that the joke had gone far enough. Once I nearly suggested that her interest in this subject was unnatural, but I wasn't sure if the remark would come out as light as I meant it.

After all, a day didn't go by that month when I wouldn't pick up two or three of the CDs in the stack on the credenza I never used—the credenza on which I would toss the CDs after Kate had shared them with me—and stare at the people on the covers. I'd stare at their transgender lips or their transsexual mouths, I'd look closely at the shape of their cheeks and their noses and their jaws. I'd try and see beyond their smiles and their pouts—beyond the oddly flirtatious gaze in their eyes—to figure out whether they were indeed happy.

All Things Considered
Tuesday, September 25

DR. JEN FULLER: In my opinion, clothing is infinitely more important to a transsexual than to a transvestite. A transvestite is merely using clothing to play a role. A transsexual is using it to define himself—or herself—as a human being.

allison

I RATHER DOUBT I'D HAVE SEEN DANA AGAIN IF
I'd thought seriously about the consequences. I know I didn't have
any expectations or goals when I called him two days after he told me
his plans; I don't think I had thought as far as tomorrow.

Maybe I thought I would see him once more and hurt him. Maybe
I thought I could talk him out of it. Maybe I just never stopped loving
him. I don't know.

But I certainly hadn't expected the two of us would be living
together as the snow would start falling in earnest in early December,
or that on the very first Monday of the month I'd be called into the
principal's office after school.

"You must hate this sort of thing," Glenn said, using his metal
wastepaper basket like an ottoman for his big heavy loafers.

"What sort of thing?" I asked. I figured I'd play naive, though I
knew exactly why I was there. Glenn Frazier had only come to the

112

school that September, and in little more than a season had shown himself to be an administrative automaton and a middle-aged martinet.
We'd already had a series of run-ins that fall. We'd bickered the very
first week of school when a mother complained that I was giving my
sixth-graders too much free rein when we visited the World Wide Web
on the classroom computer, and then we'd quarreled during the second
week over my decision to allow some of the students to go swimming
out at the maritime museum when the bus wouldn't start. Two parents
had called him, and he wasn't simply concerned that I had endangered
my students' welfare: A rumor had spread that I had actually allowed
the girls to go swimming topless. Two weeks after that, Glenn prohib-
ited me from taking my class on a picnic near the cliffs behind Will's
house. I'd gone there with eighteen to twenty eleven-year-olds every
single year for almost a decade and a half, and the only accident I'd
ever witnessed had been an adult chaperone's twisted ankle. Still,
Glenn was convinced that it was only a matter of time before one of
the kids ventured to the ledge and did a cannonball over the side.

He shrugged. "Talking about your life. You must hate it. After all,
it is *your* life. I know how hard it is to live in a fishbowl."

"I live in a Victorian village house."

He rolled his eyes and smiled. "You know what I mean."

"Honestly, I don't."

He pulled his feet back from the trash can and sat up straight in his
desk chair. His office overlooked the playground, and I saw that it had
started to snow once again, and the snow was beginning to stick to the
seats on the swings and the metal bars of the jungle gym.

"Your new live-in," he said.

I nodded. "Ah."

"I had a parent call me about him today. That makes three in a week
—actually, three since last Thursday—so I figured we should connect."

"A parent of one of my students?"

"Yup."

"May I ask who?"

"Well, today it was Lindsey's dad. Lindsey Lessard."

"I don't know him."

"Richard Lessard?"

"Nope. We've never met. I know Lindsey's mom."

"Well, he's concerned."

"Why?"

"Why do you think? Because his daughter's sixth-grade teacher is living with a transvestite."

"Not true."

He rolled his chair closer to his desk and folded his hands on the blotter. "We've all seen him."

"Dana's not a transvestite."

"We're about to play a game of semantics, aren't we?"

"No. But Dana's a transsexual. There's a big difference."

"Point noted. Bottom line? He's still a guy in a dress. He's still wandering around Grand Union in lipstick and mascara."

"I don't see why Richard Lessard should care."

"I don't think he would if Dana didn't take his groceries and go back to your house."

"What does he want?"

"Richard? I'm not sure. But he's not happy. Mostly he just wanted to vent—like the others."

"And you were happy to listen."

"It's my job."

"Did you defend me?" The question seemed to catch him off guard, and for a long moment he stared at the row of Thanksgiving pictures the first-graders had drawn the month before.

"I said you've been here a long time. And most of the time you seem to have pretty good judgment."

"Most of the time?"

"I was honest. We've really only known each other since August."

"Well. Thank you for the ringing testimonial."

"You know you have my support."

"Hardly!"

"You do. But I am concerned about this relationship of yours."

"I have many relationships. Do you mean the one with my daughter? My ex-husband? My friend Molly?"

"That attitude doesn't make this any easier."

"Who lives with me is none of Richard Lessard's business."

"That's not true. You teach his daughter. He pays your salary."

"It's not like I'm shacked up with a convicted child abuser. It's not like I'm having some fifteen-year-old's baby."

"No. You're living with a man in a dress."

I could see this conversation was going nowhere good, and that remaining and arguing with him would only make things more difficult. And so I asked him what he wanted me to do.

He was quiet for a long moment, and then he shook his head. "At this point," he said finally, "I just wanted you to know that parents were calling me. That's it." And then he scrunched up his eyebrows and tried to look thoughtful. "I guess that's really all," he said, and then added, "at least at this point."

That December, Dana and I went to Montreal for the weekend with Molly Cochran and her husband, a lawyer named Clayton. We went to the theater on Saturday night, and we spent the weekend afternoons shopping for Christmas presents and clothes at the elegant department stores along Saint Catherine.

On Saturday afternoon, the four of us wandered from Eaton's to Frommer and Bristol. Clayton was in the men's department on the first floor browsing through neckties, while Molly, Dana, and I were upstairs trying on business suits and skirts. The dressing room in that section is a rarity, especially for a store as refined as F&B's: Although the individual changing rooms are private, separated from one another by long, cabana-like doors, the three-sided mirrors are in a large chamber between the changing rooms and the store floor. The result? You have to emerge into a vaguely communal anteroom to see whether the dress you're thinking about is indeed flattering.

At one point, Dana and Molly had disappeared into the dressing room, while I was looking at pleated skirts along a side wall.

When they returned, Molly was giggling and Dana was oddly self-satisfied. Almost smug.

Molly squeezed my wrist and said, "You really are a dyke." Then she kissed my cheek.

I assumed I knew exactly what had occurred and was unimpressed. "What did you think Dana would do in there? Try and find a urinal? Hide in a changing room?"

"You had to be there, Allison. This had nothing to do with peeing like a woman or simply trying to act female."

"Much more affirming," Dana added, and he pointed discreetly toward a man and a woman chatting beside a rack of blazers. As I looked more closely at the pair, I realized that the woman was actually a man in drag.

"Was he in there when you two were?" I asked, referring to the transvestite.

Molly nodded and then told us what she had witnessed. Apparently, Dana had been standing at one of the three-sided mirrors beside a woman, fixing his headband and adjusting the shoulders of the dress he was considering. The transvestite had emerged from a changing room, seen the two females before the mirrors, and abruptly grown anxious and fled back onto the store floor. The woman at the mirror beside Dana had shaken her head, clearly appalled.

"Isn't it just amazing? That guy was trying to look like a girl," she had said to Dana. "What kind of man thinks he can do that?"

When Molly had finished her story, Dana offered a small smile and murmured contentedly, "And that, dear hearts, is the difference between a transvestite and a transsexual."

Sometimes, in the month between Thanksgiving and Christmas, I felt a bit like Beauty in the story of Beauty and the Beast. Like many little girls, Carly had loved the tale as a child, and so I knew the basics of the plot pretty well.

I don't mean to suggest that I was as lovely as Beauty, or that Dana, by comparison, was as frightening as the Beast. Not at all. But I had begun to see my home as a castle, and the only spot in the world where I could feel absolutely safe. Moreover, because Dana was focused almost entirely on staying healthy for his upcoming surgery, he spent huge chunks of his day doing nothing more than taking care of the house and preparing the magnificent breakfasts and dinners we shared. And so, just as it was for Beauty once she was inside the Beast's walls, there was absolutely no work for me to do. None. Everything, suddenly, was provided for me, and I was cared for and loved with a fervor I'd never before felt in my life.

Nevertheless, while Dana may not have looked like a Beast, I did understand that he was viewed as one whenever he ventured beyond the front door of our little citadel. While he could pass as a woman among strangers, everyone in town knew exactly who he was, and all too often he was seen as a freak—a freak who was insane.

I, of course, was merely considered insane.

There was one horrible moment at the grocery store when a woman complained to the manager that Dana was touching the fruits and the vegetables. Her concern? Clearly a person like Dana was leaving some horrible disease on the grapes. Another time, at the post office, a customer whose hands were completely empty refused to open the door for Dana, even though Dana had a half dozen boxes to mail in his arms. Finally, he had to put them down in the salt and sludge on the cement steps.

And he was given two speeding tickets in the village in the course of a week. Certainly our town—like many rural villages—is a bit of a speed trap, but in all the years I'd lived there, I hadn't received a single citation. Dana, however, was pulled over once for going thirty-six in a thirty-mile zone, and then for going forty-one on a stretch where the speed limit increased to thirty-five. Both times, he insisted, he was going the limit.

But what was especially awful was the way the officer tried to intimidate Dana because his appearance no longer matched the photograph on his driver's license. His license showed a well-groomed man in his early thirties. It also had a big M beside gender.

The policeman, under most circumstances a nice enough young guy named Culberson, saw in Dana the sort of deviance that some people find disgusting and menacing at once.

"There seems to be a problem, sir. This doesn't appear to be you," Culberson said, knowing of course that it was. "I'm going to have to ask you to leave your vehicle and stand away from it with your arms at your sides."

After Dana patiently explained the situation, the officer politely but firmly continued to insist that he stand outside of his car while Culberson wrote out the ticket. He also continued to call Dana *mister* and *sir,* even after Dana asked him not to.

"So long as you have an M on your license, sir, I am going to have to call you mister. Okay, Mr. Stevens?"

Two days later, Culberson pulled him over again, and once more the officer made him wait by the side of the road.

When Dana and I were alone inside our castle, however, it was a grand month. Certainly it was for me. I was spoiled. Didn't vacuum once. Didn't clean the bathtub. Didn't pull a single seed from the spaghetti squash, or chop a single scallion.

And while the female hormones had begun to decrease the frequency of Dana's erections—as well as his ability to sustain them—they hadn't diminished his desire to love me. I would get a massage almost every night before bed, and at least half the time I would wind up on my back while he explored with his fingers and tongue the pudendum of his dreams. Moreover, I gather Dana had always had a much more powerful libido than most transsexuals, and so even when his body was filled with testosterone blockers and his sexual reassignment was barely a month away, more times than not he would still get hard when I would rub his nascent breasts, or lick my way from his wondrously hairless ankles to his thighs.

In return, all Dana wanted from me was to be a woman. To be womanly. He would watch me shave my legs and my underarms, he would stare as I pulled on panty hose or a bra. He would want to see how I sat when I talked on the phone with Carly, and to listen in when I chatted at night with Nancy or Molly or my mother in Philadelphia.

"How do you butter your toast?" he would ask, and he would be completely sincere. The fact is, women do butter their bread very differently from men.

"Let me watch you climb into your car," he would say, and I would show him.

"Brush your hair again, please."

"Would you flip through a newspaper?"

"How do you pick up a pen?"

It was never annoying: I felt, simultaneously, like a cherished possession and a goddess. A woman loved on a variety of levels. A woman loved for all the right reasons, and for ones too small to matter in any other relationship I could have. The way I held a book when I read on the couch. The fact that I would sleep on my side five or six days before my period, because my breasts would be tender. The things I carried in my purse.

And so although I adore teaching—and although I had a particularly sweet and smart group of kids that year—there were some mornings when I could barely bring myself to put on my overcoat and leave the remarkable world I had in my house.

Christmas was on a Wednesday that year, and so the public schools were open on Monday, the twenty-third, but then closed for a luxurious thirteen-day break. The students weren't due back until January sixth. Dana was able to reschedule his final pre-operative consultation with the Trinidad surgeon for Monday, the thirtieth, and the sexual reassignment itself for the thirty-first: New Year's Eve morning.

"I guess it's sort of like completing my New Year's resolution a full three hundred and sixty-five days ahead of schedule," Dana observed while finalizing the details. "This year I'm going to be organized. This year I'm going to take off ten ugly pounds. This year I'm going to lose that needless appendage between my legs."

The real reason the timing mattered, however, was that by having the surgery performed on that Tuesday, I could remain with Dana in Trinidad for four full days after the operation, and—in total—we'd have nine days together out west. Our plan was that we'd spend Christmas in Vermont with Carly and my mother (she came north from Philadelphia every year), and then Dana and I would fly to Colorado on Friday, the twenty-seventh. I would return home alone on Sunday, January fifth, in time to teach the following day.

Dana, then, would still be unable to leave the hospital bed. Sexual reassignment is not minor surgery, and Dana wouldn't be allowed to even stand up until Monday, the sixth. Discharge—just another new woman emerging from Mount San Rafael, a hospital operated by the

Catholic Sisters of Charity until 1968—wouldn't occur until the middle of that week.

I would have liked to stay to help Dana, but I didn't dare miss a day of school—especially if my reason was my transsexual lover.

When Dana and I were first working out the details of the trip—the timing, the flights, finding a motel—I would try and tell myself that he wouldn't, in the end, go through with it. But as Christmas neared, I began to realize he would. He left for Florida to see his parents and his sister the weekend before the holiday, and once he was gone, the notion that he was going to spend two and a half days in a dress with his dreaded family signaled for me the irrevocability of his decision.

And so the Friday before Christmas, almost the moment Dana got into his car to drive to the airport, my magic little paradise evaporated. Poof. Beauty without her Beast. Dana had left, and everything seemed to disappear at once. And I began to cry. I cried off and on that whole weekend, even though Carly was home from college and might be watching TV in the den, or reading, or simply trying to sleep on the couch after her first semester as a college freshman.

"Mom, he'll—I mean *she'll*—still be Dana. You said so yourself," Carly reminded me any number of times that weekend, sometimes rubbing my back or patting my arm.

I was still weeping as the weekend came to an end.

"Why are you crying?" little Missy Thompson asked me when she saw my eyes tearing Monday morning as we wandered up the front steps of the school together at the start of the day. The building was long and low, and the bricks were a patchwork of rust and red. There were white pines surrounding the parking lot, and apple trees lining the front walk. The school was shady and cool in the summer, warm in the winter, and always very, very comforting.

"Because everything's so beautiful this morning," I lied, and I motioned toward the snow that had silenced the world the day before, and for a time had made all of the sidewalks in town look like church runners.

I don't think I was crying because I cared so much about Dana's penis, or because I gave a damn about the idea that some people would think I was gay. It was the notion that once the surgery was done, it could never be undone. Sure, some people went back, but the surgically built penis wasn't the same. It was a little bell cord, a third of a suitcase grip.

Limp, it looked fine. The rebuilt man could use it to pee standing up. But it didn't grow hard on its own, it didn't really get any bigger.

Here was yet another unalterable fact of transsexuality: Surgeons could do an astonishing job transforming a man into a woman, but the techniques weren't nearly as good when a woman—either genetic or surgically wrought—wanted to become a man. At least not yet.

Especially when the genital nerves had already been rearranged and transplanted once.

And so what if Dana was making a mistake? What if he really was, merely, a transvestite? Or an effeminate, heterosexual male? Or, perhaps, a gay male who, for some reason, was incapable of admitting the truth to himself?

And what if I was repulsed by Dana after the reassignment? I might be. No matter how many pictures he showed me of OR-sculpted vulvas, no matter how many Polaroids we received in the mail of the surgeon's fine work . . . the truth was, I had never in my life been sexually attracted to a woman. At least not seriously.

"Do you love me?" Dana asked on the phone that weekend from his parents' house in Florida.

"I do," I said.

"Do you have fun with me?"

"Of course."

"I make you happy?"

"So happy," I whispered, determined not to cry on the phone.

"Then we'll be fine," Dana said.

But once we'd said good night and the line had gone dead, my eyes welled with tears and I started to sniffle. Once again I was crying, and I don't think I stopped for more than a few minutes at a time until he returned Monday night, and made me laugh with his tales of his parents, his adventures in the ladies' rooms in airports and shopping malls, and his brief time on the beach in a sundress.

All Things Considered
Tuesday, September 25

DR. THOMAS MEEHAN: You really want to know? Let's see, there must be at least half a dozen different "-ectomies" alone. There's the penectomy and the vaginectomy. The orchidectomy and the oophorectomy. F2Ms, of course, all have a salpingectomy, a hysterectomy, and a mastectomy.

Actually, that's an exaggeration: Not *all* have the mastectomy. Some will just have reduction mammoplasty —and now we're getting into the "-plasties." Reduction mammoplasty. Augmentation mammoplasty. Phalloplasty. Vaginoplasty. Labiaplasty.

And then there's the procedure that I guess you'd have to call the phonetic wild card. But it's a biggie. Certainly it's something that mattered to Dana Stevens.

CARLY BANKS: And that is?

MEEHAN: Castration, of course.

14

dana

IT COULD HAVE BEEN WORSE: NEITHER OF MY parents had a stroke and died. When I was on the airplane, I thought there was a distinct possibility that at least one of them would.

My mother had wanted to pick me up at the airport, but I had insisted she couldn't. I'd said I'd rent a car. My parents thought that was ridiculous. And so we had compromised: My sister, Isabel, would take the day off from the television station where she was a producer and get me. She was even going to bring along her little daughter—my niece—and the two of them would spend the morning bonding at some big public pool with a series of water slides before picking me up.

I'd told my parents beforehand exactly why I was coming and what I would be wearing, but it's one thing to be told that your son—who you believe is merely a disgusting pansy, though he continues to claim he is something else entirely—will be traveling in a pair of almost indecently comfortable floral leggings and a pink cardigan sweater, and it's quite another to see it.

"I'd ask to borrow that," Isabel said, fingering one of the sweater's small wooden buttons as we walked through the airport in Miami, "but I think I'm a tad too small in the shoulders and a tad too big in the chest. Too busty."

Her daughter, Olivia, was about to turn five, and she hadn't seen me in close to two years. She had no real memory of me as a man. Both her hair and her mother's hair were still damp from the pool.

"With any luck, someday I will be too—too busty, that is."

Since I was only going to be in Florida for three nights, I'd brought along only two carry-on bags. Nevertheless, it had shocked me how many more things a woman needed to pack than a man. My cosmetics and blow dryer and curling iron alone took up half a satchel.

"Let me take one of those for you," Isabel said, motioning toward my little bags. At first that part of me that had grown up as a male refused. But then I realized that Isabel's *sister* would most certainly have allowed her to take one of the totes, and so I handed over the lighter of the two.

Olivia kept looking up at me as we walked, as if she wanted to ask me something. As if something about me confused her. I had thought I'd looked pretty good that morning when I'd gotten dressed, or at least pretty female. And so her gaze was shaking my confidence a tiny bit.

Finally, as we were emerging from the air-conditioning into the tropical heat—I could literally feel the waves rising up from the asphalt—she took my free hand and said, "Aunt Dana, your earring is awfully dangly. I think it's gonna fall off."

I touched my lobe, and she was absolutely right. It was about to fall off. And so there in Section B of the parking lot I stopped and knelt and planted a big, lipstick-laced kiss on her cheek.

I slept in the room that had been my room as a child, though it looked nothing like it had two decades earlier. Once I started graduate school and it was clear to my mother that I'd never be living there again, she converted it into a bedroom for guests—of which they've always had

scads. That meant that everything was now an equatorial white, like
every other room in the house, as if we didn't have air-conditioning
squalls roaring through the place twenty-four hours a day.

My mother grew orchids and had placed two of her more spectacu-
lar plants in the room to cheer me.

I hadn't been back in two Christmases, and I'd seen my parents
only once that whole time. The autumn before I'd met Allison, they'd
flown to Vermont for a week of leaf peeping, and we'd had breakfast
and dinner together two days in a row when they were in Burlington.
It wasn't a disaster, but they complained constantly about how much
colder Vermont was than Coconut Grove, and it didn't help at all
when, the first night we went out to eat, our frolicsome waiter overheard that my parents were from Florida and welcomed them with
great histrionics to the "Queen City." My father was convinced that I
knew the fellow and had put him up to it.

"No, Dad," I'd said, "that really is Burlington's nickname."

"Queen City?"

"Yup."

"Is that why you settled here?"

And my mother kept hugging herself, as if she were freezing to
death on an ice floe. "Polar tundra," she kept saying. "You must have
absolutely no growing season here!"

She also couldn't believe that there wasn't a man in my life I was
hiding.

"You get checked for AIDS, don't you?" she asked before they continued on their way to Stowe. "It's very controllable now, you know,"
she said, and she gave me the sort of perfunctory squeeze that she con-
ferred upon her women friends when they'd run into one another at
charity events at Viscaya or the Playhouse.

Early that afternoon when Isabel and I arrived at the family
hacienda—a faux adobe that mixed white stucco walls with black
wrought-iron railing—both our mother and father were home. I
wasn't surprised Mother was there, since her tennis games were Tuesdays and Thursdays, and she rarely did lunch on a Friday. Her
women's group met Wednesday mornings.

But I was shocked to find Father there, too. Isabel was also. We had both assumed that I would take a runway walk first for my mother and then, once whichever tranquilizer she was on that day had had a chance to mellow her out, unveil the new me for dear Dad. One parent at a time, that was my plan, in each case with lovely, supportive, maternal Isabel as my emotional brace.

Well, it didn't happen that way. Apparently Dad had run out of things to develop, at least for the afternoon. It looked as though the Everglades, so long as I was in town, would be safe.

"Well, Dana," he said as we walked in the front door, "you really are one very brave . . ."

"Yes?" I asked when he couldn't bring himself to finish his sentence.

"Let me look at you," my mother said, and I put down the bag I was carrying and offered a demure little spin in their entryway.

"I saved Aunt Dana's earring," Olivia cooed in the brief silence, and my father picked her up and kissed her. He was wearing tennis shorts, and I realized he probably hadn't gone into the office for even a few hours that morning. I was very flattered.

"Oh, good for you! I'm sure your Unc— I'm sure Dana was very grateful," he said.

"Have you had lunch?" my mother asked.

"Lunch?"

"It's the meal we eat between breakfast and dinner," my father said.

"Though *meal* isn't exactly the right word for Mom's midday fare these days," Isabel added. "I'd say it's more of a drink: eleven fruits and vegetables in a juicer."

"Sometimes I add yogurt, sweetheart."

"You asked to look at me, and you haven't rendered any opinion!" I said. I tried to make it sound as if my indignation was a joke, but I was still hurt that my mother hadn't told me what she thought.

"You've lost a lot of weight," my father said. "Too much, I think. You're as bad as your—"

"Mother?" I said, wondering whether I was trying to be helpful or throw a bomb.

"Yes."

"You're a big man, Father," I said. "I don't want to be either."

"Either?"

"Big. Man."

"I get it."

Olivia climbed down from his arms and started petting Coconut, one of the two springer spaniels my mother had brought home from the animal shelter a few years earlier. As usual, Coconut—like her sister—had a buzz cut. Springers are hairy little pups, and my mother hated pulling tufts of fur from the rattan, or finding matted hair on her white upholstery.

"You don't want to get sick," my mother said.

"I won't get sick!"

"Are you getting exercise?"

Isabel—a woman who, clearly, should be raising her sweet child in some embassy overseas because she is indeed a born diplomat—took my hand and squeezed it. "I'll tell you what I think," she said to me. "I think you'll have to tell me where you got those leggings. And you'll have to tell me what you do to make your skin look so damn healthy!"

Before I could answer, my father said it was officially Friday afternoon and he was going to go get a beer. Clearly, however, it wasn't that he wanted that beer or he needed a drink. It was the *going* part that mattered, it was his need to leave the hallway where we were standing. I looked at my watch: His urge to flee around me had kicked in barely two minutes after my arrival—conceivably a record, I thought.

"So, Mother, tell me: Do you like my new look? Is it better or worse than you feared? I want to know. Honestly."

My mother looked down at her granddaughter and then back at me. She sighed, and then her eyes started to water: big drops meandering down a face that looked elderly but wrinkle-free. The face-lift visage.

"You look fine, honey," she whispered, her words partly lost in her throat. "So fine I don't think you need to do the rest."

"The rest?"

"You know," she mumbled, wiping her face with her fingers. "The operation. I don't think you need it. Please don't. Please. Don't."

Olivia looked up from Coconut and asked her mother, "Is Aunt Dana sick?"

And though my sister quickly smiled at her little girl and shook her head no; though my mother turned away from us, hiding her face in the painting of a spiky cockscomb shrub by the stairs; though my father was in the kitchen, taking as long as he could to pop the top of a can of beer; I knew that if any one of them had been asked the question alone—even my truly dear younger sister—they would have said, with varying degrees of sympathy and support, "Yes, Olivia. Your aunt Dana is sick."

Though my father would not have used the word *aunt*.

The closest thing my mother has to an office is the terrace by the café at Viscaya—the massive "villa" James Deering built on Biscayne Bay almost a century ago. It isn't quite as jaw-dropping opulent as Hearst Castle, but it isn't shabby: thirty-four rooms, tons of marble, and ten acres of formal gardens and fountains. It's now a museum, which is why my mother lunches there with some frequency: She's on the board.

That, I imagine, and the fact that she likes to watch the fashion photographers do their clothing shoots. It keeps her a season or two ahead.

When my parents took me there Saturday morning, a group of young things were preening in gauzy lingerie in a roped-off corner of one of the white marble balconies overlooking the ocean. It wasn't the sort of fashion shoot that was going to interest my mother, but I was happy for my dad. Though he had to have breakfast in public with me, he at least had the pleasure of watching young girls in tiny panties pretend they were harlots.

Truth be told, it wasn't bad for me either. As usual, I lusted. I learned. I coveted.

But my father was all business and may actually have paid less attention to the models than even my mother. He was hoping he could talk me out of my surgery, and he was going to play what he thought was his last card. Not necessarily what he believed was his best or even his second-best card—he'd played those the night before, asking me first if I understood the physical complications that were possible after the surgery, and then whether I'd really and truly digested its finality.

He ordered a ham and cheese croissant, asking—as only my father can—for extra ham and mustard. My mother and I had the tomatoes stuffed with tuna salad.

"I know you think you have to do this," my father began, "and I know you think your mother and I are opposed to it simply because we view you as our son."

"Uh-huh."

"There's more to it than that."

"Okay." A new model appeared in a white camisole and a very demure pair of white cotton panties. As the stylist, a man, was adjusting them, I realized that the woman was actually wearing two briefs so there wouldn't be any bulges or bumps from her pubic hair. It made for an almost preternaturally smooth presentation. I wondered if the transgendered had discovered that little trick. I knew I hadn't.

"You have to understand that there are some things you're going to experience that you can't possibly have endured. Things your mother and sister have had to go through. Things no person should have to tolerate."

I considered placing my hand on my father's and saying something flippant: *Father, don't worry. I won't start getting a period at thirty-five.*

Father, don't fret. I'll live if a construction worker pats me on the ass.

But he was so sincere that I held my tongue. My father may not approve of me—he may think I'm completely insane—but I don't believe he has ever stopped loving me. And his delivery was so earnest that a part of me actually feared that something profoundly horrible had indeed happened to my sister and my mother. A mugging, perhaps. Maybe they'd been victimized by a pervert in a trench coat.

Perhaps it had been something much, much worse.

Based on my father's tone, it was certainly possible. Yet I assumed I would have heard if such a thing had occurred. One would have thought that someone would have gotten on the phone and told even me, the transsexual disappointment in northern Vermont.

"I'm a businessman," my father continued, "and I'm in a business where I see a lot of men and women. I see a lot of men and women working together. And I know a little bit about what goes on at the TV station where your sister works. I know people there."

My mother watched her tuna and her tomato, instead of looking at either my father or me. I realized we were all wearing sunglasses, and I wondered if we looked like a family of drug dealers to the tourists who were at Viscaya to see the house and the gardens and the scantily clad models. Mid-morning, we were the only people on the terrace who were actually eating.

"I hope you're not about to tell me something hideous has happened to Isabel," I said. "Or to you, Mother."

My father finished his orange juice and sat back in his deck chair. "I'm talking discrimination, Dana. In business. In life. I can tell you flat-out as a businessman that discrimination remains a fact of life in the workplace. In the world! There's a producer at Isabel's station who must earn seven or eight thousand dollars a year more than she does, even though he isn't half as good. Know why?"

"Let me guess: because he's male?"

"Damn straight. And while I try to make sure that the women in my firm are on the exact same pay scale as the men, I know how the companies we work with behave. I know how they treat their women."

"Most of the businesses you work with are construction companies—a group not exactly known for their forward-thinking personnel practices."

"They work with banks, too," my mother said softly.

"Look, I know the statistics," I said, careful to keep my voice even. "I know women earn less than men. I know the numbers."

"And they're not treated as equals. Ever. And you can't know what that's like, having been born a man and treated as a man. Do you have any idea how difficult it is for your mom to be heard in some of her committee meetings? Sometimes the men don't let her get a word in edgewise."

"So no one's been mugged?" I asked. "No one's been attacked?"

"Attacked? Why would you think such a thing?"

"For a moment I'd been afraid that was where this conversation was going. I'm very relieved."

"Dana, we just don't think you have the foggiest idea what it's going to be like to simply conduct your life nine to five. The business world—"

"I'm not in the business world, Father. I'm a tenured professor at a fine university."

"Must you interrupt me?" my father said.

I sat back and folded my hands in my lap. "I'm sorry. I didn't mean to be rude."

"If you go through with this, it's going to be much harder than you realize to do almost everything," he said. "I can't wait till you try and get your next car loan. Or a mortgage."

My mother pushed her sunglasses back against the bridge of her nose and turned to face me. "And just watch what happens the first time you bring your car in for a tune-up," she said. "They'll find things wrong with parts of the engine that you didn't even know existed."

"Let me make sure I understand this: You two think I shouldn't have my reassignment because an auto mechanic might charge me for some gasket I don't need?"

"That's an oversimplification," my father said.

"And it may be a small thing," my mother added, growing animated for the first time that morning, "but most of the time, life is nothing but small things. Getting the oil changed in your car. Convincing the plumber to come and fix a leaky shower. And it's harder when you're a woman. A lot harder. I know. I've been doing it for almost sixty-one years."

My father glanced at the models and then back at me. Then he took a deep breath and said, "Will you do me a favor? One small thing?"

I knew exactly what was coming, and so I lied: "Of course I will."

"Think about this some more. Think about how hard your life is going to be. How difficult. Would you at least reconsider your plan?"

I knew I had forty-eight hours to go in scenic South Florida, two more days with my parents. And so in the interest of making the visit as pleasurable for them as possible, perhaps even keeping the peace for the remainder of my stay, I pursed my lips and tried to look thoughtful. Pensive. Sincere.

"Okay," I repeated. "For you two I will."

But, of course, I didn't.

I strolled up and down the streets of South Beach Saturday afternoon, and I was blissfully invisible. Perhaps there were people who knew or suspected what I was, but on South Beach they saw such things all the time. I loved the warmth from the sun on my shoulders and my arms. I loved to have my toes naked but for my finely woven sandals. I loved the *whoosh* my dress made against my legs as I walked.

My parents were so relieved by the notion that I would reconsider my plans that I began to fear lying to them had been a mistake. I probably shouldn't have gotten their hopes up, since I'd be dashing them again so very soon: In only six days I would be getting on an airplane for Colorado.

Briefly I wondered what would happen if I didn't tell them. In theory, they'd never have to know I'd had the reassignment. After all, I wouldn't exactly be wandering around their house naked when I next returned, I wouldn't be flaunting my new vagina. They hadn't seen me without my clothes on since I was seven or eight years old, and there was no reason to believe they would ever see me that way again.

And withholding the truth would certainly make my lifestyle less frightening to them. It would certainly make them happy. Well, happier. They could always tell themselves that at some point I might return to my senses, that someday I might climb back into my clothes as a man.

"And Allison really doesn't mind?" my father had asked me Friday night as he'd stared at the pictures of her I had brought.

"She isn't sure if she minds or not," I had answered. "She just knows what I'm going to do."

"She's so feminine," my mother had said, unable to mask her surprise. I have no idea what she had imagined Allison would look like, but I have a feeling she was still expecting me to bring south photographs of a man. "She's so pretty."

"I'll tell her you said so."

"And if you go through with this, she's going with you?"

"When I have the operation? Indeed she is," I had said, and—to be completely honest—I know there was pride in my voice. Unattractive, I realize. Downright manly.

But it wasn't simply the idea that I was involved with or possessed a beautiful woman. It was the idea that I was involved with a beautiful woman who had volunteered to stand beside me through my operation.

That was more than my parents had offered to do.

I stopped into one of the faux deco bars across the street from the ocean and sat down at a small table by the window. I ordered a cranberry juice and club soda, and watched the people go by. In six days, Allison and I would be in Trinidad, and four days after that I would have my reassignment. Ten days. At that exact moment in ten days, I would in fact be flat on my back in a hospital bed, woozy from anesthetics and painkillers, my body just starting its road back from the knife.

I decided I had to tell my parents the hard truth. Here I was having the procedure because I was tired of denying who I was. What I was. It certainly didn't make sense now to encourage my parents' continued denial, or to place myself in the position of having to lie to them for the rest of my life. It wouldn't be fair to Isabel, who would certainly know what I had done, and it wouldn't be fair to Allison. If she could be brave, so could my mother and father.

I decided I would tell them Monday morning. Over breakfast I would tell them that I'd thought long and hard about my decision for almost forty-eight hours, and I hadn't changed my mind. There wasn't a single lingering doubt anywhere inside my gray matter. I was going to live what I hoped would be the rest of a long and healthy life as a woman.

And then, after telling them, I would hug them.

I looked at the polish I'd applied to my nails. I sipped my drink. And I think I glowed.

All Things Considered
Tuesday, September 25

DR. THOMAS MEEHAN: The bed nucleus is a tiny region in the part of the brain called the hypothalamus. It's no bigger than a BB, really. But here's what's so interesting. The study found that in men—gay, straight, it didn't matter—the bed nucleus was two-point-six cubic millimeters. In women, it was around one-point-seven cubic millimeters.

And in male-to-female transsexuals? One-point-three. Imagine, half the size. That's telling.

Of course, we're not sure whether those differences are the result of something that occurs in fetal development, or something that occurs years later. At least I'm not.

Moreover, there's a problem with the study. It only included six transsexual brains. And it took the researchers eleven years to track down even that many.

carly

"There was a very wealthy woman in Philadelphia who wanted to look like a cat. And they did it. The doctors, that is. It took three or four operations—maybe more—and Lord knows how much it all cost. And how much it hurt. But she looks a bit like a cat now," my grandmother said, shaking her head.

"Whiskers, too?" Dana asked.

"Very funny. Mostly they worked on her eyes and her cheek-bones."

"Would you like more sweet potatoes, Mother?" my mom asked, clearly hoping to change the subject.

"Oh, why not. They're delicious, Dana."

"Thank you."

"Isn't Dana an awesome cook?" I said.

"Very good," my grandmother said. Unlike the rest of us, she was still wearing a dress. After the Christmas Eve service—the early one, the one that began at seven o'clock—my mother and Dana and I had all climbed into slacks or, in my case, blue jeans.

"I guess you can see my point," she went on.

"I can," Dana said. "But, honestly, Mrs. Cronin, I'm not doing this simply because it *can* be done."

My grandmother has always been very sporty, perhaps because she'd been a surgical nurse until age forced her to retire. Nothing in the world, it seems, can faze her. The Christmas before my mother met Dana, my mom's friend Nancy Keenan spent Christmas Eve at our house. After drinking a little too much eggnog, Nancy told all of us—including my grandmother—about her brother's car accident the month before. He was going to be fine, but he'd had to be cut out of the car by the rescue squad, and so everyone saw exactly why he'd wrapped his Subaru around a telephone pole and broken both of his arms: He was using this thing called an Auto Suck, and he'd lost control of his car when he came. Very stupid, it seemed to me. And I couldn't believe that Nancy was telling us the story in front of my grandmother.

But my grandmother hadn't seemed bothered at all.

"Did it use batteries?" she'd asked Nancy.

"Nope. Plugged right into the cigarette lighter."

"See?" my grandmother had said. "No good has ever, ever come from smoking."

Nevertheless, I was still amazed by how comfortable she was discussing Dana's plans Christmas Eve, and offering her opinions. She was, after all, somewhere in her early seventies.

"This isn't a nose job, Dana," she went on. "This has to be a major operation."

"Oh, it is."

"What would you do if the procedure didn't exist? If it wasn't possible?"

"Suffer."

"Is that what—and I want to use the right word—transsexual people did until someone figured out how to do it? They just suffered?"

Dana took a piece of bread from the basket and delicately broke it in half. "Essentially, yes. They lived very unhappy lives."

"So there was a . . . demand for the procedure? Some doctor some-where thought it was something we needed to figure out how to do?"

"Market forces at work," Dana said.

My grandmother sat back in her chair. "When it's done, will you tell the next man you meet how you came to be who you are?"

"I don't think I understand what you mean," Dana said, and then motioned for my mother to pass the butter.

"The next time you fall in love with a man, and things proceed to the bedroom: What will you tell him? Or will you have told him already? I guess this is a question about sexual etiquette. Obviously it wasn't an issue for my generation."

I glanced at my mother, and she was already looking at Dana. Dana looked crestfallen: doe-eyed and sad and surprised. Clearly my mom hadn't told her mother that she and Dana were lovers, and somehow my grandmother had missed the fact that they'd slept in the same bed-room the night before—or, if she had noticed, she had simply viewed it as two middle-aged gals bunking together.

Dana sat up very straight, turned back to my grandmother, and said in a tone that was as controlled as it was polite, "I'm having this operation so I won't have to hide who I am. I like to believe that I'd only fall in love with a person who's completely comfortable with that. With me."

I don't know if my mom was planning to tell my grandmother about Dana and her and just hadn't yet found the right moment, or whether she was hoping she'd never have to mention it. But I could see how hurt Dana was, and certainly my mom could, too. And so she ral-lied. She took Dana's hand in hers and said, "And I'm that person, Mother. Dana and I have been dating since the middle of the summer."

My grandmother pulled off her eyeglasses, folded the ear pieces flat, and placed them on the dining room table. "I didn't realize," she said.

"It's true," my mom said. Dana, I saw, was actually blushing.

"And you're having the surgery next week?" my grandmother asked.

"A week from today, as a matter of fact."

My grandmother nodded, and I thought that for one of the few times in her life she was actually embarrassed. But I was wrong. She was displeased, but she wasn't flustered. "Well, dear," she said to Mom, "we all need to try new things now and then. Let's face it: The first person to eat a lobster must have been a very brave man."

"Or," Dana said, smiling, "very, very hungry."

I stayed up watching television well past midnight Christmas Eve, and so I was the last one to go upstairs. For a long moment I stood in the dark at the top of the steps, and then I tiptoed down the hall to my mom's bedroom. There was a string of light under the shut door, but I didn't want to disturb them and so I didn't knock. But I stood there for a long moment, entranced, wondering what was going on at that exact moment on the other side. Were they reading? Had one or both of them fallen asleep with the light on? Were they, at that very moment, making love?

I tried not to think about Dana naked, but I did. I tried not to think of either the breasts that were starting to blossom, or the penis that would soon be gone. But I did. I thought of both.

I imagined Dana and my mother were having a variant on make-up sex: Dana, in my mind, was filled with gratitude because my mom had announced at the dinner table that the two of them were lovers, while my mom was, finally, liberated from the guilt she must have been feeling for days at having hidden that very fact.

Nevertheless, I found it interesting that my mom was still so uncomfortable with her relationship with Dana that there remained people from whom she hid the gory details.

It may have been the apparent fixation of everybody around me on genitals, and it may have been the odd tensions and euphorias that filled the house; it may even have been the simple fact that I'd finally gotten some much-needed sleep after my first semester of college; but I realized, suddenly, how powerfully horny I had become, and I retreated as fast as I could to my bedroom. If it hadn't been Christmas

Eve and if I hadn't known it would have sent my ex-boyfriend, Michael, exactly the wrong message, I would have called him up that very moment and told him to come over to my house and fuck me silly.

The women in my family have always seemed to do okay without a man permanently under the roof. My mom hadn't lived with one since I was in elementary school, and her mom hadn't lived with one since my grandfather died when I was a toddler.

Nevertheless, I knew my grandmother was very disappointed when her daughter and Will Banks had divorced. She liked my dad a lot.

We went for a walk through the village early Christmas night, just the two of us, savoring the lights and the decorations on the houses that ringed the green. Mom and Dana had prepared another monster dinner and refused to let my grandmother or me do a thing—even help clear the table when we were done.

"We don't get snow like this in Philadelphia," she said, and she waved at the white quilt on the commons, and the drifts piled up against the gazebo. "I wish we did."

"Trust me: It loses its luster in February. Sometimes you're pretty sick of it by March."

"Do you know what kind of weather they'll have in Colorado?"

I was careful to walk pretty slowly, because there were little patches of ice on the sidewalk and I didn't want my grandmother to fall and break her hip. Aside from the damper it would put on the holiday, it would have complicated my mom's travel plans in a big way.

"Cold, but not too cold. Twenties and thirties at night. Forties during the day. And there's no snow where they're going right now. They might get some, but supposedly it wouldn't last."

"Like Philadelphia."

"Maybe."

"I still can't believe what doctors can do today. And believe me, I've seen a lot of changes over the years."

"Me too. It's pretty amazing."

"What do you think of him?"

"Dana?"

"Excuse me. *Her*."

"It's okay. None of us can keep up with the pronouns. Except for Mom."

"Well, she is a teacher."

"I like Dana," I said.

"Oh, I do, too. But do you think she's normal?"

"Nope."

"Me either. I think she's as crazy as a loon."

"Still, you'd be surprised how quickly you can get used to the weirdness of it all."

"Have you?"

"Gotten used to it? Not always. But most of the time. And the important thing is that she makes Mom happy."

"For the moment, anyway," my grandmother said. "No one, it seems, has been able to keep your mother happy forever. I guess your father still holds the longevity record."

"I guess."

"What do people in town think of Dana? Not much, I'd wager."

"I was gone most of the fall, so I'm probably not a good person to ask."

"That was a very tactful answer, dear. Forgive me. I didn't mean to try and make you rat on your mother."

We passed by a massive yellow and blue Victorian house that had been a bed-and-breakfast for as long as I could remember. There were electric candles in every single window, and small wreaths on the shutters.

"I really haven't had to talk to anyone about Dana," I said, and then thought to myself, *yet*. I knew it was only a matter of time.

"Not even your father?"

"Well, Dad and I have talked."

"What does he think?"

I shrugged, though my grandmother was so focused on the sidewalk she probably didn't notice. "You know, my sense is he isn't going to like anyone my mom likes," I said.

"You're probably right. Your father enjoys his torch. He'll carry it to his grave."

"Oh, I think he loves Patricia."

"In a way, maybe. How is she?"

"She and Dad seem to be at odds a bit lately."

"What a surprise."

"But I guess she's okay. Busy."

"So, your father's met Dana?"

"Uh-huh. But Dana wasn't wearing women's clothes yet."

My favorite high-school English teacher and her family drove by, and she gave me a little wave. Somehow she recognized me under my wool hat and my scarf.

"I'm glad I didn't know about them last night," my grandmother said. "I thought they were just friends."

"You mean when we were at church?"

"Exactly. I think if I'd known the truth, I would have convinced myself that every single human being in the sanctuary was staring at us."

I nodded, and kicked a little piece of ice off the sidewalk. I didn't have the heart to tell her they were.

16

will

THINK ABOUT IT, AND JUST IMAGINE THE POSSIBILITIES:
You think you're a Caucasian trapped in an Oriental's body. You
know for a fact that your hair is supposed to be blond, you know your
chest is supposed to be a forest of tawny curling hair. A mass as thick as
steel wool. And so you're miserable. Wretched. Perhaps even bitter.
What do you do? You have cosmetic surgery so you look like a WASP.
You dye the ebony mass on your head the color of straw, you have hair
plugs implanted into your chest. You have your eyes rounded.

But are you no longer Taiwanese? Chinese? Japanese?

Of course not.

Better still: You're convinced you're a black man imprisoned inside
a white guy's skin; you're absolutely sure that a gigantic error's been
made. Really, that's what you believe. And so you go to a dermatologist
to find out what can be done to make you look black.

Or walk with me a few generations into the future. You're a short man. You're barely five feet. And you are sick to death of being treated as . . . small. Especially since you are so big inside. So tall. You know it. You sense it. You feel it. Perhaps when you were a teenager and no one was home, you once went so far as to sneak into your father's armoire, and you pranced around the bedroom in his suits. Forty-two longs. Trousers with an inseam of thirty-six.

You looked ridiculous, and certainly all that fabric bunched up around your ankles and shins didn't do a whole lot to facilitate the illusion. But there was something there if you half closed your eyes and you gave your imagination free rein. It was a bit like visiting the fun house at the county fair and standing in front of the mirror that stretched you like a rubber band.

Now, however, the science is there to build you a body that would get you a tryout with the Knicks. Make you the tall man on the outside that you know you are on the inside. And so you have the surgery. Or you take the drugs.

Are any of these ideas stranger than the notion that with hormones and a knife we can change a person's gender? When I first met Dana, I didn't think so. To be honest, I'm not completely sure I do now.

The fact is, no hormone was going to turn Dana Stevens's Y chromosome into an X. No surgery in the world was going to offer him the particular history that went along with growing up female. No procedure was going to give him the joys or the terrors that must accompany pregnancy—that must, for teen girls, make sex a walk over Niagara Falls on a tightrope.

In my opinion, learning to mince through a mall didn't make him female, rouge didn't make him female, a barrette in his hair didn't make him female.

You simply couldn't, it seemed to me, change a biological imperative.

When I realized what Dana was going to do, I saw at best a parody of femininity. I saw the sort of man who could set the women's movement back decades. *Look at me,* the transsexual screams, *I'm a girl! I'm wearing a dress!*

The problem? The male transsexual wants only to be as womanly as possible. He wants to be ultra-feminine. Half the transsexuals in this world would probably have looked right at home at a Junior League luncheon in 1961. The only giveaway? Their bigger hands would have been holding those teeny-tiny watercress sandwiches. Their bigger mouths would have been eating them.

Dana, no matter what, was never going to know what it was like to grow up female. He was never going to be molded by the sorts of challenges that confronted Allie twenty and thirty years ago, or that face Carly right now. Dana was never going to be formed, at least in part, by the fears and frustrations a woman inevitably endures throughout her life. Nor, for that matter, was he ever going to know her real joys.

I did my homework, and it struck me that Dana's problem was as much on the outside as it was on the inside. A big part of his predicament was his world. Instead of living in a place where it was perfectly fine to be a man who feels like a woman (or, for that matter, a woman who feels like a man), he was part of a civilization that would rather castrate certain men and remove the ovaries from certain women. We're just not very comfortable with people who, for example, lack that second X chromosome and therefore sport facial hair and a penis, but would rather wear stockings and a skirt than a pair of pants.

And yet it wouldn't be that difficult to learn to be comfortable. What would it take? A generation? Maybe two?

Look at me. I've changed.

And even if we never, ever grew to approve of them, you have to admit: Tolerating them is far better than mutilating them. Chopping apart their genitals. Disfiguring their bodies.

Here's an irony too good to pass up: The last name of the surgeon who in 1952 turned George Jorgensen into Christine?

Hamburger. The guy with the knife was named Hamburger.

The logistics of Allie's and my friendship are only complex when other people are involved. I don't think Patricia ever minded too terribly when I dropped in on Allie—or, at least, I was always able to convince myself that she didn't. For some reason, however, I was very uncomfortable the one time that Patricia and Dell, Allie's mother, were together in the same room. Some years earlier, when Mrs. Cronin had come north for a long Fourth of July weekend, she and Allie and Carly had all dropped by our house on a Sunday afternoon. I think Patricia felt outnumbered—she saw an ambush, three generations of women descending upon her from my ex-wife's family—and so it had been a very tense forty-five minutes.

Consequently, the day after Christmas I went to Allie's house to say hello to Mrs. Cronin. I went late-morning, because Allie had told me that Dana would be in Burlington then, doing his last-minute shopping before they left for his big event in Colorado.

The four of us had a very nice visit together, and I said nothing uncivil when Carly mentioned her mother's and Dana's trip. I simply nodded politely and reminded Allie to bring along Dramamine. Once, when we'd been married, she'd forgotten.

Mostly we talked about Carly's growing interest in broadcast media, and the video she had completed about the battery factory in Bennington. That morning may also have been the first time that I heard the full details of the part-time job Carly would have in the spring at a little radio station in southwest Vermont. I was, of course, thrilled.

And then I left. I went straight from Allie's to the Grand Union to replenish the pantry that Patricia's nieces and nephews had pillaged Christmas Day. It was there that I ran into the principal of our local elementary school.

I did not, as some people probably believed at the time, call Glenn Frazier on the telephone. I did not make a special effort to see him, I did not tattle on my ex-wife.

I simply bumped into him in the cereal aisle, our carts almost clanking together as we met. And at some point in our conversation— when we were beyond the holiday pleasantries, when we were done praising the original Shredded Wheat biscuit—the topic invariably turned to my ex-wife. How could it not? People were aware that we were still friends, and people knew who she was living with now. People knew what she was doing with her life.

And since Glenn seemed to know so much about her involvement with Dana, it was perfectly reasonable for me to assume that he knew as well what Dana was planning to do in a couple of days in Colorado. And that my ex-wife would be with him.

Certainly I wish now I'd kept my mouth shut, because the last thing I ever want to do is to complicate Allie's life—or mine. (We seem to do that well enough on our own.) The fact is, when I opened my mouth and started talking about Allie's and Dana's trip, I had no idea that Glenn didn't know where they were going, or that he would have such a strong reaction to their travel plans.

I had no idea that events, after that, would sprout beyond anyone's control—certainly beyond mine.

It was all a bit like mushrooms in a wet summer.

In a way, it was a bit like the transgender tapes. My station devoted a whopping twenty-two minutes to transsexuality over two days in March, and most of it was focused on Allie's battle with some local parents. Later that year NPR would see in the story five days of programming on the nature of love.

At that moment, however, on the day after Christmas, I wasn't thinking about programming. I was merely making small talk in a supermarket. Nothing more, nothing less. To me, it was just a little grocery store banter.

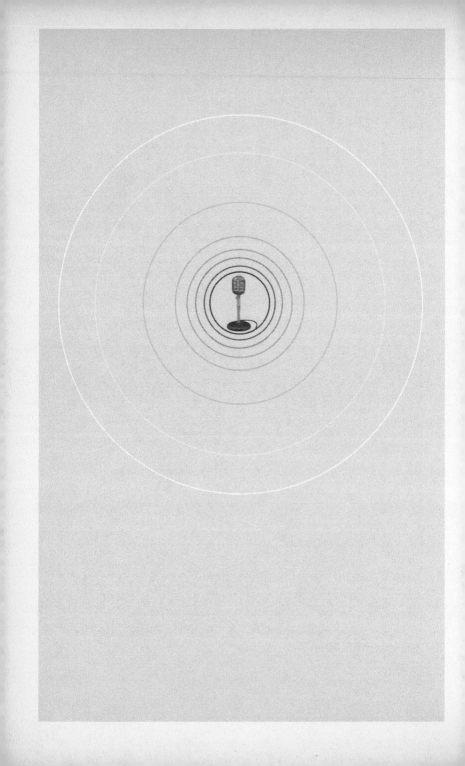

All Things Considered
Tuesday, September 25

DR. THOMAS MEEHAN: If you get beyond what some people consider the grisly details of the surgery, there's something very primal going on here, something very basic. A profound human desire. And that's my point. We—and I mean the doctors, but I guess the same could be said for the patients—are all playing Creator. Some of us do it better than others, some of us do more of it than others.

But man has always wanted to remake man. Look at the Frankenstein archetype. Look at the whole history of bioengineering.

Let's face it, right now we put the genes of arctic fish in tomatoes, we clone all kinds of mammals. You and I both know it's only a matter of time before we start cloning humans.

And that's a big part of the enticement science has for the scientist—or, in my case, for the surgeon. That sense of creation. Of control. The whole idea that we're doing something that's never been done before.

Hell, in that regard, what I do is nothing compared to a lot of my peers. Compared to them, I'm just a cut-and-paste pieceworker.

CARLY BANKS: And yet like all surgeons who perform sexual reassignment, among Dr. Meehan's critics are those people who insist he is taking advantage of transsexuals—who suggest he is, in essence, preying on a mental illness.

MEEHAN: Preying? God, no. I'm healing. Or at least trying to heal. I'm giving them their best shot at a normal, happy life. Therapy doesn't cut it with these people. Surgery does. That's the reality, whether you like it or not.

dana

THE FIRST THING YOU SEE ARE THE HUAJATOLLA—
Ute for "breasts of the world." You'll be driving south on the interstate, and suddenly you'll notice a pair of massive geologic hooters
rising from the rough plains. The Huajatolla are northwest of
Trinidad. Igneous rock. Twin mountains that tower well above twelve
thousand feet. Ghost white in the winter, an almost neon green in the
summer.

There are tales that gold can be mined in the rivers that snake
through them, but my guess is they're packed mostly with coal, just
like the other peaks that circle the town to the south and the west and
the north.

I've met trannies who hated Trinidad and simply couldn't believe
they had to go there for their surgery. I know one girl who actually
chose Palo Alto for the sole reason that it was in California, and
another who went to Portland, Oregon, just so she wouldn't have to

spend a couple of weeks in a shell-shocked little mining town in southern Colorado.

But I rather liked Trinidad, and I liked it for all sorts of reasons. Certainly the karma felt right. Not only does the approach to the city have mountain-sized mammaries to greet you, but the river that weaves through Trinidad is called the Purgatoire—an ever-flowing boa of water whose very name celebrates the betwixt. The between. The transgendered.

And in ways the city will never admit, it likes the transsexual business. For a time, the town lived off the mines and the railroads, but no more. The last mine went belly up in 1995. And while there will always be boosters who will try to bring tourism to "historic Trinidad"—Gateway to the Rockies, Bat Masterson Territory, Kit Carson's Personal Rest Stop—the fact is, the town is in the middle of nowhere. Southeastern Colorado. Nearest city of any size? Pueblo, eighty-five miles to the north. And, as far as I can tell, lawman Bat Masterson only tried to keep the peace there for a year. He actually lost his bid for reelection as marshal, having taken the townsfolk for a thousand dollars each month playing cards.

And while Indian fighter Kit Carson indeed visited Trinidad throughout his career, my sense is that coming *in* Trinidad mattered much more to him than coming *to* Trinidad. He'd struggle in after who knows how long on the Santa Fe Trail, and climb into a hotel bed with some company for as long as the money would last.

Once, when the mines were thriving, a good thirty thousand people lived there. Now there's barely a third that many. For a time, the city had boasted a two-level Main Street that stretched four solid blocks, and the shops possessed lower floors that were accessible from the sidewalk. When the population dwindled, however, there was no longer a need for all that space, and the underground was buried in cement—literally drowned in mortar and sand and stone, and then paved over with asphalt. You'd never know it was there, except for a tiny section of one subterranean block that has been preserved—two dark store windows—and may be accessed by an unmarked flight of steps on the corner of Animas and West Main.

Trinidad's big employers these days? A junior college. A prison. And the hospital where people like me come for our surgery.

Certainly, there are upright citizens in Trinidad who don't approve of the surgeons who help the trannies who pass through the town, but most of the folks are tolerant and helpful and kind. They need us and we need them. The relationship is downright symbiotic.

Allison and I landed in Colorado Springs just after lunch and arrived in Trinidad about three in the afternoon. Trinidad is 130 miles south of Colorado Springs, but the speed limit on the interstate is a glorious seventy-five, and the weather was fabulous: a cerulean blue winter sky, a balmy forty degrees. The driving was easy. And though there was plenty of snow on the mountains to the west, there was absolutely none on the ground in our strip of the state. All in all, it made Vermont seem positively glacial.

And so we were settled into the Holiday Inn just south of the city by the time the sun had set, and we were wandering down Main Street hand in hand in search of a restaurant for dinner by six.

The next day, Saturday, we went sight-seeing, and that must have killed a solid forty-five minutes. It isn't that Trinidad has nothing to see, but there isn't a whole lot that's open in December. Trinidad History Museum? Closed. Old Fire House Number One? Doors shut and sealed. The Archaeology Museum at the junior college? A vault. And the illustrious A. R. Mitchell Museum of Western Art? Boarded up— like a lot of the city, it seemed.

Fully half the storefronts in the town were vacant, the glass either replaced by plywood, painted over by children as part of a school art project, or filled with some unrealistically optimistic real-estate agent's large lease or FOR SALE sign.

In all fairness, the city does have a great many buildings from the early boom years that are absolutely exquisite, and practically the entire downtown—*El Corazon de Trinidad*—is a National Historic Landmark District. I especially liked nineteenth-century cattle rancher Frank Bloom's Victorian mansion, which I am quite sure was the inspiration for the home in which the kindly Norman Bates would live with his mother in *Psycho*.

But my favorite structure, of course, was the five-story stone bank building where I knew Dr. Meehan had his offices. Arched windows, magnificent detailing along the pediments. My surgeon toiling away on the very top floor when he wasn't in the operating room at Mount San Rafael. The building was constructed in the 1920s, in the waning years of the Trinidad coal country heyday.

Mount San Rafael, the hospital that would be my address for a little more than a week, was about a mile outside of town. Allison and I went there Saturday afternoon, and we visited the shrine on the small bluff above it. The Ava Maria Shrine. It looks down upon the two-story hospital. The Trinidad Ava Maria is inside a little white stucco chapel, rich with the exterior detailing we expect from our most cherished roadside art: neon lettering, a neon star, a life-size painted statue of a monk.

The chapel was locked, but there was a little grotto beside it. Allison and I sat for a moment on one of the blue benches and looked at the icons of Jesus and Mary under glass. We were both quiet for a long moment, and then Allison asked me if I'd been praying.

"No," I said. "But I will before we leave. I think I'd feel guilty if I left here without praying. And with major surgery in a couple of days, it seems to make perfect sense to hedge my bets. And you?"

"Me?"

"Praying: Were you praying?"

"As a matter of fact, I was."

"May I ask what for?"

She stared at the plaster Christ on the cross and took my hand. She found it without looking.

"I was praying for you to be happy. For this to be the right decision," she answered evenly.

"That's very sweet."

She clicked her tongue in her mouth. "I'm one hell of a sweet girl."

There was a slight edge to her voice that I'd come to recognize: Frustration. Incredulity. A hint of despair. Instantly I convinced myself that in reality Allison had been praying that I would yet change my mind. Maybe have a last-second submission to the chromosomes and plumbing I'd been given at birth. Perhaps accept the shell I'd endured for three and a half decades.

"You're so good to be here," I said. "I will always be more grateful than I can tell you. You know that, don't you?"

"I do."

"And if there was any way in the world I could change my mind . . . well, for you, Allison, I would. I surely would. But I can't."

She took back her hand and placed it inside her coat pocket. It was just cold enough that we could see our breath when we spoke—little curls of steam that rose up in the air and disappeared amidst the white latticework that surrounded us.

"Don't worry," she said, "I wasn't praying for that. I don't pray for things that specific."

"No?"

She shook her head. "I see no reason to court disappointment in this life. It seems to come often enough on its own."

There's a story that one night in 1908, when Trinidad physician John Epsey was leaving the hospital, he saw a flickering light on the hill before him—despite the snow and the wind and the fact that at the time there was nothing but scrub pine and rock on that bank. And so he wandered toward it, perplexed, and discovered there the 250-pound statue of the Virgin Mary that is still a part of the chapel today. No one knew where it came from, no one understood how it got there.

Inspired, that very year the townsfolk built the grotto in which Allison and I sat for a few minutes our first Saturday in Trinidad.

Today, some of the locals insist, if you come at the perfect time of the day or if the moonlight is right after dark, it looks as if the statue of the Virgin is crying—sobbing, in theory, because of the surgery that occurs right in front of her. Literally, right under her nose.

Allison and I were told these stories when we were having a cup of coffee after visiting the shrine. The waitress at the diner regaled us with stories about Trinidad, especially the tales she'd heard about the trannies who'd come before me. Initially, I was a little perturbed that she saw so quickly what I was; I was a little frustrated by the fact that I had so clearly failed to pass.

"Is it really that obvious?" I asked.

"Oh, don't be upset," she reassured me, and she smiled at Allison. "It's your friend's nails that gave you away. They're just bitten to shreds."

When my sister, Isabel, was four and five years old, we'd act out fairy tales together. She was always the princess—Snow White, Cinderella, Sleeping Beauty—and I was the appropriate heavy. The Hag. The Stepmother. The Witch.

We'd find a shady spot by the palms in our yard, or we'd play inside in the den. For some reason, we never played in Isabel's room, and I have memories of lugging the trunk in which she kept her stash of dress-up clothes all over the house. I was only nine and ten myself, of course, and so half the time I had to drag the chest like a body through the hallways, or along the cement that bordered the pool.

I was already too tall for any of the dresses, but I would wear the big, loopy clip-on earrings and the scarves and the shoes my mother no longer wore. Isabel would get to wear the shiny polyester gowns with the pouf ballroom sleeves, and the diminutive wedding dresses with scooped necks.

Then, depending upon the role, I would stamp my feet and whine, or I would snarl and hiss and shout. I spent a lot of time seething, and Isabel spent a lot of time collapsing and pretending to cry. It was a good arrangement.

To most of the world, I probably looked like a patient and imaginative and exceptionally loving older brother. How many ten-year-old boys, after all, are willing to drape a nylon scarf over their heads and pretend they're the evil fairy Maleficent? How many male fifth-graders are content to spend time casting spells on poor little Aurora, a.k.a. Sleeping Beauty/Briar Rose/Kid Sister Izzy?

Sometimes Isabel would grow bored of the games before I would, and I would have to return to a world in which I was supposed to care about Little League baseball, books about tank battles, and loud, smelly go-carts.

Over dinner those nights, my mother might mention how I had spent my day, and my father would mumble distractedly, "You're a good brother."

"Yup."

"Want to go see the Dolphins this Sunday? The Jets are in town."

"No, thank you. I have a ton of homework to do."

"Okay. I'll take Jack," he would say, referring to one of my cousins who lived in West Palm Beach. Jack was in high school by then, and played tight end on the football team.

And so a few days later, while my father would be watching a football game with a boy who understood and appreciated the rites that accompany an NFL Sunday, I would be alone in my room, probably waiting for my sister to return from a play date so I, too, would have someone to play with.

All Things Considered
Tuesday, September 25

CARLY BANKS: The costs mount quickly in Trinidad, especially if the transsexual is having more than genital surgery: a tracheal shave, for example, or a nose job. Dr. Meehan's fee begins at a flat $7,500 and starts climbing from there: $2,900 for breast implants, $2,250 for a rhinoplasty, $1,800 to reduce the appearance of the Adam's apple.

In addition, the anesthesiologist will charge between $1,300 and $1,800.

And then there are the hospital costs, which begin at $6,200 and often reach $10,000—even when there are no serious complications.

Moreover, it is unlikely that any part of the operation will be covered by insurance, and neither Dr. Meehan nor the hospital accept personal checks. The business runs almost entirely on cashier checks and cash.

18

allison

WHEN I AWOKE IN THE HOTEL SATURDAY MORNING, without thinking I reached under Dana's nightgown and cupped the penis and balls I found there in my hand. I did the same thing on Sunday, though this time I was very conscious of what I was doing. I wanted reassurance. I wanted to know they hadn't disappeared in the night.

We lay there like spoons, Dana inside my arms, the palm of my hand and my fingers protecting testicles and spongiosum and glans.

On Monday we had breakfast in the hotel restaurant, and then we drove into the town we'd gotten to know well over the weekend. We were able to get a parking space right in front of the building in which Dr. Meehan had his offices, and then we rode the antique elevator to the fifth floor.

Dana's surgeon had the weathered skin I'd expect on a cowboy, but his hair was thick and full and the color of sepia ink. I guessed he was in his mid to late fifties.

He told us he'd been an army surgeon in Vietnam in the early 1970s and wound up in southeastern Colorado after he was discharged because he'd fallen in love with a nurse in his unit whose father had run one of the last remaining Trinidad mines.

"I didn't study this at medical school," he said, smiling. "But I learned from the best," and he motioned toward a photograph on the wall behind his desk of the founder of the Waterman Gender Clinic.

"How'd he wind up here?" Dana asked, just a hint of unease in the question. It wasn't Meehan himself who was making us uncomfortable, it was the place where he worked—his clinic. The walls of the waiting room were decorated with bullfighting posters and the yellowed covers of half-century-old *Wild West Weeklies*. The Venetian blinds on the windows were brown with dust, the tile on the floor was cracked with age, and the Naugahyde chairs that lined three of the walls had seen their best days before my daughter was born.

There were magazines from an earlier presidential administration.

"Same way, more or less. The mines. They drew most of us here. Only difference was, Cordell Waterman was a mining company recruit. Brought here a good twenty years before me by the mining company itself, because there wasn't a surgeon in the whole city at the time. He started doing the reassignment work about a decade and a half after he arrived when a chef in town who everyone thought was a woman dropped the bombshell that he was a man. At least anatomically. And the fellow had heard that Johns Hopkins was doing sex change operations, and he wanted his penis transformed into a vagina."

"Why didn't he just go to Johns Hopkins?"

Meehan shrugged. "Money, I guess. And he trusted Cordy."

"And so Dr. Waterman did it?" I asked.

"That's right. The surgeon in Baltimore sent him the diagrams, the instructions. Told Cordy exactly how to do it on the phone. And throughout the 1970s, the word just spread that here was the place to come if you'd been dealt the wrong cards at birth—especially once Johns Hopkins stopped doing the procedure."

He rose from behind his desk and poured a stack of Polaroid pictures from a greeting card envelope into his hand, and then fanned them together as if he were about to perform a magic trick. They were not unlike ones Dana had been sent earlier that fall.

"We really do very good work here," he said as he glanced at the pictures himself. "Mostly these are M2Fs, but there are some recent F2Ms as well. Really, really nice jobs—if I say so myself."

I expected him to offer the pictures to Dana, but instead he gave them to me. "Dana and I are going to spend some time talking with my nurse now, Allison, so would you mind waiting in the reception room?"

I stood, smiled at Dana, and—though I had no interest in them at all—took the Polaroids with me. I didn't want Dana's doctor to think I was a difficult partner.

Meehan's receptionist was closer to my mother's age than to mine.

"How long have you been with Dr. Meehan?" I asked. Her desk was across from the elevator, instead of a part of the tiled waiting room with the posters of bullfighters and cowboys. I didn't want to be alone, and so I decided to wait in the hallway with her.

"A very long time," she said, without looking away from the computer terminal before her. She had pinned a plastic iris to the lapel of her blazer like a corsage. "I mean, I started with Dr. Waterman. I was here before he even began doing his work with the trannies."

"Are you from Trinidad?"

"I was born and raised here. Brought up my four kids here. I still have a daughter and two grandchildren living about a mile from my house."

"I'm sure it's a lovely place to raise a family," I said.

"Trinidad's coming back, you know."

"I'm sure."

"Now, as I recall from our correspondence with Ms. Stevens, you two aren't related."

"Nope." *Just friends,* I almost added, but I stopped myself. Still, I couldn't bring myself to say the word *lovers*.

"She seems very nice," the receptionist said.

"She is."

For the first time she looked up from her keyboard and terminal. "And you are very nice to be here," she said. "Usually the trannies come alone. Completely alone. Not a soul with them. No mom or dad. No girlfriends or boyfriends. No friends of any kind."

"That's sad."

"Imagine. Eight or nine days in the hospital, and no one you know with you. Terrible, isn't it?"

"It is."

"My name is Rose."

"Allison. Allison Banks."

She smiled and then noticed the envelope of photographs in my hands. "Would you like me to take those for you?" she asked.

"Thank you."

"Sometimes Dr. Meehan gets so carried away with his work that he forgets that some people don't need quite so much information. But he just loves his trannies. Meehan Maidens, he calls them. He just adores his Meehan Maidens. I don't think there's any work in the world he'd rather do."

"Why?"

"Excuse me?"

"Why?" I asked. Initially the question had been a reflex, but then I repeated the word with deliberation. "Why? Why does he love his . . . work so much?"

She tilted her head and seemed to grow thoughtful. It was as if she were about to try and explain to a preschooler why the sky's blue.

"Well, I guess I could say, 'Wouldn't you?' but I suppose in this case that wouldn't be true. Would it?"

I shook my head. "Nope."

"You know, a lot of people in this town say terrible things about Dr. Meehan. And you can imagine the sorts of things they used to say about poor Dr. Waterman. Awful. Just awful! Some people would look at all of Dr. Waterman's horses or Dr. Meehan's house—it has an indoor pool and its own fitness center, which I'm sure you can under-

stand are very rare in these parts—and they'd say they just did it for
the money. But between you and me, there are a lot of people in this
town who drive very nice cars, thanks to this clinic. *Very* nice cars. I
think Dr. Meehan could probably be mayor of Trinidad if he wanted
the job. He really could. It's just that all the people who love that man
and the work he does keep their thoughts to themselves."

There was a window on the wall beside the elevator, and I could see
it was starting to spit snow.

"So why does he love to work with transsexuals?" I asked again.

She shrugged and gave me the smile that it shames me to admit I
probably offer my sixth-graders a hundred times every year: Tolerant.
Patient. Condescending. "He makes them happy," Rose told me. "In
some cases, he makes them happy for the very first time in their lives.
Imagine being able to give that gift to someone. It's a blessing, it seems
to me. It's a blessing."

The bed beside Dana was empty, and the patient advocate who
brought us there told us it would probably remain empty, barring a
bus accident or a natural disaster.

The advocate was a tiny woman named Maura, whose hair was a
massive waterfall of silver and blond wings and waves that fell to her
waist. "You have no reason at all to be nervous," she told Dana. "Dr.
Meehan does this all the time. It's like a tonsillectomy. Why, last week
he took care of an airline pilot, and a seventy-seven-year-old girl
who'd been living in a camper-trailer for twenty years while she saved
her money for the procedure. They're both still here if you'd like to
meet them."

"If there's time, certainly," Dana said, pulling up the blinds on one
of the windows. Despite the clouds, in the distance we could see the
Huajatolla.

"Now, you're here for bottom and top—well, partial top."

"Excuse me?" Dana said.

Maura looked at her clipboard. "We call it bottom and top. I
was just confirming that you're having the genital reassignment

tomorrow as well as a tracheal shave. But you're not having any breast augmentation."

"That's right. My breasts seem to be coming along just fine, thank you very much."

"All you?" she asked, glancing at Dana's chest.

"All me. Well, all hormones, I guess."

"How long?"

"Not quite a year."

She nodded, and I think she was impressed. "The main thing I want you to know is that I'm here for you," she said. "I'm your representative. You can't ask nurses to mail a letter for you and you can't ask Dr. Meehan to get you a magazine in the gift shop. But you can ask me. You're going to be in bed for a week or so after your bottom's been done, so you're going to need some help. Well, I'm that help." Maura turned to me. "How long will you be here?" she asked.

"I leave Sunday."

"Wow. It's really sweet of you to stay that long. You're a lucky girl, Dana."

"Lately, it seems."

"No, really. I almost never see out-of-towners stay in Trinidad a full week if they don't have stitches to hold them."

The airline pilot was going to leave the next day, and hoped to be flying again by Easter. She had an ex-wife who no longer spoke to her, and twin boys whom she apparently scared. They were in the third grade. They were, she said, her only regret.

The woman who'd lived in a camper had a little dog for company and didn't seem to mind that she wasn't healing as fast as Dr. Meehan would have liked.

"Even if I die today, it won't be so bad," she said, petting the little terrier who was allowed into her room for parts of each day. "After all, I'd be leaving the world the way I was supposed to come into it. That's not a bad exit."

Then she showed us a beautifully embossed surgical record that

Dr. Meehan had issued so she could have her birth certificate updated. At seventy-seven, she'd been reborn a girl.

Dana was settled into his hospital room by quarter to three, and I offered to go back into town to get the sorts of provisions we realized would be necessary in the hospital. I think I was looking for an excuse to get away.

The snow hadn't stuck to the ground, so the little city seemed particularly haggard and gray. Even the Christmas decorations in the shop windows looked tired to me. I wandered into the drugstore on Main Street, surprised at first that it was open: Some of the tubes of fluorescent light along the ceiling had burned out, and I'd thought for a moment that the store had closed early for some reason.

I had the list of cosmetics and magazines Dana had requested, most of which I figured I could find at the pharmacy, but I knew I'd have to drive to the electronics store in the strip mall north of town if I had any hope at all of finding an AC adapter for a laptop computer.

I had been staring at the mascara and eye cream a long time when I realized the pharmacist was talking to me. I saw a clock on the wall over his shoulder and was surprised to see it was almost three-thirty.

"Do you need some help?" he asked gently.

"No, thank you," I murmured, and I tried to smile. "I guess I was spacing out a bit."

"Are you okay? Would you like to sit down? A glass of water, maybe?"

I shook my head. "I'm fine," I lied. "I was just lost in thought for a second."

"Try ten minutes."

"Ten minutes?"

"Uh-huh."

The aisle was narrow, and I allowed myself to lean back against the pegboard rack of dusty brushes and combs and hair clips. I kept seeing that seventy-seven-year-old's surgical certificate in my head, and I realized that in the next week Meehan would issue a new one for

Dana, too. The male Dana would really and truly be gone, the original Dana would no longer exist. Instead there would be a Meehan Maiden, a born-again woman with a legal piece of paper from the doctor who'd made her to commemorate her birth.

"It's been a really long day," I told him.

"It's almost over," he said, trying to comfort me. The pharmacist was Native American, with a magnificent aquiline face: long and narrow, and the color of a mesa at dusk.

"It is, isn't it?"

"The sun probably fell behind the mountains while you were shopping."

Supposedly, you can't prevent a person from killing himself, if that's what he's determined to do. If someone is resolute in his decision, there's no way in the world to stop him. The same, apparently, was true of the transsexual. Of Dana.

"I should get back," I said.

"You're not from around here, are you?"

"No."

"Visiting someone at the hospital?"

I nodded, and I could tell instantly that he understood.

"You on any medication?"

"No."

"Okay, then," he murmured, and he led me to a corner of the store filled with vials of tiny pills and little bottles of brown tinctures. "I don't normally do this," he added.

"Do what?"

"Offer unsolicited counsel," he said, and he handed me a bottle labeled St. John's Wort. "Each capsule's four hundred and fifty milligrams. Take two a day."

"What will it do?"

"Maybe nothing. Maybe something. It's a natural antidepressant."

"Okay," I said, and I was grateful. There in the store I peeled off the plastic that was pasted around the lid, and I swallowed the first pill that fell into the palm of my hand.

Tuesday morning before Dana was wheeled from the room, we kissed. I could tell I had the orderly's sympathy.

In Trinidad, it seemed, I had everyone's sympathy. Regardless of whether they imagined that Dana and I were siblings, or whether they assumed we had once been married, they felt sorry for me. They felt for my loss, and they viewed me as some wondrous angel of a person for staying with Dana.

"If anybody comes along with the trannie," Maura had said when we'd had a cup of coffee Monday evening, echoing Dr. Meehan's receptionist, "it's Mom. Sometimes Mom will stick around for a few days, but that's about it. And she's usually numb. It's like she's the one who's been given the anesthetic."

Back in Vermont, of course, I didn't have anyone's sympathy. There, I knew, I was merely viewed as a lunatic—or, in some people's minds, as a pervert. Someone who shouldn't be allowed in a classroom with children.

When I could no longer hear the gurney as it squeaked its way down the corridor to the operating room, I sat down in the chair in the corner by Dana's bed and stared out the window at the mountains. I realized it had been almost exactly thirty-six hours since Dana and I had made love for the last time. Quickly I corrected myself: made love for the last time in a way that most people did. Or, at least, could.

We'd had sex before going out to dinner. Despite the hormones and the testosterone blockers—despite the surgery that was imminent—Dana had left one last erection.

"Isn't hotel sex hot?" Dana had asked when we were through, and I'd simply purred my concurrence. I didn't dare open my mouth and say a word, because I knew my voice would break and I would cry if I did. And so neither of us said anything about the fact that this was the last time Dana would ever be inside me.

We might be together as a couple for months or years or even decades; it was possible we'd be making love again by Valentine's Day. ("I tend to heal very quickly," Dana had told me. "Physically, anyway.") But never again would Dana sink into me, or would I reach down and open myself up to—and the pronouns are everything here—him. Never again would we move our hips together the way we once had, never again would I sit upon him and ride him and be, literally, filled. Never again would we be together as a woman and a man.

Dana had reassured me constantly throughout the fall and then as winter arrived that nothing would change between us, except for that act. With the exception of one of the ways we made love, nothing at all would be different.

"It's not like the person is changed on the inside," Dana's friend Jordan said to me once. "When Dana's wheeled into post-op, it'll be the same old Dana. Oh, a fraction of a pound lighter, maybe. But trust me: It will be the same human being underneath all that surgical gauze."

On one level, I prayed that would be the case. But I also realized that my life would be easier in so many ways if Dana was changed and I didn't love the new person Meehan was about to start sculpting in the operating room down the hall. Perhaps the two of us would simply go our separate ways, and people would kid me when we met on the street in Bartlett:

"Was that a weird phase, or what?"

"Allison, we thought you had lost your mind."

"What were you thinking, girl? What *were* you thinking?"

If Dana turned out to be different and we were no longer in love, I could resume the life I had known before we had met, and I would no longer have to plumb those parts of my psyche that were probably best left unexplored.

A male nurse I'd never met before put his head into the room and asked me if I needed anything. I shook my head no. Suddenly I wanted to get away from the thin little bed in which Dana had slept, the sheets still stained with the rust-colored antiseptic that had been painted the night before upon groin and torso and thighs.

The hospital gift shop wasn't open yet but the cafeteria was, and I went there to read newspapers and sip coffee, and to wait for the doctor to finish with Dana.

19

dana

IT'S EASY TO REMOVE THE TESTICLES. YOU SIMPLY make a small midline incision across the scrotum, tie off the spermatic cords, and exhume the testicles from their little balloon of a purse. This is known as an orchidectomy.

It is considerably more difficult to transform a penis into a vagina.

Slice open the penis, beginning a scant two centimeters from the anus. Remember, the balls are no longer a buffer. By now they're in the container with the hazardous waste—though, interestingly, you will have preserved a good measure of scrotal skin, because this parchment will become both the new labia and a free graft to help lengthen the tunnel that will become the vagina.

The incision will run the length of the penis (*longitudinal* is the word the surgeons prefer), extending all the way up to the glans. It is at the perineum where the cut is the deepest.

You will then excavate all of the pulpy, erectile tissue beneath the skin, careful not to inadvertently hack the penile urethra. After the organ has been all but hollowed out, you may clip the tiny tube that links bladder with bathroom. Now, once and for all, sever the flap that is the cylindrical seat of one's life—axis, locus, hub, regardless of whether we are gay or straight, regardless of whether we are happy with the genitalia that accompanied us through our mother's vaginal canal or miserable with the little hermit crab who pokes out its head at the damnedest moments in time.

With the penile skin put aside for the moment—though carefully preserved—you will insert a urinary catheter, a guest who will reside in your patient's groin for almost a week.

At this point, you will shift from doctor to miner, though this may be, in fact, the most difficult part of the operation. It demands both patience and skill. You will bore a vagina, dissecting a crawl space between rectum and bladder. This is the part of the procedure where complications are most likely. There is bleeding. Tissue resistance. And it is easy here to nick the lower intestine, to pierce the fine and sensitive terminus of the hose line that weaves its way through so much of the torso. Fistulae are possible. Abscesses are not uncommon.

Neither, I imagine, are pleasant.

Once the cavity is complete, you will take the penile skin you have painstakingly conserved, and you will turn it inside out as if it were a sock. Bear in mind that though the penile and scrotal skin help line the tunnel, they alone do not determine the ultimate vaginal length. You may want to graft skin as well from buttock and thigh. Pare off a fingernail-size piece of the glans—sensitive, reactive, just bursting with nerves—and insert the rest inside the burrow before you.

Next, take that section of glans and affix it upon a little bulb of spongiosum just above the vagina, as if it were a piece from a little box of Colorforms. This will be the clitoris.

Now, remember that birch bark–like skin that once housed the testes? Pretend you're back in preschool and fashion from it a two-dimensional sugar doughnut. Make sure it's slightly more oval than round. Voilà! Instant labia. Apply around the vagina like a life preserver, hooding the clitoris at the top.

Finally, pack the vagina with antibiotic gauze. Be generous; this is no time to cut corners or costs. Expect to load it with at least ten feet, and be prepared to fill it with twenty. The last thing you want is a spanking new vagina that becomes infected or (worse, arguably) begins to narrow before your patient can begin her regime of postoperative dilation—the routinized use of dildos to prevent the tissue inside her from closing.

You will want to sew the packing in place with heavy silk or nylon sutures. Don't fear: It will all be gone in six or seven days. Catheter, too.

If the genital surgery has gone well, then proceed with the ancillary work. Enhancing her breasts. Shaving the trachea. Touching up her cheeks or her nose.

Altogether, it shouldn't take more than a morning. It takes much less time to make a vagina in an operating room than in a womb.

All Things Considered
Wednesday, September 26

DANA STEVENS: Amazing, isn't it? A university with eight thousand students gives me absolutely no guff. Doesn't do a thing to complicate my life. But a little elementary school with two hundred and ninety kids? They practically run the transsexual and her paramour out of town!

carly

One afternoon between Christmas and New Year's, my boyfriend from high school told me he had a male cousin who'd had pillowcases and sheets with ballerinas on them when he was growing up. The boy had in fact had two sets, one that was yellow with blue dancers, and one that had pink dancers on white.

"I think he turned out okay," Michael said. "I mean, he seems normal enough now. His family didn't come to our house for Christmas this week, so I haven't seen him in over a year. But he never seemed freakish to me as a kid. Maybe a little effeminate. But I always assumed he was straight."

Nevertheless, his cousin's desire for ballerina bed linens had clearly become a part of that family's mythology. The boy had been five and six years old at the time, and he'd outgrown his interest in the sheets by the time he was in second grade. But it was, apparently, something that came up whenever Michael's family gathered as kin.

I heard lots of stories like that while Mom was in Colorado. My friend Rhea showed me a picture of herself in a family photo album in which she was wearing a plastic army helmet that she had camouflaged with fallen leaves and small branches. She thought she was nine when it was taken.

"It was just a phase," she explained. "War got pretty boring once I discovered boys."

And Heather, who I really hadn't been friends with since seventh grade, insisted I come over to her house and into her bedroom. "Boxer shorts," she said, opening her lingerie drawer to me and pulling aside a top layer of bikini briefs. "I started wearing boxer shorts at college this fall."

"Why?"

"It turns me on."

"No," I said, shaking my head. "Why are you telling me this?"

She shrugged. "I thought you'd understand."

Moreover, when my friends weren't sharing with me their tentative forays across the Great Gender Divide, their parents were volunteering their opinions about Dana.

"I don't normally have time for those daytime talk shows," Rhea's mom said, "but when my foot was operated on a few years ago, I watched them a bit. They're addictive, they really are. And one day, one of them had on a group of transsexuals. They seemed very nice. They really did. But it's so clear they're no happier now than they were before they were changed. And none of them has the slightest idea how to dress."

And, of course, the really frightening wolves came out of the forest en masse once my mom and Dana were gone. People I barely knew wanted to tell me what they thought.

"He must know how inappropriate it is to dress that way around children," a teller at the bank told me. "Of course I cashed his check for him, but he made everyone in line very uncomfortable. Especially Joyce Lavigne. She came in with her little girl when your mother's friend was here, and when she saw him, she turned on her heels and left. And I can't blame her, Carly. Really, I can't. Can you?"

A day later I was at the service station getting Dana's car inspected, since I knew she wouldn't feel up to it when she returned, and the fellow who worked there said he didn't think Dana should be allowed on the road.

"And why not?" I asked.

"If he had an accident and there was blood all around—his blood, I mean—it would be a hazard to the rescue folks. They shouldn't have to worry about such things."

I explained that Dana wasn't HIV-positive, but I might just as well have been insisting that a moment earlier I'd returned from a magical land with a tin man who talked and a scarecrow who danced.

And on New Year's Day when I wandered from Dad's house to the pizza parlor to get a slice mid-afternoon, an elderly couple I didn't know stared at me while I waited for it to be reheated. Finally the man got up from his booth and said, "Our granddaughter is in your mother's class at school. None of us are happy about that, you know."

"No," I said, "I didn't know." But certainly I did. I'd been hearing that sort of thing for almost a week.

I had never met my mom's new principal, but I knew she didn't like him. And so I didn't either. I knew they'd had run-ins, especially over some field trip to Lake Champlain in early September.

Of course, my mom had had run-ins with his predecessor, too, but I always had the sense that my mom and Mrs. Dixon liked each other. Mrs. Dixon was considerably older than Mom, and I think she viewed her as a sort of charismatic but renegade daughter. She was always telling Mom that she didn't understand the politics of her job, and it mattered when a parent complained—even if the complaint was unfounded. I remember one spring Mom did a unit on the homeless in Vermont, and she took the class to a part of the Burlington waterfront that hadn't been gentrified and then to the emergency shelter. She had a social worker and the manager of the shelter with her all the time, but you can't be everywhere every second, and a homeless person on the waterfront said something off-color to a couple of the kids.

Inevitably, some parents protested, and my mom and Mrs. Dixon had one of their chats.

But I'm certain that their chat was, in the end, pretty amicable.

Even if my mom and Mr. Frazier didn't get along, however, I always tried to be polite when he called. He was, after all, my mom's boss. By the time he phoned the Friday after New Year's, I was half expecting his voice on the other end of the line. It had been that kind of week.

"She's not here," I told Mr. Frazier as I surveyed the little mountain of clothes on my bed. I was trying to decide what should stay in Bartlett, and what should come with me back to college. My dad was going to drive me there later in the month, so I could pretty much take whatever I wanted. "Should I have her call you?"

"Is she still in Colorado?"

I hadn't realized he knew she was there, but I shouldn't have been surprised. The whole town seemed to know.

"Yup."

"Does she return tomorrow or Sunday?"

"Sunday."

"Well, let me think. Even if she gets an early flight out of—what, Pueblo?"

"Colorado Springs."

"Of course. Even if she gets an early flight out of Colorado Springs, she won't be home until dinnertime."

"Actually, it will be after dinner. I think her plane lands around eight-thirty."

"And that's if there aren't any delays . . ."

"Right."

"I'll be up late. Would you ask her to call me, please?"

"I'm sure I'll talk to her tonight. Want me to have her call you tomorrow?"

"From Colorado? Yes, absolutely. That's a great idea."

"Any message?"

"No. Just have her call me. It's important."

At dinner that night, I told my dad and Patricia that Mr. Frazier had phoned.

"He sounded a little annoyed," I said.

"I'm sure he is," my dad said, slicing a ravioli in half with his fork. "He's the new guy in town, he has to establish himself. And your mother's little escapade has made his life very difficult."

"But don't worry, Carly," Patricia said quickly, "there's not a thing he can do."

"Why is he angry?" I asked. "Because people are talking about Mom and Dana?"

"Oh, some are doing more than talking. There's a petition going around. Some parents of her students started it when they heard your mother and Dana had gone to Colorado—and why."

I felt my stomach get a little queasy, and so I stopped eating. "What kind of petition?" I asked.

Patricia did something she almost never did: She took my hand. She put down her fork and she reached over and rested her hand gently on top of mine. "Your mother is part of the teachers' association," she said to me, looking me straight in the eye. "The school wouldn't dare do anything stupid. Between the association and the ACLU— between the association, the ACLU, and me—they would face considerable opposition."

I nodded. "Is her job in jeopardy?" I asked.

"Just your house, sweetheart," my dad said. "Just your house."

"Will!"

"That was a joke, I'm sorry."

"It was an idiotic one," Patricia told him. "All I think your father meant is that Glenn said he thought your mother and Dana would be better off if they didn't live smack in the center of the village."

"He wants us to move?" I asked, looking at my dad.

"Oh, probably not seriously. But it's clear he doesn't want every parent in the community watching Dana prance around town in a dress and then go home to your mother's house," he said. "People rarely want their children taught by someone they think lives with a sexual deviant. And so Glenn's concerned—not without cause—that parents will get mad, and it will affect their kids' schooling. After all, if Mom and Dad don't approve of the teacher, what are the chances the kids will—especially at their age?"

"That's nonsense," Patricia said. Her fingers were still upon mine.

"Maybe," he said to Patricia, "but it's clear he'd prefer they lived elsewhere."

"So your ex-wife and her partner should move twenty or thirty miles out of town—Allison should give up the house she's lived in for two decades—just to make Glenn Frazier's life a little easier? That's asinine. Completely asinine."

"Well, that's how he feels."

"But they won't fire her," I said. "Right?" I wasn't surprised by how nervous my voice sounded, but I wasn't pleased.

"They can't," Patricia reassured me. "Not over something like this. They won't even try."

"But her life is about to get even more complicated, Carly," my father said, "and you might as well understand that. There are a lot of parents who aren't happy about this, and I don't think it will end with a petition. Some are planning to come to school Monday morning. And Glenn—Glenn and the school board, really—will have to do something to appease them."

"They will not," Patricia said.

"Oh, maybe not legally," my father said before taking a big bite of the doughy pasta. "But politically they will. That's a fact."

"What does the petition say?" I asked.

"I haven't seen it," he said. "But I think it asks the school to insist upon a certain basic morality from the teachers it hires."

"Allison and Dana have done nothing immoral," Patricia said.

"I agree. Unnatural, yes. Immoral, no."

"Will! What is your problem?"

"Look, I'm every bit as appalled as you are. And, unlike you, I also have to live with the fact that I was the one who told Glenn where Allie was going—"

"You told him?" Patricia said, and she glared angrily at my dad for a long second.

"Yes, I did. But it wasn't like I was some confidential informant. I ran into the guy at the supermarket. I'd just seen Allie and Dell, and I happened to mention the trip in passing. I think I figured he knew."

"You think?"

"For God's sake, if he didn't hear about it from me, he would have heard about it from someone else." He turned to me and said, "The bottom line, Carly, is that there are some very conservative elements in this town. At the very least, every kid whose family goes to that fundamentalist church in East Medford is going to be home-schooled if Dana doesn't move out."

I considered reminding him that Mom was an excellent teacher and had taught at the Bartlett school almost as long as I'd been alive. I considered mentioning that there had to be hundreds of people who would be vocal on her behalf—both parents of the kids she had taught, and the kids themselves, now grown into young adults.

But those sentiments seemed both obvious to me and naive. Nevertheless, I decided that I'd talk to Molly Cochran after dinner and see what she could tell me. Molly was one of my mom's best friends, and she'd started teaching six-year-olds at the school almost the same year that my mom had started teaching the kids who were eleven.

Then, once I knew what Molly knew, I'd call my mom in Colorado.

We sat on the couch by the woodstove, and Molly showed me class pictures.

"Lord, Chrystal's in sixth grade now," she said, shaking her head. "I adored Chrystal. Still do. She would bring me a drawing every day when she was in my class, including these absolute horrors she made with something called Blush Art."

"Blush Art?"

"It's just like it sounds. Little pads of cosmetic blush you pat on your paper. It comes with stencils, so the pictures are pretty generic. Unicorns. Cakes. Women with very big hair. The problem is that the stuff stains, and so the year I taught Chrystal, I had a dry-cleaning bill that rivaled the national debt. Humongous. Just humongous. But I love that girl, she is incredibly sweet."

"And her parents are behind the petition?"

"I don't know if they're behind it. But I promise you they've signed it."

Molly lived in a house that had once been a barn, on land that had once been a cornfield. She lived about a mile and a half outside of the village, so I had borrowed my dad's car and driven there. And though I had called first, Molly and her husband had two boys in elementary school—one in the second grade and one in the fourth—and so their house was completely trashed, despite the warning they'd had that I was coming. Every time either of us moved, we were gored by one of the plastic aliens her kids had left in the cushions of the couch.

"I don't know the family," I said.

"You probably wouldn't. They live out in New Haven. And you can bet that if your mom and Dana stay together, your mom won't get to know them real well either: They'll either begin to home-school their little Chrystal, or they'll demand that she's transferred into Carolyn Chapel's class," she said, referring to the school's other sixth-grade teacher. When I was eleven, Mrs. Chapel had been my teacher.

"It must be really hard to home-school a kid," I said.

"It is. As a parent, you have to feel awfully strongly about something to do it."

Upstairs we heard a thump and then laughter. I must have looked up toward the ceiling reflexively, because Molly was quick to reassure me that it was only her husband, Clayton, and the two boys. They were supposed to be reading, but it was clear they were wrestling.

"Let's see, Audrey LaFontaine: Her family won't be happy about this either."

"No?"

"Nope. Fundamentalists. They're also in that church in East Medford. Same with the McCurdys. Of course, there could be worse things to happen to your mother than to lose Brian McCurdy."

"A difficult child?"

"Actually, just the opposite. But needy beyond belief, and guaranteed to fail. Your mom always cares way too much for kids like that. She lets them bring her down."

I didn't know Brian McCurdy, but I did know his older sister. Terry. Terry was the sort of girl who was never invited to the really good parties, and tended to accessorize badly. She was also from a house where it was clear bathing was optional, and so she wasn't very popular. Nevertheless, I'd always felt bad for her, and in eleventh grade I'd made it a personal self-improvement goal to eat lunch with her at least once a week in the cafeteria. I'd even suggested we take driver's ed together, though it had meant sitting in the backseat of a Dodge Dynasty with her for an hour a day in the spring, a formidable task given her family's evident indifference to laundry and soap.

Of course, self-improvement has its limits when you're sixteen: I never had her over to my house.

"What's Terry doing now?" I asked.

"Haven't a clue. But working somewhere, I imagine. She was, in her own way, very industrious. Unlike her brother, who's merely exasperating."

I knew that Brian and Terry were part of a pretty large brood, and so it crossed my mind that poor Terry was simply spending her life baby-sitting.

"Let's see," Molly murmured as she flipped open another folder with another class picture. "The Duncans will be trouble. And so will the Hedderiggs."

"Are you worried?" The question had come out abruptly. I'd meant to ease into my concerns more gracefully, though I'm sure Molly knew I was anxious. That was, after all, why I'd come by.

Without looking up from the picture she answered, "A little. But it's like your stepmother said: They can't do anything. Really, they can't."

"They can just, what . . . circulate a petition?"

"Actually, they can do something much worse than that," she said, and she looked straight at me and her face became serious. "Much worse."

"What?"

"Meetings, Carly Banks. They can make us have meetings."

21

allison

IN THE DAYS IMMEDIATELY AFTER HER SURGERY, I grew accustomed to talking to Dana while her feet were higher than her head. Three times a day her bed was tilted this way, while warm pads soaked in saline were applied to her new vagina. She'd fold her arms across her chest and I'd sit in the chair with the view of the Huajatolla, and we'd chat about nothing. The weather in Trinidad. The weather in Bartlett. Whether her painkillers were better or worse than a daiquiri.

Sometimes she'd reach over for my hand, and she'd kiss the tips of my fingers.

Outwardly, she didn't look any more feminine than she had a week or two earlier, and in some ways she may have looked less: She wore little makeup in the hospital, and her hair had fallen flat because she couldn't wash it. But she seemed more womanly to me, and sometimes she seemed downright maternal.

"You are taking care of yourself, aren't you?" she asked me Wednesday night—New Year's Day—barely thirty-six hours after her surgery.

"Of course I am," I said. That night when I returned to my hotel room, waiting for me were chocolates and flowers and a half dozen paperback books she'd ordered for me before we'd even left Vermont.

The surgery had gone well, and there seemed to be no postoperative complications on the horizon, and so on Friday morning Dana suggested that I take our rental car and go for a drive. She thought it would do me good to get out—out of the hospital, and out of Trinidad—and she reassured me she would be fine. She said she had plenty to read.

I considered driving northwest toward the Huajatolla themselves, but I was warned that there was a chance of snow in the forecast, and decided I probably shouldn't go sight-seeing at twelve and thirteen thousand feet.

And so I drove south through the Raton Pass—a mere seventy-eight hundred feet—and into New Mexico. Suddenly I was in the desert and it was warm. Amarillo, the green sign said, was only 214 miles distant, and I estimated that the westernmost edge of the Texas panhandle was barely two hours away. I decided I would go there. I would go east. I had no expectations that I would ever see Amarillo—nor even the promising red dot on the map called Dalhart—but I thought I could reach a little black speck called Texline by early afternoon.

Sometimes I'd listen to country music, something I never did in Vermont, and for an hour mid-morning I listened to a radio shrink I picked up on a talk station out of Denver. Usually the people who called into those shows struck me as pathetic and predictable at once: They were men who had extramarital affairs and now had gonorrhea, women who had fought with their husbands and then slept with their brothers-in-law, aunts (never uncles) who were annoyed that their nieces and nephews never sent thank-you notes.

Often there were men who wore women's clothing in secret and were wondering if they should tell their wives . . . but none that day. Frequently there were women who were toying with the idea of a lesbian dalliance . . . but not that morning. Regularly, it seemed, there were women and men who were involved in a relationship that no one around them seemed to understand . . . but no one that Friday seemed to have such a dilemma. For the first time in my life, my problems actually seemed bigger than theirs.

Though, of course, every bit as self-created.

"You got yourself into this mess, and it's up to you to get yourself out of it," the doctor told most of the callers. "It's your life."

Yet the sun seemed higher in New Mexico than in Colorado, and I realized I was warmer outside than I'd been any moment since early October. It was seventy degrees in the town of Clayton, and I bought a sandwich at a diner and sat alone at the picnic table in the parking lot. I convinced myself that I really didn't have any problems at all.

In the days immediately after Carly was born, I couldn't imagine Will would ever want to have sex with me again. He'd been in the delivery room with me, and I feared he'd been present for too much bloody show to view me as something sexual. To find me arousing.

"Not true," he insisted, and he was comforting and sweet. "The mind compartmentalizes that sort of thing. Besides, I'm a guy. I spend my life in heat."

Sure enough, six or seven weeks after Carly had joined us, we were making love while she slept in the nearby bassinet. Though at first we were both nervous and tentative, we got the hang of it again soon enough. Will, it was clear, was able to separate the vulva from which his daughter had emerged from the vulva he would make love to as a husband.

I wondered if I could do the same thing with Dana. I worried. I couldn't stop thinking about the gauze and the fluids and the blood. I couldn't stop thinking about the surgery.

On the steps of the library in Texline, I ate some of the chocolates that Dana had given me. They melted fast in the sun, and within moments the chocolate had the consistency of mayonnaise.

There I fantasized that I would climb back into my rental and drive on to Dalhart. Hartley. Dumas. I would reach Amarillo by dinner, I imagined, spend the night there, and then continue east along old Route 66. I would lose myself in a Texas town with the magical name of Shamrock.

Shamrock, on old Route 66.

Or, perhaps, I would veer south of the highway and sleep in Goodnight. Maybe, instead, I'd decide to spend the rest of my life in Groom, an interstate diamond almost exactly equidistant between Shamrock and Amarillo.

Groom, Goodnight, and Shamrock. Was there a patch on the planet with three towns with more promising names? Not likely.

Of course, I went to none of those places. I turned around and headed back into Colorado. I went west and northwest, for a time driving straight into the low winter sun.

But in Capulin I did stop and visit the crater from a ten-thousand-year-old volcano, and there I wished that I'd worn sandals as I walked through the chokecherries and brown field grass that surrounded it. And in Raton I watched children in short pants climb upon a cluster of playground dinosaurs, each of the sculptures painted a cheerful pastel.

I watched the children, I realized after the fact, for close to forty-five minutes.

Though I hadn't run away into Texas, I had managed to spend the day sleepwalking.

I was back at Mount San Rafael barely in time to watch Dana eat the apple cobbler that had come with her supper, and have a cup of coffee with her while she finished her dessert. She was disappointed that I hadn't had dinner with her, but she said she was happy that I'd had the chance to spend the day in the southwestern sun.

"And you made Texas? Okra, fried food, and trucks with big tires. Lord, Allison, I wish I'd been with you," she said, joking, but I couldn't find it in me to laugh. I'd liked my few minutes in Texas.

We watched an hour and a half of television together in her hospital room, and I was back at my hotel by quarter to nine. I saw immediately that the little red light on my phone was blinking, and I learned from the generic voice that hails from computer message centers everywhere that I had received a call. My daughter had phoned only moments before, calling from her father's house around ten-thirty at night her time.

Though I knew she'd be awake, I wasn't sure about Patricia and Will, and so I almost didn't return the call that evening. But I did, and I'm glad. Looking back, I don't regret that decision at all. I simply wish the news of the petition hadn't made me so testy with Dana during our last day together in Colorado.

Testier, actually.

Let's be honest. I hadn't been very pleasant around her on Thursday or on Friday night when I returned from my drive. Then, when I looked into the face of my girlfriend and I saw what I feared was my future, I experienced what I can only describe as buyer's remorse.

dana

I AM NOT A SENSATION. I AM NOT SENSATIONAL. I have never appeared on a TV talk show.

The last thing I want to do is draw attention to myself as a transsexual. As a woman in a doctor-built body.

But I would have risen from my bed—ripping my stitching to shreds—and returned to Vermont with Allison to defend her if I had thought such a thing would have made her life one tiny bit easier.

I would have.

But we all knew that my going there then would only have made her life worse.

All Things Considered
Wednesday, September 26

MOLLY COCHRAN: Once we joked about it. Maybe twice.
She knew there were people in the community who
wouldn't be happy about her decision to stay with
Dana.

But she was in love. And true love's supposed to
conquer everything, isn't it? I mean, really, isn't it?

23

will

IT'S NOT ALWAYS EXPLICABLE WHAT ATTRACTS US, and what doesn't. There are the basics, of course, certain universal tenets of beauty. The doctrine of symmetry. The dogma of slim.

At the time that my second marriage was starting to crumble, I had slept with only three women. Allie. Patricia. And exactly one lover between my two marriages, a woman whose face I can now barely remember. That had been it.

And Allie and Patricia really look nothing alike. Patricia is shorter, smaller, more petite. She is darker. Less serene. I won't say she is less beautiful than my Allie.

My Allie.

It is probably owing to the fact that out of habit I occasionally use that construction that I now discuss my second marriage in the past tense. Not literally, of course. Patricia didn't leave me because I used the words *my Allie* once in a session with our therapist toward the very end of January. But it didn't help. It made the remainder of that meeting needlessly hostile.

That afternoon—it was a Thursday—Patricia informed me that she needed a few days apart from me, and one of us needed to leave the house for the weekend. She said she'd be happy to go, but I insisted it should be me. After all, I had a conference that night with our listeners' advisory board anyway, and the meeting was going to be in Woodstock. And so I spent that night at the Woodstock Inn, and then on Friday I drove south to Bennington. Carly and I had dinner together on Friday night and then went to a movie, and we had breakfast together the next day. She took me to the radio station where she'd begun working earlier that week, and introduced me to the Saturday-morning deejay.

I wasn't sure what to do with myself once I had taken Carly back to her dorm, and so I decided to go skiing. I went to Stratton, rented a pair of skis, and spent the afternoon on the mountain. After my last run I called Patricia to see how she felt about the notion of my returning home. I got our answering machine. I went to a restaurant down the road from the resort, ordered dinner from the bar, and—when I was finished—tried Patricia again. Once more I got the answering machine.

That's when I checked into the motel across the street from the restaurant. But I wasn't ready for bed, and I certainly wasn't sleepy. And so I walked back across the road, planning to get potted in the saloon while people a generation younger than me flirted and danced and went back to their own motel rooms to have sex.

I didn't succeed in getting smashed, however, because one of those young women close to Carly's age started coming on to me at the bar. She was not beautiful but she was cute, and she had very short hair and a stud in the side of her nose. She was studying to become a paralegal.

When she put her hand on my thigh while telling me about how much she liked to dance alone—meaning, I realized, perform for a lover as foreplay—I asked her why in the name of God she was coming on to what had to look like a middle-aged, burnout drunk in a bar.

"I've always liked older people," she said.

"Ah, a daddy complex."

"And a mommy one."

"I have a daughter who's roughly your age."

"So? I have a father who's roughly yours."

I took her hand off my blue jeans and held it for a long moment. It was small and soft, and there was a thin gloss of moisture on her palm. I studied her face carefully, since I was about to reject her and I wanted to say the right thing. Suddenly she seemed to me more than cute. She seemed sexy and wanton and I imagined that whatever I was about to give up in a motel bedroom would have given me all manner of memory for years to come. She had grown more attractive in the few minutes we'd been together for the simple reason that she'd wanted me. Physically.

No other woman on the planet seemed to. Certainly not Patricia. Not Allie.

"Look," I said. "I think—"

She pulled her hand from mine and put her finger on my lips.

"I think you need to relax," she murmured.

"I do. And as much as I loved having your hand on my thigh, it wasn't relaxing me."

"Know what would relax you?"

I nodded and stood up. "I do," I said. "You're a very attractive young woman, and I am very attracted to you. I have every confidence you could relax me. But I'm married and I'm a father, and—"

" 'Nuff said." She surprised me by kissing me lightly on the cheek, and then took her beer and disappeared into a group of people near the band.

People will have intercourse with anything. Especially men. Take Chinese foot-binding: Men would literally fornicate with the deformed cleft of an adult woman's size-three or -three-and-a-half foot.

When I went back to my motel room, Patricia still wasn't home. I realized then she'd gone somewhere, too. I wondered if she simply couldn't bear to be around even my things anymore. The reminders of me.

And so I decided to call Allie, even though it was ten o'clock on a

Saturday night. I told myself I was merely phoning because I was going to report on how Carly's first few days back at Bennington seemed to be going.

But Allie was out for a brief walk around the green when I called, getting some fresh air before going to bed.

"She'll be sorry she missed you," Dana said. "Should she call you?"

"Yeah. If she doesn't mind."

"No, she wouldn't mind at all. You'll still be up?"

"I think so," I said, and offered the number of the motel. Then, perhaps triggered by remorse for having mentioned Dana's plans to Glenn Frazier, I surprised myself by asking, "So, how are you feeling?"

"Pretty good, actually. Thank you."

"Do they have you on painkillers?"

"Don't need them. I haven't needed them for a couple of weeks now."

"That's good."

"It is."

For a long moment we both were quiet, and I was about to thank Dana for passing along my message and hang up, but Dana said, "Your station did a nice job with that farm story this week."

"We did, didn't we?" I said. "Moira's a good reporter." Three days that week we'd examined how a once-rural village had lost every single one of its dairy farms since the Second World War and become a distant but tony suburb of Burlington. I was very proud of that package. Still am.

"She is. But it was beautifully produced, all of it. The music. The timing."

"I'll tell the producer. And Moira."

"How's Carly doing?"

"God, Carly's fine. We should all be so together."

"You and Allison have done an absolutely stunning job with her."

I agreed, and we continued to chat about my daughter and radio. I learned a little more about the two books Dana had written, and why I should consider reading George Sand. I don't think either of us consciously avoided discussing the Bartlett Elementary School, but the fact is, classrooms and school boards and disgruntled parents never came up. Transsexuality never came up. It was such a pleasant conversation that we were still on the phone when Allie got home, and I had largely forgotten that I was speaking with a person who'd been born a man.

That night when I was falling asleep in the motel bed, it seemed instead that I'd been talking to some female friend of Allie's. A woman, perhaps, who'd come into her life after we had divorced and who—like most of Allie's friends—was intelligent and interesting and . . . attractive.

Quickly I disabused myself of this notion.

Some men in this world would fornicate with anything, I reminded myself. But I wasn't among them.

24

allison

IT WAS POSSIBLE FOR ME TO GO TO SLEEP THE Sunday night that I returned home from Trinidad and convince myself that there was at least a chance the petition was merely a nasty rumor. Ugly but—happily—untrue. After all, no one I spoke with had actually seen it: not Carly, not Molly, not Will. Not even Glenn, our school principal, who told me that he thought it was possible the last straw had been my decision to go with Dana to Colorado.

"People were not happy when they heard," he said.

"Well, how did they hear?" I asked.

"How would I know?" he answered, but I could tell by the sudden churlishness in his voice that he was lying. I had a feeling they knew because he had told them.

Nevertheless, I did believe him when he insisted that he hadn't yet seen the petition. He—like Carly and Molly and Will—had simply heard that one existed: It was just outside the Grand Union. It was being passed around in a church. Someone had seen someone holding one while standing in line at the post office.

Sometimes there was the added conjecture of a name behind it. It had to be the Hedderiggs, it was likely the LaFontaines. The Duncans? Good chance—though it was possible that because Al Duncan was a member of the school board, he might have felt it was inappropriate to initiate a little grassroots activism against one of the teachers. Regardless, no one had in fact seen anyone soliciting signatures in a parking lot.

Nothing had really changed in the thirty-six hours since I'd called Glenn from Colorado, and I doubt the petition would have even come up when we spoke Sunday night if I hadn't mentioned it. Mostly Glenn phoned because he wanted to discuss the meeting we were going to have with some parents Monday morning, and to chastise me once more for not, as he put it, "keeping him in the loop." He thought I should have warned him early that fall that I was in the midst of what had the potential to become a controversial relationship.

"I just wish you'd told me back in September or October," he said again. "I just wish you'd warned me. That way I wouldn't have been blindsided."

"I understand," I said.

"I should know about these things before the PTA. I should hear about them before the school board."

"You're right," I agreed. Because he was. Without fail I would have sat down with his predecessor, Sue Dixon, and explained to her that I was seeing someone who might raise some eyebrows in the town. But Glenn and I had barely known each other; we'd worked together less than three months when Dana moved into my house. Moreover, the little contact we'd had had been unpleasant: fights about field trips, squabbles about the Internet.

And, of course, Glenn was male, and I'm sure that had entered into it, too. In some way, it would have seemed oddly deferential of me to have gone to him. It would have seemed like he was my father, and I needed his approval or his permission to see my new heartthrob.

The fact is, at my age, there are few people in this world whose approval I court or whose permission I need. Perhaps, on some level, I still look to my mother for approval. But I certainly can't imagine looking to the likes of Glenn Frazier for permission. Especially that winter, when we barely knew each other.

"I haven't talked to Judd," Glenn continued on the phone, referring to our school superintendent—the fellow who supervised all of the public schools in our half of the county. "And I haven't asked any lawyers to be there. I don't think we're at that stage yet, and I think it would be inflammatory to have someone there. So, please, don't even bring that sort of thing up."

"Why would I bring up a lawyer?"

"Defensiveness, maybe. Self-preservation."

"I'm not defensive. And I don't see what good a lawyer would do."

"Fight or flight, Allison. You go with fight, you might bring up a lawyer. I can see it. I would."

"I won't do anything of the sort. The idea hadn't even crossed my mind."

"With any luck, it won't even come to that. With any luck, they'll talk, we'll listen, and we'll all go home friends."

"That's all you want me to do tomorrow morning? Listen?"

"That's all I want *us* to do. My hope is that once they've had a chance to vent, they'll get on with their lives."

In the living room, I heard Carly turn on the television.

"I would love to get back to my daughter," I said. "I've only seen her about ten minutes since I got home."

"How was your flight?"

"Bumpy."

"Sorry to hear that."

"Oh," I said, "I'm sure it was no worse than tomorrow morning's meeting will be."

I told Carly about Trinidad, and how nice it had felt to be outside and warm on Friday. I told her how pretty the mountains were to the west, and how flat the landscape was to the east. I told her how sometimes it seemed the town was nothing but beauty salons and bars—almost everything else was boarded up or closed—and what a young man who worked at a bakery said people did there most Saturday nights: "They get liquored up and they get their hair done. Sometimes they do it in the proper order. But not always."

I told her how I thought Dana was feeling, and about the sponge baths and the hospital food and how well she was handling the post-operative pain. I told her that Dana had taken her first, tentative steps as a woman the night before—a day and a half early, technically, but she had wanted me present for the commencement.

I did not tell Carly about the gauze, or the dilation that would be necessary once the gauze was removed. I did not tell her about the catheter.

Carly, in turn, told me about the snow that had fallen in my absence, and the days she had spent skiing. She told me about a New Year's Eve party she'd gone to.

We spoke briefly about my conversation with Glenn, but Carly was careful not to bring up the things people in town were saying about me. Nor did she ask, I noticed, when Dana was planning to return.

I met Glenn at his office early Monday morning, fifteen minutes before any of the parents were due to arrive. He was in the midst of taking down the drawings the kids had made weeks earlier of menorahs and snowmen and Christmas trees.

"Now, I don't know for sure how many people will actually show up for a seven A.M. meeting," he said as he worked, sometimes pulling the masking tape off a picture so he could return it intact to the student. "It's supposed to be a small group. Emissaries, you might say. But as a precaution I said we'd meet in the cafeteria."

"The cafeteria? It sounds like you're expecting a mob!"

"Not at all. But I want to be sure there's a table big enough for nine or ten people—just in case."

I said nothing but I wasn't reassured, and he must have sensed my dismay.

"I doubt anywhere near that many will come," he added.

"I hope you're right."

He paused when he realized he had in his hands Lindsey Lessard's beautiful painting of reindeer. Lindsey was one of my students. "Her dad's coming, that's for sure," he said, and he held up the picture for me so I could see who he meant.

"Is there anything you want me to do?"

"Aside from finding a new boyfriend?"

"That was really a despicable thing to say, Glenn."

He sighed, exasperated. "You asked. Probably common courtesy should have precluded me from answering."

"Or common sense."

"Probably. I'm sorry."

I nodded, as if his apology made everything okay. But of course it didn't. I'd known he wasn't going to be my friend or my ally when we went into that meeting, but I'd thought it was possible he might at least view himself as a mediator. As somebody neutral.

I realized I'd been kidding myself. Glenn Frazier was anything but a disinterested party.

Al Duncan sat beside Bea and Ken Hedderigg, while Rich Lessard somehow wound up at the head of the table. Audrey LaFontaine's mother—whose name, I realized with some embarrassment, I didn't know—sat next to Glenn, and I sat next to her.

While two of the women who worked in the school kitchen started preparing lunch—the meal was still five hours away, but it takes time to make pizza and coleslaw for 290 children, even if the cabbage has already been shredded and bagged—Glenn chatted amiably with the parents about how they had spent their Christmas vacations. I smiled and kept my mouth shut. No one needed to be reminded of where I had been.

The Hedderiggs, the Duncans, and the LaFontaines all went to the same church in East Medford, a congregation known throughout the county for its conservative theology and Republican politics. The men were solid. The women were deferential. And the softball team was amazing, because the teens in the church never missed a game.

The Lessards, I thought, were members of the Catholic church in town, but religion really didn't have anything to do with Rich Lessard's antipathy toward Dana. He simply thought my lover was a pervert. Rich was, he informed me, a liberal Democrat with a very high threshold for tolerance, and the firm belief that gays should be allowed to be out in the military. He was the chief financial officer for the largest employer in town, after the lumber mill: a crunchy granola manufacturer of all-natural shaving soap and toothpaste and talc. His company's products rested inside my medicine cabinet and inside my daughter's backpack. The enterprise gave an impressive percentage of its profits to charity each year, and the employees—even the highest management—came to work in blue jeans and flannel shirts.

Of course, religion was at best only a small part of the reason why even the assemblage from East Medford was concerned about Dana. Certainly they thought she was unnatural, and at one point Ken Hedderigg implied that he considered her a tad presumptuous to believe she understood better than God what sort of genitalia she was supposed to have. But, like Rich Lessard, most of their repulsion was triggered by the simple belief that Dana was twisted and freakish and sick. She may even have been, on some level, the sort of sexual predator who might not physically abuse children, but was likely, by her mere presence in the community, to encourage all manner of aberrant sexual practices. The fact that my students were in the sixth grade was especially troubling to the group: Here my kids were on the very cusp of adolescence and sexual activity, and there before them was a grown woman they respected—their teacher, of all things—who was involved with a transsexual.

"He—" Ken began at one point, referring to Dana.

"She," I corrected him, careful to keep my voice light.

"No. He. You can call him a girl if you want, but I'm not going to do it," Ken told me, before continuing his thought: "He is clearly way too fixated on that part of his body. He is way too fixated on sex. And you can talk all you want about gender, but the fact is, you two didn't go to Colorado so he could have a gender change. You two went so he could have a sex change."

We only had half an hour, so Glenn steered the conversation as quickly as he could to the specifics of what the parents wanted, and what they had in mind.

"Mostly," Rich said, "we want to hear what you're planning," and he turned his attention to me. They all did. Even Audrey LaFontaine's mother, a lovely young woman who it was clear was reticent and shy and had mustered all the courage she had to come and confront me, pulled her beautiful wool shawl tightly around her shoulders and stared at me.

I tried to smile, but I'm sure it looked forced. The room seemed, suddenly, too warm. It was the first Monday in January, and I was feeling flush. "What I'm planning to do about . . . what? About Dana?"

"Obviously."

"My personal life, in other words."

"Look, Allison, you're a teacher," Rich said. "You live smack in the center of town. That means—and it kills me to say this, because I really do view myself as a very open-minded person—your personal life has a public component."

The room smelled of canned tomatoes and sweet basil, and I realized that at some point one of the women in the kitchen had turned a radio on softly. I heard country music: a crying steel guitar and the plaintive lament of a young fellow who has been jilted. The radio was, I decided, an act of courtesy: The pair hadn't wanted to eavesdrop.

"Well, I'm not planning to do anything," I answered, and I crossed my legs under the table. I didn't dare cross my arms. "What am I supposed to do? Tell her she can no longer live in my house because some people don't approve? Tell her we can't be friends because we have some neighbors who don't like her?"

"No one has said anything of the kind," Glenn said.

"Of course not," Bea Hedderigg added.

"Then what?"

"Can I say something?" Audrey LaFontaine's mother asked, her voice as small as a girl's—Carly's, perhaps, when she was in elementary school. We all turned to her.

"I can't speak for anybody else," she began, "and I don't want to. If you want to live with this person, Allison, that's your right. But my

daughter really looks up to you. You're so important to her . . . you just
don't realize. And so I don't want her confused by your personal life, I
don't want her getting the wrong message. I don't want her getting the
idea that because you want to live with a person like that, it's okay—"

"Though it most assuredly doesn't speak well of your judgment,"
Al Duncan said, cutting in.

"No, but that's not my point," Audrey's mom said.

"But it's an important point," Al said quickly. "Seriously, Allison,
what's going on here? Why are you doing this? It doesn't show a
whole lot of common sense."

"All I want her to do is move," Audrey's mom said, raising her
voice a tiny bit to be heard.

For a moment the table grew quiet, and everyone looked down at
their shoes or into their laps. They looked at the red exit signs over the
doors, or the posters that explained how to help someone who was
choking on their breakfast or lunch. They didn't look at one another,
and they certainly didn't look at me.

"You want me to move?" I asked.

She nodded and then spoke very slowly. "I don't mind you teaching
here," she said. "Really, I don't. I don't mind you teaching Audrey, or
teaching any of the other kids—"

"Oh, I think we still need to discuss that," Al said.

"No, I really don't mind. I just don't want Audrey to see you living
with that person."

"So I'm supposed to sell my house and commute?"

"Everyone knows he has an apartment in Burlington. Why can't
you live there if you want to be with him?"

"And drive back and forth?"

"Folks do it," Rich Lessard said, shrugging. "Your ex-husband
does it."

"I like my house. I don't plan on moving. Even for a short while."

"No one's said you should," Glenn said.

"No, I did," Audrey's mother said. "That's exactly what I said."

"But even that doesn't get to the real heart of the matter," Rich
insisted. "Look, I'm in favor of gay marriage. Really. That sort of thing
probably doesn't matter in some professions and in some places. But it

does matter here. In this case. As parents, we have a moral obligation to ask ourselves whether we want our children taught by someone who's comfortable living in the center of town with a transvestite."

"Transsexual," I corrected.

"A man—"

"A woman—"

Glenn put his hand on my wrist and reflexively I yanked my arm away. "People," he said, as if nothing had happened, as if I hadn't pulled away from him as if he were a leech, "we're not here to solve anything this morning. We're not going to. We're here to listen, and here's what I'm hearing.

"First of all, there's some concern about Allison's judgment. She shouldn't have been so public about this new . . . relationship. Is that a fair word, Allison?"

"It's fine," I said, sighing.

"Second, there's some concern that her relationship, even if it had been completely private, may be inappropriate for a teacher."

I looked at Glenn, unable to hide my astonishment. I couldn't believe he would say such a thing in front of parents.

"Is that accurate?" he asked them, and some of them nodded.

"A teacher is indeed a role model," Al Duncan said.

"And, third, you're worried that her effectiveness in the classroom might be compromised—impaired, perhaps—by this relationship because she will no longer have the support of her students' parents. Right?"

"I don't think anyone said that," I said.

"No, but it's an excellent point," Rich Lessard agreed. "And very true."

"Now, I understand a petition is circulating," Glenn went on. "Is that correct?"

For a moment nobody answered, and then the men at the table seemed to move their heads just enough to suggest it was true.

"What does it say?" he asked.

Al Duncan pushed his chair back from the table for dramatic effect. "Before anyone says another word, I should note that I am not here as a member of the school board," he said. "I'm just here as an interested parent, because my son is in Allison's class."

Glenn smiled cordially. "Point noted."

"It doesn't cite you specifically, Allison," Bea said after a moment, when it was clear that no one else was going to open their mouth. "The petition, that is."

"Oh, good."

Rich folded his hands on the table, as if he were in a business meeting. "It says, very simply, that we expect a certain level of moral decency and propriety from our teachers. Nothing more, nothing less."

"Did you define it?" I asked.

"Did we define what?"

"Moral decency?"

"No."

"Don't you think you should have?"

"Look, I know what you're getting at," Rich said. "Morality is fluid. Morality is vague. Morality differs wherever you go. But there are certain parameters, and—at least in this community—there are certain expectations. That's all we're getting at."

"And somehow I've violated them."

"One man's opinion," Ken Hedderigg said, "but yes, I think so."

"Okay," I said, and I resisted the urge to liken myself to Hester Prynne. But I thought instantly of the painting of Prynne that adorned the cover of the paperback edition of *The Scarlet Letter* that Dana had had us read back in July. In the painting, Prynne was holding her infant daughter, and she looked at once defiant and soft: a usually sweet, demure woman driven to anger by her community's moral condemnation.

Prynne was, of course, dressed largely in black. Unfortunately, the A pinned to her breast looked more like a varsity sports letter than the scarlet brand she'd earned for a crime.

Hester Prynne, varsity athlete. All-county field-hockey forward.

"Okay, what?" Rich asked me.

"Okay," Glenn said before I could open my mouth, "Allison's heard your concerns. I've heard your concerns. Right, Allison?"

"Right."

"What do you plan to do with the petition?" the principal asked.

"When we're done circulating it, we'll take it to the school board and see what they have to say—unless you give us a reason not to," Ken said. When he'd begun his response, he'd been looking at Glenn, but in the space of his sentence he'd turned his attention to me.

"How many names do you have so far?" Glenn asked.

"That's hard to say, because there are at least three copies floating around."

"We're only doing this because we love our children," Audrey's mom said. "You understand that, don't you?"

"Of course."

"I mean, you have a daughter," she said. "Carly, right? I know she's away at school now. But I have to ask: What would you do if your Carly came home from college with a transsexual boyfriend or girlfriend?"

It was a great question, one that had certainly crossed my mind that winter. But it was also one that I'd been careful not to answer, always relegating it to a remote crevice in my brain. That won't happen, I'd tell myself. It would be like getting daggered by lightning twice in a night. But the question clearly frightened me, because I knew on some level that regardless of whatever my final answer turned out to be, my initial reaction would be a shudder. No parent wants their child to fall in love with a transsexual. For the vast majority of parents in this world, the only thing worse than having a transsexual for a son- or a daughter-in-law would be to have one for a child.

"If Carly came home one evening with a transsexual friend," I answered, not exactly lying but certainly not telling the truth, "I would offer to make them both dinner. And then I'd put out clean towels in the bathroom."

"I couldn't do that," Audrey's mom said, and I thought her voice was going to break. "I'd be too busy crying. I'd be too busy crying for her and for me, and for her new friend."

I curled my lips against my teeth, moved by her candor. I knew in my heart I'd cry, too.

25

dana

AT FIRST MY NEW VAGINA HURT LIKE HELL. TRULY. And it seemed to hurt more after Allison left Sunday morning. The pain would begin like a bruise—and much of the area was indeed black and blue—but it would grow into something far more pronounced: the biting ache of a broken bone. But, of course, there were no bones involved. The hardest thing down there was gauze.

Until Dr. Meehan stopped by Monday morning while making his rounds, I feared that I'd done something awful when I'd insisted on standing up for Allison on Saturday night. I was afraid I was going to pay some horrible price for my hubris, for what I can only imagine was a last vestige of male arrogance.

A few times, I had phantom pains where I had once had a penis. Ah, my old friend, I would think, the words a regal British accent in my mind because I'd been reading so much Jan Morris in my hospital bed, even in absentia you manage to trouble me.

Now that the penis was gone—most of it, anyway, and the parts that remained I'd already begun to view as vagina—I could regard it with the sort of benign affection we have for our friends' big sloppy dogs. It was no longer a massive goiter between my legs. It was, instead, that Alaskan malamute who insists on clomping into your yard, inadvertently trampling the rosebushes, and then—without any ill intent whatsoever—pooping right outside your front door.

Maybe husky is too grandiose an image. I certainly didn't have a poodle of a penis, but I also don't want to suggest that Dr. Meehan had in the stirrups before him one surgical morning the big dog of dicks. Picture instead a good-sized springer spaniel. Or, perhaps, a petite golden retriever.

I stayed in bed all of Sunday, but on Monday morning Dr. Meehan made his rounds and told me it was time to stand up. I didn't tell him I already had.

"If I may say so myself," he murmured as he checked his stitching, "I do very nice work. You are going to have a perfectly lovely little vulva."

Then he suggested I walk as far as the nurses' station, and I suggested we push the envelope and try for the gift shop.

"There's no reason to press. You'll only risk bleeding," he said. "Maybe later today you can go, if you feel up to it."

When I swung my legs off the mattress and pushed off with my hands, I realized he was right. It felt like there was a bowling ball dangling from my groin, and it felt like it was hung there with fish hooks. I couldn't believe there were women in the world who would voluntarily pierce their labia to add gold or silver rings.

"It should smart a bit," my doctor said, his voice betraying absolutely no concern.

I nodded. "It does." And while the pain was reminiscent of the soreness I had felt when I stood for the first time on Saturday night, it was considerably more pronounced. I realized with some bemusement that I'd been running on some sort of desperate adrenaline the night before my lover was due to leave. I was so determined to show her that I was getting better—growing stronger by the minute, so she needn't fear for a second that she'd be saddled with an invalid when I returned to Vermont—that I had performed a feat damn near Herculean.

Still, despite the pain, for Dr. Meehan I walked. I walked as I had years earlier, when I hiked to the summit of Mount Washington one day with two friends from college: I shuffled, my knees barely moving, my feet as flat as two irons. I took baby steps, and still I found myself grimacing.

But I plodded forward, out the door of my room and then down the hall to the nurses' station. Two of the nurses looked up and offered a polite golfer's clap. I hung on tight to their counter, rested, and tried to smile back. Then, much to my surgeon's surprise, I motioned with my head to the corridor that led to the gift shop and insisted on pressing on.

"You think you can do it?" he asked.

"I do."

"I don't want to have to scrape you off the floor with a spatula. I don't want you to undo all that good work I did between your legs."

I shook my head. "I'm fine," I insisted. Suddenly I had to get to the gift shop, and I had to get there for no other reason than the fact that I wasn't supposed to. I wanted to exceed Dr. Meehan's expectations. My expectations. Everyone's expectations. I wanted to get there for Allison.

Wasn't it bad enough that she was living, in the eyes of her village, with a freak? I knew Allison hadn't been happy in Colorado, and I knew she was having second thoughts about me. I couldn't blame her. And so the last thing I wanted was for her to be burdened with a freak who was sickly: I wanted to get better fast, and the first step seemed to be walking.

Dr. Meehan did not—as he put it with such delicacy—have to scrape me off the floor with a spatula. But my legs felt like Jell-O when we reached the shop, and I thought my vagina had been swabbed with battery acid. I gave my doctor my arm once I had touched the brass rack with the gums and candies and mints—home base in a children's game—and allowed him to help me shamble back to my room. I walked like a desperately old lady, but I was smiling inside as if I had just hiked every dirt- and loam- and mud-covered inch of the Appalachian Trail.

When I was settled back in my bed, Dr. Meehan told me that another girl would be arriving at the hospital around lunchtime, and she would be having her final reassignment Tuesday morning. I could tell that he wanted me to visit with her, and so before he even made the suggestion, I offered to go and hold her hand that afternoon.

There had been other transsexuals in the hospital when I was there, including an airline pilot who checked out soon after I arrived, and an elderly woman who left the day before Allison. I knew that a set designer for Las Vegas hotel shows had had her reassignment on Friday. But Allison had been with me until Sunday, and so I had made no effort to meet any of my peers. I had Allison, and that was all the company I needed.

By mid-afternoon, I felt sufficiently recovered from my marathon walk to the gift shop to go visiting. I hobbled first to meet Sasha, the girl from Vegas who was on day three of her road to recovery, but it was clear I would be unable to stay with her for very long.

"If I were taller, you know, I'd have been a showgirl," she insisted, smearing a small tub of an "emergency" line cream into the wrinkles that ran like little dry riverbeds around her eyes. "I have just boodles of energy."

I smiled in agreement and left as quickly as I could: I have never been very comfortable around people who use words like *boodles,* even if they claim gender dysphoria as their excuse. Transsexuality is no reason to talk like a moron, or to presume that energy and height are the only prerequisites to becoming a showgirl. Still, I was happy to see that she, too, was getting better.

Then I went to visit Melissa, the new girl, and I understood instantly why Dr. Meehan had wanted me to say hello. She was a petite, anorexic young thing from Dallas—no more than twenty-six or twenty-seven years old—who had just finished getting her master's in English at SMU. Now, before forging ahead on her doctorate, she was having her reassignment. She was completely alone in Colorado, and she was scared to death.

"If I ever told my father what I was doing, he would never forgive me," she said.

"I almost didn't tell my parents either," I said.

"But you did?"

"I think you have to. The whole reason you're doing this is so you can be yourself—stop living the big lie."

"He's a high-school football coach. He climbs mountains."

Almost instantly I felt like her big sister. I was sitting in one of those hideous orange hospital chairs, the kind in which Allison had practically lived for a good part of the preceding week, and I leaned forward and rested my hand on her smooth, smooth shin. I gave her leg a squeeze.

"He hasn't climbed a mountain anywhere near as tall as the one you have to get here," I said. "Never in his life has he done anything as difficult as you have. Never."

"Your parents forgave you?"

"They will. If they haven't already. And, honestly, you shouldn't even talk like that. Neither should I. After all, if you had schizophrenia or depression, would you feel this need for your parents' forgiveness? Of course not. If you had some crippling disease, would you? God, no."

We shared our lives with each other for the rest of the afternoon, and I think I was able to convince her that someday her parents would indeed understand her decision (which may or may not have been true, but it was something she needed to believe that day), and that she would be able to manage the post-operative pain. A little before eight, just after the nurse had given her a pill to ensure that she would sleep, I went back to her room and gave her a sisterly kiss on her forehead, and brushed her hair to relax her.

When I saw her next, I reminded her, her surgery would be behind her. I did not have the heart to tell her, however, that by the time she had swum completely back to the surface from that insensible, underwater realm of anesthesia—a world of slow-motion dreams and vivid memories that in fact never happened—I would be gone. Oh, she might wake up off and on throughout the afternoon, and she might even be sufficiently awake for a small dinner on Tuesday night. But it would really be Wednesday afternoon before the drugs that had knocked her out would be fully cleansed from her system and the pain would be retreating toward bearable.

I might see her, in other words, but she really wouldn't see me. I was going to be discharged Wednesday morning, and then I was planning to spend one last day at the Holiday Inn south of the city, recuperating before my long journey home to Vermont. With any luck, I'd be back with Allison by dinner Thursday night, and we'd begin what I hoped—no, what I expected—would be a long and glorious and serene life together.

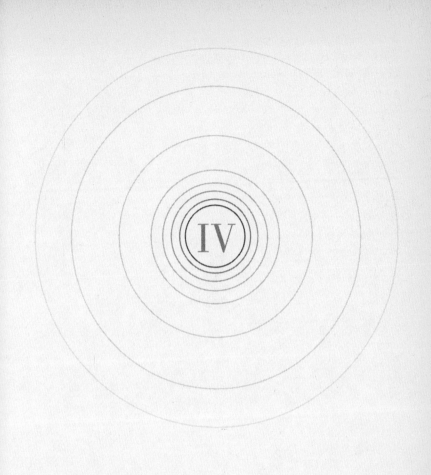

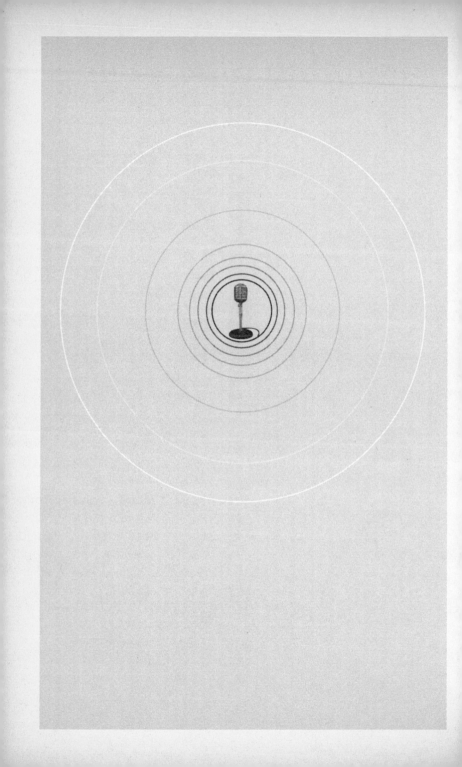

All Things Considered
Wednesday, September 26

RICH LESSARD: None of us would have cared if he——Dana Stevens——hadn't been so brazen. What he wanted to do in the privacy of his bedroom was entirely up to him.

The problem, in my opinion, was that he was parading around Bartlett in women's clothes, and the little kids could see him. All the time. Then he had that operation, and he was pretty darn brassy about that, too.

It just didn't show very good judgment. Not on his part. And not on Allison's.

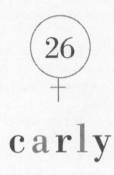

26

carly

THE MOON IN THE SKY LOOKED LIKE IT WAS underwater; it bobbed beneath a gauzy haze like a Caribbean jellyfish in the shallows by a beach. It was a sickle moon. There was still some daylight left, but the sky was moving quickly from purple to dusk. It was a little past five in the afternoon.

I climbed into my roommate's sporty little Camry and started back up the hill toward the college. I knew I couldn't make a habit of borrowing June's car, because I just didn't like her enough to incur that kind of debt. Come March, I figured, I could bicycle back and forth between my dormitory and the radio station in town, but I wasn't sure what I would do until then. A full third of January still remained.

The station where I was going to work that spring was on the top floor of a brick building about three blocks from the battery factory in Bennington. It used lots of syndicated material, and it seemed like we ran almost every PSA we received. Especially overnight. Mostly the station was known for classic rock, the sort of stuff my mom would play at her parties and listen to when she was cleaning the house—there were album covers all over the walls, and the waiting room looked like a head shop from an era way before my time—but throughout the day it offered a five-minute local news roundup on the half hour. Then, at twelve-thirty and five-thirty, it actually had a fifteen-minute news program, which was what drew me to the station in the first place.

Jim Blosser did both of those broadcasts. He was the station owner as well as the station manager, and he was, I am sure, a much better salesperson than the person whom he actually expected to sell time. He paid me a dollar above minimum wage and gave me plenty to do.

At first I simply typed up ad contracts and called local retailers to get merchandise we could give away on the air. But once Jim saw I could write and put together a story, I started drafting news for the deejays and Jim to read: Direct-mail clothing merchant to open outlet in Manchester. Three cows die in sudden snowstorm. Diner to offer discounts for seniors.

Moreover, after I got my FCC license later that spring, Jim allowed me to go on the air with Jamie Sloan whenever she wanted the company and I had the time. Jamie was somewhere in her mid-thirties, and her real job was as a shift supervisor for some valve factory in Hoosick Falls. But she loved rock and roll music and she loved being a radio "personality," and so she did the station's afternoon program during the week. Jamie was great fun to be around because she understood that we were a ten-thousand-watt station with, at any given point in the day, somewhere between eleven and nine hundred listeners. Jamie also generated a fair amount of ad revenue herself because of her spontaneous and bizarre on-air additions to the commercials she was handed to read:

"I'm telling you, the rhubarb pie at the Blue Benn is out of this world. The best. If *60 Minutes* ever does an exposé on the valve factory in Hoosick, I'm serving Mike Wallace that pie. Truly. Mike Wallace? He gets the pie. It's one of a kind. Top it with the Blue Benn's homemade ice cream, and you won't mind the angioplasty that'll come with dessert. You just won't care."

My first day there—the day I saw the sickle moon in the sky—was a Monday. My mom had been home two weeks and a day by then, and Dana had been back for a week and a half. To be honest, I was somewhat relieved that I had had an excuse to leave Bartlett. Certainly a part of me wanted to be home to cheer up my mom and to continue to help Dana with her recovery. I had insisted on making dinner every night for two weeks, and I'd brought Dana breakfast in bed her first Friday and Saturday home so she wouldn't have to struggle down the stairs as soon as she woke up in the morning.

But I couldn't bear to hear my mom insist that she didn't care about what people were saying and doing, when it was so clear that she was devastated. And Dana, who wanted nothing more than to be treated like a woman, was acting, it seemed, more and more like a man.

"We need to respond," she kept saying, "we need to do something!"

"Oh?"

"Yes! We can't just let them pillory you. We can't just let them put you in the stocks."

"They're not pillorying me."

"That petition is heinous. Its implications are appalling."

"It's meaningless. It's names on paper."

"Do you want to talk to my lawyer? Let's do that. Let's talk to my lawyer. That thing Al Duncan said in the paper? It's libel, I know it is."

That particular day there had been a short article in the Middlebury newspaper because Al Duncan had said publicly that he thought my mom should be fired. His comments were news because he was a member of the school board, and because it was obvious that he wasn't alone in his opinion. But the article also had a quote from Judd Prescott, the school superintendent, that made it clear that as a member of the Vermont NEA—the Vermont National Education Association, the group that acted, in essence, as the teachers union—my mom couldn't possibly be let go because she was living with Dana.

"I have a lawyer," my mom said. "Thank you."

"Then let's call him. Let's schedule a time to see him right now."

"Her. My lawyer happens to be female."

This conversation was repeated, more or less, over and over during the first few days Dana was back. Finally, over dinner one night, I snapped at the two of them: "You're like an old married couple!" I said. "You're having the same fight every day. If I want to watch two people argue all the time, I can just hang out at Dad's."

Dana apologized, and my mom gave me a hug. I felt bad comparing them to Dad and Patricia, and I regretted my inference that their squabbling was going to drive me away. The fact was, my dad was taking me back to school in a couple of days in any event, because my job at the radio station began on the twentieth.

Nevertheless, I can remember climbing into Dad's car on a Sunday afternoon and—despite the snow that was swirling in little gusts and the measureless gray in the sky—feeling downright happy. As soon as I got to Bennington, I realized, I would no longer be the daughter of the teacher who lived with the transsexual.

The words in the petition that most rankled Dana were *perversion* and *prurience*.

"Of course I'm deviant," she said, shaking her head as she scanned the petition her first weekend home. "Every transsexual is. But perverted? I think not. And I'm certainly not prurient."

The copy we had hadn't been circulated, so we couldn't see the names of the people who had signed it. Apparently, however, the school board had been presented with three petitions and a total of 725 signatures—or, roughly, almost one out of six people in the town, and a much higher percentage of the adults. Moreover, 210 of the signatures were from parents of children who attended the school, including seventeen parents of the kids my mom taught. Since my mom had nineteen kids in her class, and since it was likely that sometimes a child's mother and father had both signed the petition, I calculated that the parents of somewhere between a half and two-thirds of her students had offered their signatures.

The petition was only two paragraphs long, and it was the kind of thing any sane person would sign if he didn't know the politics behind it:

We, the undersigned, believe that teachers are role models. Their behavior in the classroom and their behavior in their community influences the children in their care.

We therefore believe that teachers must act morally, honorably, and decently in their private as well as their public lives. They must not court obscenity, prurience, or deviance. They must not advocate perversion.

Let's face it, no one wants a teacher who advocates perversion. No one wants a pervert teaching their kid how to read or write or find the Solomon Islands on a map.

But everyone in Bartlett knew that the petition was all about Dana and my mom, and that meant there was a lot of not-in-my-backyard hypocrisy fueling it, too. And while I know teenagers are supposed to see adult hypocrisy everywhere, in this case it was pretty evident. A lot of people who would support gay rights in the abstract were very uncomfortable with a little in-your-face gender bending. Everybody who signed the petition was saying publicly that they believed my mom was courting obscenity and advocating perversion. They were saying they didn't want my mom in the classroom so long as she was living in Bartlett with Dana.

When I left for Bennington, however, there really didn't seem to be a whole lot that anyone could do other than sign the petition and make some noise. My mom said she thought some parents might see if they could have their kids transferred into the other sixth-grade class, and some might even withdraw their children and home-school them for the remainder of the year. But the storm would pass, and eventually everyone would get used to Dana. After all, hadn't the school superintendent himself said that her job wasn't in any jeopardy?

I think, on most levels, I believed that. Yet I continued to worry. And I was glad to get away.

allison

A ROGUE SENTENCE: "I WISH THINGS COULD BE the way they had been in the summer."

A rogue thought: *This whole business is freakish.*

I kept the thought to myself, but not the sentence. I was lying in bed with Dana the night Carly had returned to college, watching her flip distractedly through a magazine. I'd closed my own book at least a half hour earlier and placed it on the nightstand on my side of the bed. I wasn't sure at first if I'd actually verbalized the words that had formed in my mind, or whether I'd kept them inside me.

"That's a loaded idea," Dana said, without looking up from her magazine. She was sitting up. I was lying on my tummy.

"I didn't mean anything by it," I said, beating a hasty retreat.

"Certainly you did. What?"

"Nothing. Really, nothing."

"Do you simply wish it was warm again? Is that it? Are you sick of the snow and the ice and the cold?"

"Yes."

"You're lying," she said, her voice considerably lighter than her words.

"No. I do want it to be warm."

"But that's not what you meant."

"I guess not."

She rested her magazine on top of her knees. Her nightgown had teacups a delft-blue, and her hair hung loose like the drapes.

"Do you know what you meant?" she asked.

"Probably not," I said, though when I pressed the side of my face deep into my pillow, I realized I knew exactly what I meant. We both did. And then I had another rogue thought, one that had been floating just beyond my consciousness since Trinidad but had never landed with such explicitness in my sentient mind: *I will never be fucked again.*

At least as long as I was with Dana.

She read for another few minutes and then turned out the light and lay down beside me, pulling the quilt over us both. She rubbed my back and massaged my shoulders until, finally, I fell asleep.

"You're a beautiful woman," I told Dana at breakfast Monday morning.

"I wish," she said, delicately spreading raspberry jam on an English muffin.

"No, you are," I insisted. She was healing quickly, getting better fast. She was walking with the same sure, long-legged gait she had had before surgery. She was going to start making dinner for me again soon.

"My hands are too big. My nose is a man's."

She was wearing a sea-green cardigan with glistening pearl buttons. Her leggings were sleek and crisp, and they matched her sweater: They were a beautiful shade of turquoise. She made me look shabby in my loose thermal dress.

"I should go," I said. "My eleven-year-olds await."

"Tonight we really must talk," she said.

I nodded. I smiled. I kissed her on her cheek.

I wished, I realized, that I, too, were gay. With confidence. With assurance. Without reservation. I wished that I could be the lesbian of her dreams.

Or, if I wasn't, that I could decide whether such things really mattered.

But we didn't talk that night, and later in the week she licked me and I came, and she entered me with a dildo and I came again. Some evenings she would rub an oil made with neroli and black pepper into the backs of my legs; one time she painted my toenails a shade called cerise. In bed we would sip fruit shakes made from the strawberries I'd picked half a year earlier, thawing the red brick from my freezer in the microwave before dropping the fruit with bananas and ice into a blender.

I did nothing for her in return, and still we did not discuss our relationship.

Yet I would lie awake at three in the morning and I would think to myself, I'm not a lesbian, repeating the words like a mantra. But I knew I couldn't tell her such a thing in the middle of the night, and—more important—that was the only time that I felt completely sure. As long as we were savoring fruit shakes in bed, or the sheets were still wet from my orgasm, a part of me would remain open to the possibility.

When I was alone that week, walking to and from school or preparing for class, I would wonder at how things had changed since Christmas. Outwardly, Dana's final sexual reassignment had changed nothing: She was wearing the same clothes, the same shades of lipstick and nail polish, the same boots when she ventured outside. She read the same magazines and books, she liked the same foods. She held my hand the same way when we walked upstairs together in the evening.

I had not yet seen her vagina, and I wouldn't until there were absolutely no traces of the surgery—until her vagina would look, more or less, like mine. Dana was adamant about this, and I was content with her decision.

But the surgery had changed everything. It had to, it was inescapable. You can't say to yourself, much as you might want to, *It's just a penis, it was just one small part of our relationship*. It didn't matter whether we actually used the penis for sex twice a week or once a month, it didn't matter if I saw it or felt it a dozen times a year or over a hundred. The fact remained that it was there, and I knew it was there.

Moreover, it was also true that had Dana been male—no gender dysphoria, no need to wear a dress, no woman in the soul under the flesh—and lost his penis because of an accident or a disease, I wouldn't have felt as acutely its loss. Because then, I imagine, Dana would have continued to live as a man. It isn't the penis solely that makes someone male: Just ask a female transsexual, a woman with gender dysphoria. Just ask a self-proclaimed trans-man.

As recently as late December, however, Dana had still had a penis, and on some level I must have been continuing to cling to the fantasy that the sexual reassignment surgery would never actually happen. I may have been living with a person who wore makeup and skirts, but the person beside me in bed had a penis.

I could play all the mind games I wanted, I could intellectualize and rationalize forever, but, pure and simple, Dana's castration changed something. It no longer made sense to me to rest my head on her shoulder the way I had as recently as Christmas, or to lay my head in her lap when we watched a movie in the den. I did that sort of thing with men. I'd sat in her lap any number of times the summer we met—the summer before I'd known her plans—and I couldn't imagine doing such a thing now. It just didn't seem like the kind of thing a woman did with another woman.

But then I'd remind myself how happy I'd been sometimes in the fall—how remarkably, blissfully happy—and I'd try and convince myself that little in reality was different. We had the same breakfasts, the same dinners, the same long talks about movies and books. There was the specter of the people in the town who disapproved of Dana, but inside our home—that little fantasy palace—once more I was Beauty. I was fed. I was pampered. I was stroked.

I was—with wands, batons, and vibrating scepters—fucked.

And I came. Some cold nights in late January I'd tell Dana, No, I don't want that, and I'd turn away, but then I'd feel something oiled and new sliding between my cheeks or I'd hear an unfamiliar hum, and almost instantly I'd grow wet.

One night she would blindfold me. One night she would keep the room black. One night she would light the bedroom only with candles.

One night, when she'd been home almost a month, she climbed on top of me and entered me with a vibrator she had somehow attached to her groin, and she fucked me the way she once had. I was able to move my hips against someone the way I had for—oh, God—a quarter century. I was able to reach my hands up and over my lover, squeezing and stroking her neck, her shoulder, her back.

Nevertheless, something seemed wrong—off, to be precise—and I couldn't find that place I'd known well in the fall and the early part of the winter, that place where I had been . . . happy.

I think, ironically, that if people like Rich Lessard and Glenn Frazier hadn't tried to drive Dana away, I might have given up on the relationship within weeks of our return from Colorado. Had I not felt that I was being bullied and Dana was being harassed, at some point in January I might very well have confessed to Dana that I wasn't as happy as I thought I should be—certainly I wasn't as happy as I had been in August or November. And then, perhaps, I might have asked her to leave.

Or, until she was absolutely and completely well, to move into the guest bedroom. And then leave.

After all, I have always been very capable when it comes to ending a relationship, or asking someone who loves me to go. Just ask my ex-husband. There are at least three—maybe more—men in this world who believe that I am at once among the crueler women who walk on this planet and the quickest to throw what they deemed as happiness aside.

The Rich Lessards and Glenn Fraziers of the community did challenge me, however, and I have never been good at acquiescence. I have never, ever done something simply because somebody wanted me to, or because it was the easy way out. And because they couldn't tolerate Dana's presence in my life, I decided that she was more than welcome to be a part of it. No matter what.

Despite the reality that she lacked a penis.

Despite my belief that I wasn't gay, and that somehow that mattered.

Despite the fact that I was coming in the night with an apparently endless assortment of sex toys.

The paper was a single sheet in the midst of a stack of stapled exams, the conclusion of our small unit about the Canadian maritime provinces, and on it was a four-color image printed from the Internet and a pair of words scribbled in red crayon: *Fucking perverts.* The image was a photograph of a naked transsexual—pre-operative, in that the person had a penis and breasts—standing before a dated couch and the sort of home entertainment center you buy at a big discount department store. It looked like a photo from an Internet personals ad. Or, perhaps, from the transsexual's home page.

The words had been scrawled over the picture, in letters that were thick and bold. It wouldn't have taken a handwriting expert to conclude that they had been written in anger—each letter looked like an obscenity—but I know I couldn't decide whether they had been written by one of my eleven-year-olds or by someone considerably older. Someone who was trying to disguise his age.

The fact that the final word was plural made it seem particularly odious and hurtful, acknowledging, as it did, the notion of Dana's and my consensual involvement. The missing words? *You're. Both.*

The full insinuation? *You're both fucking perverts.*

Yet the worst part wasn't the accusation. It was the primitive, childlike drawings that had been added to the photograph with that very same crayon: A dagger poised at the transsexual's penis, with the sort of dashes and chit marks surrounding the blade that a child might use to convey sharpness. A second knife aimed at the transsexual's breasts—or, perhaps, at her heart. I couldn't decide.

I stared at the words and the pictures for a long time, numbed, sometimes only dimly aware of the photograph that shared the page with them. When I heard the sounds of people in the hall, I slipped the paper under my desk blotter and sat back in my chair and tried to think.

I remembered my students had placed their tests in a small in-box at the front of my desk as they filed past it on their way to my class-room door just before noon. Together, we had then filed down the long corridor to the cafeteria for lunch. That meant the exams had been in the tray for close to three and a half hours before I picked them up and thumbed through them at the end of the day. Moreover, they'd been alone in my classroom for almost an hour during lunch.

And so I decided it was possible that the paper hadn't even been left there by one of my students. Clearly it hadn't been placed in my in-box by either the student whose exam was below the slur or above it. That would have been much too obvious. And when I thought about the two students whose work surrounded the paper, I concluded that nei-ther could have been responsible in any event. Neither was the type to surf the Internet in search of this sort of smut, or the kind of person who would—who could—call someone a pervert. Neither was the type to use the word *fucking*.

Certainly there were other students in my class who had that capa-bility. But not those two.

Nevertheless, I thought back to the moment the kids had filed past my desk with their tests: I'd been standing by my door at the time, I'd been a good fifteen feet away. I certainly hadn't been watching them carefully as they shuffled past it, dropping their tests in the tray that I kept at the front for this purpose. And so while I was sure it hadn't been either of the students whose exams were nearest the image, it was clear that virtually any other student could have slipped the paper in the pile at almost any point. I wasn't paying close attention. I really wasn't paying any attention at all.

But then once more I would convince myself that it couldn't possibly have been one of my kids in the first place. It just couldn't. Someone else had to have wandered into my classroom during lunch and placed the paper there. A teenager, maybe. Perhaps even a grown-up. It was, in fact, probably left there by someone who barely knew me. Maybe someone who'd never even met me: The parent of a student in another grade or the other sixth-grade class, perhaps. Someone who had just seen me in the hallways. Or in the auditorium. Or walking to and from school.

I wanted to throw the paper away, simply excise it from my life, but I didn't dare. It seemed important to keep it. If I thought I would have had any support at all from Glenn Frazier, I would have shown it to him that very moment. He was, after all, my administrator. My principal. But I didn't have his support, and I had a sense that sharing it with him that afternoon would only make things worse.

Of course, I also didn't want to defile my house by bringing the picture home. And so once the people in the hallway had long passed—once the world had grown so quiet that I heard only a distant ringing somewhere in my ears—I pulled the image from beneath my desk blotter and placed it in one of my lower desk drawers. Then, for the first time in my entire career, I locked my desk.

I knew eleven-year-old Jeremy Roscoe had a crush on eleven-year-old Renee Wood, and I knew Renee and her friends would talk about nothing but kissing when they had lunch in the cafeteria.

I knew Audrey LaFontaine wished she were one of Renee's friends, but Renee's family had money and Audrey's did not, and so a friendship between the two had been unlikely since the pair left preschool. But I knew also that Audrey was smart and Audrey was loved, and Audrey would do fine without Renee's friendship, assuming she ever learned not to care.

A tall order, that. But, I hoped, one that was possible.

I knew Schuyler Brown wrote surprisingly lovely poems in the writing journals I had the kids keep, even if they were often about his in-line skates and his snowboard. I knew he wrote one about his grandmother after she'd died that was particularly sweet: She was buried in a plot beside a hydrangea tree, and he likened the blossoms to lawn darts and pink cotton candy.

I knew Ethan LaPree thought he looked fat in the turtleneck shirts his parents made him wear, the sleeves often damp from his nose. For a week in December I'd placed a Kleenex box by his desk—he sat in a row against the wall with a counter—but he clearly preferred the cotton on his cuffs.

"It isn't a cold," his mother insisted. "He's allergic to airborne indoor pollutants."

Oh, but Mike Deering did have a cold. He had had a cold throughout the fall and into the winter, and the fact that his boots had holes didn't help. I pretended I was his Secret Santa and bought him a new pair, but he wore them only one time that I know of.

I knew Sally Warwick was reading and understanding the same sorts of novels that sat on my nightstand and was capable of polishing off the "young adult" books she was expected to read in a day. I recommended at least a dozen books to her that autumn and winter, and took her to the public library in the village three times to show her my favorite authors.

I knew Sam Reynolds was beginning to grasp algebra and starting to solve binomial equations.

I knew no one was able to concoct more rules for Capture the Flag and permutations for Red Rover, Red Rover than Lindsey Lessard. I knew that, in spite of her father, she was a delightful little person with a smile that was infectious. She had, even then, movie-star eyebrows.

I knew Dan Hedderigg didn't like me, in part because his parents didn't like me, but also because I insisted he learn how to spell.

I feared Roberta Beaudet would be pregnant before she could drive: I knew she was in desperate need of affection, and no teacher alone could fill the giant maw in her heart.

Brian McCurdy, too. I don't mean, of course, that I feared someday soon he'd be pregnant. Rather, I worried that his need for human kindness would simply drive him to extremes. He was one of too many children in a trailer in a five-acre floodplain of decrepit mobile homes some people called the Tin City. There wasn't a father to be found in the bunch. Brian's dad, too, was long gone.

But Brian was what we have come to call a "good kid." He worked hard. He played well with his friends. And when he wasn't paying attention to me, he was at least drawing harmlessly in his salt-and-pepper notebook in the back of the class.

I knew my students well, and I cared about all of them. Some, in a teacher's way, I probably loved.

Not long after Carly had left for Bennington, two days after I found the picture of the transsexual in my in-box, I met with Glenn Frazier and Evelyn Newman over lunch. Evelyn was chairperson of the school board, a group of five adults from the community who worked with school administrators and teachers on a variety of issues: Staffing. Extracurriculars. The budget that would be presented for approval each year at the town meeting in March. The group was paid a modest stipend for their work, but not nearly enough, in my mind, to justify the aggravation that came with the job, or the amount of time it demanded. They were elected officials, which meant they actually ran for their jobs every other year.

We met in Glenn's office, eating egg salad sandwiches that came from the cafeteria. I had taught Evelyn's son, Tim, now a freshman in high school, and there was an even chance that I would teach her daughter, Casey, the following year. I'd liked Tim a lot, despite his mistaken belief that sixth-grade boys looked good with the back of their hair shaped into a rattail, but I could always count on him to stroll to the chalkboard and tackle even the most complex open-ended math problems, and I had always assumed that he'd liked me. I had every reason to believe that his mother was fond of me, too. Consequently, I'd been looking forward to the meeting, because I thought it was possible that Evelyn might be able to rein in board member Al Duncan and convince the rest of the group to take my side in what had the potential to become a particularly nasty clash with disgruntled parents.

I was wrong.

"Isn't my job already thankless enough, Allison?" Evelyn asked early in the meeting, and I heard annoyance in her voice. Evelyn was a Realtor, and usually her people skills were pretty good. She had to be deeply irked to try not to hide it.

"No one ever likes the budgets we present," she went on, "no one's ever pleased with what we spend on special ed. It's either too much or too little. The classroom computers are too expensive for some people, they're too old for others. Every year it's something. Every year."

She paused to nibble her sandwich and took a small, inconsequential mouthful that demanded she barely part her lips—what Carly and I had called a rabbit bite when she was a little girl. She was holding the triangle of half-sandwich with both hands.

"Well, the good news, then, is that this issue doesn't have anything to do with budgets or computers or special ed," I suggested. I hoped I sounded helpful.

"Really, I thought I'd seen everything," she said, ignoring me. "I must admit, I was leaning against running again this spring, but now my mind is made up. Firmly made up. There is no way on God's green earth I want to deal with this lunacy for another term."

"Am I the problem, in your opinion? Or is it Al and the parents who've been calling you?"

"Oh, please," she said.

"Really, I don't know."

"My answering machine wouldn't be filled every single night with irate moms and dads if it weren't for you! It's not just Al—come on. I have a petition with over seven hundred names on it in my hands. Seven hundred."

"So you think I'm the problem. Not their intolerance."

"Tolerance is an awfully squishy notion, Allison," Glenn said. "It's meaningless, completely meaningless." He'd finished his sandwich and was wiping his fingers on a brown paper napkin. "I'd wager you couldn't find two people on this planet who are tolerant of the same things. God, my wife thinks I'm way too tolerant of our new puppy. A really delightful black Lab, but dumb as a doorstop. He chewed her slippers to rags yesterday, and I just wasn't that upset. After all, the dog's only three months old."

"This isn't about dog tolerance," I said.

"Of course it isn't. But people tolerate different things. You'd probably be much more tolerant of your daughter if she came home from college with a nose ring than I'd be if mine pulled the same stunt."

"Please, Glenn—"

"Seriously, hear me out. All of those parents who you just called intolerant? If their sons and daughters decided to get married at nineteen, they'd be much more tolerant than you would if your daughter told you tomorrow she was going to get married in the spring. I'm quite sure of that. Tolerance has a tendency to drift, no matter how hard we try and anchor it with political correctness."

"There are some standards. Some basics."

"Gotcha!" he said, sitting forward in his chair and slam-dunking his napkin into his wastepaper basket.

"Gotcha?"

"Yes! There *are* some standards," he said, "there *are* some basics. And you've crossed a line! Maybe in a perfect world it wouldn't matter who you lived with. But in this world it does. In this world there are people who don't want their children's teachers living with people like Mr. Stevens. Are they intolerant? Maybe. Unreasonable? Perhaps. But I have to tell you: Most of the world wouldn't think so."

I looked at Evelyn to see how she was reacting to Glenn's little speech. She was nodding her head just the tiniest bit, while continuing to gnaw at the white bread around her egg-yellow mush.

"First of all, I don't live with a mister," I said, and then took a deep breath to try and calm myself. I was growing furious, but I was still just this side of rational behavior. "Secondly, I'm getting really tired of defending my lifestyle."

"This isn't about sexual preference," Evelyn said.

"I didn't say it was," I said.

"You used the word *lifestyle*. Isn't that one of those euphemisms for *gay*?"

"No! Since when does *gay* even need a euphemism?"

"Personally, I think *gay* itself is a euphemism—and my brother-in-law's gay," Glenn said.

"Look, Allison, I would defend you completely if this were just about being a lesbian. I don't care if you like women or men, really I don't. But it's not about that."

"Though I'm sure for some parents that, too, is a factor," Glenn added.

"What concerns me is that this Dana person is something else. A transvestite, a transsexual, I won't make that distinction—"

"How can you not? It's like not making the distinction between carrots and peas! They're both vegetables, yes, but otherwise they're completely different!"

"They're not *that* different!"

"But they are different!"

"Look, I really don't care, I simply—"

"You have to care!"

"Allison," Glenn said, and when he first said my name, I assumed he was about to try and calm me down. Looking back, however, it's clear that he saw I was on the edge and with a single thought he could send me over the side. "The man had his penis cut off. You're romantically involved with a human being who voluntarily had his penis cut off."

"That's enough!" I said, and I slammed my hand down hard on his desk—so hard that my palm started to sting and the bones in my fingers started to hurt. Some pencils rolled onto the floor. "How dare you?"

"How dare I what?"

"How dare you suggest that what I do with my life is wrong!"

"I didn't!"

"Right now, locked in a drawer in my desk, is one of the most childish, disgusting, and mean-spirited—really, mean-spirited— things I've ever seen! Someone printed a picture off the Internet, defaced it, and then left it for me in my in-box! And now I have to listen to this? How dare you?"

I was trembling, and both Evelyn and Glenn grew quiet. Finally

Evelyn asked, her voice surprisingly wobbly, "What is it? The thing in your desk?" She ran her hands over her skirt, as if she were flattening the sheets on a bed.

"It's a picture of a naked person," I began, and I realized that my breathing had begun to sound like a whimper: an endless chain of short little pants and gasps, with an occasional, embarrassing wheeze. I sat back in my chair to compose myself, and then I described for them the photo and the drawings and the insult that had been scribbled upon it.

When I was through, Evelyn told me she was sorry that I had had to endure such a thing, and Glenn said no one should ever be treated that way. For an instant, I actually began to believe that the photograph might, in the end, turn out to be a godsend. For whole seconds I imagined the incident was going to rally the school board and my principal and the community behind me. Perhaps, I thought, I had turned some sort of corner. Maybe, I fantasized, by March Dana and I would be playing bridge with the Fraziers, or military whist with the Newmans. Hadn't stranger things happened? Didn't stranger things happen every day?

"As a matter of honor," I heard Glenn saying, "I like people to look one another in the eye. Settle their differences like grown-ups. I think the fact that it was anonymous is as troubling as the subject matter itself. It's downright menacing."

"Have any laws been broken?" Evelyn asked.

"Probably not," Glenn said. "It's not illegal to take a naked picture of an adult off the Web."

"But what if it was a student who found it? Wouldn't the Web site be responsible for . . . something?"

He rocked back in his chair and waved his hands at his side. "Oh, maybe. I don't know. But it doesn't matter, that's not the issue in my mind. What do you want me to do, Allison?"

"About the picture?"

"Right."

"Nothing," I said. "That's not why I told you. I'd like you to keep this among us."

He shook his head. "That's understandable. But that's the one thing we can't do. We have our newsletter going out to parents next week, and I think we should mention it. Tell the folks what happened, and ask the person who did it to come forward and apologize."

"No, I'd really rather we didn't—"

He held up one hand like a police officer commanding me to stop, and continued, "We simply can't have your authority any more undermined than it already is. Even now we know that some parents are undoing a good deal of what you do on any given day in the classroom. Nitpicking. Carping. Criticizing. Surely you've noticed. It seems to me, if parents think someone can get away with leaving a piece of smut in your in-box, you're finished."

I honestly wasn't aware of any unusual nitpicking, but I didn't contradict him. I was too busy marveling at how deluded I'd been just a moment before, and digesting the fact that my own principal was actually going to use the picture to cripple me further in the eyes of the town.

That night Judd Prescott called me at my house just after dinner. Dana answered, with the result that the school superintendent was mildly flustered by the time Dana handed me the phone. I have to assume that Dana was the first transsexual he had ever spoken to.

"I have what I hope is good news," he said, trying to get back on track. Judd was a huge man, not so much fat as massively boned. He was probably in his late fifties, but I knew he held his own in a twice-weekly basketball game with much younger teachers at the Middlebury College gym. He was well-liked, and I'd found him perfectly nice the few times our paths had crossed. He had a statewide reputation as a first-rate administrator.

"I could use some," I said.

"I've talked to our lawyer, and he says we can offer you a paid leave of absence. Full salary, full benefits. The works."

I was in the kitchen, leaning against the refrigerator. Dana and I had been cleaning the dinner dishes when he called.

"Is that so?" I said, trying to think. I could feel a little lurch in my stomach. I took the cordless phone with me and went into the hallway, both to escape the sound of the pots as they clanged together in the sink and so Dana wouldn't see me turning pale.

"Yes."

"Why would I want such a thing?"

"Glenn told me about the unseemly picture someone left you—which, not incidentally, you should turn over to us as soon as you can. I'm sorry for you, Allison, really I am. It must have been very frightening."

"The picture?"

"A part of me can't believe someone would threaten you like that. But then, another part of me is never surprised by how low people can fall."

"No one threatened me."

"Not in so many words. But that picture was clearly—"

"It was most clearly not a threat."

"But there was a knife in it, correct?"

"It was obscene and degrading and childish. But it wasn't threatening."

"Well, we can let the experts decide that. In the meantime, while we investigate this, you don't have to be in the classroom—you don't have to put up with such nonsense, or be treated with such shabby disregard."

In the kitchen I heard the low rumble from the dishwasher as Dana switched on the machine.

"You're blowing this way out of proportion, Judd. I don't need a leave of absence, and I don't want one."

He paused. "There are other reasons, of course."

"Such as?"

"Do I really need to elaborate?"

He didn't; I knew exactly what he meant. Still, I considered making him say what he was thinking; I almost made him express his distaste for my lover. But I decided I'd be better off in the long run if I kept quiet.

"No, probably not," I said simply.

"Seriously, Allison, don't you think you might be doing everyone around you a colossal favor if you accepted this offer? Your students, for example. This whole controversy can't be good for them."

"My students are fine."

For a long moment he was silent, and I imagined him looking at a note card in his hand. I wondered if he had written out his remarks ahead of time.

"In that case, may I offer you one more enticement to consider the proposal?"

"An enticement? To stop teaching? I love teaching, I love what I do. And the kids really don't care who I'm living with. It's their parents who are so bent out of shape! I think the world of my students, and I would never do anything to jeopardize their education, or hurt them, or put them at risk. I would never—"

"Let them swim in Lake Champlain without lifeguards?" he said, finishing my sentence for me. "That was clearly putting them at risk."

"Are you talking about that field trip to the maritime museum back in September?"

He sighed so loudly I could hear his breath on the phone. "Look, if you take this leave of absence—paid, I should remind you—I can assure you that you will be in no trouble for violating the contract over that fiasco at the lake."

"Violating my teacher's contract?"

"You endangered children by letting them swim, you—"

"I did nothing of the sort!"

"And you let them swim topless."

"That's not true!"

"Individually, either of those episodes might merit disciplinary action. Together . . ."

"Together . . . what? Are you suggesting my job is in danger?"

"All I'm suggesting is that you should consider a leave of absence right now—over this picture. Nothing more."

Dana appeared in the hallway, drying her hands in a dish towel. Without speaking she mouthed the words *Is everything okay?* and her eyes were small rifts of concern.

"It's not an option, Judd, I'm sorry to disappoint you. If you investigate that field trip, you'll see it's a nonissue. A complete nonissue. And so while I appreciate your concern for my welfare, I am not taking a leave of absence, and I am not going to leave my classroom. Do you understand?"

A moment later, after we had both hung up, I allowed myself to fall into Dana's warm and sheltering arms. She told me later I was so mad I was shaking.

28

will

PATRICIA WAS GONE WHEN I GOT HOME SUNDAY
morning from Stratton, and I really wasn't surprised. Her note said
that she was with the Brighams, a family who lived in a restored farm-
house out in Waltham. Marshall Brigham worked in her law firm, and
she was friends with both Marshall and his wife. She said she'd prefer
that I didn't call her, and that she'd be back after work Monday night.
I noticed that she hadn't written she'd be *home* after work Monday
night. She had used the word *back,* which I concluded could mean
everything or nothing. Was her decision to not use the word *home* a
conscious signal that she no longer considered the house in which we
lived her home? Or was *back* the signal, and the word meant that she
planned on coming *back* to our marriage?

I decided I was probably reading way too much into the word
either way. For all I knew, she'd simply scribbled the note in half a
minute and hadn't been thinking about anything but the fact that she

was miserable and sad and she had to get out of the house that very moment.

And so I unpacked my small bag and read the mail that had arrived on Friday and Saturday. And then, because Allie will always be my best friend no matter who I am married to (or separating from), I called her to tell her that Patricia was gone until Monday, and I had a sick feeling that I was about to see my second marriage collapse.

"You probably don't want to rattle around your house all alone this evening. Would you like to come over here for dinner?" she asked.

I hesitated for a moment, wondering why I would want to have dinner at a table that would also include Allie's strange paramour. Had I really fallen so far so fast that I was about to turn for comfort to a support group of two that included our esteemed town's ultimate outcast? Maybe, I thought, I would be lucky and Dana would spend the whole time in the kitchen. Wasn't he the cook and cabana boy in their little arrangement? But then I recalled my conversation with Dana the night before on the telephone and remembered how, after the first minute or so, it really hadn't been all that awkward. Moreover, it was clear that there were people—including my own daughter—who could deal just fine with my Allie's new friend.

Consequently, I agreed, though not without healthy measures of both trepidation and self-loathing.

"Sure," I said. "Why not?" My voice sounded odd to me: simultaneously embarrassed and apprehensive.

"No reason. Dana's making a vegetarian lasagna."

"Okay," I said.

"It's a school night, so how's six o'clock?"

"Fine."

"Good. We'll see you then."

"You will," I said, and I hung up the phone. And then I turned on the radio and decided to change the sheets on the bed and vacuum the house. If Patricia decided, after all, to come home—to come back—and I wasn't there, I wanted to be sure that the house was inviting and clean.

❦

My radio instincts aren't brilliant, but I've been in the business for so many years that longevity alone has given me a reasonable sense of what will work and what won't. And Dana Stevens, I'd begun to think, would work well. Gender dysphoria, I'd decided, interested people—even if it repulsed them. Even if it angered them.

And, certainly, it angered Rebecca Barnard, my Wednesday-morning commentator.

"You can't be serious," she said when I told her my idea.

She'd finished taping her commentaries for the next two weeks, and we were sitting in my office having coffee, and watching small softballs of snow fall from the blue spruce trees outside my window. It was a week and a day since the Punxsutawney groundhog had retreated from the sight of his shadow, and the temperature was climbing into the high thirties for the first time in a month. It was glorious.

"I am."

"You're going to give him radio time?"

"Not just Dana. Dana and Allie. Maybe Dana and this Burlington support group. The Green Mountain Gender Benders, I think they're called. Maybe Dana and some doctor in Montreal who specializes in sexual reassignment."

"There's a doctor in Montreal who does that?"

"Yup. Dana said he's very good. Even considered using him. But the guy in Colorado had a lot more experience."

"God, experience. Gross. He'd hacked off more penises, you mean."

"Call it what you will."

"Do you know how many listeners you'll piss off?"

"Listeners like controversy, especially in the context of news. Listeners like conflict. And most of our listeners are pretty darn nice. Statistically, the vast majority of them disagree with every word you say, but still they tolerate you. Some, I'd wager, even enjoy you."

"I'm your voice of reason."

"Perhaps if you like Ethan Allen."

"Have you asked him about this? Have you talked to Allison?"

"Nope."

"What makes you think they'll do it? It sounds like they're already getting a lot more attention than they want. I understand there are a lot of angry parents in your peaceful little hamlet."

"I think that's exactly why they will do it. They can tell their side. They're both smart, charismatic people, and they'll sound great on the radio. And those nitwits I call neighbors will look like a lynch mob."

"Those nitwits are reasonable adults and concerned parents. And since when is there anything charismatic about a man in a dress?"

"Even if they're right," I said, referring to my neighbors, "they're still acting like nitwits."

"Someday I should do a commentary about him. Or, better still, about Allison. About the vital role of an elementary-school teacher in a small community."

My antennae had gone up the moment she said my ex-wife's name, but I was still confident she was merely trying to annoy me. "You do what you want," I said. "Just don't slander anybody."

"I wouldn't. You know that."

"Thank you."

"Though that would take all the fun out of it now, wouldn't it?"

"Probably."

She smiled. "Have you spoken to the illustrious Professor Stevens since he returned from Colorado?"

"Yup."

"I assume the surgery was successful?"

"Apparently."

"Appalling," she mumbled, shaking her head.

"In some ways. But you know what? We had dinner—"

"You had dinner?"

"Yes, we had dinner. A week ago Sunday."

"God, I wish I'd been a fly on the wall for that little outing. Was this in public?"

"No," I said, and then added, "Not that it would matter."

"Let me guess: at your ex-wife's?"

"Yes."

"I see. You weren't interested in seeing Professor Sex Change. He just happened to be at the table."

"I guess that's true," I said. I started to fold my arms across my chest, but stopped myself when I realized how defensive I'd look. From her years in the classroom, Rebecca Barnard was an expert on body language.

"And it was at that dinner that you concluded he'd be good on the radio?"

"It was," I said, nodding. I didn't volunteer the information that we'd spoken three times since then on the telephone, including once in the middle of the day when Allie wasn't even home.

All Things Considered
Thursday, September 27

DANA STEVENS: What was I feeling? Guilt, mostly. But not completely. I was angry, too.

I think I was angry that I was being made to feel guilty.

dana

WHEN LINDSEY LESSARD AND DAN HEDDERIGG were transferred into Carolyn Chapel's class, and when Audrey LaFontaine's parents withdrew their daughter from the public school, I offered to move out.

I volunteered again when Allison lost a little girl she liked very much named Chrystal. But Allison dug in her heels and insisted I stay. It became, in her mind, an act of principle.

"I really don't care about principles," I told her. "I care about you being happy. And you're not. You're miserable, and it's entirely my fault!"

"It's not," she said. "I don't want you to go anywhere. I'd be even more miserable if you left."

But the attrition in her classroom made her heartsick, and she was shattered by the mean-spirited way that Glenn Frazier and the school superintendent and even Carolyn Chapel were refusing to defend her.

I think the idea that Carolyn didn't stand by her was particularly dispiriting. Carolyn had been at the school for six years, and she had sufficient tenure there that she could have stubbornly refused to take in any more kids. The fact is, that's what the teachers association wanted her to do, and I think that's what they assumed she would do. Show a little solidarity. A little support. A little spine.

"I'm only trying to do what's best for the kids," she said to Allison. "I don't want to see Lindsey or Dan home-schooled. I don't think it's in their best interest."

I wanted to pick up the phone and tell her that it wasn't in the kids' best interest to grow up in a community of small-minded bigots either, but I held my tongue.

And so Carolyn got two more students, and the teacher's aide she had Tuesdays and Thursdays started coming five days a week. Somewhere the school board found the extra money in the budget. Imagine. And when the McCurdys and the Duncans heard that Carolyn Chapel now had a full-time aide, they had their children transferred into her class, too. It was appalling. I hate to even speculate about what the kids who were left with Allison must have been thinking. They'd seen a third of their class vanish into their homes or the room across the hall.

"Would you like me to write the superintendent? Or those people on the school board?" I asked Allison. "Teach them a little about gender dysphoria, maybe? Explain to them that I'm not some evil child abuser?"

But she said no, she couldn't believe that would help. Nor would she let me write letters to the editors of the local newspapers.

"In that case, maybe I should go to the next school board meeting," I suggested. "Maybe if we all had a chance to talk in person, they'd see that I'm not so bad. They could ask me questions."

But she declined that offer, too. She didn't say that my speaking out on her behalf would make things even more difficult, but it was clear that she felt that way.

"I don't think they'd listen to you," she said simply. "They'll see you in a dress—"

"I could wear slacks."

"They'll see you in women's clothes, and they won't hear a word you say. Whatever small part of their minds that might still be open will close up completely."

Meanwhile, some lackey from the superintendent's office interviewed the four parents who had chaperoned a field trip to the Lake Champlain Maritime Museum back in September—September, for God's sake!—to see if Allison had been encouraging the kids to swim the length of the lake in their Nikes and then strip for some prepubescent orgy. It was ridiculous, but the parents were interviewed separately over the course of a week. Then, when this mangy fellow was done with the parents, he started nagging the bus driver and some poor museum docent.

The purpose was evident: Stretch the "investigation" out as long as possible, and thereby inflict maximum torment upon the teacher. Make her so mad, perhaps, that she'd take that leave of absence and just go away.

But Allison was certainly not going to budge. And why should she? She hadn't done anything wrong! Her lawyer—whom she finally called and met with at some length—reassured her that she was on solid ground and she couldn't possibly be compelled to take a leave of absence against her will. At least not because of her transsexual girlfriend. She—Allison's lawyer—didn't believe the field trip would result in any sort of disciplinary action either, but she cautioned Allison to wait and see what the superintendent did next before responding. For all we knew, after talking to the parents who'd been with the kids at the lake, everyone would see that she'd acted responsibly and the trip had been harmless.

Inside our home I did what I could to make her happy, and that, at least, gave me some pleasure. I tried to make her house a secure little oasis in which she was pampered and pleasured and cared for. I wanted her to feel every moment that she was living with a person who loved her madly and saw her as the most beautiful creature on the planet.

Some days and nights, I think, I actually succeeded. Not all, but some. I think there may actually have been weekend mornings and weekday evenings when she was able to forget the way her professional life was unraveling. Of course, that may be a fantasy of my own. I'll never know for sure whether she was honest with me those nights when she would say she was fine and allow me to rub her back till she fell asleep, or whether she was just being kind.

I stopped going out in public in Bartlett. I thought that might help Allison.

I started doing the grocery shopping in Middlebury instead of at the Grand Union within walking distance of Allison's house. The Middlebury supermarket was exactly 17.4 miles from the edge of the driveway, and I never left once without checking the odometer so that my anger at the world would be fresh when I squeezed peaches and tossed toilet paper into the cart.

I no longer used the Bartlett post office or the hardware store, I no longer went to the local pharmacy. I had my prescriptions for my hormones transferred to the drugstore beside my new supermarket. I no longer even filled up my car at the gas station in town, or stopped there for mints or a magazine. I no longer went to the video store.

The damnedest thing was, by Valentine's Day I'd started to look pretty good. That's an awful thing to admit, but it's true. One morning when Allison was at school, a day or two before Valentine's Day, I finally had the courage to swing open the full-length mirror on the back of the closet door in our bedroom and stand before it bare naked.

Not buck naked, obviously. This is a semantic difference of some importance to me.

But I stripped off my sweater and my blouse and my leggings, and I pulled off my panties and my bra. And then I surveyed the goods.

I knew my vagina was coming along nicely, because I saw enough of it every day during dilation. It had the dreamy, flowery look of endive, or the abstruse but beautiful edging of the bud vase that might come with a Middle Eastern princess's breakfast tray. My biggest— only, really—concern with it aesthetically? In the little thicket of pubic hair that was returning I had counted a half dozen gray strands. Not quite thirty-six years old, I thought, and I have to start thinking about hoary pubes.

Certainly there were other things that I knew about my transformed body, too. I could see my arms were ungainly for a woman—not chimpy, but a tad longer than I would have liked. I understood that my feet were large, though my ankles were oddly, unexpectedly exquisite. And I knew that I now wore a B-cup bra, because I'd bought Allison and me some new lingerie at the end of January to cheer us both up.

But I hadn't really studied my breasts, or considered them in the context of my whole physique. I hadn't explored my new body *in toto*.

I'm sure there are myriad reasons for that, but the big one was fear. Pure and simple, I'd been afraid to strip and stand nude before a mirror and really examine how I looked post-op. After all, I'd done virtually everything I could now with the unit I'd been given at birth, I'd gone about as far as possible. Oh, there might be minor surgical alterations, there might be forays into the health club (though sure as hell not the one in Bartlett), and there might be diets. But this was pretty much the body that was going to take me through middle age and then start to sag and fall apart.

As Valentine's Day approached, however, I finally decided to take the plunge. The little holiday would fall on a Friday, and it crossed my mind that it might be as good a date as any to allow Allison to touch my new vagina—that is, of course, if she had any inclination. Though I'd been making love to her for almost a month, it was only in the last week or so that my own libido had returned, and my Meehan-made vulva had come of age and was now ready for its metaphoric deflowering.

And so I peeled, prepared for all manner of disappointment and emotional devastation.

Instead I was pleasantly surprised. Really. I noticed instantly that my nipples were much smaller than a genetic woman's, and the areolae—though a shade of bay that was not unlike Allison's—were flatter. Flatter in dimension, and flatter in shade. But my breasts were a delight. They were—dare I say it?—downright perky. Let's face it, they were as new as a teenager's and so they had an unfair advantage over their generational peers. They floated before me just below the yoke of my collarbone, two happy orbs still oblivious to the ravages of gravity.

I didn't have womanly hips—which, ironically, would probably have made some genetic females jealous of me—and so a part of me would have liked a few extra inches down there. My figure was slender, but it wasn't the hourglass I'd been trained to worship.

My tummy was flat and firm, and my legs were hard-body luscious. Long, too.

I liked what I saw, I realized, I liked it a lot. Really, I did. I looked good: Womanly. Feminine. Ladylike.

And sexy as hell. Honest to God.

Forgive me, but it's an amazing sensation to feel for the first time that you are an object worthy of some desire. Especially when you don't feel such a thing until you're knocking on the door of thirty-six.

There were people who stuck up for Allison. All those parents who kept their children in her class showed their support. A lot of them may have signed that despicable petition—most of them, actually, a legitimate majority—but they weren't about to give up the chance to have their kids taught by Allison Banks.

And there were the now-over-the-hill, former hippies. Allison and Will were only two of the dozens of Middlebury and UVM graduates who'd settled in Bartlett. The hippies had begun arriving in the late 1960s and early 1970s, a decade before Allison and Will, and lots of them had chosen to stay. They'd taken their prestigious degrees and gone back to the land on the defunct dairy farms in the area. They'd built geodesic domes, they'd married, they'd divorced and married again. They'd faced middle age, usually with rebellious teens of their own, and then had to figure out what it meant to grow up and old all at once. Few of them worked in Bartlett, but almost all of them had impressive jobs in Burlington, Montpelier, or Middlebury. Some were successful entrepreneurs, and some were lawyers. Others opened funky clothing boutiques and trendy restaurants. Some became architects.

And, bless their hearts, many of them defended Allison Banks's right to live with a transsexual lesbian. They wrote letters to the school board and to the despotic pinhead who ran her school, and they started a petition of their own—copying exactly the first paragraph from the original petition:

> We, the undersigned, believe that teachers are role models. Their behavior in the classroom and their behavior in their community influences the children in their care.
>
> We therefore support teachers like Allison Banks: Teachers who are tolerant and open-minded; teachers who have the courage of their convictions; and teachers who are receptive to the many kinds of beauty that can be found on this planet.

The wording in the second paragraph was a little too goopy for my taste—a little too peace-love-and-tie-dye—but the sentiments behind it made me weepy. I was very, very happy for Allison.

Allison, on the other hand, had decidedly mixed emotions about the petition. A big part of her was extremely uncomfortable with the notion that her name was in it. Certainly she knew she was a *cause célèbre,* especially after that noxious doctrinaire of a principal had suggested in the school's newsletter to parents that she was getting obscene hate mail in her own classroom. But at that point she still didn't want to see her plight become any more public than it already was, and clearly she didn't want to be viewed as some standard bearer for gender tolerance. The personal, in this case, was anything but political, particularly since she'd first fallen in love with a person she had assumed to be male.

The second petition didn't get nearly as many signatures as the first, but that was due at least in part to Allison's reluctance to allow anyone to go house to house with it, or to solicit signatures in the grocery store parking lot. The petition simply sat on clipboards at the front register of the health-food store and the little bookstore in town, shops with clienteles somewhat more sympathetic to Allison's situation. No one ever actually asked anyone to sign it. Still, close to two hundred people eventually penciled their names and addresses on the little black lines under the second paragraph.

The pastor at Allison's church also stood by her. He was an elderly gentleman who was considered somewhat conservative among Baptist ministers in northern New England, but he thought the world of Allison and Carly. And so he and his wife came to her house for brunch after church on the last Sunday in January, walking there directly from the sanctuary so everyone in the center of town could see them. Then, a week later, he devoted his sermon to that beautiful moment in Acts when Philip baptizes the eunuch.

And the newspapers in Burlington and Middlebury both ran editorials that were sharply critical of Glenn Frazier, Judd Prescott, and the school board for allowing students to transfer from Allison's class into Carolyn's. The Burlington paper even chastised those parents who withdrew their children—though, of course, they didn't actually rebuke anybody by name.

My sense is that Allison and I would have been a very big local news story those first months after we returned from Colorado if either of us had been willing to speak to reporters. But we refused. We refused the *Burlington Free Press* and we refused the *Addison Independent*. We passed when a writer from an alternative weekly in Chittenden County phoned us, and when a reporter from the Montpelier daily paper showed up at our door. We said no to the NBC television affiliate, and we said no to the two radio talk-show hosts who called. We both wanted our privacy, and we both expected that eventually the tempest around us would pass. Maybe I just had to lie low a little while. Maybe if we could reach the end of the school year without a major explosion, people's interest would dissipate over the summer. Maybe, just maybe, people would grow to like me.

People, after all, had seemed to like me just fine in the years before my sexual reassignment.

Were we kidding ourselves? Perhaps. But I just wanted to get on with my life as a female—I certainly didn't want to remind people that I'd been born with male genitalia—and Allison simply wanted her old life back. She wanted nothing more than to teach, and visit with friends, and (I like to believe) relax in the evenings with the woman she loved.

And while people who listened to Vermont Public Radio that March might have assumed it was the obscenity someone had spray-painted on our front door that changed all that—that made us both willing to talk to the media—the truth is, we had changed our minds five days before we discovered what some horrible person had done. The front door had been vandalized on February 21, and we had found it on the twenty-second. But we had already agreed to go public on the seventeenth, one of the nights Will Banks had come to our house for dinner that month, and the very evening he had proposed his idea for a story.

"You *are* beautiful," Allison whispered to me in our bed on Valentine's Day, just after she pulled away from my mouth. I opened my eyes and looked up at her, and despite what I'd seen of myself in the mirror, I knew I wasn't nearly as lovely as she. Wasn't possible. She was smiling, the light from the candle dancing across her cheeks, but there was something going on in her eyes I couldn't quite decipher, a mystery in the tiny lines emerging along the sides of her face.

She rested her weight on her elbows and combed my hair with her fingers and then closed her eyes and kissed me again. I tasted blue-berry brandy. I allowed myself a small purr. And then through the silk of my chemise I felt her running her fingers gently over my nipples, and down my ribs and my abdomen until she reached the hem at the end of the material. The hem at the end of the world, I thought. There's no place else to go but . . . there.

I was wrong, and she dallied along the insides of my thighs a long while, sliding her body down mine so she could rub my legs and caress my ass with both of her hands and with her tongue. I spread my legs for her, telling her it was okay, signaling her that I was ready if she was.

She put one of her lovely slender fingers into my mouth, and I sucked it for a long while. She gave me a second, and I sucked them together, coating them both with all the saliva I could muster.

That night she made love to me with fingers steeped in spit, and with a little pink vibrator coated with orange-scented lube. I didn't come, but it didn't matter. It all felt heavenly, especially the notion that I was spreading my legs and there was a vagina—moistened and open and just oozing with nerves—telling my lover I loved her.

"God, I adore you," I murmured later when we were lying in each other's arms. My thigh was snuggling against her vulva, and her thigh was nestling beside mine.

"I know," she said softly. "I know you do."

She smiled at me again, and without any design revealed the otherwise inexpressible secret that was lurking in her eyes: She was sad. She was pitifully, earnestly, seriously sad.

Misery had softened Will Banks. Made him a whole lot nicer. Who knows? Maybe every arrogant man simply needs a good woman to humble him once in a while by walking out—though in Will's case, I guess, it took two.

But when he came to our house for dinner for the third time in two weeks, he actually extended his hand to me and gave it an appropriately gentle squeeze. And then he hugged me. He sure as hell wouldn't have done that when he'd joined us for lasagna two weeks earlier.

"That's a beautiful headband," he added, and I was flattered. "Blue and yellow look nice in your hair."

Granted, Allison got a much bigger and longer hug than I did, but the two of them had a lot more history together. I think it was in fact that evening that for the first time I really saw the friendship that had developed over the years between Will Banks and Allison, and finally understood it. After all, that first evening he joined us for dinner was the weekend Patricia had left, and he was just a basket case. The second time, too. Mostly, Allison was offering him emotional triage.

When he had dinner with us that third time, however, he was already pulling himself together and preparing to get on with a new phase in his life. There was a big cutout in the wall between the kitchen and the den, and I watched them chatting while I finished preparing dinner. They looked almost like siblings.

At least that's what I told myself then. God forbid they should look like lovers. The last thing I wanted was to somehow effect a reconciliation between my girlfriend and her ex-husband. I know well how distress can breed romance—I don't especially like support groups, but I know what can happen—and those two people were certainly in the midst of periods in their lives that could only be called blue. And so when I saw the two of them reminiscing about their years in college together or pondering the self-possessed young woman who was in actuality their daughter, I had a few pangs of apprehension: As I peeled the pears for the fruit salad. As I set the table. As I opened a second bottle of wine.

The two of them seemed to laugh so easily together that I actually felt guilty about the way my presence had strained their relationship throughout the fall.

Dinner, however, reassured me. Allison sat at the head of the table, surrounded on either side by her current and her former lover, and she sat just a hair closer to me. Twice she stroked the back of my hand when she spoke, and she squeezed it lovingly during dessert, after she tasted the white chocolate mousse.

Will was charming, and downright chivalrous when he talked about Patricia. Penitent, too. He understood what mistakes he had made, and his self-deprecation was utterly endearing.

But he hadn't come to see us to discuss the wreck of his marriage. He'd come to our house to talk about radio. Midway through dinner he brought up his idea for a program about us, and I was fascinated by the way his hands and face were transformed when the subject changed from the turmoil in his personal world to his professional passion. Suddenly his hands came to life. I realized that prior to that moment he hadn't once used his hands or his fingers when he'd spoken: It was as if he was conditioned from two decades in radio to understand that hands weren't helpful in conversation.

But clearly I was wrong. He was simply more restrained—his

hands, too—when he was talking about himself. When the subject was radio or radio programming, however, he was like an orchestra conductor: His eyes grew animated and his head practically swayed with enthusiasm. He put his knife and his fork down and leaned into the table when he first began outlining his concept, and his fingers practically danced with excitement. All ten of them. It was like he was playing the dining room air.

When he was done, I was sold. I don't court publicity, but I saw the short series as a wonderful way to defend my ladylove. I know, that sounds butch. But it's exactly how I felt. I was looking for the chance—any chance—to do something to help.

Allison, on the other hand, was somewhat less enthusiastic. "Absolutely not," she said.

"Think about it. Just think about it for a few days," Will said.

"No. Absolutely not," she said again.

"Okay," Will said, and he leaned back in his chair, and his hands and his face wilted. He picked up his fork and returned to the curried carrots.

"These really are delicious," he told me.

I wasn't surprised by Allison's aversion to the notion of a radio story, but I was shocked by how quickly Will had backed down.

"Allison," I said, "this is a great opportunity. This is a chance to make the world see how horribly you've been treated!"

"Why do I want to advertise that?"

"Because people shouldn't be allowed to treat you that way."

"Our lives are private."

"People shouldn't be allowed to treat *anyone* that way," I said.

"I would think you'd be used to all this," she said.

"Dear heart, I didn't mean me. I meant your students. That Lindsey Lessard child you care so much about. That Audrey LaFontaine. They've lost a great teacher."

"Your opinion. There are parents who'd disagree with you."

"Oh, Allison, all I'm saying is that there's a human cost here, and we're not the only humans involved. But we are the only ones who can present a certain perspective. People need to know what you're feeling.

What I'm feeling."

"I really don't want to be a poster child."

"And I don't think Dana is saying you should be," Will said. "But she's right. There are people behaving very badly in this town, and if the rest of the state knew you—and I mean both of you—I think it would shame some of our neighbors into decency."

Allison and I didn't look at each other as he spoke; I don't think either of us wanted to call attention to what had just transpired. But we'd both heard it, we'd both caught it. *She's.* Will had used a feminine pronoun. He had referred to me as a woman.

It was that moment, I believe, that changed Allison's mind about being interviewed. Not the horrid piece of paper someone slipped into her in-box, not the frustrating meetings she seemed to have to endure almost weekly. Not the vicious graffito that would appear a few days later on the front door. It was the realization that she was no longer alone when she looked at me and saw a woman.

allison

WE HELD A TALENT SHOW THAT YEAR TOWARD the end of February to break up the monotony of winter. We'd never had one before, but one of the teachers and I—for wholly different reasons, of course—were feeling that the season had conspired with the town to make winter seem particularly claustrophobic, and we needed to do something to take our minds off the cold and the snow and the ubiquitous road salt.

Glenn Frazier was comfortable with the idea, but when we were alone he told me that he had heard rumblings about some skit one group of my sixth-graders had performed some time ago during the annual end-of-the-year production for parents.

"It wasn't some skit," I said. "It was the finale. And it wasn't a small group. It was my entire class."

"They were in bathing suits?"

"And grass skirts. We were doing African dancing."

"Well, just remember. We live in rural Vermont."

I restrained myself from reminding him that I'd lived in Bartlett far longer than he. Instead I reassured him: "It'll be fine. Everyone will have a wonderful evening."

The kids were always given a fair amount of rope to do whatever they desired in those June performances, though we adults always worked with them to make sure that their dancing or their skit had at least a semblance of choreography and cohesion. But it was still a pretty casual affair, and that was pretty much what happened that February.

A group of the youngest girls in the school who took ballet together in Middlebury did a few twirls and pirouettes, while their male classmates jumped around the stage like movie ninjas. A few children played the piano, and one little girl played the flute with her mother. Twin boys played the violin.

A fifth-grade class that was in the midst of a unit on global climate change performed a truly disarming skit about the frightening numbers of three-legged frogs that were being discovered throughout the Lake Champlain Basin. A fourth-grade class built a sugar house onstage out of cardboard, and wrote two surprisingly clever songs about maple syrup and mud—without question, Vermont's two most salient features in March.

"Busby Berkeley Visits the Ozarks," Dana dubbed that part of the production later that night, but she did admit that the kids looked pretty cute when they danced around in their mud boots and checked flannel shirts. She watched the show from the back corner of the auditorium, standing in the dark about six feet from a lit exit sign. She wanted to come, but she didn't want to be seen. And so she arrived a few minutes late and left a few minutes early, which meant, unfortunately, that she missed the curtain call.

My own students had wanted to do something to support me, but I had refused to allow them. I didn't want them any more involved in my situation than they already were by the nature of the fact that they'd wound up in my class six months earlier. Instead the group fixated upon aliens (Was there a connection in their opinion between my situation and a Martian's? They denied that they thought so) and asked me to help them develop a series of hip-hop moves that would, they hoped, look slightly robotic. I did, and the skit went off without a hitch.

But then there was the curtain call. I was working backstage, and after the final sketch I went to help Molly Cochran round up her six-year-olds. My eleven-year-olds, I knew, were capable of marching back onto the stage in a line, holding hands, and bowing once or twice during their parents' applause. We'd gone over it during the dress rehearsal, and it was clear that they understood the drill.

Besides, most of them were veterans of the June theatricals.

Consequently, I was as surprised as the audience when my entire class—granted, it was a small class by then—reappeared on the polyurethaned wood floor in drag. All of the girls had changed into pants and were wearing their fathers' neckties and blazers, and Sally Warwick and Renee Wood had gone so far as to paint black mustaches just above their lips with eyeliner. And the boys? There was Jeremy Roscoe in his big sister's field hockey kilt, and Schuyler Brown in what must have been one of his mother's summer skirts. Ethan LaPree had climbed inside a dress that was covered with sunflowers, and Sam Reynolds—my gifted young mathematician—had found a blond wig somewhere and was wearing a hoop in each ear the size of a bracelet.

They paraded onto the stage with the rest of the kids as if there was nothing unusual about their costumes, and for the first time in my life I understood that expression about a lump in one's throat. Somehow, swallowing and weeping were connected.

"You did okay with those kids, Allison," Molly whispered beside me, and she patted my back.

In the audience, small groups of parents stood up for them, and others whistled and hooted. The boys in the dresses loved it, and Schuyler and Ethan and Jeremy did a few kicks together as if they were cancan dancers or Rockettes.

"I'm going to assume you had nothing to do with this," Glenn Frazier said to me. His hands were clasped behind his back, and he looked more bemused than disgusted.

"Of course not," I managed to murmur, though I was still unsure what would happen when I opened my mouth.

"Didn't think so," he said.

I realized I was very lucky that moment to be a sixth-grade teacher. The girls, of course, would wear masculine shirts and pants at least some days for the rest of their lives. But the boys? If they had been a single year older and started junior high school, they wouldn't have been caught dead in women's clothes. Likewise, if they'd been a year or two younger, they wouldn't have had the confidence and the wherewithal to pull off this sort of statement.

At eleven, however, for both the boys and the girls the absurdity of dress was still clear. It was all costume. It was still fun to dress up. It just didn't matter if the person with whom I lived happened to outfit herself in what we called a blouse or a shirt, pants or a skirt. It was, most of the time, all just denim and cotton and wool.

When we finally pulled the curtain shut in front of the kids, my students ran to me, giggling and giving one another high fives as they approached.

"How do I look?" Ethan LaPree asked.

I bent over slightly so we were at eye level. "I think yellow's your color," I said as earnestly as I could. "And sunflowers in February are a very cheery statement. Thank you."

He shrugged, and before I could say another word to Ethan, I had to compliment all of the boys in their dresses and all of the girls in their pants, and then—at their insistence—take a group picture for the class photo album.

"Were you surprised?" Sally Warwick asked me.

"Absolutely," I said.

She grinned, and she was still blinking from the flash. For a moment the image was strobelike, surreal—a scene from a film from the Weimar Republic. *Cabaret* done by dwarfs. But the moment passed, and suddenly Sally was once again just a smart little girl with a drawn-on mustache. I hugged her and she hugged me, and then I embraced every single one of my students.

The next morning, we found the words on the door. Dana discovered them just before breakfast, when she was getting the daily paper out of the newspaper box.

I'll never know if it was a response to my students' show of support the night before—a message, perhaps, to remind me that though a dozen eleven-year-olds were on my side, a large part of the town was still very angry—or simple coincidence.

Saturday morning we had woken up together, happier than we'd been in a very long time. Dana was disappointed that she'd gone home before the curtain call, but she was nevertheless touched. I think she even thought we might have begun winning over some of the more reactionary personalities in town. Certainly that hope had crossed my mind.

But then we wandered downstairs, and I shuffled into the kitchen to make a pot of coffee and warm up the banana muffins Dana had baked the day before, and she went outside to retrieve our newspaper. When she joined me in the kitchen, I could see instantly that she was seething: Her eyes were slits and she was red in the face.

"What?" I asked. "What happened?"

She rolled the newspaper into a tube—a baton as thick as a baseball bat—and swatted the top slat of a ladder-back chair.

"People are pigs," she said. "They disgust me. This provincial piece-of-shit town disgusts me. You know what? We really should move. Get the hell out of here. Get the hell out of Bartlett. Out of Vermont. Go where nobody has the slightest idea who we are," she raged, and then she sat down in the chair and put her head on the table.

"Outside?" I asked, and I motioned toward the street. I understood that whatever had happened had happened outdoors—someone had said something to her, perhaps, or shouted something at her—but she'd revealed little else.

"God, I'd clean it off before you could see it," she continued. "But I can't. It's dry. It's paint, and it's dry. We'll probably need a new door."

I put down the butter dish and left her in the kitchen. I tried to look calm, which meant walking down the hallway, though I wanted to run. When I swung open the front door, I saw there were two words spray-painted upon it in massive red letters, and for a second I assumed I was reading a pair of nouns—oddly, it seemed, a singular and a plural—but then I realized the first word was meant to be an adjective.

A part of me wanted to curl up in the cold on the stoop; a part of me wanted to roll into a little ball and close my eyes, hoping—like a child—that when I opened them it would be gone. I'd never seen such a thing written so big. But it was a small part of me, and mostly I was fine. Really. Maybe if Dana hadn't been so angry that she was close to tears, I might have lost my composure. But I doubt it. Instead I simply closed the door and took a deep breath and then returned to the kitchen.

"It's completely inarticulate," I said. "We'll just paint over it."

"It's February! It's too cold to paint over it!"

"We'll put a heater on the porch. We'll—"

"We can't make it go away! Not till the spring! Don't you see? You can spray something like that on a door in this weather, but you can't really . . . paint."

Perhaps I would have been as enraged as Dana if I hadn't already been called a pervert in my own classroom. If I hadn't already found myself referred to as a kind of obscenity. Perhaps the Internet picture someone had left in my in-box had helped to prepare me for the affront on my house.

But I think there's also a chance I would have been fine even without that warm-up, or without the need to be strong for Dana. The night before, I'd been given a gift by my students that made the slur on the door seem particularly small-minded and stupid. Juvenile. The night before, my students had shown me they cared for me, regardless of what the adults around them may have thought, or what their peers may have been saying.

Moreover, I realized with an almost intellectual detachment that the two words on the wood had far more power when they were used separately. Individually, each was offensive—one was probably the word most universally and thoroughly despised by women. God knows it had always made me bristle. And the other, though less potent, certainly had the potential to generate a good amount of hostility in heterosexual men.

But together? They were by no means laughable. But they were also oxymoronic. Implausible. And, in a way, as silly as they were grim:

FAGGOT CUNTS

"We will cover it up," I said to Dana, and I pulled a chair beside her and sat down. "I'm sure the hardware store will have something."

"God, it's horrid. Horrid!"

"Seriously, it won't be that difficult to cover up. Trust me, I'm sure."

"It's just so mean. Why would someone do such a thing?"

"You know the answer to that."

"Really, I don't."

"Well, trust me: The hardware store will have a solution. It will."

She sighed. "I hope so. God, I hope so."

"It will."

She put her head on my shoulder and I stroked her hair. "Why do you put up with me?" she asked.

"You bake," I said. "I don't."

"Seriously. Look what I've—"

I put two fingers on her lips to shush her. And then I resumed petting the back of her head, and I tried to focus on nothing but the extraordinary softness of her hair and the smell of the freshly brewed coffee that was filling my kitchen.

All Things Considered
Thursday, September 27

DANA STEVENS: The thing is, I never was one of those Times Square transsexuals. It's not like I was hanging around street corners in Bartlett or Burlington, dressed like a slut and trying to seduce mixed-up teenage boys.

Or, I imagine, mixed-up grown men. The sexually . . . confused. I never was the sort of transsexual—the sort of *person*—who abused people, or tried to take advantage of them.

Of course I knew transsexuals like that. I knew—I know—prostitutes. I know transsexuals who will do whatever it takes to get the money they need for their reassignment, and I know transsexuals who are simply so . . . bewildered by their own sexuality that they're content to fill their bodies with female hormones, and keep their penises intact. They'll seduce anything that moves.

But there are people who aren't transsexuals who are like that. Not straight, not gay, not bi. Omnisexual, I guess. Megasexual.

Either way, that's not me. I've always been as domestic as a balloon shade or a perennial garden. And just as harmless.

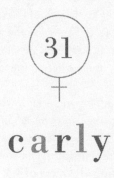

carly

MY VIDEO ABOUT THE BATTERY FACTORY WON A college journalism award that spring, and the local PBS station wanted to air it until I told them I hadn't gotten release forms from the people I interviewed. To this day, my dad says it's that prize that got me the NPR internship, but I think he could have gotten me the gig no matter what. He's very well-connected, and I really did have honest-to-God radio experience. Besides—and maybe this isn't beside the fact at all—I was willing to work for peanuts.

Still, I was very proud of that award, and when I came home for a weekend early in March, my dad and my mom and Dana took me out to dinner. We went to a "bistro" in Montpelier because, my dad said, it was the very best restaurant in the state. Personally, I think we went there because he still wasn't wild about being seen with Dana in public: There wasn't an overhead light in the whole dining room, and the place was forty-two miles from Bartlett.

Actually, 42.5: My dad's pretty compulsive, and he set the digital tripometer in his Explorer before we left Bartlett early Saturday night.

Nevertheless, I was surprised that my dad was even willing to have Dana along for the celebration—and, likewise, that Dana even wanted to eat a meal with my dad. Apparently, however, in February the two had become downright chummy. Maybe *chummy* isn't the right word, because it makes it sound like they would have played golf together if there hadn't been eleven feet of snow on the ground. But it was clear that they were no longer at odds, and people who didn't know their history together might even have gotten the idea into their heads that they were friends.

After all, it was my dad, my mom said, who had arrived at Mom's house the Saturday morning after the talent show with a kerosene heater and a big can of Bulls Eye Primer Sealer Stain Killer, and set up shop on the front steps. He and Dana worked a good part of the day together, first covering all traces of the obscenity on the door, and then—I guess since they had the heater and all that sealer—scraping and priming the wooden banister that hadn't been painted in years.

Throughout the month, the two had continued to get to know each other. Once Patricia had decided to move out, my dad ate dinner more and more often at Mom's. And in the last week of February, my dad and Dana spent a fair amount of time together because of the radio tapings. The radio series hadn't aired yet when I came home in March, but the interviews were complete and the key segments had been cued. The station was planning to air the story over two nights in the middle of the month.

Still, I wasn't prepared to see my dad and Dana hanging together like in-laws. That's really what it felt like in the car: Dad and Mom and Aunt Dana. Ol' Aunt Dana: my mom's sister, Dad's big buddy.

Was this wishful thinking? I guess. I was nineteen, but apparently on some level I was still harboring delusions that my mom and dad were going to reconcile someday. And the seating in the car didn't help. It was my dad's car, so he was driving, and because I was the youngest, I climbed into the back before anyone could stop me. It seemed like the natural thing to do.

And Dana certainly wasn't about to sit in the front seat, so she got in with me. The result? My mom and dad were together in the front seat, and Dana and I were in the back. It felt very fifties. Me and my maiden aunt.

Yet the strangest moment of the night wouldn't occur until we were back in Bartlett. Dinner had actually seemed pretty normal. My dad got a bottle of champagne to toast to my award, and the waitress at the restaurant looked the other way when he poured the bubbly into my water goblet. Dana translated for all of us the two items on the menu that we couldn't decipher.

Midway through the meal my head was so fuzzy from the alcohol— I've never been able to hold my liquor—that I almost told Dana how well she passed. She was looking, I realized, less and less like an aunt and more and more like a sister. My sister. I knew she was thirty-five, but she now looked considerably younger. She looked closer to my age than to my parents'; she certainly appeared a lot more than seven years younger than my mom.

And, I realized, she was beautiful. Really beautiful. A stunner. Her skin was softer and smoother than mine, and it practically glowed with good health. And so while there may have been diners in the restaurant who thought she was my aunt and diners who assumed she was my sister, there wasn't a soul in the place who didn't think she was a lovely young woman.

Yet it wasn't then that I realized my dad might now have seen her that way, too. That wouldn't happen until we got back to Bartlett and he was dropping the three of us off at my mom's house. That was the moment that to this day has struck me as so bizarre.

We pulled into the driveway, and my mom invited my dad in for a drink. At first he said that would be nice, and he got out of the car with all us gals and started up the bluestone walkway with us. But then he stopped midway between his car and the door and said he should probably take a pass.

"It's fine to come in, Will," my mom said, wondering exactly as I was why he had changed his mind so suddenly.

Did she then follow his eyes and see what I did? I doubt it; she doesn't think like that. But maybe she did. We never talked about it.

"No, I think I'll go home and get some sleep. I'm really very tired," he said, and he gave me a hug. For the first time in maybe half a minute he took his eyes off the front steps about fifteen or twenty feet away, and the image of Dana that was there. She hadn't bothered to put her coat back on for the walk from the car to the house, and so she was standing on the top step in her leather boots and her skirt and her blouse. The porch light was casting her face in shadow but silhouetting the shape of her breasts, and I swear she looked like a fashion model. Tall and slim and proud. She was, without any intent at all, radiating sexuality like the confident, seductive women of all ages who fill the ad pages at the front of glossy magazines. *Vogue. Mirabella. Vanity Fair.*

She was prettier than my mother, she was prettier than me.

And while I don't think my dad made those sorts of comparisons, he couldn't help but notice she was gorgeous. He couldn't help but see, suddenly, that she was almost too beautiful to be around.

In Plato's *Symposium,* Pausanias tells his drinking buddies that homosexual love is inspired by the "heavenly Aphrodite," the daughter of Uranus, and is far superior to heterosexual—or "common"—love. Gay lovers are in their way, therefore, the progeny of Uranus.

We read *The Symposium* in a philosophy class, and of course every straight boy in the lecture hall thought Plato's inadvertent pun was a howl: *Of course queer partners would turn to your anus!*

But from a digression in the course I learned the tidbit that Uranus was in fact the origin of the word some transsexuals use to describe themselves: *urnings.*

"It rhymes with yearnings, doesn't it? I think I like it," Dana said when I shared with her my newfound knowledge. The term was a revelation to her, and so I felt very special when I unveiled it. "It's downright onomatopoetic," she added.

"It sounds to me like a kind of turtle."

"A baby turtle."

"It was actually a pretty common word in late-nineteenth-century

Germany. It seems there was a big homosexual-rights movement there a century ago."

"Big, perhaps, but apparently not very successful. I guess that little scuffle in Sarajevo deflected attention."

We were sitting in the den at opposite ends of the big couch after our dinner in Montpelier, sipping orange spice tea. My mom had gone straight to bed, and I had felt badly for Dana. She'd seemed so awake. And so I'd offered to keep her company for a few minutes.

"A world war will do that," I agreed.

We were both quiet for a long moment, and I was very content. The room was warm and outside it felt like spring wasn't too many weeks in the distance.

"She goes to bed early often these days," Dana said, staring down into her mug, and I was surprised by her candor. She had confessed this to me as if she were admitting a personal failure.

"This is the low point of the school year for her—in terms of energy," I said. It was an ad-lib, but I didn't think it was half-bad. "There's still a long way to go, and she's exhausted from the winter."

She had kicked off her boots in the front hall, and for a brief second my perception of Dana as a mesmerizing beauty was shattered, since her feet were almost as big as my dad's. But then she curled up her legs underneath her and once more she was that striking woman from dinner. The one who was complicating my mom's life, and I could tell was worried now that she was going to lose her.

"You're sweet," she said, but she sighed.

"It's the truth."

"We'll see."

"Really," I went on. "Spring's coming. That always cheers her."

"This weather is just a tease. A brief thaw."

"Before you know it, you'll be having sugar on snow at somebody's sugar house. Maybe the Murphys'. My mom likes the Murphys." Every year the Murphys invited us to watch them boil maple sap into syrup, and we'd drizzle the hot sugar onto the snow. It was delicious.

Along with the sugar runs, of course, there would be mud. Weeks of quicksand and slop. And though the first crocuses would soon rise from the flat, brown grass and open themselves up to the sun, soon after that they'd be pummeled by snow. It was inevitable. A crocus lives a short, hard life in Vermont. Tulips do better, but the tulips wouldn't arrive for at least another five weeks. Maybe six. They came at the end of the spring.

The last time there had been tulips, I realized, I had broken up with my boyfriend. That was how long it had been since I'd been involved. Almost a year.

"I think there's more to it than cabin fever," Dana said.

I shrugged. "Even if there is, I wouldn't worry. My mom is who she is, and there's not a thing you can do about it. You can't change her." There was a boy at Bennington who wanted to get serious with me, and we'd slept together twice in February. He was from a suburb of New York City, and his hair was a nuclear shade of orange. All of his courses freshman year had focused on biology and theater, which was actually a pretty normal combination for Bennington. But I just wasn't all that passionate about him. At least not yet. I thought he was cute underneath that hair, but I had a hard time seeing past all the henna.

"You're a very wise girl."

"I just know my mom. I just know how Banks females think."

"Are we growing apart? Is it possible?"

"She'd have told you if you were. Honest. My mom has never been afraid to end a relationship."

"This is different."

I understood, and I nodded. Breaking up in this case would be tan-tamount to capitulation. It would allow all those parents who had taken their children out of my mom's class to conclude that they had been right; it would allow the awful people who had spray-painted an obscenity on her door to believe that they'd won. It would give license to the hundreds of adults who'd signed what my mom had come to call the "perversion advocacy petition" to presume that she agreed now that she had made a colossal mistake—that she fathomed the error of her ways and she saw how clouded her judgment had been.

"This is very, very different," she repeated.

"My mom's tough."

"She is," Dana said, and then she looked at me intensely, her eyes just barely above the lip of her mug. "But the fact is, she didn't grow up as an . . . urning. She never had to develop an urning's protective shell."

The next day, I asked my mom what she thought caused someone to become a transsexual.

"Ask Dana," she said.

"I will," I agreed. "Still: Tell me what you think."

We were walking around the green late Sunday morning, listening to the sounds of snow melting. Water running from the roofs to the rain gutters. Water flowing by the curb along the side of the road. Water splashing under tires and dogs' paws, and under the boots of the little kids who suddenly were everywhere. Winter was clearly coming apart, and I don't think it could have begun to end at a better time for my mom.

"I don't think transsexuals *become,*" she said. "I think they just *are.*"

"They're born?"

"They're born. It's not like Dana's mother or father did something wrong, or made some horrible mistake while they were raising him as a boy. It's not like, I don't know, they gave him the wrong toys when he was a boy growing up."

"What do they think of Dana's decision? Do you know?"

"Well, I gather they're not very happy about it. But they don't blame themselves. They once did, apparently. At least her mother did. Her mother was convinced it was all her fault. She'd drunk too much when she was pregnant, and the alcohol had damaged some chromosome. Or she'd paid too much attention to Dana when she was little. Or she hadn't paid enough attention."

"But they got over it?"

"Well, they say they have."

"I'm glad for them."

"Me too. Though Dana does believe her mother has a screw loose."

"Really?"

"Uh-huh. But I think that's natural. All children think their parents are nuts. I assume my mother's nuts. Don't you think I am?"

"Gee, Mom, why would I think that? Just because you invited a transsexual to move in with you?"

"See what I mean?"

"But you believe it's biological—being a transsexual?"

"Yup," she answered, and she shrugged. "There are those theories about the size of some part of the brain. And there are people who say it's a chemical thing. Or a chromosome thing. Who knows? Maybe someday when they finish that human genome project, they'll have found the 'transsexual gene.' Or genes. But my sense is, whatever it is that makes someone gender dysphoric—I have no idea if that's a real word, but you get my drift—it probably begins with nature. Not nurture."

"Hemingway's mom always put dresses on him when he was a little boy. Really frilly dresses. Made him look like a little girl."

"Your point?"

"There's a lot of transgender role-playing in *The Garden of Eden*."

"Really?"

"At least in bed. And at the barbershop. We read the novel last month." It dawned on me that transsexual literature was peppering my classes at college. First Plato, now Hemingway. It was like discovering a new rock group: Suddenly everybody seems to be listening to them, too, and wherever you go, you see their faces.

"I don't think Hemingway had transsexual leanings," my mom said. "I suspect he had his gender demons, but I don't think he'll ever appear in the transsexual pantheon."

"Probably not," I agreed, yet then I surprised myself by suggesting, "but I do think we all want to cross over a lot more than we realize. We all want to be . . . other."

My mom nodded and then asked abruptly, "Am I wrong about parenting? Did I make my little Carly a transsexual?" Though her voice was light, I could tell she was uneasy.

"No," I reassured her, "you don't need to add that to your worries. But I'm lucky. It's so much easier to do guy things as a woman than it is to do woman things as a guy."

"I like being a woman. I like being feminine."

"I do, too. Sometimes. But not always."

She sighed and put her arm around my shoulder as we walked. "I like being a woman a lot. Really, a lot. And you know what? I like being with a man. It pains me so much to say that. But it's true. It is, for better or worse, just who I am. A gal who likes a man's lap once in a while."

"Are you going to break up with Dana?"

"I should, I really should. But I can't. I wouldn't know what to say, I wouldn't know where to begin. Because I do love her. It's just that . . ."

She didn't finish her sentence and I didn't finish it for her. I didn't know how. And so we continued to stroll around the commons, listening to the birds that were coming back, and savoring the warm midday sun on our faces.

I returned to Bennington on a bus late that Sunday afternoon, aware that in eight days my mom and Dana's story would air on VPR. My dad told me that the program would be two segments broadcast on consecutive nights, beginning a week from Monday. Each segment would be about eleven minutes long and would begin at five thirty-one.

The first part, he said, would be mostly about Dana and gender dysphoria, wrapping up with her romance with my mom. That was the word he used: *romance.* He said it without any sarcasm at all, like he viewed their relationship now as one of the world's great love stories.

The second part would be about my mom's confrontation with the school, and there would be interviews with parents on both sides of the conflict.

"Given my friendship with your mom, I've scrupulously avoided listening to any of the tapes that will be used in that segment, or making any suggestions about content," he said, smiling. "Call it journalistic recusal."

On the bus, I wondered if the show was yet another reason why my mom didn't want to break up with Dana. The program had grown to mean a lot to both Dana and my dad, and maybe she figured that breaking up with Dana now would ruin their effort.

But I also understood that it was a lot more complicated than that.

The next day, I decided to wear makeup and a skirt to my classes, and then to the radio station in the afternoon. The skirt was short and my tights were black, and so no one said anything about that. But some people noticed the lipstick and eye shadow, and tried to figure out what kind of statement I was trying to make. Neil Shorter, my new friend with the nuclear lid, thought it looked very sexy and said I should let him henna my hair that night, and I almost said yes because he made it sound just like foreplay.

The only person who I think sensed what I was doing was Jamie Sloan. She wasn't usually at the radio station on Monday, but she stopped in after work to get some new CDs to listen to at home so she could decide whether they were worthy of airtime.

"Aren't you the little Barbie," she said when she saw me.

"Overkill?"

"No, not at all," she said. "Very, very feminine."

That night Neil and I had sex for the third time, and it was incredibly hot. Dressing up, I decided, was fun. It made every day seem kind of like Halloween.

32

will

PERHAPS BECAUSE I HAD A FIRSTHAND FAMILIAR-
ity with divorce, I didn't view myself as particularly romantic at
midlife. Maybe, I decided some moments, I never had been.

Yet my sense was we were all pretty romantic when we were
young, and I didn't suppose I had been an exception. There had certainly been a time, after all, when I had convinced myself that we were
all destined to meet that one special person, and I had my Allie. As a
young man, I had imagined that Allie and I would spend our entire
lives with each other on this planet, and then, in some way I could not
begin to fathom, we would spend our eternities together someplace
else. Somewhere else. If we hadn't met at college, then we would have
met at the radio station or a restaurant or . . . a car wash. But we were
fated to find each other.

Then, when it wasn't Allie, I was sure it was Patricia. Allie had
been a mere detour. Patricia was my actual soul mate.

I think it would take a lot of grit to get through this life and not believe such a thing—to believe instead that we are, in essence, completely alone, and there is no one person out there whose fate is inextricably linked with our own.

Or, what might be an even worse interpretation of the same revelation, to believe that there are in fact uncountable legions of people out there who could offer us all exactly the same quotient of happiness (or unhappiness), and it just doesn't matter with whom we finally tell ourselves we are in love. Which might be why, arguably, the only people who are more romantic than the very young are often the very old.

At almost all the funerals I have attended for parents and grandparents—mine and others'—and for elderly friends who have died, invariably someone has remarked on the depth of the love that linked the deceased and his wife.

Or the deceased and her husband.

"They were meant for each other."

"They were perfect together."

"I've never seen a love quite like theirs . . ."

It really may only be when we are in our forties and fifties, when we're old enough to know better but still young enough not to need pretense and fancy and sham, that we can be so determinedly unromantic.

And yet . . . and yet . . . a part of me never did let go of the hope that there really was one very specific woman out there for me. People—including, unfortunately, Patricia—assumed that the problem was that I had never let go of Allie.

I think that's incorrect, and I think I understood that with some clarity after Patricia's and my marriage had unraveled. I was having dinner with Allie and Dana once or twice a week, it seemed, and Allie and I were chatting with some frequency on the phone. Was there still a small part of me that fantasized about waking up one morning—morning after morning, really—and finding Allie beside me in bed? Perhaps. But did I actually believe that such a thing might happen, given my experience with her over the past decade? No.

Allie and I were meant to be friends, not lovers. That's what I had concluded. We'd be like cousins who were close. Perhaps we were meant to be together long enough to bring Carly into this world, and then we were meant to do our best to raise her from our small, separate perches.

But there was no invisible tie linking us, since there was no place in Allie's psyche upon which that tie could be fastened. There just wasn't, and I think I knew that.

The problem, if that's even the right word, is that I was still clinging to the fallacy of the one perfect woman—perfect, that is, for me. There was an animus out there enclosed in sinew and flesh that was an exact fit with whatever intangible abided within me.

Moreover, the more time I spent with Allie and Dana together, usually on the pretext of the radio series or in the context of their story, the more I realized that a small part of me was hoping their relationship would survive into their old age. Things were hard for the pair right now, but in time, perhaps, they might become nothing more than the village's eccentric elderly. That odd pair of old ladies you saw shuffling together behind a wire grocery cart in the supermarket down aisle six. Waiting for their prescriptions at the pharmacy. Asking too many questions about the scones or the bread at the bakery.

It was the animus that mattered, not the shape of the shell that housed it. If Dana wanted a reconfigured husk, so be it. The husk doesn't last.

When I would have these visions—in the car or my office or as I'd wander about my empty house—I would wonder if I was a romantic after all. Or whether, maybe, I was trying to focus upon anything but the fact that I was beginning to fear I was going to grow old all alone. I was never going to find that kindred spirit who would make everything right.

I never sat in on the recordings, and I didn't listen to any of the tapes until the final product was brought to me for review. But I had lunch with Allie and Dana the day they both came to the station, and I had breakfast with Dana the next morning, when she alone was needed in the studio. I also went with Kevin Gaines to Bartlett when he wanted to spend some time with Allie and Dana at the house in which they were living, and I stayed for coffee with them when Kevin left to begin interviewing the folks who thought Allie shouldn't have allowed or encouraged a transsexual to move in.

This meant, in all fairness, that I had a sense of how the programming was coming together. I knew how Kevin was structuring the short series in his mind.

Once, Kevin came into my office and shook his head. "He really can pass for a woman," he said.

"I know," I said, and I could tell that Kevin was experiencing for the first time something I had been feeling with increasing frequency—and if not yet with increasing discomfort, then certainly with increasing bemusement.

"He's almost pretty," Kevin went on.

I smiled and shook my head. "Not almost," I told him, stating the obvious.

"It's true. You expect the ugly duckling, and you get this swan."

Kevin was about a decade younger than I was, and he had two small daughters at home. He was, I assumed, happily married. "We'll have to make that clear on the radio," he continued. "Normally what someone looks like doesn't matter. But it does here. We need to make it clear he isn't a drag queen and he isn't a—"

"Use a feminine pronoun," I suggested.

"Do you mean on-air?"

"Yes."

"We'll confuse our listeners."

"Just think about it. As you work on the narrative, see how it sounds."

"It'll sound weird."

"So? Their whole story is weird."

He was sipping coffee from one of our fund-raising mugs, and he ran a finger around the swirl that comprised the radio station's logo. "This must be very, very strange for you," he said, his eyes on the porcelain.

I'd known Kevin for perhaps half a decade, since he'd come to public radio from the CBC in Montreal, and he had probably become one of my closer friends. At some point, I had imagined, I was going to move on to another station or to NPR in Washington—whenever Patricia and I had discussed it, we always assumed it would be once Carly had left for college—and Kevin would become the station G.M. Already he was doing as much managerial and programming work as he was reporting. Maybe more.

"Which part?" I asked him. "The part about my ex-wife, the lesbian? Or that part where my ex-wife sleeps with a man and a woman who turn out to be the same person? Of course, there's also the part where my daughter comes home from college and finds out her mom has invited a transsexual to move in. That's a little strange, too."

He shook his head, and I could see that I had depressed him a tiny bit. I hadn't meant to. "It all comes back to Allison, doesn't it? Even now," he observed.

I knew what he was driving at, and I ignored it. "In this radio series, it shouldn't. At least in the first half—on day one—Allie is completely irrelevant. Completely. On day two, she should certainly come into focus. So should a lot of people. But, in my mind, she's only a part of the program."

"I wasn't talking about the program."

"I was aware of that."

"Okay, fine. Has Patricia found a new home yet?"

"She has. She has a glorious apartment. In Brandon, of all places."

"Lousy spot to meet people."

"Ah, but it isn't Bartlett, and I think that's all that mattered. She wanted out of our little town, and I really can't say I blame her."

"Have you seen it?"

"Her place? No. But I know the building. It's gorgeous. She has the top two floors of some monster Victorian near the library. Right now she's planning to stay there for a couple of months and regain her bearings. Through the summer, probably."

"And then?"

"I don't know. But this isn't a trial separation. I wish it were. Sometimes. But it's not."

"I'm sorry."

"Me too," I said, and I tried to recall the last time we had made love. I couldn't, and for some reason that scared me. I knew it had been in December, but our last few intimate moments had blurred together like so many leaves on the collages Carly would make in the autumn when she was a little girl. Quickly I returned to the subject of the radio series. "Explain that she can pass for a natural woman. Dana, of course."

"And leave it at that?"

"Tell people she's attractive."

He sipped his coffee and then nodded. "Yeah, I think that's important."

"It is for the radio," I said. "But not in reality."

Oh, but it was. Whenever I saw Dana, and I saw her quite a lot in February and March, I would have to remind myself that she was a transsexual. I would have to focus upon the phonetics of the word, murmur it to myself in my mind, and conjure the genitalia that once had been there. Otherwise . . . and sometimes I would cut the thought off right there:

Otherwise . . . otherwise, nothing.

And I would allow myself to hug her as a friend. I would touch her the way I might have touched any of Allie's or Patricia's female pals, or the various women I knew who were married to my male friends. I would give her an embrace that was warm but not overtly sexual. I would shake her hand gently. I would not touch her legs or her hair, which for male friends are off-limits, but I would graze her arm with my fingers when it was appropriate.

But aren't even those touches sexual?

That was the *otherwise:* For men, on some level it's all sexual. It might be that way for women, too, but I can't speak for women. For men, however, it's always about sex. We are what we are. Whenever I thought about touching Dana, I realized that I hadn't ever touched a woman without understanding on some plane that we were different genders, and succumbing to the sexual charge—sometimes awkward, sometimes teasing, sometimes downright thrilling—that was as involuntary as it was inevitable. It was, in its own way, *pro forma*. Men don't hug women without thinking of sex. It may be for the merest second, the flutter of a hummingbird's wing. But it's there and it's real. After all, that's a woman's shoulder blade you are touching or patting or caressing for the briefest twinkling. Those are a woman's breasts that are pressed against your chest when you squeeze her to you after a dinner party. That human being in your arms for an instant? Your bodies fit together, and the genome that limned you and the memes that control you . . . they understand this and crave her.

And so when I'd hug Dana or touch the inside of her palm with the inside of mine (a handshake, yet so suggestive) or my fingers would find their way to one of her arms, I would experience a sexual ripple and wonder why I had felt such a thing—why I had *courted* such a thing. And the answer would be because she was pretty and she was smart and she was feminine. The *otherwise* that was the euphemism in my mind for penis and balls and a chest with a rug would be subsumed by the scent of her perfume and the softness of her skin. The small of her back. The feel of her body forming itself next to mine for the split second that it takes to embrace as . . . friends.

Even the word *transsexual* had grown less disconcerting. Less foreign. It began to seem less like a scientific abomination—man into woman with the aid of hormones and scalpel—and more like medicine. A woman healed.

One time when Dana was with Kevin, and Allie and I were alone, I asked her if she thought she was gay because she was attracted to Dana.

"No," she said, and then she asked the question of me that only my Allie would ask. "Do you think you are?"

I wasn't sure what I expected when I went to see Glenn Frazier. Probably I shouldn't have called first. I should have surprised him. But he knew I was coming and he knew why I was coming, and so he was ready.

I stopped by his house after dinner. He'd said his family was usually done eating by seven or seven-fifteen, and so we agreed upon seven-thirty.

His house was part of a small, relatively elegant development that had been built on what was once a modest dairy farm just outside of town. Ten or eleven houses, all one- and two- and three-acre lots. They'd been built in the early 1990s, and they were vaguely Colonial: inappropriate for northern Vermont, but they were well landscaped and they were not unattractive.

The Fraziers had lived there just about eight months. They were the second family to live in the house. I knew Glenn because Bartlett is a small town and we were men about the same age, and because he worked with my ex-wife at the school. We knew each other well enough to make small talk when our paths would cross at the bakery in the morning or—obviously—when we ran into each other at the supermarket. But we weren't friends, and I had never before been to his house.

When I arrived, Glenn's teenage son—a boy a few years younger than Carly—was doing some sort of math homework in the den off the front hall. He left me standing in the entryway when he went upstairs to tell his father I was there. And then, a moment later, he came back downstairs and informed me that his father was on the phone and would be with me in a minute. Then he returned to his homework, stopping once to pet the side of a puppy that was asleep on the floor by the woodstove.

He seemed like a nice enough kid. Awkward. Not particularly well socialized for a fourteen- or fifteen-year-old. But the fact that he was doing schoolwork at seven-thirty at night was encouraging to me. I read nothing into the fact that he didn't invite me in to sit down, or offer me something to drink. I read nothing into the fact that his mother didn't appear to say hello while Glenn wrapped up his conversation on the telephone.

At least I didn't at first.

I leaned my back against the front door with my coat in my arms and wondered if I should take off my shoes. Then I decided not to:

The boy had his sneakers on. And my loafers were reasonably clean. I glanced around the hallway, noting the way the brass fixtures still had a bright shine to them, and the wallpaper on the stairs had not yet begun to separate at the seams. There was a copy of the day's newspaper, unread, on a small table by a mirror.

At twenty to eight, I asked the boy in the den if his mother was home.

"Yup. You want me to get her?" he asked.

I shook my head no. "Just curious."

He nodded, donned a pair of small headphones, and continued to work.

At a quarter to eight, I decided to read the newspaper. I had already read the paper once that day, and so the articles I read at the Fraziers' were the stories that hadn't interested me at first. In most cases, they still didn't. But the waiting was less awkward when I had something to do with my hands, when I had something to look at other than the wallpaper and the fixtures and a boy with his homework.

At ten of eight I sat down on one of the bottom steps on the stairs, still holding the newspaper and my coat. I resolved not to give Glenn the satisfaction of sending his son up for him again, and I resolved not to leave. I resolved I would not be stood up.

But at eight o'clock Glenn's son took off his headphones, snapped shut his math book, and turned on the television. He was watching a prime-time soap opera aimed at teens, and I found the dialogue I could hear in the hallway unbearable. I didn't believe the boy was a part of a little conspiracy his father had engineered, I didn't believe he was intentionally trying to torment me, but the show was quickly growing unendurable. Adult angst is bad enough; teen angst is pure torture.

And so at ten after eight, when I'd been kept waiting for forty minutes, I finally yelled up the stairs:

"Hello? You off the phone yet, Glenn Frazier?"

I'd tried to keep my voice light, but I doubted I had. At the very least, I saw, I had made the dog's ears twitch, and I might very well have sounded livid. Because, of course, I was. I was furious.

The boy came out of the den and said he'd go see what was keeping his dad. Then, a moment later, they both appeared at the top of the stairs. The boy retreated back into the den, and Glenn stood before me for a moment in the hallway. He managed not to apologize.

"That phone call was endless, wasn't it?" he said.

"Yes, it was. It must have been very important."

"Actually, it wasn't. I just couldn't find an out to escape," he said, and he shook his head as if he felt bad. But it was clear he didn't feel bad, and it was clear he wanted me to understand that.

"Where would you like to talk?" I asked.

"Will this take long?"

"It shouldn't."

He looked around the hallway, and for a second I thought he was going to suggest we stand where we were. Finally he motioned toward the kitchen, and so we went there and I assumed we were going to sit around a mahogany table fresh from an Ethan Allen showroom. But he remained standing, his back to a sliding glass door.

So I stood, too, still with my coat in my arms.

"I guess you know why I'm here," I said.

"You were pretty clear on the phone."

"Was I?"

"Yeah. Perfectly. Is there something you want to add?"

I considered asking him how I had insulted him in that conversation, but I knew that wasn't the issue. The issue was that I had told him I wanted to stop by to discuss Allie and Dana, and that I wanted him to give them his support. To stop making their life any harder than it already was. Perhaps, I had even hinted, to intervene with Judd Prescott and the school board, and get them to stop pressuring Allie to take a leave of absence.

And, somehow, that had not simply irritated him: It had, in his mind, demeaned me. In his eyes, I had become a traitor to the cause. Gone native, so to speak.

I realized that I had endured the indignity of standing in his front hall for forty minutes for absolutely nothing. There was no reason for me to be polite, because there was no way I was going to change his mind. There was no way he was going to ask anyone or anything to back off. Not the school board, not the parents. Certainly not his own sense of right and wrong.

"I guess not," I said, "I guess I was clear." Then I walked myself to his front door and I left. I figured he was still standing in his kitchen when I started my car.

Usually by the time a program we have produced has aired, I've lost interest in it. By then it has come up in so many meetings at the station and I've heard it in so many stages that it no longer holds any surprises. Moreover, by then I'm usually immersed in something else: the next series, the new hire, the latest transmission crisis.

The story about Allie and Dana was different, in part because I had made the professional decision to distance myself from it as much as possible during production. But there were other reasons, too. The subject matter was—as Kevin had said—all very strange, especially since it was a story that hit so close to home. Certainly I had understood that when I first had the idea, and then when I proposed it to Allie and Dana. But I hadn't realized how much I would change as the program date drew near. Something was different for me now, and I wanted to grasp what it was. I wanted to fathom that strangeness.

Moreover, I actually wanted the program to help Allie and Dana. I wanted it to get the people in Bartlett off their backs. That was a lot to ask of a story, and I honestly didn't have any expectations that it would accomplish such a thing. Has any newspaper editorial ever changed anyone's mind? I doubt it. And it didn't seem fair to put that kind of pressure on this series.

But I did.

I listened to the program alone in my office because it seemed inappropriate to listen to it with Allie and Dana. They, I knew, were planning to be at their home those two days when it aired, and I imagined them listening in their warm and cozy den. Twilight in March. Allie home from school, Dana home from . . . well, just home. Knowing how embattled Dana was feeling those days, I imagined she hadn't gone anywhere.

Carly, I knew, was going to listen to it in her dorm.

And Patricia? I had told Patricia about it, and I figured she would listen as well. Despite the breakup of our marriage, I believe she would have gone to the legal mat for Allie and Dana, if only on principle. Principle and the fact that she didn't dislike either of them, even if she believed my interest in Allie was excessive and unhealthy. Probably, like me, Patricia would be in her office when the programming aired.

The one time I may have crossed that Berlin Wall between station president and Allie's ex-husband was when I decided the Wednesday before the two-day series would begin to increase the rotation of the prerecorded promos. Normally, we might have run the spots five or six times in the course of a day, but I suggested to the program director that he might want to double it—especially during *Morning Edition* and *All Things Considered,* the big drive-time news shows we bought from NPR. Allie and Dana's story would in fact be run during one of our local ATC cut-ins, just after five-thirty in the afternoon.

Nevertheless, when the program finally aired the third Monday in March, I was hearing it very much like my listeners. Some parts of it were as new to me as they were to them: There were moments in the first section, such as when a surgeon was explaining Dana's operation in some detail, when I found myself crossing my legs. There were portions during day two when I shook my head in astonishment: *Had someone really spray-painted such a thing on their door? Had I really helped clean it up?* Yes and yes. But already those events seemed to have occurred a very long time ago. Not necessarily in another life. But clearly one when a simple little thing like voluntary castration and the surgical creation of a vagina could make me queasy.

Dana phoned right after the first segment aired and told me she loved it. She said she was embarrassed by all the attention and didn't believe she was as interesting a person as Kevin had made her seem. But she was very happy. And so, therefore, was I. It was good journalism, and Dana was pleased.

I hung up and shut down my computer for the day, and prepared to leave. Briefly I marveled at the idea that when Dana and I were through talking, I hadn't asked to speak to Allie. A part of me was oddly self-satisfied—I had finally stopped courting the approval of a woman I hadn't been married to in years—and a part of me was quite sure that I must have simply assumed that Dana had phoned on behalf of them both. But I did call back to speak to Allie, telling myself that it had been rude not to ask her what she thought. We chatted for a warm fifteen minutes, and I was glad that Allie was enjoying the story, too. Then I went home.

Later that night, however, while eating my dinner alone and then getting ready for bed, I wondered at what I had not done in that first call, and the things I hadn't felt the need to ask. A part of me wondered if I should view this as emancipating. But another part of me worried that I should be scared.

dana

AT FIRST THERE IS NOTHING SEXY ABOUT DILA-
tion. It is, alas, akin to flossing; it's simply a part of one's better hygiene
regimen. You brush your teeth, you wash your face, you dilate your
new vagina. Sometimes, in fact, it was downright inconvenient,
because it takes fifteen to twenty minutes, and you need to do it four
and five times a day those first months!

But, almost imperceptibly, something began to change when I
would work the different dildos inside me that spring. I began to
understand the desire for—radical feminism be damned—penetration.
Anal penetration still held no allure, but I began to understand how
the biological pieces might fit together for a woman born straight. The
line between dilation and masturbation grew increasingly hazy, and
I'd stare at the wand in my hand when I was through—still wet with
lube, and slippery with me—and in a fog I would wonder what my
new body was trying to tell me.

Marisa, one of my trannie friends from Burlington, had wanted us to call the police about the obscenity someone had spray-painted on Allison's door, but of course we didn't.

"It's a hate crime!" she'd insisted.

"Almost all crimes are hate crimes," I'd said.

"No, it's a legal hate crime," she'd continued. "There's a statute against exactly this kind of personal attack."

A part of me thought she was right and we should phone that fine young gentleman who insisted on giving me speeding tickets and calling me sir, if only to make the bastard sit in our house and act deferential. But mostly I agreed with Allison. The last thing she wanted was to draw further attention to it, especially after the wondrous show of support she'd received the night before at the talent show.

And so we never called the police, and Will and I had the door looking as good as new by two-thirty or three that very afternoon.

Nevertheless, sometimes when I absolutely had to go out in Bartlett, I'd try to look people in the eye to see if they were the ones who had been responsible for defacing the door. I'd glare. I'd walk to the Grand Union for the butter I'd forgotten to buy in Middlebury, and I'd stare back at the teen boys who were staring at me, or at the parents who I knew had signed that abominable first petition. The adults, it seemed, always looked away when they saw me looking at them, but sometimes the teen boys could hold my gaze for a moment or two. But they always blinked first. And while my angry scowl may not have made those forays to the grocery store any more pleasant, it certainly made them more interesting. An irate gape competition? What fun!

Ironically, though Allison and I never told the police or newspaper reporters what had been scrawled on the door, without any discussion beforehand we found ourselves telling the VPR reporter. Somehow it seemed the right thing to do, especially since we hadn't made a big deal of it publicly when it happened. As a result, we sounded magnanimous. Charitable. Forgiving.

The days before the Vermont radio program aired, I began to wonder seriously what effect the story would have—if any. Certainly I'd gotten my hopes up before that things would change and people would come to accept me, and so I tried not to expect too much. In truth, I tried not to expect anything. But I would still find myself hoping, despite what all experience had taught me, that things would be different once people heard what I had to say. I began to tell myself that it might somehow make the town more tolerant of me. Maybe it would actually cause the more rabid of my critics to leave me alone— to leave Allison and me alone.

I think that's why I decided to see Mr. Judd Prescott myself. It was a Friday morning, and the show would air in three days. I was hopeful. I didn't know then that Will had already visited Allison's principal, and I'm glad. I suppose if I'd known what had happened at Glenn Frazier's house, I wouldn't have had the audacity to appear unannounced at the office of the school superintendent.

Oh, maybe I would have gone anyway. Who knows? I'm not sure what I expected would occur, but I thought it was unlikely I'd make things any worse. And I had to do something for Allison, I had to at least try and help.

And so that morning I arrived at his office, wearing the most androgynous khakis in the closet, a bulky ski sweater that any man could have worn, and just enough makeup to smooth out my skin. I put my hair back in the sort of mannish ponytail I'd worn just before I'd begun my transition. I wanted to look unthreatening and conservative, and—odd, isn't it, how much baggage we bring to clothes?—like a woman who didn't need to flaunt her femininity. I was afraid that if I wore the sorts of skirts and dresses that gave me the most pleasure, I'd look, in his eyes, as if I were trying to throw my sex change in his face. And I didn't want to do that.

Allison had no idea I was there. I didn't tell her beforehand because I knew she would have asked me not to go. I decided I would tell her that afternoon when she came home from school, and I would imply that it had been a very spontaneous decision. The superintendent's office was right around the corner from the Middlebury grocery store where I would be doing our shopping in any event. I'd tell Allison I had just wound up there.

Inevitably, the superintendent was in a meeting somewhere else in the building when I arrived, and so I sat in a little chair by a table without a single magazine for over an hour—until eleven-thirty, when he came back to his office to return phone calls before going to lunch. I didn't make his secretary uncomfortable, and I thought that was a promising sign. She was a young thing, barely three or four years older than Carly, I guessed, and a little on the plump side. But she was immensely professional, and not at all disturbed by the fact that the odious transsexual from Bartlett, the one who was complicating her boss's life, had arrived without an appointment. She simply kept typing some report into the computer on her desk, answering the phone, and asking me every so often if I'd like water or coffee or soda. I'd have to pay for the soda from a machine down the hall, she said apologetically, but the water and the coffee were free.

"I'm fine," I'd say, and I'd smile broadly. I wanted to keep her as my friend.

Finally Judd Prescott appeared, coming through the very same door I had passed. At first he didn't know who I was, and I was thrilled. But when I stood up and his secretary introduced us, his back arched and his mouth hung open for a very long second. He was a big fellow, with a wonderful thick crop of silver hair, and he was wearing the sort of gray tweed blazer in which I had once lived.

Quickly he regained his composure and asked me into his office. "We don't have long," he said. "But, please, come in." He took with him a thick pile of phone messages, and a small part of my heart went out to him. He spent his life putting out fires, and here I was before him, a bone-dry plot of forest and a blowtorch.

His office was small, but it was in a corner of the building and as nicely appointed as a college dean's: heavy leather chairs, the desk crafted from fine cherry wood, and a pair of attractive oil paintings of Vermont mountains on the two walls without windows—Mount Mansfield in one case, Camel's Hump in the other.

"So, Monday night we become radio celebrities," I said, hoping I was offering us some commonality. I knew he, too, had been interviewed, and I tried to present our radio experience in a neutral sort of light. "I'm a little nervous."

"Oh, these things come and go. Whenever a newspaper reporter misquotes me, I get angry, but a day or two later no one even remembers what I didn't really say."

"Did you like Kevin?" I asked, referring to the VPR reporter who had interviewed Allison and me. "I did."

"Nice young man."

"Yes."

"So." He folded his hands on his desk blotter. "Why are we here? This meeting is about . . . what?"

"This meeting is about the very best schoolteacher in the Bartlett Elementary School. A dedicated and thoughtful and hardworking sixth-grade teacher who is absolutely beloved by her students."

"All twelve of them," he said with a sigh.

"Thirteen," I said, correcting him.

"All thirteen of them, in that case. Forgive me. But I hope you see my point."

"I do."

"Okay, then. What about Allison Banks?"

"I feel that you're trying to punish her because of me, and I don't want you to do that. Surely you understand that she doesn't want to take a leave of absence."

"So she's said."

"Why are you making her, then?"

"I'm not making her. I'm simply encouraging her. And I'm encouraging her because right now there are two sixth-grade classes at the Bartlett Elementary School and—as we both just determined—one of them has thirteen students, and one of them has twenty-five. That's not a good situation. And it's not going to change next year. Nor is the distraction that is currently rippling through the entire school. That's not going to go away either. Over seven hundred people signed that petition this winter. That's a lot. Make no mistake: That's a lot."

"And so now you're using some field trip from the fall to try and bully her out. Is that fair?"

"I would have investigated the field trip regardless of whether you were living with her. That's the truth."

"But you wouldn't have pressured her this way, I believe. Is that true, too?"

He stood up and motioned for me to remain where I was. Then he put his head out the doorway and asked his secretary if the lawyer had gotten back to her on what he called the Banks letter.

"Yes. I think you're all set," I heard her say. "He had one tiny change, and I typed it in this morning."

"May I have a copy, please?" he asked, and a second later he walked past me once more and returned to his heavy leather chair.

"You can't take this with you," he said, handing me a piece of letterhead, "but I'm going to let you read it. You can tell Allison what's in it if you'd like. She'll get her copy on Monday."

The letter was short and to the point: After reviewing what had occurred during the field trip to the maritime museum in the fall, the superintendent's office had determined that although she should not have allowed children to swim without parental consent—and never should she do such a thing in the future—she had done nothing in direct violation of her teacher's contract and no disciplinary action was needed.

I nodded happily, unable to hide my surprise. "Oh, this is cheering news. I expect it will please her very much."

"That wasn't my intention."

"I know."

"I was just doing my job."

"I understand."

"And I will still do what I can to have two sixth-grade classrooms in Bartlett with the same number of children in each, and a school where everyone isn't talking about somebody's sex change."

"Mine."

"Yes."

"So she shouldn't view this as some sort of total vindication."

"No," he said, and perhaps because he sounded so determined, I sat there for a moment expecting him to say something more. But he didn't. And so, finally, I left.

Allison didn't want to make a big deal of the radio show, but she was always home well before five-thirty in the afternoon, and so she didn't have an excuse not to savor every minute with me. That Monday I baked cinnamon and vanilla *Mandelbrot* and prepared hot chocolate with just a hint of Amaretto. We listened to the program together, sometimes giggling and sometimes groaning, but there really wasn't a single moment in it that either of us thought could possibly make our lives any harder.

The reporter, a fellow a tad younger than me named Kevin, began with just a bit of foreshadowing about what his focus would be on Tuesday night—the fact that my little decision would cause a third of Allison Banks's sixth-graders to be pulled by their parents from her classroom—but mostly he educated listeners about gender dysphoria. I thought he did a fine job, and I was very pleased that Jordan and Pinto had nice little roles in his story, too. It meant that I wasn't his only transsexual. And I was glad that he'd gone to Montreal to meet with the surgeon there who specialized in sexual reassignment. The doctor made the surgical grail that colors the existence of so many transsexuals sound like a sensible and wise life goal.

Throughout dinner and into the early evening, I felt very close to Allison, even though one or both of us was always on the phone. The phone rang a lot, and not one call was from a crank or an anti-trannie kook. They were from Allison's friends and my friends, and people I knew at the university. They were from my acquaintances in the Gender Benders, and from people Allison had gone to school with more than two decades earlier. It was a hoot, and I understood why there were people in this world, including far too many transsexuals, who actually solicited this sort of attention.

More important, based on the calls that just kept coming and coming and coming, I couldn't imagine the narrow-minded people who were plaguing us would dare to say an unattractive word about transsexuality or sexual preference ever again—at least within the confines of scenic Bartlett. Moreover, the best was yet to come! Tomorrow night those bigots would really be put through the radio wringer!

That night in bed, however, Allison wasn't interested in making love. And that surprised me at first. And then it began to alarm me.

Obviously we didn't have sex every night—not even every other night, or, some weeks, even every third or fourth night—and so the notion of a night without sex wouldn't alone have concerned me. Besides, I knew well the struggles Allison had been having since I had returned from Colorado, I understood her confusion about who I was and what that meant in bed.

But I was hot-wired from my hope that people were about to back off. I was aroused by my fifteen seconds of fame.

Unfortunately, something was different that night for Allison, and she resisted my caresses and kisses and suggestions that we couple. When we turned off the lights by the sides of our bed, I pulled her to me and for a moment we lay there like spoons, my arm wrapped around her tummy.

"Good night, love," I said.

"Good night, Dana."

She never called me Dana in bed. And I never called her Allison. Think about it: Do lovers, especially lovers with any history together at all, ever use their partner's name when they're alone together in that small, erotic world of pillows and blankets and sheets? Of course they don't. First of all, unless you're into threesomes or multiples, there are only the two of you present. You don't *need* to specify to whom you're speaking. Nor do you need to get someone's attention across a big room: You're cozy. You're intimate. Your bodies are probably touching, for God's sake.

Moreover, unless your parents were inhumanly cruel and named you Sweetheart or Punkin or Honey, you probably don't have a name that's appropriate for the close quarters of a bed. Terms of endearment? They make the most sense in the boudoir, and they sound best when one is on the verge of sleep.

And so the simple sound of my name—two syllables, one vowel used two ways—was disconcerting. And hurtful. I had to work hard to resist the urge not to murmur something defensive or accusatory in response. In my head, however, I heard myself whisper, "Good night, Allison," and it had an edge to it that I just didn't like.

No one on the school board was interviewed for the second part of the series, because Glenn Frazier and Judd Prescott had determined for legal reasons that they alone should represent the school district's "official" take on the story. A small part of me was disappointed: I would have loved to hear a loose cannon like the school board's Al Duncan shoot off his gaping maw of a mouth one more time and embarrass those Babbitt vulgarians who were tormenting Allison and me. Still, parents like Rich Lessard and Bea Hedderigg—parents who had pulled their children from Allison's class—were plenty happy to talk, and offer listeners their misguided and angry opinions.

But there were also parents of some of the children who had remained in Allison's care, and they were eloquent and lovely to listen to. They said all the right things about Allison's competency in the classroom, and her right to live her life the way that she wanted when she was at home. And Allison's voice on the radio Tuesday night was a dream, much, much prettier than my oddly husky little bark.

"Your voice sounds nice," Allison insisted, but I disagreed.

"Hah! I sound like some over-the-hill tart—a brothel madam, maybe!"

There were considerably fewer phone calls during dinner that night, in part, I imagine, because so many people had phoned us Monday evening. But I think there was another reason, too: Bartlett had been a tad bloodied by the second segment. Even if you agreed with Rich Lessard or Glenn Frazier, they still sounded a bit like a lynch mob. And no one likes to hear about a rural village trashing one of its own: It happens all the time, of course, but public radio listeners don't want to be reminded that Norman Rockwell painted only one aspect of small-town America.

And the real star Tuesday night was neither Allison nor me. It turned out to be Sally Warwick, the eleven-year-old mastermind behind her class's cross-dressing curtain call. The kid just stole the show, especially when she talked about sneaking one of her dad's neckties from his armoire, or taking advantage of the fact that one of the boys in her class—she wouldn't say who—had a crush on her, and she knew she could use that to her advantage when she showed him the earrings and the skirt that she wanted him to wear.

"We figured if I was the one who asked him, he'd go along. You see, when you think someone's cute, you do really weird stuff," she said, expressing a wisdom well beyond her years, and Allison laughed so hard that I thought she was going to spill her hot cocoa.

Will joined us for dinner Tuesday night and brought with him a bottle of champagne. Together Allison and Will phoned Carly in her dorm room to make sure she was okay with her mom's continued notoriety, and then we let the answering machine handle the calls for the rest of the night.

"To you two," he said, raising his flute. "Thank you for being such good sports."

Midway through dinner, I think Will noticed what I'd suspected for days: Allison was beginning her retreat to that place she'd gone to years earlier without him—a place where he wasn't allowed—and that place I'd always feared she'd go to without me. Without discussing it, we both began trying to be almost neurotically charming and cheerful, but neither of us were able to make Allison laugh the way Sally Warwick had.

Who knows? Maybe we were simply trying too hard. Maybe that had been our problem all along: We'd always tried too hard. Once separately, now together.

Certainly a part of me had known from day one that eventually Allison and I would separate. Let's face it: If she had felt about a boyfriend the way she did about me, he probably would have been back in his own apartment by Groundhog Day. Maybe, if he was lucky, he could have hung on by his fingernails until Ash Wednesday.

I sometimes wonder if it was in fact the very cruelties rendered by the Rich Lessards and Officer Culbersons of the world that had prolonged my stay in her house.

Yet never—never!—did I imagine in February or March that it would be the Vermont radio program itself that would eventually lead to our separation, or that I would be the one who would initiate our disunion.

34

will

ALLIE AND DANA WERE GOING TO BREAK UP. I
suspected it when I was leaving their house after dinner Tuesday
night, and I was sure of it when I woke up the next morning and I
thought back on the evening we had shared. I knew as well as anyone
the signs that a relationship was in its waning days, and I knew as well
as anyone the cast of Allie Banks's face when she was unhappy and trying to figure out why—and what to do about it.

And so when I was shaving Wednesday morning, I resolved to put
some distance between me and the transsexual.

That was, in fact, the word I used in my head as I looked at my
aging eyes in the mirror. Not *Dana,* not *Allie's girlfriend.* The *transsexual.* I wanted to remain focused on what Dana was because those feel-
ings that I had once viewed as merely ironic had become unpleasant
when examined in the context of Dana's availability. That morning I
was no longer sure why I was spending so much time with her—there

was that pronoun again, haunting me with its anatomic specificity—
and my motives had grown somewhat muddied. Clearly it was no
longer about radio, and it was no longer about being around Allie.

It was, I feared, simply about being around Dana.

And the last thing I wanted was to know what really existed
beneath that blouse or behind the folds of her skirt. Especially if, suddenly, Dana was going to be single and unattached.

I did not miss the humor—sobering though it was—in the notion
that when I contemplated the sudden availability of one half of the
relationship, the first person I thought of was Dana. Not Allie. For the
first time in years, both Allie and I were going to be uninvolved, and
yet the first thought that crossed my mind had not been reconciliation.
It had been something else. Something about that transsexual.

When I threw cold water on my face and rinsed away the last traces
of shaving cream, I resolved that I would no longer initiate any contact
with the professor. I would not allow myself to be seduced by the illusion that had been created by some prescription pills and a surgeon
and a little makeup.

No, not a little makeup. A lot of makeup, probably.

At least that's what I told myself.

Yet even then an image crossed my mind: Dana in a silk slip before
an Art Deco vanity mirror, applying lipstick. A glamour girl from
bygone Hollywood. A knee crossed, and the smooth skin of . . .

I dressed quickly and went downstairs to brew a pot of coffee. I
focused on *Morning Edition,* and wondered at the calls that would have
come in overnight on our Reaction Line to the second part of the
transgender story.

And I decided that although Patricia's and my divorce was months
from completion, I was going to date all the women I wanted. I
wouldn't care if they were my age or they were young. I wouldn't care
whether their noses were pierced and they took pride in their daddy
complexes. I wouldn't care if they listened to VPR or to the shock
jocks on competitive radio stations.

And I reminded myself that I might be wrong about Allie and me.
Wasn't it possible, despite my conclusion that my first wife and I were

not destined to be together, that at some point in the not-too-distant future we would indeed be working our way back to each other? Certainly it was. Of course it was. Absolutely.

I realized I was angry at the transsexual for the chimera she had created, and for the unfullfillable fantasies that she offered.

Dating other women—dating real women, including, possibly, my first wife—with that mind-set would actually be rather easy, I decided. Especially now that I was over my youthful romanticism and reconciled to the belief that there wasn't one consummate woman out there who was meant for me. It was all random.

And though it wasn't exactly meaningless, it was all merely adequate.

dana

WE DIDN'T MAKE LOVE AFTER THE SECOND NIGHT
of the radio story either. I had thought that we might, and when we
didn't, I asked Allison what she was thinking. The bedroom smelled
faintly of hand cream, and I could feel the shape of the vibrator
through the pillow where—ever the optimist—I had placed it.

"I'm thinking that I want to go to sleep," she answered, her face
toward the wall.

"You're thinking more than that."

"Not by choice."

"Then what?"

She sighed, and I stroked her shoulder and the back of her neck
through the quilt.

"Are you tired of all this?" I asked, careful to keep my question
vague. I wasn't sure myself what I meant.

"Here's what I'm thinking," she murmured. "I'm thinking we shouldn't have this conversation at eleven o'clock at night."

"You never want to talk in bed."

"No, I don't. I don't like that kind of stress here."

"Will this be a stressful conversation—when we have it?"

"Dana: Stop. Please."

"Stop touching you?"

"Stop asking me questions. I want to sleep."

I took my hand off her and fell back on my pillow. "Can I say one more thing?"

"I doubt I can stop you. I've never stopped you from doing anything, now have I?"

An allusion to my surgery? Probably. But I ignored it. "I just want to make sure you know that I appreciate everything you said on the radio. About personal choices. About teaching. About me. All of it." And then I turned off the light and assumed that would be the end of it for the night. Who knew what the morning would bring? Half the time when we said we'd talk about something the next day, we never did, and so a part of me was quite sure this conversation was over for the foreseeable future. Allison was just tired. Tomorrow, once more, everything would be fine.

Oh, but not that night.

I'd placed the vibrator on the nightstand on the far side of a pile of books and rolled over onto my side, and I'd begun to try to clear my head so I could sleep. Exorcise those demons that dog us every day, banish those moments—the good ones as well as the bad—that keep one awake. I thought only of the fact that I was warm in the bed and the pillow felt good, and tomorrow I might bake some walnut-and-beer bread. I'd bake bread and read the manuscript for a new biography of George Sand a friend of mine at another university was writing. I'd wait for people to call with the news that they'd heard Allison and me on the radio, and to declare that the town was indeed behaving badly. It would be a glorious day.

"I'm done with radio," Allison said suddenly, and in an instant I was wide awake.

"Go on."

"No, that's all there is. I'm glad I spoke my piece and said what had to be said. And now I'm done. No more interviews. No more discussion."

"Good," I said simply, but I wondered if it would really be that simple. Tomorrow that would be all anyone would want to talk to her about.

"No more," she continued, and her voice broke abruptly. A crack on the *m* that drew the syllable out into a long stutter, a little cry punctuating the final exhalation. And then she was crying soundlessly, her face buried deep in her pillow, her shoulders twitching away from my touch as if I had leprosy.

"Allison, my Allison," I said softly, "what is this?"

"No!" she hissed, and she turned toward me and then sat up in bed. "I'm not *your* Allison!"

"I didn't mean anything, I'm sorry. Just tell me—"

"I'm not your Allison, I'm not Will's Allison! I'm nobody's Allison but mine!"

I sat up, too, but she wouldn't look at me. She had pulled her legs up toward her chest and buried her face in the covers on her knees. "I understand," I said. "I'm sorry. Really, I'm sorry." I tried to touch her, but she wouldn't let me. She didn't exactly swat at my hand, but she brushed aside my fingers like so much dandruff or dust.

"Just tell me why you're crying," I murmured, and then—because I couldn't find the words to pacify her, and I was feeling useless and ineffectual and utterly (the word here is chosen with care) impotent— I added, "I've never seen you cry!"

I realized that I needed her help: I needed her to tell me how to help her—to tell me exactly what to do—because I was hoping, even then, to be her Savior Male. Imagine: Almost three months after surgery, and I was still having postmortem penile reflexes.

Unfortunately, as I would understand in a moment, those few words were the single worst thing I could have said, because of all that they revealed about me. About who, in so many ways, I still was.

But for a time Allison ignored me and continued to cry, her body shuddering with her sniffles. Finally she allowed me to drape my arm over her like a tent, but I was engulfing her more than touching her, and—though the thought crossed my mind—I didn't dare try to kiss the back of her hair.

How long did she cry? I can't say. Time is pure torture when you're that sad, just ask any transsexual. It's excruciating and it's endless. A sailboat on a lake with no wind. Was it a mere ten or fifteen minutes, or was it considerably longer? Could she have cried without stopping for fully half an hour? Perhaps. Those tears, I know now, had been welling inside her since Trinidad.

No, they'd begun gathering even earlier than that. They'd begun congregating on a ledge up in Lincoln that autumn afternoon when I first told her my plans.

Finally she said in a voice barely above a whisper, "Never seen me cry?" It was a question, but it was asked in astonishment.

"No," I said.

"There have been whole days—weekends—when I cried all the time!"

I nodded to myself, the words echoing in my head as if she had shouted them in a cave, and I realized something as disturbing as the fact that I had missed so much of her misery: I wasn't crying. And I should have been. I should have been crying, too. Sympathy sobs. An empathy wail. Some wholly justifiable weeping.

But I would have had to will those tears from the reservoir; they weren't going to come on their own.

And that meant something, too.

I didn't dare speak, because I knew if I did, I would acknowledge what we both understood: It was time for me to leave. I knew it, and so did she. And this time, I was quite sure, she wouldn't stop me. Because she'd made her point. She'd refused to be bullied. She had, with the help of her ex-husband of all people, stood by her woman.

And now she needed to get on with her life. And I with mine.

At some point I did speak. And, unlike when I broached the subject in the past, she didn't offer even token resistance to the notion that I should return to my home in Burlington.

Of course, it wouldn't have mattered if she had. I would have left regardless of what she said, because it was time. The experiment was over, and it had failed. That sounds harsh, but it reflects the reality of how I felt my last night in her bed. Not only was I the wrong person for Allison—gay, straight, I wasn't even focused that moment on monikers—the two of us together had replicated one of the most onerous male/female paradigms in the history of gender.

A nurturing woman had given way too much to an insensitive creep of a man. She had been my teacher and my nurse and the one person in the world who had been there for me—no matter what. She had endured all manner of derision on my behalf, she had risked her place in her community. She had jeopardized her career, her future, her sense of herself.

So much for transcending a few millennia of sex-role socialization, I thought to myself.

Well, bully for us! Bully for me!

Oh, I could tell myself that I had vacuumed for her and I had cooked for her. I could remind myself that I had even done windows.

But in reality Allison hadn't gotten anything from me that she couldn't have gotten from a first-rate domestic.

For a long moment she was quiet when I told her what I was going to do, and then I saw her nod. It was small, almost invisible. But it was real. Soon after that I believe she fell asleep—exhausted, I imagine, by all those tears and by the emotional toll that living with me had taken—but I would be awake through the night. At four in the morning I finally climbed from the bed that was already feeling foreign to me, and I tiptoed downstairs to the kitchen. There I put a kettle on the stove for hot tea and baked that walnut-and-beer bread, and then I wandered through the rooms on the first floor of the house. I touched things as if I would never touch them again—the candlesticks on the dining room table, the couch in the den, the kitchen ladles and whisks and tureens that had become my unduly gynecic line in the sand—because I understood that I would never be back here again.

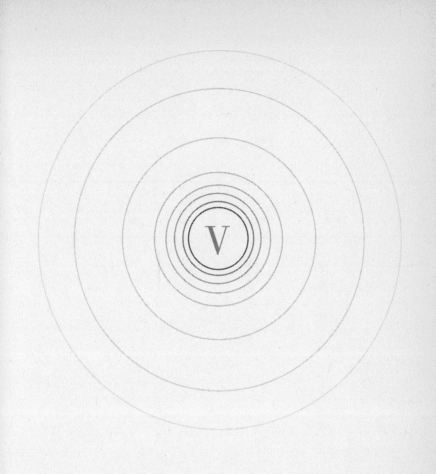

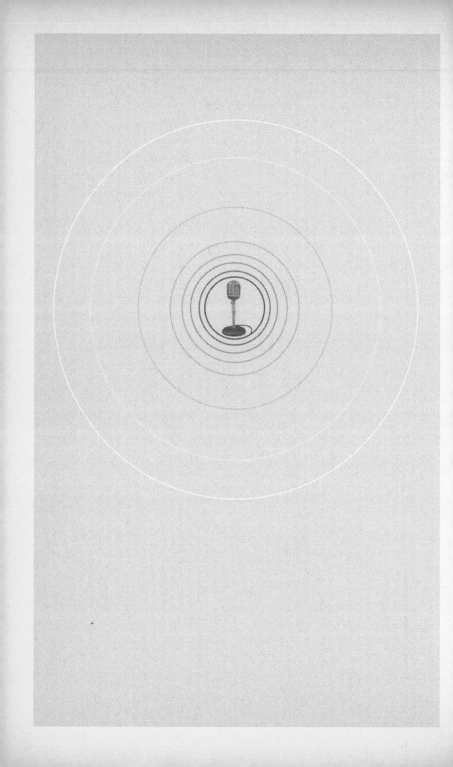

All Things Considered
Friday, September 28

DR. JEN FULLER: I've heard some transsexuals liken their transformation to a butterfly's. They wake one day and they have wings. They're beautiful and they can fly.

But it's not usually like that. You're too awkward, too insecure. You're still experimenting with your new identity.

Usually it's much more like . . . adolescence.

36

allison

IT WAS AS IF DANA HAD NEVER LIVED WITH ME. I would wander through town or I would walk to the school, and nobody seemed to view me anymore as the local sex renegade or pariah. I was, once again, merely a schoolteacher. One of the dozen-plus who lived in the town. I was a neighbor. I was Allison Banks—Allie (still and always) to one of the village's more prominent citizens.

When Rich Lessard and I would run into each other at the post office, we would make small talk. We were courteous to each other, we were polite. When Al Duncan and I would pass each other on the street by the bank or the bookstore, we would chat. We would laugh about the weather. Or his family's new minivan. He would ask me how Carly was doing at college.

Once more, Glenn Frazier and I bickered only about my curriculum and field trips—though I no longer had the cloud of the maritime museum excursion hanging over my head. But Glenn and I stopped discussing my life, because, after all, my life no longer mattered to him. Or to anyone. I wasn't exactly invisible—one can never do what I did and not become a part of a little town's mythos—but I believe I was no longer actively discussed. The corkboards and counters at the stores that had once held petitions debating the importance of a school-teacher's morality now had flyers for piano teachers and typists and young people looking for roommates. The petitions themselves were buried deep in someone's gray metal filing cabinet.

My house seemed, suddenly, way too big for one person, and in late April I considered putting it on the market. But Carly came home from school two and a half weeks later, and though she only stayed with me until Memorial Day—that Monday she left for her internship in Washington—I was glad we had so much room. Neither of us is a big person, but somehow we manage to take up a lot of space. And so I decided I wouldn't even consider selling the house again until Carly had finished college.

And then? And then who knew.

The fact was, in less than a year I had met and lived with a trans-sexual, I had had sex with a woman for the first time in my life. I'd been excommunicated by a good measure of my community and then taken back into the fold without anyone saying a word. Without anyone even acknowledging what had transpired.

I had been, for better or worse, on the radio two nights in a row.

I had seen my daughter go off to college.

Consequently, I wouldn't even conjecture about where I might be in three years, or who I might have become. Especially with that wild card called midlife looming large.

For a while I was angry with Dana, and I felt I'd been used. She'd needed someone to take care of her during transition, she'd needed a woman to tutor her in the finer points of my gender. She'd seen the way I'd fallen in love with her when she was my male professor, and taken advantage of me.

I found it interesting that when I was most angry with Dana that spring, I would inadvertently revert to male pronouns and a male image—to Dana Stevens before her reassignment. He used me, I'd think, and the image in my mind would be the man I'd once known who wore his hair in a ponytail.

But then I would think to myself, How? How had he used me? Yes, I'd wound up as his model woman—*her* model woman—but I was the one who had called Dana back in September after she revealed to me her intentions on a cliff high in Lincoln. I was the one who had proposed that she move into my house. I was the one who had suggested she would need company in Colorado, and offered to go with her.

And, in return, I had received a very great deal. I'm not sure other people would see it that way, I'm not even sure Dana would. But I did, and I don't mean simply the company or the conversation or the way my house seemed to smell of freshly baked bread all the time. Nor am I referring to the sex, which, though it often confused me, always left me deeply satisfied. More than any of that, first he—and then she— had given me the faith, however brief, that I might not wander unescorted through the rest of my life. We had been in love, and for months and months I had had hope—one of the greatest gifts you can give someone on the far side of forty.

When I would realize that, my anger would dissipate. I would no longer be mad. I would even feel a twinge of what might have been guilt. Or, at least, disappointment in myself. What did it say about me, I would wonder, that I could only love Dana as a man? Was I really that intractable, that emotionally obstinate? Or was sexual preference so profoundly ingrained in my gray matter and soul that even the desperate attraction I had felt for Dana the preceding September—a desire that in the days before our hike to the cliff may have bordered on rapture—couldn't budge it?

The irony there was inescapable. It was the man who had made me angry, but it was also the man whom I seemed to love.

Still, I refused to see Dana that spring. Maybe in the summer when school was out, we would meet for coffee in Burlington. Maybe in a few years we would actually be friends—not unlike the way Will and I, over time, had built a friendship that transcended the fact that we shared a daughter.

In April and May, however, I simply wanted to reclaim a semblance of normalcy. And that meant only seeing people who had no plans to challenge what had once been a biological absolute.

Carly told me that she had listened to Dana's and my story on VPR in her dorm room. Listening with her were her roommate and a few of her friends—including Neil Shorter, a boy I could tell she was growing interested in, either because of or in spite of the pleasure he derived from coloring hair. Apparently, that spring it was a traffic-tape orange. Carly and I spoke on the phone both nights the programming aired, but she called me again on Thursday from the station with the news that we—her mother and her transsexual girlfriend—were all over the wires in two- and three-hundred-word increments. I wasn't surprised. The newspapers in northwestern Vermont had called my house and the school throughout Wednesday, though I continued to refuse to speak to reporters.

I told Carly then what was the real news in my life: There would be no more stories about Dana and me, because we'd decided Tuesday night to separate. Dana had already moved back to Burlington. She asked whether there had been any specific trigger, and I told her there hadn't.

"Just a chemistry thing, huh?" she said, using the expression she had heard me use perhaps a half dozen times when I would break off a relationship that had had some duration, or when I would report that a first date had been a bore.

"Yeah, a chemistry thing," I said.

"Were yesterday and today really strange?"

I admitted that there had been awkward moments both days, but word travels fast in a village like Bartlett. People had seen Dana loading up her car in the morning. And so by the time I had started to walk home from school Wednesday afternoon, by the time I had stopped at the supermarket and the bank, I had the sense that everyone in town knew Dana had left. I could see it in their faces: In some cases they were masks of sympathy, in others there was relief they couldn't hide. The trannie was gone, and the sixth-grade teacher had regained her senses.

Of course, it was nowhere near that simple. Regained my senses?

Maybe, but with reason came despair. Before I knew it, I was in mourning, and the mourning grew deeper through April and May.

Nevertheless, somehow I was able to stave off the full brunt of the depression until after Carly had left Bartlett for Washington on Memorial Day. But then it hit me like a train, and I was a mess through a good part of the summer. I'm not sure how I endured the last two weeks of school, how I managed to get dressed the final nine or ten mornings: I know there was one period when I went four nights without washing my hair. There was one day when my eyes were so red from crying, I wore a pair of old eyeglasses to school that were supposed to change from dark to light when you wandered inside, but they hadn't functioned properly in years. But that was exactly the point: I knew even indoors they would remain a dull gray and hide my eyes.

Once school ended in the middle of June, I rarely left my house. At some point I planted my vegetable garden, but I have only the vaguest memory of kneeling in the dirt with a spade and a claw. And one day I must have planted the annuals that would fill in the gaps between the perennials that line the front walk, but I have no recollection of visiting the nursery where Carly had worked the summer before.

I know Molly Cochran and Nancy Keenan brought me cold soups and salads, and Will came by for visits. I know Dana wanted to come by, though I wasn't ready to see her. Was there anyone else? Probably. But visits from other people were rare—and always unsolicited.

I don't remember the Fourth of July, though every year there is an impressive fireworks celebration at the high-school athletic fields, and usually I sit on my terrace with friends and we watch the pyrotechnics in the sky. Not that summer. I don't even recall hearing the explosions high in the air above Bartlett.

There's an expression that a bulb will burn brightest just before it burns out. Certainly that was true in my father's case. I was twenty-six years old when he passed away, and Carly was just about twenty months. He died of pancreatic cancer, and two days before he died—though he had opened his eyes no more than a slit in twenty-four hours, and his body probably had more morphine in it than blood—he sat up in his bed and told my mother and me and the hospice worker who was visiting that he wanted to be hoisted into his wheelchair and taken to see the lights on the boathouses that line a small stretch of the Schuylkill River near the Philadelphia Art Museum. The houses are outlined in white Christmas lights year-round, so you can just see their silhouettes against the night sky, and they look like giant gingerbread cookies held vertically against a black backdrop. Sometimes you can see their reflection in the river as well.

My father had been a rower, and when he was younger, he would participate every year in the local regattas: the Dad-Vail and the Head of the Schuylkill. When I was very young, he would take me with him for more leisurely rides.

And so we took my father to see the boathouses, and he smiled and was not unhappy. Somehow he had rallied, and briefly he resembled the man who had raised me. And then we came home and he slipped into a coma, and less then forty-eight hours later he died.

My last months with Dana were something like that: I got sicker and sicker in January and February, but the night of the talent show—and the morning after, when our front door was vandalized and one last time I had to be there for her—I burned bright. I was strong and spirited and yet oddly serene. I was, briefly, at peace.

And then I burned out.

People believe that I have only a small role in the version of our story that aired nationally in the fall on *All Things Considered* because I refused to be interviewed through most of the summer. But that's only partly true. Yes, I had reclaimed my personal life, and the fact is, I probably wouldn't have talked to Carly about Dana and me with a producer and a tape recorder present in July. But both Carly and Will also understood how uncharacteristically fragile I had become, and they both made it clear to everyone in Washington that I would—that I could—have nothing to do with the programming until at least August. And even then there was no guarantee.

That's the real reason why you hear my name often but only rarely my voice in those stories. It wasn't simply that I didn't want to make a longer statement (though that, too, is true): Pure and simple, I couldn't.

Honestly, I just couldn't.

37

carly

AT FIRST I FELT A LITTLE DISLOYAL AGREEING TO have a drink with Dana when I came home from college in May. But she said she simply wanted to see how I was doing, and it was okay to tell Mom.

Still, I didn't. I just didn't think Mom wanted to know.

My dad kept telling me that my mom would be okay, and I tried not to worry. But I'd never seen her like this. One night she brought home a big stack of tests to grade, and she plopped herself down on the couch in the den with the pile in her lap. She began about eight-thirty, and she was still at it at ten o'clock. Finally, a little before midnight, I asked how she was doing, and she told me she hadn't started. She'd finished her tea, but otherwise she hadn't done a thing but sit there and daydream with the tests in her lap.

"Do you miss Dana?" I asked. I promised myself that I wouldn't share a thing that she told me with Dana.

She shook her head. "I miss the Dana I met last summer."

"The man."

"Yup. I like the woman she's become very much. But I'm not sure I'm prepared to be her friend."

"I can see that," I said. Then, without thinking, I asked, "Is it really okay for me to go to Washington this summer?"

"Okay? Why wouldn't it be? I'm very proud of you."

"I know. But a part of me thinks it would be really fun to do something brain-dead this summer in town. Maybe work at the nursery again. And hang out with you."

"I'm not an invalid," she said. "I'm a little shell-shocked, but I'll be fine. Don't even think of turning down that internship for me. I'd be furious with you if you did. Furious."

"I'd be turning it down for me. I'm sure I could do it next summer. And I worked really hard this year at school. Maybe I've earned a rest."

"You're talking nonsense," she said. "This is a great honor, and you'll love it. You'll love every minute of it."

I went upstairs to bed a few minutes later, and when I fell asleep, she was still in the den. When I woke up, I heard her in the shower getting ready for school, and I made a decision. I would check the book bag that would, inevitably, be hanging off the top of a ladder-back chair in the kitchen. If she had finished grading her kids' tests, I would go to Washington that summer. If not, I would stay.

I tiptoed down the stairs, though I couldn't imagine she could hear me in the shower—and, if she did, why it would matter. Sure enough, her canvas bag was in its usual morning spot on a kitchen chair. And then, for the only time in my life, I snuck a peek at its contents.

The papers were all done. They were corrected and graded, and my mom had written little notes on the ones that were particularly good or bad. And so a few days later I went to Washington. I left convinced that my mom was mending and very soon would be her old self.

It was perhaps a month later that I would learn I'd been wrong, and that my mother would in fact have to get worse before she'd get better.

"My dad says she's grieving," I told Dana. We met in Burlington, at one of the tables in the bar of an elegant restaurant on Church Street. The awnings were up and the windows were open, and the spring air felt terrific. We could watch people as they wandered up and down the pedestrian mall smack in the center of the city.

"He says it's like her lover has died," I continued. "You, that is, when you were a male."

"Your father is a very smart man."

"Yeah, he is. But he said he was only repeating what Mom had told him."

"Oh."

"It doesn't matter who said it. It makes sense."

I was having an iced coffee, and she was sipping a glass of wine half filled with club soda.

"She hasn't answered any of the E-mails I've sent her. Or any of the letters," Dana said.

"Have you called her?"

"I have. In early April. She begged me not to."

"My mom doesn't beg for anything."

"Forgive me: She *insisted* that I not call her again. She told me she'd call me when she was ready," Dana said, and she looked down at the slender goblet on the table.

I wondered what people saw when they saw us. It was like that night at the restaurant in Montpelier. She was too young to be my mom, but too old for a friend. And I was incredibly underdressed next to her. Her silk blouse alone must have cost more than my top and sandals and jeans combined.

Maybe they saw an older stepsister. A sister from a first marriage. Or maybe people recognized her as that professor from the university who had had the sex change, and they thought I was one of her students. She still had another three months of her sabbatical remaining, but maybe they thought I was going to be one of her advisees.

And maybe they thought I was a transsexual, too. A young and slim, newly made woman.

It didn't matter, of course.

But for a moment I liked the notion, bizarre as it was, that if people understood that Dana had once been a guy, then perhaps once I could have been one, too. I liked the idea that gender could be that fluid. Maybe in reality it wasn't, but Dana was pretty and Dana was feminine and the Dana before me across a little table was never again going to be mistaken for a man.

"And she will call you," I told her. "My mom's good about her word."

"I know. Your mother is an amazing woman."

"Well, so are you," I said, and I was completely serious. I meant it.

"Thank you," she said, and she gave my wrist a gentle squeeze. "I'm so glad you're so together about . . . well, about everything. Are you still seeing that boy with the bright hair?"

"Sort of. His name is Neil. But he lives just outside of New York City, and that's where he'll be this summer. So we'll only see each other a couple times over the next few months, I guess. A few weekends, maybe. So who knows if it will last. But I like him. He's smart and he's cute. And you?"

"Me?"

I smiled. "Yes, you. Are you dating anyone?"

"Oh, there have been a few girls. But nothing has really clicked."

"Are you happy?"

"You know what? I think I am. I'm actually looking forward to teaching again. I honestly can't wait to get back to the classroom."

"And everything else?"

She raised her eyebrows. "What do you mean?"

I shrugged, embarrassed at my imprecision, at the way I had shied away from asking what I really meant. "The sex change. Was that the . . . the right decision?"

"Oh, God, yes! Carly, you'll just never know how good it feels to wake up every day with the right body, unless you've spent a few decades in the wrong one. Oh, it was worth it, it was worth it: Everything I endured over the last year, it was worth it. Everything. And you know what? I'd be grateful if you would tell your mother that for me. Everything she did? Well, it was more wondrous than you can imagine, and more important. I think she knows that, but would you remind her for me?"

I nodded and smiled. Somehow it would have been hurtful to inform Dana that my mom didn't even know we were having a drink together, and I had no intention of telling her anything.

I discovered my first days in Washington that my dad had a ton of friends at NPR. He had been working for public radio for almost as long as I'd been alive, so a part of me wasn't at all surprised. Besides, my dad's a nice guy. So why wouldn't he have a lot of friends?

Still, I was very proud to meet so many people so far from home who knew him. I was always introduced as "Will Banks's daughter," and I liked that. It made me feel more like I belonged there, and less like a complete nobody from Vermont.

Or, even better, that it was possible to be from Vermont and be cool.

Of course, being Will Banks's daughter also meant that everyone seemed to know about Mom and Dana. Either they knew because Will Banks had once been married to a woman who had gotten involved with a transsexual, or they knew because they had heard the tapes of the VPR stories that had aired in March. The tapes—literally, the plastic-housed spools of magnetic ribbon—had a certain underground cachet to them, and I saw copies here and there on credenzas and desks my first week in Washington. I'd be introduced to somebody, and they'd hear my name and instantly grab the cassette from underneath some pile of papers or a magazine, and say, "Your mom? Really?"

And I'd nod.

I guess it was only a matter of time before someone was going to ask me how well I knew Dana. I guess it was inevitable.

And it was probably pretty likely that it was going to be Nicole Wells. I spent lots of time with Nicole because she was only eight or nine years older than I was, and she had also gone to college in New England. She did a lot of the softer, lifestyle stories for *All Things Considered* because she was still pretty young. But she was a comer, that was clear, and I was really flattered that she was willing to spend so much time with me.

We were in a cab together when she asked the question. We were on our way to interview a chef whose restaurant had crickets and grasshoppers on the menu. Kirsten Seidler, a woman who produced a lot of stories with Nicole, was with us. I was in the middle. I didn't know Kirsten very well, and so of course the conversation began the way most of my early discussions with NPR people began:

"Your mother sure had one heck of a winter, didn't she?" Kirsten asked, though she didn't really expect an answer.

"Sure did," I agreed, and for maybe half a minute we bumped along in the taxi without speaking, staring out the windows and listening to the Middle Eastern music that was on the car's radio.

Then, without looking at me, Nicole asked, "What was it like living with Dana?"

It wasn't the first time that Nicole and I had talked about Dana, but I honestly believe it was the first time that Nicole had seen in my mom and Dana's story something other than the chaos and confrontation that had been the focus of the Vermont version. Nicole isn't especially romantic, but she was the one who had the very specific idea of seeing if my mom and Dana's experience might work as a part of *ATC*'s "The Nature of Love"—a periodic series *All Things Considered* had been running throughout the year.

"Most of the time," I answered, "when it was only the three of us, it was like I was just hanging around with my mom and one of her friends. That's it. It was only strange when there was someone else there."

"Like your father?" Kirsten asked.

"Like that," I said.

"Exactly how well do you know Dana?" Nicole then asked, and I understood instantly why she wanted to know. I don't know how I knew, but I did. Really, I did. Maybe it's because on some level I'd been hoping someone would see what I'd seen since arriving in Washington. Maybe it's because in so many ways I really am my dad's daughter. But I knew that very second that Nicole saw the same potential for

programming in my mom and Dana's relationship that I saw, and
once we were done with our feature about "microlivestock" and a
restaurant that served a mealworm bruschetta, we would discuss the
idea further.

Maybe—and this may only be hindsight—I knew even then I was
going to ask Nicole and Linda Wertheimer if I could be involved.
Seriously involved. Maybe not. But I think I understood from the very
beginning that if I worked on the story, I could make sure that the tale
was told right and that nothing was done that would embarrass my
parents.

All Things Considered
Friday, September 28

DANA STEVENS: Oh, I learned things. Really. For
starters, I learned just how much closet space my
apartment really had. Once I'd given all of my suits
and ties and Dockers pants to the Salvation Army, I
had absolutely massive amounts of closet space. Massive! It was like I had this whole new apartment.

dana

DOES THE SOUL HAVE A GENDER? I BELIEVE IT does, but my friends in the university Religion Department have given me books that argue it doesn't. And I came across one extraordinary essay that contended that the soul is androgynous: It wasn't simply without gender, it had elements of both genders.

There were moments after Allison and I separated when I would like that idea a lot.

But then I would have a drink with someone in the Psychology Department, and afterward I would labor over the distinction between spirit and soul. Suddenly semantics would preclude me from resolving the issue in my mind. The soul was something other than me, it was something autonomous, it was certainly something over which I had no control.

And so, for all I knew, it was indeed completely free of gender. It didn't give a roiling damn about chromosomes, or genitalia, or which side of the shirt had the buttons.

Today? Today I tend to believe that there is a spirit within us that is without question either female or male. Unequivocally. Not neither. Not both. It is one or the other.

How's that for male hubris and assurance?

"You gotta understand," I hear my old, masculine voice insisting dogmatically.

"You gotta . . ."

But I do indeed believe—at the moment, anyway—that I will be a woman in heaven. No mistakes there.

At least that's my sense today.

Tomorrow? Who the hell knows what I'll believe tomorrow. I sure don't. I've given up completely trying to predict what I'll believe even two hours from now.

Ah, but for the moment . . . for the moment, I am confident that I will be a woman in paradise.

After all: It wouldn't be paradise for me if I had to be a man.

I must have heard from a dozen newspapers and magazines after the stories ran on Will's radio station, including some of the national news and entertainment weeklies. But I didn't do any more stories.

Besides, Allison and I had parted by then, and so I really wasn't newsworthy anyway. I was merely another transsexual.

And that's not news. The truth is, we're everywhere.

And so I got on with my life. I accepted the blessing of the time I had been given with Allison, and the reality that it was a blessing with boundaries. I had one summer, one fall, and one winter. I stopped calling her and E-mailing her, which was what she wanted, and I settled back into my life as a university professor in Burlington—albeit one who was still on sabbatical, which meant I had way too much time on my hands.

Consequently, I went to movies and I read, and I prepared lesson plans with a thoroughness that absolutely shamed my previous decade and a half in the classroom. When I strolled the streets, I was not exactly anonymous, but I was able to shop without obvious glares, and without the need to stop and discuss my decisions. By the end of June, I imagine, I was actually blending in fairly well.

And, of course, I continued to date. Not a lot. But I met a few women, and we went out. One girl knew I was a transsexual before I told her; two others simply assumed at first that I was merely statuesque. All three were slightly uncomfortable with the notion that I had been born a man, and one of them came right out and told me that she thought her interest in me was inappropriate. Politically incorrect, if you will.

Twice I went out on second dates, but I never made it to a third.

One of the girls I saw a second time kissed me when I walked her back to her apartment. She was a dermatologist who lived about six blocks from me, on the edge of the university campus. As you might expect, she had the most beautiful skin.

She kissed me on the steps to the brick house in which she lived. Her apartment, she said, was most of the second floor. I feared that she was going to invite me upstairs when we pulled apart, but she said—as if she could read my mind—"This isn't going to work, is it?"

I shook my head. It wasn't.

Though, in all fairness, I was prepared to give our relationship a third or fourth date to see if things might improve. At the very least, I knew, she would have incredible advice about my complexion, and what to do with a face that had endured so much electrolysis.

Still, it was clear to us both that in too many ways she still viewed me as a man, while my mind—my libido—was elsewhere. Unengaged, if you will. A part of me simply wanted to pine for Allison Banks forever. A part of me felt some moral responsibility to remain uninvolved, almost as if I were widowed. After all Allison had done for me, it seemed wrong in some way to see other women.

Moreover, I had begun to realize that although I wasn't exactly confused about my sexual predilections—no one simply wakes up in the morning and decides that she's no longer gay—preference is inevitably more fluid than gender. Let's face it, I had never been confused about gender: I knew as a little kid that something screwy had happened and I'd been dropped inside the wrong skin.

Now, however, almost half a year post-op, I was clearly continuing to metamorphose. The thoughts and images I would find arousing grew, well, more diverse.

Some days I'd wonder if there was more to hormones than I realized, and it was the chemicals I was swallowing that were suddenly making me find different stimuli so interesting. I realized, for instance, that while I still thought women were beautiful, my daydreams were becoming increasingly peopled with the male of the species. I pondered on more than one occasion what it would be like now to be kissed by a fellow with a hint of stubble on his cheeks, to be held by a man whose arms were stronger than mine. One Sunday afternoon I grew way too interested in those TV commercials for home fitness machines, the ones that showed men whose stomachs were rippled with muscles, and whose arms had mountains and valleys shaped by thew, flesh, and brawn.

I even began to fantasize about sex with men, and to imagine a penis inside me. For a woman—and, before that, a man—whose sexual reveries would have made much of the world just a tad uncomfortable, it was downright disturbing to have desires for such basic meat-and-potatoes sex. Intercourse in the missionary position? *Moi? Oh, please! At least hoist my ankles in your hands, you big brute, and take me off the bed!*

The whole idea that a penis might offer sexual gratification sometimes gave me the giggles, and I'd find myself more than a little bemused when the image of Dana Stevens having Doris Day sex would pop into my head.

Oh, but pop into my head it did. Increasingly often.

And while I could objectify the male torso and the male arm, while the very notion of an erect penis could interest me, in the end it wasn't anonymous male body parts that were turning me on, I decided. If I was going to have a casual dalliance with someone who mattered to me solely as a sexual partner, I still think I would have wound up with a woman. It's what I knew, it's what I loved.

No, it was, in the end, a single man who was inadvertently leading me astray. It was a fellow I saw more and more often in April and May, and who I knew was as bewildered by me as I was by him. After all, we were introduced when I was still living my life as a male, which meant we were more likely to repulse each other than find each other attractive.

Yet attracted to each other we were. We were. It was undeniable. We both knew something was happening: We could feel our dinners together were growing charged, we could sense the way the coffee we would share some afternoons was oddly electrifying. He had never seen my apartment and I had never seen the inside of his home.

But I was quite sure it was only a matter of time.

It was just before the Fourth of July weekend when Carly called me from Washington. I was painting my toenails when the phone rang, and I was savoring something genetic women take for granted: My breasts and my thighs would press together when I curled a knee and dabbed polish upon the tiny stamps at the ends of my toes.

I hadn't spoken to her since we had a drink together in late May, and it was an absolute joy to hear her voice. She sounded very happy— and very professional.

But then we finished with what I realized was small talk, and she got around to why she was calling. At first I thought she was trying to warn me, but then I understood she was actually exploring my interest in the idea: She was gauging my willingness. How public was I feeling? Would I talk to another reporter? Would it help if she came along?

I wondered if her father knew she was calling, and I realized he couldn't. He didn't. He would have told me if he had any idea what the folks at NPR were thinking.

But it was possible her mother was aware of what was going on. In fact, it was likely: I could imagine Carly calling me before her dad, but—given her mother's and my history together—not her mom. Her mom had to know.

"What does your mom think about all this?" I asked her.

"She knows she's welcome to talk about it, but she doesn't have to. I made that really clear. I told her they might not even do anything with the story."

"I don't see how they could if she didn't talk to them," I said.

"Uh-huh," she agreed.

What was it in the two grunts that comprised her response? Was it evasiveness? No, I don't think so. Carly is not an evasive young woman. What you see is what you get.

Rather, it was the calmness in the acknowledgment. The aplomb. I understood then that she knew more than I did. A lot more. And so—though I do it rarely and am therefore not particularly good at it—I listened and allowed myself to be led. She knew what she wanted, and she knew what the real story was.

Suddenly, I realized, I was just along for the ride.

All Things Considered
Friday, September 28

WILL BANKS: Hey, I was wrong before. I'm smarter now.
Simple.

39

will

WHEN I WAS ALONE, I WOULD FIND MYSELF TAKING deep cleansing breaths. I would take them when I would fall asleep and when I would wake, and I would take them when I would climb into my car.

I stayed away from the edge of the airport runway as if it were a crack house and I were a recovering junkie. But the planes would come in low near the station, and I would wander outside in the warm spring air with a cup of coffee, and I would watch them circle and approach and descend.

I thought of my daughter in Bennington, and my ex-wives in Brandon and Bartlett, and the fact that both of my parents were dead. I found myself wishing that my brother and his family hadn't moved to California. I wished, at the very least, that they lived in New England.

One day my assistant wandered outside, and she asked me what I was doing. A pair of National Guard F-16s had flown by a moment before, and before that a United 737 bound for Chicago.

"I'm watching airplanes," I said.

"Why?"

"I think I've lived in Vermont too long," I answered, which may have been a more honest response than she wanted.

For a good part of March and April, I viewed myself as a predator. I slept with a woman I met at a public radio conference in Seattle—an executive from another station whose husband had recently died—and I slept with the woman who was the CFO of one of our largest underwriters. It was reckless and stupid. But we fucked in a hotel room chair overlooking Lake Champlain, and every single moment was as good as the sunset we watched.

I slept with two different members of the Vermont Symphony Orchestra on consecutive nights, when the VSO was in Burlington for a pair of concerts. Both women were younger than me, and they both wore white shirts with pearl buttons. I loved to undress them.

In the space of a couple of weeks, I had more than doubled the number of women with whom I had slept in my life.

I wasn't sure whether I was proud of myself or I hated myself.

I tried to stop having coffee with Dana, but I couldn't. Sometimes we had dinner together. She'd call and we'd talk—I was never impolite—and before I knew it, we had firmed up a place and a time to (and I loathe this word, really I do) chat.

Always when we would part I would vow that I would never see her again. Never. I was through. And then I would try and seduce an attractive woman who was—and the word's letters would form in my head one by one—real.

For three weeks in May I dated a woman named Beth, a public-relations manager for a hospital in central Vermont. We had sex on our first date and on every date thereafter, and I stopped trying to seduce every new woman I met. Beth was intelligent and thoughtful and giving in every imaginable way. She was more beautiful naked than with her clothes on.

Still . . . I feared I was losing.

When we made love for what I knew would be the very last time, I turned on a light in a corner of her bedroom, and—much to her surprise and increasing discomfort—I just stared and I stared at her body. When I went down on her, I never once shut my eyes: I wanted to know forever what her vagina looked like, I wanted to see her tummy in repose. I wanted to have a picture in my mind of her clitoris when she was aroused, and of the way the pink drapes around it would glisten with moisture.

Sex therapists and psychiatrists say men are more visual than women.

I wanted images I could take to my grave.

Does that mean I knew what I was doing? Or, to be precise, does that mean I knew what a small corner of my brain was thinking? Anticipating? Planning?

Perhaps. But it may also mean I was merely desperate. Afraid.

Perhaps I was simply trying to convince myself that nothing in the world could compete with the real thing.

Dana suggested that I read *Little Women* because she said she was feeling a little bit like Laurie.

"You know, Laurie?" she explained when she made the request, because I must have looked puzzled. "The lad who lives next door to the March girls?"

"No, I don't know," I confessed. "I never read *Little Women*."

She pretended to be incredulous; she pretended to be appalled by my unfamiliarity with what she considered a seminal work in the transgender canon. But, the fact is, I knew the basics and I understood what she meant. I knew that in Alcott's story Laurie spent years wooing the tomboy Jo March, and then, after she finally rebuffed him, he simply moved on to her kid sister Amy and married her. He believed that he was destined to become a part of the March clan, and it was the last name that mattered more than the first.

In Dana's eyes, the parallels were obvious.

"Allie's not a tomboy," I said.

"You're a philistine," she told me. "And a literalist."

I did not kiss her then, but I found myself gazing at her mouth as she spoke, at the lipstick that looked like burgundy wine. My sense is that had we not been in a coffee bar north of Burlington, had it not been three-thirty in the afternoon, I would have kissed her at that moment. I would have leaned as far as I could across the wrought-iron table, and I would have pressed my lips against hers.

I have no doubt that people were talking. I have no doubt that people like Rebecca Barnard, one of Dana's peers on the faculty and my station's right-wing radio pundit, were murmuring that Will Banks had lost his mind. Or, at the very least, that he was intent in some way on the destruction of his career and his life.

First it was Allison, his ex-wife. And now it's him. There must be something awful in the drinking water in Bartlett.

But throughout April and May, Dana and I were merely having coffee or dinner together. That's all that was happening. We went to one movie together.

And always, at the end of the night or the end of the day, we went our separate ways. Often when I would see Dana in the afternoon, in the evening I would go out on a date—a real one. Never did Dana come back with me to Bartlett.

Together, we talked often about Allie. There was my Allie and there was her Allison, and we compared notes about what we loved in the woman and why we would always worry about her.

Together, we talked about her career and mine. We talked about Carly, and we talked about Dana's family in Florida. We talked about teaching and radio.

We did not, I realized, talk about my divorce, and I wondered if there was nothing there I needed to discuss. Briefly that concerned me, and I worried that I had grown cold. She reassured me I hadn't.

At some point I confessed that I needed desperately to get out of Vermont, and I was planning to extend feelers that summer throughout the NPR station network. She understood there would be advantages for her to leave Burlington, too, not the least of which would be the chance to begin her life as an anonymous woman, versus Dana Stevens, the local teacher-transsexual. But she wasn't sure that she ever would. She had tenure where she was. Now that she had her sex change, would she ever get tenure anyplace else? She wasn't sure.

Did we flirt? I don't believe so. But one's mind can't help but wander to sex around a transsexual, if only because you know the person beside you has had a sex change. Your mind will, of its own volition, wonder about the penis or the vagina that once was there and now is gone, and the penis or the vagina that has replaced it.

Even now I wonder if that's the real reason why transsexuals make the rest of us so uncomfortable. Though many are wholly indifferent to sex, they think more about genitalia than everybody else, and they are considerably more comfortable with that reality.

Nevertheless, I am quite sure that only a small percentage of my attraction to Dana was lust. Like a holograph image that mutates with the flick of your wrist, in an instant the beautiful woman before me could become a man with a ponytail—a man I hadn't much liked. All it would take was a tiny movement: Her fingers on her chin. A deep inhalation. An adamant nod.

And then the notion of kissing her would become considerably more unappealing. And unlikely.

In June I invited Dana to the edge of the airport runway. Recently I'd started taking my laptop there, and I would write the necessary station memos from the front seat of my car—memos about fund-raising and programming, about personnel hires and the use of our new performance studio—while the planes departed and arrived.

"You need a vacation," she said when I suggested she join me. We were having coffee together at a shopping mall in a restored woolen mill just outside of Burlington, and the mall was near enough to the airport that the planes roared overhead no more than four hundred feet above the ground.

"I need more than that," I admitted. "But it's more fun than you'd realize. Little kids love watching the planes come and go. Teenagers are hypnotized by them. It's just grown-ups who won't allow themselves to be wowed by the miracle of flight."

"That's not why you sit there."

"I don't know why I sit there," I said. "But that is at least part of it."

It was nearing late afternoon when we finished our coffee and left the mall. By the time we got to the dirt by the chain-link fence near runway one-five, it was after four o'clock. The wind was warm and the sky was blue, and we leaned our backs against the front grill of my Explorer. I told her what airplanes were due momentarily, and which ones were worth waiting for: I didn't much like the angry whine of the engines that powered the Delta Connection's Saab 340s, but I enjoyed watching their slow, gradual ascent. There would be three before dinner. And there would be a pair of the smaller Dash 8s. And USAirways would have a DC-9 arriving from Philadelphia and a 737 from Pittsburgh, and everything about the planes—their size and their speed and the noise from the jet engines almost as tall as a man—would dwarf the opening acts.

There was no haze that afternoon and there weren't any clouds.

I realized that because she was wearing her loafers, Dana and I were about the same height. Had she been wearing heels, she would have been taller.

We were completely alone. And when the first of the Saabs had flown over us, their propellers whipping up just a hint of dirt and dust, I kissed her. My hands were folded across my chest as if I were bored, but that's simply how I keep my hands when I stand. I don't recall exactly where hers were. We pulled apart briefly, and then I kissed her a second time, and when I did, her hands came up from wherever they'd been, and I felt them on the back of my neck. They were gentle and soft and there wasn't a hint of strangeness.

I knew then that I would see her apartment for the first time that night, or she would return with me to Bartlett for the first time since March. But my sense was, we would go to her apartment in Burlington. My home was too close to Allie's. My home was too close to people who'd loved Dana and people who'd hurt her, and to that period in her life when she had bid farewell, once and for all, to the man in whose skin she had lived for thirty-five years.

When we pulled apart, I was aware that my tongue was tingling and my legs had started to shake.

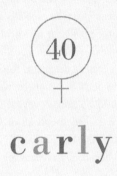

40

carly

MY MOM HASN'T DATED MUCH THIS FALL, BUT I don't read anything into that. She hangs out with her friends, mostly. And she's happy to have her classroom packed with students once again. She'd forgotten how much she likes the chaos, how much she thrives on the energy you get from a roomful of kids.

Because of *All Things Considered,* I only came home for three days before I had to start my sophomore year. I got home from Washington late on a Thursday night and was home through Sunday afternoon. And I actually worked a good part of Friday morning, listening over the telephone to segments of tape that Kirsten and Sam—the producer and the engineer—were splicing together on the computer.

But my mom and dad didn't mind that I was only home for a couple of days, because they'd gotten to see me in late July and the middle of August, when I returned to Vermont to interview both of them and

Dana and some of the people who'd been a part of their story earlier that year.

My dad was going to leave for New Mexico a few days after I'd returned to Bennington for the fall. He was going to be the general manager of the public radio station in Albuquerque and Santa Fe, and I think he was very excited. He'd been running Vermont Public Radio for a long time, and it was clear he needed a change. And so he'd rented his house to a young professor at Middlebury College and her husband for the coming year, while he decided whether he liked the Southwest enough to move there once and for all.

Dana, too, I guess. The plan was that she'd fly out there a weekend a month, and my dad would fly home every third or fourth week for a couple of days. They expected to spend all of their vacations in Santa Fe, so they could see if they liked the area.

They actually talked about Dana moving west when the spring semester was over.

The main thing that struck me about Dad was how happy he was. This is an awful thing to discover when you're nineteen years old—pretty close to twenty, actually—but it's true: It was only when my adolescence was all but over that I figured out how unhappy my dad had been for most of my life. It was only when I was a grown-up myself that I understood the fog in which he'd been living since I was about seven years old.

And so I loved seeing him that weekend at the end of the summer.

The fact is, I had loved seeing him in July when we all descended upon him and Dana with the microphones and tape recorders, and when we spent hours in the studios of his very own station. Nothing at all had seemed to faze him, and he was a much funnier man than I'd realized. He held hands with Dana when they were walking down the long corridors between the offices and the studios, and he hugged her in the parking lot as if they were married when we were done with a segment and Dana had to return to the university for some committee meeting.

Sometimes people asked me how I felt about my dad's decision to head west with a transsexual. Molly Cochran said she thought it was the most interesting midlife crisis she'd ever seen.

I told her—I told anyone who asked—that I didn't think it was a crisis at all. I told people I was very proud of my dad.

And, in a lot of ways, I was proud of Dana, too. Just like Dad, she had to see past the anatomy. She had to give whatever spark they shared some kind of chance, despite the fact that my dad's a man and she'd always been interested in women. That can't be easy, especially since Dana had always labeled everyone and everything, and put us all in these neat little boxes. Gay. Straight. Transsexual lesbian.

Let's face it: In reality, it's all just about muscle spasms that feel really good.

My sense is that my mom will start dating again when she's ready. She's smart and she's beautiful and she's an incredible amount of fun to be around. She'll never have trouble finding men.

Or women either, I guess, should her interests ever wander that way.

But she, too, seems pretty happy these days, and that's great to see. I'd worried about her in July. We all had. But she's resilient. She's tough.

And someday she might even fall in love.

All Things Considered
Friday, September 28

WILL BANKS: . . . So far I like the Southwest. I could settle down here. I think we both could.

DANA STEVENS: Definitely. It's so warm, I could wear a sundress almost year-round. I like that idea: I think my collarbone is among my best features.

CARLY BANKS: Stevens insists that she wouldn't mind giving up tenure at the end of the school year if they decided to stay.

STEVENS: It would be a trade-off. But I'd be fine. Hey, I've done far crazier things in my life—at least in some people's eyes.

CARLY BANKS: For love?

STEVENS: Nothing—and I mean nothing, Carly Banks—is crazy if you're in love.

Acknowledgments

I want to thank the members of the transgendered community—transsexuals, their partners, and in some cases their parents—who were kind enough to endure my questions, and read all or parts of this novel in manuscript form. I am especially grateful to D. C. Merkle, Kara Forward, and Liz Trumbauer. Ms. Forward and Ms. Trumbauer allowed me to spend time with them in not one but two states.

I also want to thank two transsexual surgeons: Dr. Stanley Biber of Trinidad, Colorado, and Dr. Sheila Kirk of the Transgender Surgical and Medical Center in Pittsburgh, Pennsylvania. Their knowledge (as well as their patience) is astounding. I am deeply indebted as well to their assistants. Pamela Kirk—who is Dr. Kirk's life partner as well as professional assistant—is a thoughtful, sharp, and encouraging reader. Marie Pacino, who works with Dr. Biber, is as indefatigable as she is resourceful.

Other readers offered different—but no less important—varieties of technical counsel, especially Phoebe Barash and Bill Jesdale, each of whom is an educator and school principal; Ken Neisser of the Gersh Agency; Mark Vogelzang, president and general manager of Vermont Public Radio; and Tom Wells, attorney and bookseller. Writers Jay Parini and Dana Yeaton were also kind enough to read early drafts of the novel and share with me their wisdom.

The transgender canon is large and (not surprisingly) diverse, and most authors who plumb the subject bring experiential passion to the subject. Some are more supportive of sexual reassignment than others, and some are more likely to link sex and gender with politics and power. The books that I found most helpful as a novelist— because of the author's insight, wisdom, or honesty—included: *In Search of Eve,* by Anne Bolin; *Gender Outlaw,* by Kate Bornstein; *Sex Changes,* by Pat Califia; *Body Alchemy,* by Loren Cameron; *Speaking As a Woman,* by Alison Laing; *Conundrum,* by Jan Morris; *Transsexuals: Candid Answers to Private Questions,* by Gerald Ramsey, Ph.D.; *The Transsexual Empire,* by Janice G. Raymond; and *The Transsexual's Survival Guide I* and *II*, both by JoAnn Altman Stringer.

Four novels were particularly inspiring and thought-provoking: *The Extra Man,* by Jonathan Ames; *Stone Butch Blues,* by Leslie Feinberg; *The Illusionist,* by Dinitia Smith; and *Myra Breckinridge,* by Gore Vidal.

Finally, I want to thank Random House, and six people there whose continued faith in my work will never, ever cease to astonish me: Shaye Areheart, Chip Gibson, and Dina Siciliano with the Crown Publishing Group, and Marty Asher, Jen Marshall, and Anne Messitte with Vintage Books.

I thank you all.

ALSO BY CHRIS BOHJALIAN

"Few writers can manipulate a plot with Bohjalian's grace and power." —*The New York Times Book Review*

THE LAW OF SIMILARS

In *The Law of Similars*, Chris Bohjalian delivers a riveting medical thriller about a lawyer, a homeopath, and a tragic death. When one of Carissa Lake's patients falls into an allergy-induced coma, possibly due to her prescribed remedy, Leland Fowler's office starts investigating the case. But Leland is also one of Carissa's patients, and he is beginning to realize that he has fallen in love with her. As love and legal obligations collide, Leland comes face-to-face with an ethical dilemma of enormous proportions. Bohjalian deftly examines the links between hubris and hope, deception and love in this suspenseful, intelligent novel.

Fiction/Literature/0-679-77147-6

MIDWIVES

On an icy winter night in an isolated house in rural Vermont, a seasoned midwife named Sibyl Danforth takes desperate measures to save a baby's life. She performs an emergency cesarean section on a mother she believes has died of stroke. But what if Sibyl's patient wasn't dead—and Sibyl inadvertently killed her? As Sibyl faces the antagonism of the law, the hostility of traditional doctors, and the accusations of her own conscience, *Midwives* engages, moves, and transfixes us as only the very best novels do.

Fiction/Literature/0-375-70677-1

VINTAGE CONTEMPORARIES
Available at your local bookstore, or call toll-free to order:
1-800-793-2665 (credit cards only).